BLACK PARADE

PARTHIAN

LIBRARY OF WALES

Jack Jones was born in Merthyr Tydfil in 1884, the eldest of nine who survived out of fifteen children. He left school at twelve to work with his father as a miner. Later he became a regular soldier and served in the First World War. His political engagement saw him act for the Miners' Federation; join the Communist Party, then Labour and then the Liberals, standing as Liberal candidate for Neath in 1929. Married with five children, he earned a living through mining, as a platform-speaker, navvy, salesman, assistant cinema-manager and writer.

His first novel, *Rhondda Roundabout*, was published in 1934. It was followed by two more novels (*Black Parade*, 1935, and *Bidden to the Feast*, 1938), a play and the first volume of his autobiography (*Unfinished Journey*, 1937). He made radio and film appearances and took on several minor acting roles. From 1946 Jones published two further volumes of autobiography, eight novels, including *Off to Philadelphia in the Morning* (1947), and a play. In 1948 he was made a CBE. In 1968 he was elected first president of thc English section of Yr Academi Gymreig. He died in 1970.

'I remember when all the *decent* people in Lichfield got drunk every night, and were not the worse thought of. Ale was cheap...'

Dr Johnson

BLACK PARADE

JACK JONES

LIBRARY OF WALES

Parthian
The Old Surgery
Napier Street
Cardigan
SA43 1ED
www.parthianbooks.co.uk

The Library of Wales is a Welsh Assembly Government initiative which highlights and celebrates Wales' literary heritage in the English language.

Published with the financial support of the Welsh Books Council.

www.libraryofwales.org

Series Editor: Dai Smith

First published in 1935

Library of Wales edition published 2009

Publishing Editor: Penny Thomas

ISBN 978-1-906998-14-1

Cover design: www.theundercard.co.uk
Cover image: *On the Coal Tips* (c 1930-32) (oil on canvas) by Archie Rees Griffiths © Estate of Archie Rees Griffiths with kind permission of Peter Lord

Typeset by logodædaly
Printed and bound by Gwasg Gomer, Llandysul, Wales

British Library Cataloguing in Publication Data

A cataloguing record for this book is available from the British Library.

LIBRARY OF WALES

FOREWORD

Merthyr Tydfil for Jack Jones was a stern and forbidding father, a nurturing mother, lover, friend and mortal enemy. His native town, built on its four great ironworks, forged his talent and purged his verbose and cumbersome prose of its impurities. The pressures of reliving his life there – not to mention the heroic efforts of his copy editors – tempered a style of steel-hard simplicity fit for the elemental story of his people pitted against the black cruelty of nature and the red-clawed savagery of Man.

The town is never the mere backcloth against which the lives of his characters are played out. With its massive heart, its indomitable soul, the Merthyr of the late nineteenth and early twentieth centuries dominates his best books – the three great novels, *Black Parade*, *Bidden to the Feast* (1938) and *Off to Philadelphia in the Morning* (1947) and the magnificent autobiography, *Unfinished Journey* (1937). Its dangerous streets provide a public stage for the great battles that conflict his families – the Morgans, the Davieses, the Parrys and the Joneses. There, the life-affirming vitality of its pubs, clubs, fairs, theatres and boxing booths and the bare-knuckled brutality of mountain-top contests howl against the constraint of nonconformity's careful Christianity.

In *Black Parade* the fight, as old as civilisation, divides the Morgan family between father Glyn, the hard-working, hard-drinking miner and his upwardly mobile, fashionably Christian eldest son, Benny and his snobbish wife, Annie.

It rages within an individual, hellraising Harry, Glyn's workshy, violent brother-in-law, a street fighter of considerable skill and reckless courage. When he is knocked down by a works engine on his way home from a night behind the coke ovens with a prostitute, he loses a leg. The judgement on his past life is reinforced when he is swept up in Evan Roberts' revival of 1905 and 'gets' religion. Glyn is no more enamoured of the new Harry, endlessly preaching his gospel, than he was of the violent old.

The same conflict raged within Jack Jones himself. His imagination was fired by the street fairs, the canvas-topped auctions, the music halls, above all by the penny-dreadful Victorian melodramas and great Shakespearean tragedies which enthralled him as a boy selling snacks to the audience in the newly-opened Theatre Royal. The pages of *Black Parade* hum with colourful characters like the disgraced headmaster 'Davies, MA,' who with his threadbare frock coat, unkempt red beard and fiery eyes busks for a few pennies by declaiming speeches from the great Elizabethan playwrights. Despite, or perhaps because of, his obvious contempt for his audiences they contribute enough to keep him drunk and to pay for his lodgings in Merthyr's notorious red-light district along the banks of the River Taff.

Ultimately the town's pagan licentiousness ends, like Davies, in a lonely and meaningless death if it is not tempered by a Christian compassion. When Saran, Glyn's long-suffering wife, hurries to join the throng gathering to listen to a speech by miners' leader A. J. Cook during the long lock-out of 1926, his overblown rhetoric is compared to the simple socialism of her Christian brother, Harry, as he talks to the old, the infirm and the simple-minded locked up in the town's workhouse. The message is reinforced by the cinematic expedient of cutting directly from the union leader's bombast to Harry's quiet sincerity.

Cook struggles to bolster the miners' confidence:

'... men are now solid again in the areas that looked like letting us down. After a solidarity campaign in which I am pleased to say that I have been supported by all the Labour MPs with the exception of a reactionary handful – and we shall deal with them when the time comes – I am now in a position to report that our men everywhere are as solid as they ever were. And I am pleased to be able to inform you that we are winning the sympathy of the British public....'

But Harry tells of the hawker he saw selling needles and cotton from door to door in Merthyr's incessant rain:

'Wet through, he must have been, and still the people who answered the knock slammed the doors in his face.'

The next day Harry sees men singing for a few pennies as they walk along the gutter. They, too, are ignored.

'No man should have to go from door to door selling needles and cotton in the rain, or sing in the gutter either. But when they are forced to do it, don't you think, brothers, that people should be kinder to 'em? Of course they should, for we never know...'

Without the Christian's compassion, wild Merthyr would end in an orgy of self-destruction. The message is as much the novelist's as it is Harry's.

An earthier love binds the Morgans' ramshackle family and its many branches. As Jack Jones makes clear in his memoir *Unfinished Journey*, the novel *Black Parade* is Saran

Morgan's book. For most of its life before publication the novel was entitled Saran, short for Sarah Ann. She is named for the novelist's beloved mother and both are the embodiment of maternal love. Like her real-life counterpart, Saran Morgan epitomises fecundity and nurturing commitment. She spends much of *Black Parade* with breast bared, suckling the latest of her brood. When her fertility ends, her daughter and daughters-in-law take over, a seemingly endless production line.

Like most working-class mothers in the Merthyr of the late nineteenth and early twentieth centuries, she suffers the most harrowing losses. One brother is killed in South Africa's Zulu Wars, another disappears, a third, the feisty Harry, is imprisoned, loses a leg and has to be rescued from the workhouse. Two sons die in the horrific explosion that kills four hundred miners at the Universal Colliery Senghenydd in 1913. Two are killed and another is maimed in World War One. Her miner husband and sons suffer through the depredations of the long stoppage of 1926. Through this martyrdom she remains steadfast, loyal, and as crucial to the support and well-being of her loved ones as pit props are to the lives of her men.

It is one of the pleasures of Jack Jones' vigorous and subtle characterisation that Saran Morgan is more than a passive Earth Mother. From the moment we meet her as a girl working in the brickyard her blunt honesty, her humour and her spirited independence beguile us. She is the financial mainstay for her ageing parents and her two workshy brothers. She may love Glyn, the handsome young miner a little too fond of his drink but she is not prepared to bend to his will. When he fails to turn up to take her to the theatre, she breaks a taboo by seeking him out in the male-only preserve of the taproom at the Black Cock public house. His outraged drinking companions suggest he should teach her some manners by giving her a pair of black eyes.

As a married woman in the early twentieth century she may accept that pride of place in the home goes to the male breadwinners, but long before the book ends she has become the de facto head of the household. She knows Glyn will disapprove if she offers their widowed brother-in-law, the feckless pub entertainer and balladeer Twm Steppwr, a bed in which to die. She does it anyway. And she rescues her brother Harry, a man for whom Glyn feels an intense dislike, from the workhouse in order that he, too, may die under their roof. In her enthusiasm for the theatre and, later, the cinema, this illiterate woman becomes the guardian of the family's cultural values as well as its spiritual and physical well-being.

As Saran and her family mature, so does that other great protagonist of *Black Parade*, Merthyr. With the appearance of its imposing Town Hall, its General Hospital, its sports grounds and great parks, its theatres and cinemas, the town grows into a new sense of civic pride. With strong and resilient families like the Morgans forming its backbone, it looks forward to an uncertain future with optimism.

In his life as well as his writing Jack Jones epitomised Merthyr's restless, often wasteful, creativity. He travelled with bewildering speed from near-illiterate pit boy to soldier, woodsman, salesman for the Encyclopaedia Britannica, internationally-known public speaker, late-flowering novelist, playwright, broadcaster and scriptwriter. During his years as a professional politician he moved from party to party searching in vain for a philosophy that satisfied him. And there were long periods of threadbare poverty on the dole worrying where the next meal for his long-suffering wife, Laura, and their children would come from.

In *Black Parade* Jack Jones lays strong claim, despite stiff opposition, to being the best fiction writer Merthyr has produced and one of the best to emerge in modern Wales. His neglect in recent decades shames us. His books are out of print, consigned to dusty, forgotten corners of the stacks stores of public libraries. This much-needed Library of Wales edition will help restore to him the reputation he deserves.

Mario Basini

BLACK PARADE

CHAPTER 1

A HECTIC WEEKEND – SATURDAY

Two stark-naked young men in the living room of the cottage singing a duet from one of Dr Parry's operas as a middle-aged woman picked up and hung away the pit clothes they had shed. They had both washed white the upper halves of their coal-blackened bodies, and the elder of the two was standing in the tub half filled with warm water washing his lower part, using the washing flannel with one hand, the other hand he used to screen his secret parts from the woman.

The duet ended, and the young man standing near the fireplace cried impatiently: 'Come on, Glyn, hurry up out of that tub so as I can finish washing. There's good beer waiting for me in a dozen places…'

'How many times have I told you to leave your talk about the beer until you get outside this house?' said his brother in an undertone. 'The end of it'll be that dad'll hear you and then... and how many times have I told you about standing about naked and showing all you've got in front of Marged. Cover up, for shame's sake.'

'Oh, Marged don't mind, 'tisn't as if she was a slip of a girl. You're not particular, are you, Marged?'

'If I said I was it'd make no difference. Do you want me to wash your back, Glyn?'

'If you please,' said Glyn, kneeling down in the tub to enable her to do so.

'Damned particular, ain't you?' grumbled the impatient Dai. 'Every night you wash his back for him. If you only knew how weakening it is; once a week's often enough to have the back washed.'

'If you had it washed as often as Glyn, then I wouldn't have to wash two of your shirts for every one of his,' said the woman as she bent over the kneeling man and started washing the coal-dust from off his back.

'Oh, so that's why you're always asking him to wash his back, is it? I thought there was something behind it.' He rubbed his week's growth of beard. 'Well, if there's many waiting in Humpy's this'll have to stay on till some time next week. I don't believe in wasting time – and holiday time in particular – hanging about barbers' shops.'

'If you leave it much longer the barber will be able to play music on it,' said Marged.

'Ay, Annie Laurie with variations,' laughed Glyn as he rose to his feet, his back clean and wiped dry. He swilled his soapy legs and stepped out of the tub on to the piece of sacking spread out near the fireplace. 'Though I was nearly as bad until I went out for a scrape last night, for I knew it would mean waiting in Humpy's a couple of hours if I left it until today.'

'I'm not waiting any two hours,' said Dai as he stepped into the tub.

'I was going to get you clean water,' said Marged.

'Never mind, this'll do. I'm not so particular as some people. You attend to Glyn, and turn him out smart, for he's going to meet his wench, his lovely Saran, today.'

'Shut up. No, not that shirt, Marged. My best flannel.'

'And his best blue pilot suit, remember, Marged; and his best silk muffler and new 'lastic-sides. Yes, turn him out smart, for he got to make up for last Saturday when he got drunk and left her waiting...'

Glyn stopped his mouth with a slap from the rough towel.

'You look after yourself, and leave me look after myself, Dai lad.'

They went on washing and dressing and singing. They were a handsome pair of young men, now that they could be seen free of the disguise of the coating of coal-dust. A bit Spanish-looking, of medium height, bodies graceful and slight, yet strong. Dark complexioned, wearing long, drooping, silky moustaches and tiny tufts just below the cleft of the lower lip. The elder wore earrings of gold wire, for his eyes' sake, he maintained; his eyes having been strained in the darkness of the mine too soon after their first opening, for he had started work in the mines – against his father's will – at the tender age of eight. The younger had two more years of boyhood, up to the age of ten, before he, too, started work in the mines under his brother's wing.

Their father, a stonemason, had wanted them apprenticed to his trade, but the mother could see no sense in her lads working as apprentices for next to nothing during the years they might be earning what was regarded as big money in the mines; and as she was a strong-willed woman, her boys went to work down in the mines after they had had a few years' schooling. For about five years they had worked from twelve to fourteen hours a shift in the mines, and each Saturday had proudly brought home their wages to her. Then, all of a sudden, she died. Marged, a girlhood friend who had never married, and who was about that time beginning to realise that her job as tram-woman on the bleak Cwm pithead was getting beyond her, came in to take care of the house and the father and two sons after her friend's death; and 'twas lucky for them she did, for in less than a year after the mother's death the father took to his bed never to leave it alive.

'He's in decline, poor fellow,' Marged told the neighbours; and there he was now lingering on upstairs, cared for by the faithful Marged – loved by his boys and his only daughter, Mary, who had foolishly married... but of her and her feckless husband more later.

The two boys had been named Glyndwr and David, but it was only their father called them by their full names, to everyone outside the home they were 'Glyn' and 'Dai'.

'Shall I wash your back, Dai?' Marged asked him.

'Not today, no time today.'

'Plenty of time, and God knows it wants washing with three shifts' dirt on it; but you're in a hurry to go out to get drunk, ain't you? Better if the pair of you went to bed to rest for a few hours after working three shifts without a break, as you two have. Rushing out...'

'Rest, my bottom,' said Dai, stepping out of the tub on to the sacking, where he stood wiping his legs. 'Plenty of rest when we're dead. Today's the beginning of August Monday for me, the only holiday worth a damn in the year. All...'

'How can Saturday be the beginning of Monday, you fool?' asked Marged.

'It is for me, anyway,' said Dai. 'From now until I start back for the pit on Tuesday morning it'll be August Bank Holiday for me. Too true it will. Only five days a year out of the pit, so make the most of 'em, I say.'

'Yes, but see you don't make as much of this one as you did of Whit Monday,' said Glyn warningly as he fixed his high-crowned bowler hat so as to leave a little of his hair 'quiff' showing on the right side underneath the brim. 'You know what I mean....' He assumed the helpless look and posture of a drunken man. 'That's what I mean.'

'You look after your bloody self,' growled Dai.

'And I can.' He crossed to the foot of the stairs and called up: 'I'm off out now, dad. S'long.'

'S'long, Glyndwr.'

'Mind you look after him, Marged,' whispered Glyn, jerking a thumb upwards as he was going out.

The sunshine made him blink at first as he stepped outside the house and started walking from the Twyn across the eminence overlooking the second largest town in Wales to where his 'wench' lived in the end house of Brick Row. He smiled and nodded his head as the sound of the organ came up to him from the fairground in the town below. 'They're at it early,' he murmured, stopping to look in the direction of the fairground. Immediately below him was the workhouse, the very thought of which made Marged shudder, he remembered, and below that again was spread out the rapidly growing and prosperous town of Merthyr Tydfil, which, he had been informed during his brief period of schooling, was the second largest town in Wales, 'stands in the centre of the South Wales Coalfield, and manufactures large quantities of steel'. He stood surveying the scene from Troedyrhiw on the left to Dowlais Top on the right until he saw a young and powerful-looking man with a bundle on his shoulder approaching. Then he started to move on again, only to be pulled up by the stranger.

'Could you tell me how to get to Bethesda Street, please?'

'Huh?' grunted Glyn aggressively.

The stranger repeated what he had said.

Glyn looked him over suspiciously. Yes, he thought, another of these farm-joskins, hundreds of whom were weekly flocking into the coalfield lured by the prospect of what seemed to them extraordinarily high wages. Glyn, like most of the native-born miners and steelworkers whose grandfathers could remember when ponies and donkeys transported what little coal and iron-ore was mined in the district, felt the reverse of friendly to the farmhands who were flocking in from the agricultural areas. They were, in the first place, generally speaking, so much bigger and stronger than the natives. And so humble, cringingly so, when the boss was about, no backbone to stand up for the rights of the miner, afraid to join the miners' and steelworkers' unions which were in formation, wouldn't... anyway, Glyn had no time for them, big yobs, timid tight-purses...

'Where did you say you wanted to get to?' he snapped.

The stranger pulled out of his pocket a piece of paper on which an address had been written. 'Here it is,' he said, holding out the paper to Glyn after reading what was written thereon again. 'Amos Davies, 46 Bethesda Street. That's what Amos hisself wrote down for I when he were down home Christmas-time. Told I to mind and be sure to come to him as soon as I got here; and that he would most certain find I place to stay and a job of work.'

'Humph. Where you from?'

'From Hereford way, I be.'

'Off a farm?'

'That's it, Edwards, The Croft... maybe you know it?'

Glyn, now beginning to thaw, shook his head. 'And been doing a bit of walking by the look of you?'

'More'n a bit, I been movin' since daybreak.'

'Well, you haven't much further to go before you get to Bethesda Street.' Glyn pointed down at the town. 'See that big building down there? No, there, man. That's the Drill Hall. Now, when you get to that... but there, come along, I'm going part of the way, so you may as well...'

Leaving whatever else he intended saying unsaid, Glyn started off with the big stranger at his side. For a time they walked in silence, then the stranger said: 'Do you think as I'll get me a job?'

Glyn laughed shortly. 'What's to stop you? You're big enough, God knows.'

'Lord, I be glad to hear you say that. And where do you reckon'll be the best place for I to start at?'

'Take your choice, stranger, take your choice, for there's plenty of places waiting for the likes o' you.' He stopped to point away to the right and went on wasting irony: 'Up there to the seven Dowlais pits – but maybe they'll be a bit far for you to travel to and fro night and morning, so p'raps you'd better start in one or other of those six pits across there. Them's the Cyfarthfa collieries, owned by Crawshay Brothers....'

'I think Amos said 'e works in one o' they.'

'Then down there to the left there's another six pits belonging to the Hills Plymouth Company.'

'My, plenty of pits.'

'Any God's amount. Of course, if you've anything against being shot down a pit in a cage every morning – which'll make you feel as though your belly's flying out of your mouth – then we've got scores of nice drifts, levels and slopes running from the surface into those mountains, where you can walk on your own two pins right from the surface into your work, right into the coalface.'

'My, that'd be grand.'

Glyn laughed. 'Would it? No, not so bloody grand, stranger. Give me the pits any day, for in some of those slopes and levels you're working up to your arse in water from morning to night. The pits are middling dry – and there's the steelworks. Drier still, they are; so if you don't like swallowing coal-dust you'd better get yourself a job in one of them. There's the Dowlais works up there, that's the biggest, though the Cyfarthfa works is nearly as big, and...

but come on if you're coming, for I've got somebody waiting for me.'

They walked down the slope leading into the town. 'Amos,' the stranger began again, 'told I that there's plenty of overtime to be had. Said as 'ow a man as is willin' can work double time all the time. But p'raps Amos was only jokin'.'

'Not him; you can work every hour God sends, work till you drop if you want to. Why, I've only just finished working a trebler.'

'A trebler?'

'Ay, three shifts down the pit without coming up for a break. That's the trebler we work to get some extra beer-money.'

'Oh, overtime?'

'You can call it what you like, overtime or beertime; but whatever you call it all I can tell you is that I was down the pit from six o'clock yesterday morning until half past two this afternoon. And I wasn't the only one by a long shot, most of the chaps do it, for the ships in Cardiff are waiting all the time for our coal.... Oh, here we are. I've got to meet somebody on this corner. You can't miss Bethesda Street now, keep to your right until you reach the Drill Hall, and then straight on. S'long, and good luck.'

'And I'm sure I be thankful to 'ee,' said the stranger gravely as he walked on alone through the crowded street, leaving Glyn standing on the corner where he had promised to meet his Saran.

Hugging the corner in the hope of avoiding pit-mates who might tempt him to slip in and have just one whilst waiting, Glyn looked down the narrow and crowded street along which the stranger was slowly making progress towards Bethesda Street. Never before had Glyn known the street so crowded with people, most of whom were strangers to him. There had been a time when he could place at least nine out of every ten persons to be met with on the street, but now he couldn't for the life of him place half of them. He stood and wondered where they all were able to live and sleep, these strangers who had flocked in from God only knew where to crowd the cottages of the neighbourhood, the beds of which had to work double shifts in order to provide rest for men more blest with work than with sleeping accommodation. Not that Glyn saw anything in the least wrong with men on the night shift waiting for the day shift to get up so as they could go to bed; neither was he aware of the wretched housing conditions of the district, conditions which were daily growing worse, and especially so in the neighbourhoods near the steelworks, those neighbourhoods upon which armies of Irish immigrants had descended; for it was the steelworks that the Irish workers favoured, very few of them ventured down the pits. But there were plenty of others coming in to feed the pits with labour power; from the north and west of Wales – and even from the west of England – there was a constant flow of men into the district, as alluring to them as Klondyke goldfields were to the penniless hordes who rushed off there.

The newcomers to the district, with the exception of the happy-go-lucky Irish, were far more sober and thrifty than the natives. Seldom did a North Walian waste his substance on riotous living; and 'the Cardies', those who came to the district from the hardbitten, agricultural Cardigan County, were even more thrifty and saving than their countrymen from the north. Those who came in from Carmarthen County were also careful in the extreme with their expenditure, with the result that after a few years' hard work in the mines and hard saving in the homes, the immigrants from the agricultural counties of the Principality became grocers, clothiers – everything bar publicans – and left the hard work of the mines and steelworks to the natives again. These same careful ones were the backbone of Welsh Nonconformity, which was daily increasing its power for the attack on the Established Church in Wales.

Yes, they were a careful set of people. Glyn noted them that day picking their way through the main street, on which there were numerous drunken and rowdy natives, as though they were avoiding dogs' messes. Glyn despised them, and grunted contemptuously as he watched them shepherd their too-damned-particular wives through the crowded street. Even carrying shopping baskets for the women, and who ever heard of a man carrying a basket for a woman before these namby-pamby water-drinkers came into the district?

Glyn looked at his Swiss Lever, of which he was very proud. Humph. She was ten minutes late. Trying to pay him out for last Saturday, was she? Well, he hadn't intended to let her down – he tried to tell her that, but she wouldn't listen – when he turned into his favourite pub to pay his weekly score and have the usual one on the house, which was the reward for prompt payment. But that pub was referred to as 'the glue-pot', anyway. So Saran had waited in vain for her Glyn. Now Glyn waited for a change, and wasn't he growing impatient. Time after time he consulted the Swiss Lever, until at last he decided to toss up to decide whether he would go and have one, or walk across to where she lived to see what was keeping her.

'Heads to get a drink, tails to fetch Saran,' he muttered, tossing a penny into the air and catching it. 'Tails.' Disappointed, he was starting across to where Saran lived when he saw her brother Shoni hurrying towards him with a bundle under his arm.

'I don't want to meet this flamer,' he muttered, bolting back to where the coal-trucks were standing at the rear of the Nelson Tavern, where he remained hidden until Shoni had passed by and down the main street. Then he went back to the corner again to wait. If he went across to the house he might run into Harry, and Harry was as bad as Shoni, if not worse. Yes, he thought, that's the trouble with me and Saran, those blasted brothers of hers.

Two of them, twin brothers – there had been one other brother, but he died fighting Zulus with the South Wales Borderers – and Glyn often wished that Shoni and Harry would join the regulars and go abroad to some place where they would die like heroes or live without worrying him. But Harry and Shoni were too cute to do anything of that sort; the nearest they were to going was when they joined the Brecon Militia, but that was nothing more than an annual spree for them, for they were in and out of the guardroom during the period of the annual training. Yes, two rough handfuls, no doubt about that, who took advantage of Glyn because he was walking out with their sister. Continually asking for the loan of money, and ordering him to buy them beer whenever he was unfortunate enough to run up against them in a pub, and it was by no means easy to refuse them what they demanded. They'd fight just for the fun of fighting – well, Harry would, but when it came to working – no, thank you. Only horses and fools worked, they were always ready to maintain in argument or bare-knuckle fight.

So they seldom worked, and when they did they contributed but little towards the upkeep of the home, of which Saran was the main support. She earned very good money, being one of the leading hands at the brickyard where she had been employed from the age of ten; and many a time she had to use the poker to defend her earnings when her brothers went to the point of physical violence in an attempt to take by force what they had failed to borrow. The only time when there was anything like peace in the home was when they were away doing their annual training with the Militia. Yet, with all their faults, Saran wouldn't allow anyone to say anything against her brothers in her presence; though at home she always shielded her wages and her parents from their attacks, outside the home she defended her brothers when people spoke against them.

Yes, a bright pair, Glyn was thinking as he saw Saran coming across the little bridge underneath which oozed along – it only ran or rushed after heavy rain – the most stinking brook in Britain. Glyn consulted the Swiss Lever again and frowned theatrically as Saran approached. She walked in the same challenging manner as her brothers, though in her case it was not swaggering. She was more than good looking. Her figure, though generously inclined, had been kept within bounds by the hard tasks imposed upon it daily in the brickyard, and her clear skin was fair, fairer even than the skin of Shoni, her brother. Open features, with two eyes, large and unwinking, set like two blue pools in her noble-looking head, which was crowned with an abundance of dark brown hair. Her feet, small and shapely, were encased in squeaky elastic-sided boots; but her hands – oh, what hands. Like a navvy's through years of brick-handling.

Glyn tingled with pleasure as she drew near to him. 'She gets to look smarter every day,' he murmured, then assumed a frown. 'And where do you reckon you've been till now?' he growled as she came up to him smiling. 'I've been waiting here since...'

'Yes, and so did I wait last Saturday, more fool me, for you. And you needn't look nasty at me, for I couldn't leave the house till one of the two had gone. First Shoni took Harry's black coat and waistcoat out of the drawer to take to pawn, and by trying to stop him I woke Harry, who was sleeping his beer off in the armchair. Then there was ructions, and mam and me had all our work cut out to stop them fighting again. So now you know.'

'Ay, I just seen Shoni rushing by with a bundle under his arm.'

'Yes, the shirt off his back, the only one he's got. Took it to pawn so as to get enough to lift the latch.'

'Well, if I had two brothers of that sort I'd...'

'Yes, I know, you've told me before; but they happen to be my brothers, see. Well, where are we going?'

'Down the fairground?'

'Not much fun down there yet; tonight's the time to go there.'

'There's nowhere else – unless we go to the Penydarren Park to see the foot-racing.'

'No, I'd rather wait till Monday to see the bicycle races.'

'Then what'll we do?'

'We can go for a bit of a walk, can't we?'

'I don't feel like a lot of walking after working a trebler.'

'That's nothing; I could do it on my head.'

'Yes, you gels can do a hell of a lot – with your mouths. Where do you want to go for a walk?'

'What if we walk to Pontsarn and back?'

'As you like. Come on.'

With his hands in the deep pockets of his flap-fronted, bell-bottomed trousers, and his head down as though ashamed to be seen in public with a girl at his side, he plunged into the crowd and pushed along, keeping about a neck ahead of Saran, who followed, not with a doglike air, but with the air of one driving a pig to market. As the horse-drawn bus on its way to Dowlais slowly came up Glyn suggested boarding it for a ride as far as the new Hospital.

'Don't be silly, boy,' Saran told him. 'What's the matter with your legs; you must havc plenty of money and want to waste some on bus-rides.'

'I tell you that I was working yesterday, last night…'

'… and today. Well, nobody forced you to.'

'That's all you know, fly-me; but what you don't know is that if a man don't put in a few shifts overtime the bosses damned soon let him know he's not wanted.'

'Well, you can go somewhere else, can't you. Plenty of work about.'

'I know there is, but a man don't want to be hopping from one pit to another all the time with his tools on his back.'

'Then don't keep on about being tired.'

'I s'pose you'll have the last word.'

'Why shouldn't I?'

He let her have it, and they pushed along in silence through the street crowded with people hurrying to get their shopping done so as to settle down to the drinking, fairing, fighting and various other diversions which made their rare holidays memorable, usually painfully so. As they pushed along they were hailed by friends, relations and acquaintances, many of whom extended invitations to drink with them or to accompany them to the foot-races, the fairground and other places. Glyn was more than once inclined to respond, and particularly when he was pressed to join one of the many wedding parties met with to drink some healths, for the August holiday was the favourite time for weddings in the district. Hundreds of young couples were joined together on the Saturday morning, and enjoyed what was a lengthy honeymoon for the likes of them before the man started work again on the following Tuesday morning. But Saran kept pushing him on past all invitations and temptations. When they were passing the new Hospital Glyn snorted loudly.

'What's the matter, Glyn?'

‘That blasted place.’

‘Well, what’s the matter with it?’

‘Plenty, butcher’s shop, that’s all it is.’

‘Don’t talk so daft.’

‘Talking daft, am I? Well, I’d as well go to hell any day as go to that place, and so would all I’ve ever worked with in the pits. Anything the matter – off it comes, that’s why there’s so many on crutches everywhere. A week last Tuesday I helped to carry Tom Roderick from the pit into that accident ward, and the next I heard was that they had taken his leg off. Phew, smell the damned place. Well, if ever anything happens to me down the pit I hope to God I either dies…’

‘Oh, shut up about dying.’

‘But indeed to God, Saran, them doctors are too fond of the knife for our good. We pay ’em twopence in the pound whether we’re bad or not, and then we’ve got to pay for the building of places like that, in which they practise on us with their knives. Humph, hospitals.’

‘Well, I think it’s a good job we’ve got one at last, and it’s a shame to think that there’s only that one for all this district. If anything happened to me…’

‘What, in a brickyard?’ Glyn laughed at the idea.

‘Lord, I didn’t know you had a laugh in you. Yes, in a brickyard; I’m as liable to get hurt there as you are in the pit, ain’t I?’

Glyn walked on in silence, looking back over his right shoulder every ten yards or so at the Hospital with distrust in his eyes, and five minutes away from the Hospital was the country, leafy, shady lanes, from the cool of which no sign of industrialisation could be seen. Woods and fields ready for the harvest. Birds singing, and rabbits hopping about. Glyn led the way into the depths of Goitre Woods.

'Quiet out here, isn't it?' said Saran from the rear.

'Ay; everybody's in town.' Glyn lowered himself to the ground. 'Let's sit here.'

Saran turned up her 'bit of best' skirt preparatory to seating herself. Couldn't risk the soiling of her 'bit of best'; the flannel petticoat was a different matter. Nobody saw that – well, nobody other than Glyn, to whom she was going to be married. So with her skirt turned up to her waist she sat in her petticoat at Glyn's side. As she sat with her knees drawn up, her legs, encased in thick woollen stockings, came under Glyn's notice. She blushed and drew down the bottom of the petticoat until it covered even the toes of her elastic-sided boots.

'Isn't it grand out here?' he murmured, reaching for her hand.

'It is that.'

For a time they sat holding hands, this hewer of coal and this handler of bricks, sat in silence for quite a time. Then Glyn said: 'Damn, your hands are as rough as mine, if not rougher.'

So they were, though they were not as dirty looking as his. For his hands were scratched and cut in scores of places from wrists to fingertips by the coal he handled daily. And out of the cuts, probably owing to the heat of the afternoon, there oozed a certain blue-black moisture; but her hands, though rougher and more cut about, by the particles of brick against which even leather-guards were not altogether effective, were not as badly discoloured as his, neither did they exude any moisture.

'Yes, quite as rough as mine,' he repeated.

'Can I help my hands being rough?' she cried angrily, pulling her hand out of his; then, as he started running his hand upwards along her leg: 'Now, for God's sake don't start messing me about.'

'Hell, can't a chap touch you?' he growled.

'Humph. Touch, indeed.'

He half turned to lie flat on his back and closed his eyes.

'As if I didn't know what would happen if I was foolish enough to let you start messing me about,' she continued. 'There's more than one gel working in our brickyard who've been caught that way; and when the baby came they were left in the lurch, with everybody pointing their fingers at 'em.' She stopped to listen, and afterwards murmured: 'Now, who'd think we could hear the fairground organ from here? Why, we must be nearly two mile away from it.' She looked down on his face, smiled. 'Well, ain't you a nice one,' she lovingly chided in a murmur which became a lullaby as she continued. 'You bring me out here to watch you sleeping, silly old boy that you are. Tired, is 'im, tired after working 'im trebler. Well, 'et 'im s'eep, den; and his Saran put 'im head in her lap and teep de old flies off 'im face. Dere 'im is....'

He slept sweetly and soundly after his thirty-odd hours' continuous labour in the pit, with his head pillowed in Saran's lap, slept for a few hours, hours during which she enjoyed herself studying his peaceful features. She murmured lullabies from time to time, as though anxious that he should sleep on; she would afterwards sit silent while she played with the long silver chain which encircled his neck twice before attaching itself to the Swiss Lever in his left-hand waistcoat pocket. She touched his face, fondled his hands. The sun was nearing the west when he awoke, and sat up.

'What time is it?' He looked at his watch. 'Damn, it's gone seven o'clock.' He rose to his feet. 'Why didn't you wake a chap? Come on, let's go back down, I want a drink, my mouth's like a limekiln.' He started off, leaving her to bring up the rear.

'So you're going on the booze tonight again?'

'I said I was going to have a drink.'

'Yes, I know; same as last Saturday. Well, you can go for all I care. I expect you'll be reeling drunk long before I'm out of the threeatre.'

'Not I.... And how many more times must I tell you that it's theatre, and not "threeatre"?'

'I'll call it what *I* like; it's me that's going there, isn't it?'

'I'm only telling you for...'

'Yes, but you needn't bother; you hurry off to get your share of the holiday beer.'

'Now, Saran, don't get nasty – I'll tell you what.' They were nearing the little wooden theatre. 'If you wait here until I've had one, and only one, pint in the Black Cock, I'll come with you. Not that I care to be seen going to the damned place, but as it's holiday-time.... What's the play tonight?' he said, walking across to a crazy little hoarding to consult the playbill.

'A gel in the brickyard told me it was *Sweeney Todd*,' said Saran as she followed him across.

‘Well, it’s not, it’s *The Dumb Man of Manchester*.’ He pointed. ‘There you are. “Saturday, August 2nd. Mr Cavendish as The Dumb Man of Manchester.” See for yourself.’

‘Well, you know I can’t read; but it’s all the same to me whatever’s on; though the gel in our brickyard said…’

‘ “Our brickyard” be damned. People’d think you owned the place to hear you talk.’

‘How many more times are you going to pick me up about my…’

‘Then talk properly and… here’s a shilling. Get yourself some oranges and nuts and wait here for me until I’ve swallowed a pint in the Black Cock. Shan’t be a jiffy.’

With her bags of oranges and nuts in her hands Saran waited about half an hour outside the little theatre, which by this time was crowded. ‘Only standing room at the back left now,’ the checker at the door, who knew Saran well, told her. On hearing that she walked down as far as the Black Cock and knowingly broke the unwritten law, the law forbidding women on pain of a terrible hiding to call a man out of his drinking place.

‘Is Glyn Morgan in there?’ she asked a man who was coming out.

‘Ay, I think he’s in the taproom.’

‘Will you ask him to come out to me a minute? Saran, tell him.’

‘Go and tell him your bloody self, you cheeky bitch you. By God, it’s coming to something when a man can’t have his pint without being bothered by flaming women. Lucky for you that you’re not a gel of mine….’

Saran pushed past him and on to the entrance to the

taproom, which was crowded. Through the smoke she could see her Glyn, forming one of a jolly group who were harmonising around a small table in the left-hand corner at the far end of the room.

'Glyn,' she cried aloud, and a deadly silence ensued. All present were shocked beyond description when they looked towards the door of the taproom and saw standing there one of the sex which should never be seen when men were devoting themselves to the serious, and almost sacred business of drinking. True, women might crowd with other women in the jug-and-bottle departments which were partitioned off from the temples sacred to Bacchus to get the liveners their husbands demanded when awakening with a fat head in the morning; and as a reward for going some husbands, though not many, went so far as to allow their wives to take a glass of something themselves, but only in the jug-and-bottle.

But here was a young woman at the door of the taproom. All the men present, after having believed their eyes, looked to where Glyn was seated with some others in the corner in a way which said plainer than words: 'Will you please attend to this matter, and deal with this female as she deserves to be dealt with. A pair of black eyes would do her the world of good, and the loss of a few of her front teeth might help to remind her of the danger of rushing in where women should never even lightly tread.'

Glyn knew very well what all present expected him to do. He rose to his feet, and with fist clenched in readiness swaggered across to the door. 'Well,' he growled, 'what the hell do you want?'

Before he could say more she had thrown the bag of oranges and nuts into his face. 'Just brought you your oranges and nuts,' she said as she turned and walked out of the place, leaving Glyn to wilt under the contemptuous laughter of those in the taproom until it forced him to leave the place.

Saran, having almost forgotten the incident, was, with two other girls who worked in the brickyard, standing at the back of the little wooden theatre enjoying Act Two of *The Dumb Man of Manchester* when her Glyn left the Black Cock, where he considered he had been made to 'look simple' by her, to walk off his temper.

By this time the narrow main street was packed with people in holiday attire, and in holiday mood. Many men, and also a few women, were already drunk enough to require the combined efforts of relatives and weeping children to assist them homewards. The dead drunks, of whom there were quite a few, Glyn noted, were like Aunt Sallies, at which scores lined up before the stalls were throwing wooden balls; they were without friends or relations, so they were merely shunted from under people's feet around some corner where they could sleep off the drink that had rendered them quite incapable. All shops and public houses overflowed with people, and there were crowds before the stalls which for over a quarter of a mile were lined up against the bank which buttressed the wall enclosing Penydarren Park. Glyn's progress through the street tight-packed with people was so slow that he was able to take in and note the various attractions, swindles, caterers and so on, lined up under the wall of the Park.

The boxing booths owned and managed by those friendly rivals, Prof Billy Samuels and Prof Patsy Perkins, around both of which were large crowds, didn't interest Glyn much, for he was not 'a lover of the noble art'; but he couldn't help hearing what Billy Samuels and Patsy Perkins barked that evening from the raised platform before the entrance to their respective booths, on which they were supported by a quartet of battered bruisers, introduced to the crowd as 'my troupe, and as fine a lot of fighters as ever were presented to Merthyr's lovers of the noble art'.

'Never mind what Patsy's saying; you listen to me,' Prof Billy Samuels was shouting. 'Patsy – he's a Cardiff man, I believe – has got one man as can fight a bit, so I'm told, but *I'm* willing to back either of these four men of mine as are standing here. Here they are, take a look at 'em...'

'... I'll back this lad here, this black man, for fifty pounds to beat either of them four old faggots Bill's shouting the odds about,' roared Prof Patsy Perkins. 'Fifty golden sovereigns...'

'... Hasn't got fifty pence,' Prof Billy Samuels informed the crowd. 'If he had, this lad of mine, this one here, would have eaten that six feet of black pudding Patsy's got over there. Here, I'll tell you what – I'm a sport, I am – and if Patsy's agreeable I'll match this lad of mine...'

Glyn had managed to push through beyond the sound of challenge and counter-challenge when a couple of giggling girls squirted water out of 'Ladies' Teasers' down his neck. He swore at them for silly fools. Buying water in leaden tubes to squirt at people. Softness, he thought. He walked past the Indian doctor's painless-extraction stand, and past the stands of other wonder-working quack medicos; on past stalls that were rapidly being cleared of their stocks of oysters, mussels, cockles; past little portable cookhouses from which steaming-hot faggots and peas were being served to those who liked their food hot even in August. Then on past the stalls catering for those afflicted with a sweet tooth, hordes of whom were shouting for supplies of cheap boiled sweets, brandy-snaps and gingerbread.

Glyn stopped to try his luck at the lucky-packet swindle that was being worked right in the open. The man running the swindle sold the packets at a shilling, 'and when you open it you may have the surprise of your life, but nobody's to open the packet until I give the word.' Having disposed of more than a score at a shilling apiece, he again gave the word, and in each of the packets the buyers of same found about twopennyworth of goods. But there were two of the buyers who proudly displayed golden sovereigns which they said they had found in their packets. Unfortunately for them and for the man running the swindle someone in the crowd recognised the lucky one as the man who been just as lucky several times on a Saturday evening a few weeks previous. Over went the stand, and down underfoot went packets, the seller of same, and his now unlucky accomplices.

The police were rushing up as Glyn moved off to where an old woman dressed in old Welsh costume was selling cockles. At the rear of her stall an 'Under and Over' gamble was being operated.

'Now, gentlemen, why not try your luck. Evens under, evens over, and three to one the lucky old seven. Come on, the more you put down the more you pick up. One chap's just walked away a couple of pound better off than he came. So slap it down, gents, and...'

Glyn moved on to where old Davies, MA, was competing with hoarse barkers on his right and left. 'Excerpts from the Classics' was the line of the old man who had blown into the district from God only knows where. Some there were who said that he had been headmaster of a high school somewhere in England; and that he had lost that job and others through his addiction to drink.... But there were all sorts of rumours; yet all that was known for certain was that he stayed at one of the many common lodging houses situated in the Iron Bridge district of Merthyr, where he paid fourpence a night for a bed and certain other easements and that he was to be found most evenings, weather permitting, declaiming in the open on some pitch or other in order to obtain the money to pay for his bed, a little food and as much drink as he could buy after he had met his food and shelter obligations.

He was a tall and physically upright old man, who wore when dressed to appear before his 'public' a threadbare frock coat. With his unkempt, reddish-grey beard and fiery eyes, he looked the reverse of appealing. Yet there was something which impressed a few of those who stood to listen to him. Glyn was always impressed though why or how was more than he could explain. Maybe it was the 'I am captain of my soul' air of the old chap. Whatever it was, there were a few who delighted in listening to him, openly contemptuous of his audiences though he was.

Glyn arrived at the old man's pitch just as he was concluding something from *Doctor Faustus*. He snorted as the faint applause with which his offering had been received died away, and with a downward motion of the hand strained his beard of some saliva he had discharged into it during his latest effort to educate the masses. Then he smacked his lips and started a gagging interlude.

'Well, gentlemen,' he commenced in a tone in which the note of sarcasm was scarcely veiled, 'I propose rendering one more of my famous masterpieces of elocution, after which, providing you have not melted before then, I will allow you to show your appreciation in the generous manner you usually do. I hardly know what next to favour you with. Perhaps it would be better if I left the selection to you, students of the Classics… ' He broke off to chuckle into his beard. 'So, I await your commands, gentlemen, but, I implore you, do not ask me to deliver "Horatius" again, for that thing is beginning to repeat with me. Come along, please,' he cried impatiently. 'What is it to be? You should know my repertoire by this time. Now.'

He looked out on the crowd expectantly; they regarded him woodenly.

'What, are you in a hurry to go across to the Nelson for a drink, Davies?' shouted one who had the reputation of a wag.

'Frankly, I am, sir,' replied Davies.

'Then give us the death of little Eva and then bugger off for your drink,' shouted the same man, who got a laugh from the crowd.

'Sorry, sir,' said Davies, 'but that lachrymatory masterpiece is reserved for female audiences.'

'What about that piece you recites about the man and his dagger?' Glyn shouted from his place in the crowd.

'The dagger speech from *Macbeth*. With pleasure, sir.'

After straining his beard once more, he cleared his throat and started to declaim, and went on until he was interrupted by a drunken fat man who staggered up to him to ask: 'Wha' you sellin'?'

"O, that this too, too solid flesh would melt," Davies murmured.

'Wha' the hell you mumbling about?' oozed the fat man.

'Sir,' cried Davies, 'I've a few more pearls to cast, so with your kind permission...'

'Oh, is tha' wha' you sellin'? I don' wan' any bloody pearls. I thought you was sellin' some o' them – some – you know wha'. Some – some – but being as you haven't – don' matter a damn, anyway.'

He staggered off towards the nearest portable cookhouse for some peas and faggots, leaving Davies to complete the interrupted soliloquy. Before the faint applause which his offering evoked had subsided Davies was pushing his old bowler hat into the faces of those who had stood their ground long enough to enable him to get to them. Most of the crowd dropped coppers into the hat, Glyn dropped a sixpenny piece, and surprised old Davies, who, after a long look at the sixpenny piece shining brightly from the midst of its humbler fellows in the hat, stared fixedly for a few moments into Glyn's face. 'And you are sober,' he quietly said.

'Well, what about it?' said Glyn in the tone of one admitting guilt.

'And you tossed a sixpence into the old man's hat. Do you know what Carlyle said about a man with sixpence in his possession?'

'No, not I. Who's Carlyle?'

'He is, well, he is not little Willie's father. He is the man who preached.... Would you be interested to hear what he thought of this place, this up-and-coming town of yours?'

'I don't care a damn what he or anybody said about it.'

Davies took a huge pinch of snuff, then held the box out to Glyn, who shook his head and said: 'I've got my pipe.'

'So did Carlyle have his, but he was never much the happier for it. He must have looked down on this town of yours on one of his bad days, for what he said about it was: "A place never to be forgotten when once seen. The bleakest spot *above* ground... a *non plus ultra* of industrialism, wholly Mammonish, given up to the shopkeeper, supply and demand; presided over by sooty darkness, physical and spiritual, by beer, Methodism, and the devil, to a lamentable and supreme extent." Yes, and this is the place in which I look like having to end my days,' cried Davies as though in pain.

'Well, whoever that man was,' said Glyn stolidly, 'he might have said our town was hell and saved all them long words. But he couldn't have known what he was talking about, for this place is the most coming place in Wales, and in years to come it'll be a rich city. And how can that man talk about the devil being here when we got more chapels than any other place in Wales – yes, more than Cardiff.'

'Chapels won't save your town from the devil; neither will this place ever be a rich and abiding city, young man. Once the earth is raped the people of substance will depart, leaving you and your sort to rot...'

'It's you are talking rot, Davies. But, there, what do you know about the place. Better you stick to your reciting.'

'Perhaps you are right, young man. Will you come across the way to have a drink with me?'

'No, not to the Lord Nelson, thank you all the same. I wouldn't wash my feet in what they sell there at the best of times, let alone the beer they get in for holiday-time.'

'Yes, I know, but I never drink beer during holiday periods,' explained Davies as he started across to the Lord Nelson, leaving Glyn to do what he pleased.

Having seen Davies disappear into the pub, Glyn again pushed his way along the crowded street. He muttered angrily when he saw his brother Dai, who appeared to be at least three-parts drunk, tossing for drinks near one of the cockle stalls with a man even drunker than himself.

What a day, Glyn was thinking during his slow progress down the street. First Saran had made him look simple as hell in front of all those chaps in the Black Cock. It would be some time before he heard the last of that. And now Dai, drunk and throwing his hard-earned bit of money all over the place before the holiday was properly started.

In anything but holiday mood he continued along the street until he reached the Eagle Hotel, the first of the huge, new-style drinking places the brewers had erected to meet the rapidly increasing demand for drinking room. Glyn thought it a fine place, so did all the finer type of young miners, that small minority able to read and fond of music. Yes, the Eagle was the place for them, for the Eagle had a large and well-conducted singing room, a bar parlour, and instead of the sand which grated so under one's feet in most of the other drinking places of the district, there was clean sawdust nearly an inch above all floors and in the bronze spittoons, into which it was a pleasure to spit. Then again, the Eagle had glass pint measures of two shapes – one could see the colour of what one was drinking.

On entering the Eagle, Glyn was annoyed to find that the ground floor of his favourite pub was almost as rough and noisy as any of the many pubs he had passed on his way there. 'Humph; the damned place is heaving,' he muttered after a peep into the long bar from the passageway, then he climbed the stairs to the singing room, before the entrance to which there were at least a score of men and youths waiting to be admitted, for nobody was allowed to enter the Eagle singing room whilst singers were on their feet. So Glyn had to wait with the others until Ike James and Shenkin Fraser had completed their rendering of 'The Moon hath raised her Lamp Above' before he could enter. From where he stood with the others near the door, Glyn helped to swell the applause before entering – for Shenkin was his only pal, and they often sang duets together.

Glyn found the singing room as crowded, and, now that the singers completed another of the items in the continuous programme, almost as noisy as the rooms below.

Shenkin Fraser crossed over to Glyn and growled: 'Come on, let's get out of this and down into the bar parlour before they call upon you or I or both of us to sing. I've sworn more than once never to sing again to a holiday crowd, and yet, damned fool that I am... come on, let's get down out of it.'

For the next two hours or so Glyn and Shenkin drank first beer, and later rum, seated on one of the broad, well-upholstered settees in the bar parlour. Glyn was sipping his third or fourth rum and wondering how Saran was getting on in the theatre when sounds of a row in the bar broke upon the refined atmosphere of the parlour. Glyn went on indifferently sipping his rum, but Shenk went out to see what the row was about.

'That was your wench's brother, Harry,' said Shenk to Glyn when he returned from the bar to the bar parlour.

'What was the matter with him again?'

'Trying to bounce beer on strap, as usual; but Mrs Morris stood up to him for once, threatened to brain him with a gallon jar if he didn't go.'

'And did he?'

'Too true he did, no doubt remembering what Mrs Morris did to Will Bevan that time. Lord, you should have seen his face.'

'What was the matter with his face?'

'Oh, knocked about a bit; had a bit of a set-to with Tim Flannery in the bar of the Anchor this afternoon, so Meurig Lloyd just told me. But they were stopped before they got going properly, he said, so they're to finish it up on the mountain in the morning; Meurig reckons it's for five pound a side.'

'Not Harry's money, I know; he couldn't put up fivepence.'

'P'raps not; but he can find plenty to put the money up for him.'

'Well, if he's wise he'll push off home and have a good sleep, for he'll have something on his plate when he meets that Flannery, who's as big as a house, and as strong as a horse. I seen him...'

'Ay, and I've seen Harry wallop bigger men than

Flannery, and I'd back him.... What say if we go to see them fight in the morning?'

Glyn finished his rum, and then sat looking into his empty glass for guidance. Presently he said: 'I don't know; the last mountain fight I saw sickened me. Besides, the police might get to know about it and...'

'Not they; if they did it'll be easy to throw them off the scent. Meurig wants me to meet him on Tom Hall's corner at half past five, so I'll meet you there.'

'But why so early?'

'Because they're due to strip at six. Flannery's bouncing about going to Mass after licking Harry. Well, will you be there?'

Again Glyn stared down into his empty glass, wondering whether Shenk would think him chicken-hearted if he said no, and whether he would voice that opinion to other chaps. Perhaps he had better go.

'Right-o, I'll be there.'

'Good. What about another?'

'No more for me.'

'Good God, so soon. Why, there's more than an hour before stop-tap. Sure you won't have another?'

'No more, I said.'

'Then I'll go back up to the singing room. Mind you're on time in the morning.'

'I'll be there. S'long.'

When Glyn got out into the open air he found himself giddy in the head and a little unsteady on his feet. 'That's through mixing drinks, that is. Damn that rum and Shenk for making me have it,' he muttered, exerting his will-power in order to maintain a dignified perpendicularity as he pushed along the now densely crowded and almost streaming narrow main street. By this time all the sober, chapel-going people were safe at home, and the town was in the hands of those who were determined to make the most of what little time they had to spend before returning to homes little more than hovels, the pits and the fiery furnaces of the steelworks. So, eat, drink, and be merry, for tomorrow.... Men carrying gallon jars filled with beer which was bought as a livener for the following morning met friends who cried: 'To hell with the morning, let's drink it *now*.' And it was drunk by the groups who seated themselves on the pavement, in the middle of the road, anywhere; and when the jar was empty one would rise and stagger off to have it refilled at the nearest pub, he and his companions rejoicing in the fact that there was another hour to go before stop-tap. They sat in the gutter and sang whilst waiting for the return of the one with the gallon jar. At the end of a song one would cry: 'What about something to eat?' To the cookshops, the butchers' shops. Pease-pudding, a loaf of bread, black-skinned blood-pudding, cold faggots, pigs' feet and hocks, chitterlings. 'And if you can't get chitterlings,' they shouted after the messenger, 'then bring – bring – any damned thing you can get to eat.' 'Shops sold out? Then get some more bloody beer.'

Groups of women swaying above the seated groups of men, sipping 'short' out of little bottles, which were kept supplied with fresh liquid by the women with good legs but no money. Every now and then one of the women would go out of sight around the corner to make water, but the men made water sitting in the gutters, didn't trouble to stand up; and whilst one was making water his companions would amuse the women swaying over them with pointed references to the man's codpiece then on view. Laughter loud and continuous.

Glyn received many invitations to 'take a swig' out of this, that and the other jar and bottle as he slowly won his way home through the crowded street; he refused every time, for he was crunching the extra strong peppermints he had bought in the hope of disguising his drink-laden breath from his father, whom he was soon to meet.

Outside their favourite pub, the Anchor, the Irish steelworkers and their womenfolk held up everything whilst they enjoyed a free fight, in the course of which gallon jars, bottles, fists, feet and fingernails were brought into play. Glyn stood to watch and listen from where he had managed to perch himself a little above the rest of the watching crowd on the hub of the right-hand front wheel of the Merthyr-Dowlais horse-drawn bus which, as was the case with several other lesser vehicles, was unable to proceed on its way owing to the fight then in progress, which looked like lasting some time.

'And where can you say the police are?' grumbled the driver of the bus from his high seat, where he sat with reins in one hand and long whip in the other. 'Not a damned policeman to be seen when they're wanted, but when they're not wanted...'

A man perched on the hub of the left-hand front wheel of the bus said he expected that most of the police had their work cut out that night down the rough Iron Bridge district and the fairground just over the Iron Bridge. 'Yes, I expect that's where most of 'em are,' he concluded.

'Then why don't they get more policemen in the district?' the bus driver wanted to know, spitting contemptuously through his teeth down into the battleground below, from where battle cries and screams came up as men and women went down. 'God help anybody as would be foolish enough to try to stop that lot,' he murmured to his nearest outside passenger.

'Why don't you drive through 'em?' said the passenger, a sober man who was on the street late because he had a stall in the market which he stayed in charge of until he had sold all he had to sell at scandalous prices to customers made gullible by drink.

'Drive through 'em?' repeated the bus driver. 'Now, what the 'ell do you take me for?' He spat down on to the back of his leading horse. 'Them three horses of mine'd be cat's meat and me bus broken up into matchsticks before I'd be halfway through 'em. No, let 'em fight it out, I say.... Oh, lord, look at that chap bleeding.'

'That's nothing; look at that woman, ah, she's down underfeet, God help her,' wailed the passenger. 'Where, where are the police?' He went on to tell the bus driver, who was an Englishman, how 'tidy' everything in the district had been until 'the old Irish' had swarmed into it. 'Never had anything like this until they came,' he concluded, pointing down to where the fight was still going strong. The bus driver grunted sceptically as he settled himself in his seat to wait until the police arrived to clear a way for him, which they eventually did, but only to make him go back the way he had come with a cargo of about a dozen of the Irish contestants, including two women, and the seven policemen to the police station.

'You'll have to settle – and salty, too – with my guv'nor for this,' he told the police sergeant who ordered the passengers off the bus so that he and his men could load up with the 'drunk and fighting, your worship' arrests they had made. 'And who's going to clean me bus after 'em, I'd like to know?' grumbled the driver as the loading proceeded. 'It'll be blood and snot from the spokes of the wheels to the…'

'Shut up; turn your horses round and drive like hell to the station if you want to avoid having to spend a night there with this lot,' said the police sergeant as he swung himself to the top of the bus.

Glyn lowered himself from where he had been perched on the hub of the wheel to watch the driver accomplishing the feat of turning his three spirited horses and the huge bus, which carried when fully loaded a score of passengers, ten inside and another ten on top, there in the narrow main street between the Anchor and the Express public houses. A wonderful feat it was; when accomplished, the bus drove off down to the police station and Glyn continued in the other direction towards home, having rid himself of the giddy feeling and general unsteadiness with which he left the Eagle by watching the fight, the arrival of the police, the truncheoning, the arrests, the turning of the bus and other sights.

When he reached home he found his slap-toss brother, Dai, in a drunken sleep on the floor in front of the fire, so he at once got hold of him under the armpits and dragged him across the floor to where the old couch was situated against the wall, and laid him on the couch. The noise he made in shifting his brother from the floor on to the couch must have awakened his dad, who called down from upstairs:

'Who is that?'

'It's me, dad.'

'Oh, Glyn, is it; and is young Dai with you?'

'Er, yes, he's here, asleep on the couch. Where's old Marged?'

'She's…' A bad bout of coughing cut him off for a while, after which he gaspingly explained: 'Sent her up as far as your sister's to see how she is. But your supper's on the table isn't it? I told her…'

'Yes, she put supper all right.'

'Good. Are you coming up for a minute – or p'raps you'll have supper first?'

'Have supper after,' said Glyn as he went upstairs to his dad, who was confined to his bed in the little room farthest from the head of the ladder-like stairs, there being no landing worthy of the name. 'Well,' he said, smiling down on his dad, 'how are we feeling tonight?'

'I'm feeling pretty good tonight, my boy.'

But his looks and laboured breathing belied his words. 'Frank, the mason' – as he was known throughout the district because of the trade he had followed from early boyhood – was one of the many in the district who were in that state referred to as 'the decline', which had set in after he had worked slopping about in water for about twelve hours a day on the construction of a culvert to carry the Morlais Brook under a main road to join the River Taff. Yes, that job was the death of him, all right. And such a 'tidy' man; never in all his life had he touched the drink, and – up to the time he took to his bed for good – as regular as clockwork did he attend his chapel and his Sunday school. He was one of the very few working men in the district that could read and write both English and Welsh; and but for him his children would have been as illiterate as most others in the district – for it was little their mother thought of learning. 'Put 'em to work,' was what she always said. But the father insisted that they should have a little education before starting work, and he made her give them each their penny to hand to the schoolmaster every Monday morning, and when he returned from work in the nights he would for a short while turn schoolmaster, too. Read to them, he would, from the Bible, then make them read in turn to him. And the two boys were getting on famously when the mother put an end to their education by insisting that they should take advantage of the good money for boys that could be got in the pits. So Glyn went to get some of it on his eighth birthday, and had gone on getting it; his brother Dai started at the age of ten; but as for the girl, their sister Mary... well, the mother couldn't do enough for her girl, spoilt – if ever a girl was. She was still in school when girls of her age were earning good money in the brickyards or by oiling and pushing trams on the pit-heads. But she was allowed to continue at school until she was twelve, and after leaving school she was at home with her mother, 'having a lady's life', so the neighbours whose girls were out working said. Then, shortly after her mother's death, when only just gone seventeen, she went and threw herself away on good-for-nothing young Tom Francis, better known throughout the Principality as 'Twm Steppwr'. 'And the bugger's never done a day's honest work in his life,' was what Glyn said when he heard from his sister that she had that morning married Twm Steppwr in the registry office down the bottom of High Street. Said he was going to knock Twm Steppwr's head off but his father called him upstairs and talked sense. But it was enough to drive a hard-working chap like Glyn mad, say what you like; for Twm Steppwr was, like his father before him, nothing more than a pub poet, musician and dancer who went around pubs, fairs and marketplaces playing on his English concertina and singing his own compositions, thrown off extempore, and more often than not forgotten for ever. Then he danced in a way that pleased some whom his singing was directed against. Some there were who preferred his singing, others his dancing, whilst others would walk a mile to hear him play the English concertina, and no wedding party in the district was considered complete without him. It was a poor enough living he made in this way, for he was paid mostly in kind – liquid kind at that. Glyn felt mad when he thought of his sister tied to such a chap, for whom she had already borne three children.

'Yes, I told Marged to slip up to see how your sister was – she's been none too well since that last baby – and to ask her to come down and spend the day with me on Monday, her and her babies,' the father further explained. 'Why don't you slip up to see her sometimes, Glyn?'

'I will tomorrow morning.'

'For sure, now?'

'For sure, dad.'

'That's a good chap.' He lay for a time with his eyes closed before he asked: 'How is it Dai doesn't come up to see me? Having supper, is he?'

'No, he's sleeping on the couch, this last trebler took it out of him more than ever I've known it to,' lied Glyn.

'Then let him sleep; you must be tired too. Ah, well, there's something wrong when men have to work like you have. Three shifts without a break for a bit of rest, and that twice a week. It's not worth it, Glyn boy.'

'Well, whether it is or not, we got to do it, dad, or be in the bosses' black books. They say the orders for our coal are pouring in from all over the world, and there isn't men enough. Now, take the heading where me and Dai works. Nine working-places in it, and they've had to stop the heading now because there's no men to work the places it goes on opening up. And this is what we've got to do. Work our own place until we're fastened by the empty place above, then move to that place so as to work off the coal as is fastening us. Back and fore like that all the time, for there's as good as two places for every man in our pit.'

'I wonder if it will always be like that?'

'It will until they get more men from somewhere, and until they do we shall have to go on working treblers and overtime. But what about your hot milk?'

'I'll have it when Marged comes. Go on to your supper.'

'I think that's Marged now.'

'It is,' said his father, with the certainty of one who has listened long to steps in a room below him. 'Off you go to your supper.'

Glyn went downstairs to find old Marged, with her bonnet in her hand, standing near the couch looking down on the sleeping Dai. 'Humph! As I thought,' she whispered disgustedly. 'A fat lot he cares about his dad up there on his bed...'

'Shut up before dad hears you,' said Glyn in an undertone. 'You're a nice one to talk about others, all the same. He might be dead for all you care, too.'

'What are you talking about?'

'Didn't I tell you not to leave him tonight?'

'And didn't he make me go all the way to Dowlais Top to see how that sister of yours was?' Glyn was silenced. 'Did you give him his milk?'

'No: he'll have it when I go up. Sit down to your supper.'

'I had a bit to eat up Mary's: I'll have a cup of tea, though.'

'How did you find Mary up there?' whispered Glyn across the table.

'Up to her eyes in trouble as usual,' Marged whispered back. 'That bloody monkey of a husband of hers haven't been anear the house since Wednesday morning, and this is Saturday. And she's worrying about him, she's more reason to worry about herself if she only would see it. Lord, didn't she want her head tied for marrying the good-for-nothing thing as he is – and I told her so. But it's like talking to the wall, for it's "my Twm" this, and "my Twm" that. I've got no patience with her. To hear her talk you'd think he was an angel sent to her straight from heaven; and to talk like that whilst she and the children are half starving up there at a time when he's living like a fighting-cock from pub to pub...'

'What this talk about starving? She knows where there's plenty to be had for the asking, don't she?'

'Ay, but she won't ask for fear of giving that Twm of hers away.'

'Well, she wouldn't take telling, would she?'

'Ah, well, it's as much your fault as hers.'

'What the hell are you talking about, woman?'

'Who brought him to this house first? You – you and him that's lying there. With his damned concertina and fine talk.... I remember your poor mother saying that we'd rue the day...'

'We brought him home with us that night to play his concertina for dad to hear him...'

'And he kept coming, but it was Mary he went on playing for; and it's her that he's half starved since.'

'Well, that's her lookout.'

'Ay, God help her, it is,' said Marged, rising.

'Here, mind you don't say anything when you take dad's milk up about Steppwr being away from her all that time.'

'Not likely.'

'I'm going up to have a talk to Mr bloody Steppwr in the morning.'

'And she's coming down here with the children for the day on Monday.'

'See you stuff 'em well with the best of everything that day. Oh, give us a hand to lug this feller upstairs to bed.' He took hold of his sleeping brother under the armpits again. 'You just hold his feet up so as they won't bump the stairs as I drag him up.'

They managed to get him up the narrow stairs and on to

the bed without waking him or his sick father in the inner room. Downstairs they afterwards went, Marged carrying an old blanket and a shawl with her, her bedclothes, for the couch in the living room was her sleeping place. Glyn lit his pipe for a last smoke before bed as Marged warmed some milk for the sick man upstairs.

'I want you to be sure to give me a shake at half past five in the morning,' whispered Glyn to Marged's surprise.

'Why, it's Sunday morning, whatever do you want up that time on a Sunday morning for?'

'Ask no questions and you'll hear no lies. I'm going somewhere particular with a chap, and I've got to be down on Tom Hall's corner soon after half past five. If I'm not there he'll be up here hammering our door and disturbing dad at that time in the morning. So, don't forget.'

'Oh, all right; but still I don't see what you want trapesing about at that time on a Sunday morning.'

She poured the hot milk out of the saucepan into a mug and went upstairs, followed by Glyn. After wishing his dad a good night Glyn went to his room, undressed and laid himself down on the bed by the side of his sleeping brother, but not to sleep for a long time, tired though he was. He lay awake thinking of Saran, of all he had seen on the street that night, of the fight he was going to witness in the morning. Then back to Saran again his thoughts returned. Yes, she was lovely. Oh, how he wished... but what was the use of wishing?

And Saran thought for long ere sleep came to her that night. She thought about all sorts of things, but mainly of the theatre, or what she persisted in calling 'the threeatre'. Illiterate brickyard girl though she was, she had for years been a regular and enthusiastic patron of the theatre, chiefly of the wooden structures which theatrical families such as the Sinclairs, the Noakeses and the Fentons had had erected on the banks of the stinking and rat-infested Morlais Brook, and in which members of the owning family managed to fill every part in the productions presented. In addition to the wooden theatre threepenny gaff productions of melodrama and farce, Saran had witnessed performances to which, as a rule, only the 'big people' of the town went. She had once paid eighteenpence to have the pleasure of being present at the Temperance Hall when Hermann Vezin played Hamlet. How she loved the play she could tell nobody, neither could she tell anyone how she hated the chilly atmosphere of 'the front of the house', where she alone wore a shawl and was unable to read. Vezin's voice she long remembered, as she did the looks directed her way from different parts of the house. Yet after the freezing she had on that occasion, she stood up to the same supercilious crowd when she went to hear an opera performed by the first of the opera companies to visit the town. At the Drill Hall, that was, the place where she afterwards went to see the Christy Minstrels perform. But her main consolation had been the wooden theatre where she had, after having thrown his nuts back into Glyn's face, that night seen performed *The Dumb Man of Manchester,* with the great little Cavendish as the Dumb Man. He, the only player who was not a member of the Sinclair family, was the regular villain, but owing to the demand for facial contortion which he alone could meet, he had to take over the Dumb Man's part, leaving the lesser villainous role to Barry Sinclair.

Saran and the other women present lapped up every drop of the play and the farce which followed, and when leaving somewhere around eleven o'clock they were all inquiring of the checker at the door the title of the play the management was presenting on the Monday.

'Why, it's *Uncle Tom's Cabin* on Monday,' he informed them. 'Got two real bloodhounds from the hound-house an' all,' he called after them.

'We'll be there to see 'em,' they assured him in chorus.

After having had some peas and faggots at one of the portable cookhouses, where she stood eating unperturbed, surrounded by drunken men who said things unprintable, Saran walked slowly home, where, as she expected, she found her old father and her two brothers as drunk as she usually found them on Saturday nights. Harry was stretched out asleep on the floor. Her father was in the low armchair mumbling something about the days when 'puddlers was puddlers'; whilst her brother Shoni was at the table stuffing himself with food. Her old mother was seated on the low three-legged stool near the fire, close to where Harry's head reposed on the hard flagstone.

'Come to your bed, Harry bach, come to your bed, will you,' she wailed.

'Leave the swine alone where he is,' growled Shoni, crunching a large hard pickled onion loudly.

'But if you say he's going to fight that old Irishman in the morning...'

'He won't have the trouble of dressing, so leave him there. About time I had that bed to myself.'

'Oh, I don't know what the world is coming to,' moaned the old man sitting in the armchair. 'In my time it was...'

'Yes, tell us about it in the morning,' said Saran as she hoisted him up on to his feet and began pushing him before her up the rickety stairs. 'Time you was in bed. Come on, up you go.'

The old puddler was easy to handle; never had been in the least blackguardish. Always a rolling stone who was overfond of drink. He had, pursuing work and wages, dragged his family up and down the country quite a lot. Had worked as a puddler in the north of England and in various places in South Wales, and one of the results of all his rolling about was that none of his children were able to read a word in any language, any more than he could. His eldest boy had joined the good old 24th and had died a hero in Zululand, and as the old man often asked afterwards: 'What better would our Ike have been if he could read as good as John Thomas, Zoar? Them old Zulus would have killed him just the same.' His other two boys, men by this time, Harry and Shoni, had picked up all there was to be learnt about pub-crawling, brawling; and the girl Saran had had to learn to look after herself. And well for all that she did, for the old man had been scrapped by new processes and advancing age; the two brothers considered everything other than eating, drinking, fighting and gambling a waste of time, so, all boiled down, Saran was the main support of the home.

'There you are,' she said, pushing her dad into bed. 'And

you get into bed, too, mam,' she told her mother, who had come upstairs.

'Then you go back down and keep an eye on Shoni,' whispered her mother. 'Harry's got money – in his waist-coat pocket. Shoni might...'

Saran went back down to see that Shoni didn't rob Harry, and stayed down pretending to do one thing and another until Shoni went upstairs, then she went through Harry's pockets to see what money he had, and took eight of the eleven shillings she found on him, which was the only way to make Harry contribute something towards the upkeep of the home. A risky business, though, for if he woke up and caught her at it, it would have been God help her. Leaving Harry asleep on the floor she went upstairs and undressed and got into her shakedown at the side of her parents' bed, under which she safely hid the eight shillings she had taken out of Harry's pocket.

For long she could not sleep, whether owing to the bolted alfresco meal of peas and faggots, the excitements of the day and night, or the even greater excitement of robbing Harry, are questions she did not trouble to ask herself. She simply lay awake, her wide-open eyes looking towards the room's one tiny window, through which the moonlight was streaming, moonlight which stirred something within her. Thoughts striving upwards from illiterate deeps began troubling her until she heard Shoni grunt and swing heavily out of bed. He pounded in three strides past his parents' bed to where the bucket stood at the top of the rickety stairs, where he stood, the moonlight showing up a section of his powerful, hairy legs as he stood scratching his stomach and making water into the bucket for a long, long time, after which he went back to his bed and slept noisily.

Saran was almost asleep when her mother awoke and asked: 'Saran, is the dog – is Gyp in?'

'Yes, of course it is.'

'Are you sure?'

'Of course I am.'

'That's all right then; for if the dog happened to be left out them rats would be up from the brook same as before and him dead drunk p'raps it's him an' not boots they'd start on this time. If you're not quite sure I'll go down myself to see.... Are you sure, now?'

Saran was fast asleep, so the old woman got out of bed and went downstairs to make sure. The dog was in.

CHAPTER 2

A HECTIC WEEKEND – SUNDAY

'Five o'clock,' whispered Marged as she shook Glyn awake.

'Right-o,' he whispered in reply.

But he did not get out of bed as quickly as he did on the mornings when called to go to his work in the pit; for in the peace of the early Sabbath morn he felt far from eager to witness a bare-knuckle mountain fight. Still, he had promised to meet Shenk; couldn't let him down now. Glyn hated the thought of letting anyone down, had a weakness that way; he'd do a thing, or stick to a course which was against his grain rather than allow anyone to say he had funked it. And supposing he decided not to go, wasn't it probable that Shenk would hammer the door and disturb his dad. Yes, he'd better go. So he got out of bed, slipped on his clothes and went downstairs, where Marged had breakfast ready for him.

'What did you want to bother putting breakfast?'

'You don't think I'd let you go out this time in the morning with an empty belly, do you?' she said, pouring out the tea.

'I don't want anything to eat.'

'You must eat a little,' she insisted.

Just to please her he forced himself to eat a slice of bread and butter and drank two large cups of tea. He was glad of the tea.

'Now, tell me, what's taking you out so early?' whispered Marged.

'Nothing as would do you any good to know. If dad wakes and asks about me you can tell him that I've gone for a stroll up as far as Pontsarn. S'long.'

'S'long.' She locked the door and went back to her couch.

Shenk was waiting for Glyn on the corner.

'Been up all night?' Glyn asked sourly, for he had been hoping that Shenk would fail to turn up and give him an excuse to return home.

'Damned near it,' replied Shenk. 'Come on, let's hurry up as far as the Musical Hall, from where we can watch Slasher Evans' house. He's going to be Harry's picker-up, so we'll be right if we follow him to where it's to come off.'

At the mention of Slasher Evans' name Glyn stopped as though something had hit him, feeling less inclined than before to go and witness the fight due to take place that morning as he remembered that it was Slasher Evans he had seen beating a Bristol chap almost to death in a fight which was staged on the Aberdare mountain on a lovely June morning the year previous. The Bristolian died, as a result of the beating Slasher had handed out to him, about six weeks after the date of the fight, and there was some talk about the Slasher and others being tried for manslaughter, but nothing came of it, for the Bristolian died in one of the Iron Bridge common lodging houses, and people who died there were seldom fussed over. And Glyn had witnessed that fight – part of it, anyway. He had forced his way out of the crowd as the Bristolian's seconds were stopping up the horrible gashes over their man's eyes with handfuls of shag tobacco before sending him up for some more of the terrible punishment Slasher was waiting to administer. And remembering that morning, Glyn said: 'Let's not go, Shenk?'

'What? After taking the trouble to get up and out this time in the morning? Not likely. Come on, you're talking like a damned baby.'

Glyn expected he would say something like that and place him on the horns of a dilemma. 'You're talking like a damned baby'; what could a chap do but go after being told that, and what Shenk would say to his face he would surely repeat to others and it would go around that he was nothing more than a damned baby who...

Shenk was legging it for all he was worth in the direction of the Musical Hall, near to which they stood with some other chaps who were there before them and others who came along after them to watch the house of Slasher Evans. At five minutes to six the Slasher came out and walked past those waiting to trail him without a word. In his pockets he carried a bottle of lotion, a small bottle of brandy, some Ringer's Shag to stop head and face wounds, and other aids. Shoulders hunched up, he walked along with pursed-up lips and eyebrows forced down until he almost made himself sightless. And there were other mannerisms which in the aggregate made him a composite picture of abysmal ignorance and the quintessence of animality. Waiting groups on every corner sprang into life as he appeared and followed at a respectful distance the 'killer' who pursued his lonely way to the immense bowl-shaped hollow just beyond where the whippet-racing took place most Saturday afternoons.

'This is the place,' said Shenk.

'How do you know?' Glyn asked.

'Well, can't you see one-eyed Ned James scouting along the top there. He can see better and further with that one eye of his than most of us can see with two, and from there he can see anybody coming a mile away. So if the police do happen to get wind of it, Ned'll give us the tip in plenty of time to...'

'Hey, you two,' shouted one-eyed Ned at them, 'don't stand there like a pair of bloody galutes, but get down there with the others out of sight.'

Glyn and Shenk hurried forward to the rim of the bowl-shaped hollow and slithered down to join the huge crowd already seated around its sloping sides. Down there in the hollow the crowd was divided into two sections, the Welsh and Irish sections. Glyn knew most of the Welsh section, bloodthirsty fight-fans all, but he only knew by sight a few of the Irish section. To and fro between the two sections there were a number of men moving along making bets, the sporting landlord of the Anchor being the most active in this.

Glyn looked all round without catching sight of Harry, but he could see the redoubtable Tim Flannery standing ready stripped to the waist in the midst of the seemingly light-hearted Irish section of the crowd. Then where was Harry?

'Where the hell is he?' Slasher Evans was asking Will Tavern.

'Damned if I know,' Glyn heard Will Tavern reply.

'The police might have pinched Harry for something or other last night,' said Shenk.

Slasher Evans was wild. 'And Flannery here ready stripped,' he was saying to Will Tavern, 'and these bloody Micks having the laugh on us. Hasn't anyone gone to fetch Harry?'

'Not as I know. He knows where to come to; shouldn't want fetching.'

'No,' muttered the Slasher, making his way up to where one-eyed Ned James was anxiously scanning the road along which Harry should have long before travelled to his corner; and as the Slasher was ascending to the rim of the hollow Flannery attracted everyone's attention by stepping out from the midst of his supporters on to the level piece of sward on which he was to fight, where he stood exhibiting his beautiful body to the crowd. Raising both hands he several times smoothed back his long sandy moustache, and in so doing revealed his muscles in play under the skin of his arms and back.

'Bounce, that's all it is,' muttered Will Tavern. 'But wait until Harry comes; he'll knock all that out of him.'

'Hwat's keepin' tha champeein of yours?' Flannery shouted up to the anxious-looking Slasher who was pacing the rim. 'Has he been overtaken with the shites, or hwat? Hadn't ye better be goin' to help the poor feller along, for we can't be stayin' here all day waitin' to lick the likes of him.'

Then with the pace of a stallion he paraded the ring to the accompaniment of his supporters' laughter and encouraging remarks. He and his supporters looked upwards when Slasher shouted down: 'You needn't worry, Tim, he'll be here all right; the longer he is coming, the longer you're allowed to live.'

Flannery replied to this by turning a number of cart-wheels, which delighted his supporters, who roared their encouragement.

'Looks a holy terror, don't he?' said Shenk.

'Yes, Harry looks like having his work cut out this day,' said Glyn.

Will Tavern was standing near and heard what they said. 'Not he, Harry'll eat the bastard and ask for a second helping,' he told them. 'These Irish, the damned lot of 'em, are like the barber's cat, all wind and piss. Big and useless, that's what they are. Haven't I seen a priest whipping hell's-bells out of 'em for not turning up to church.'

'I'd like to see the priest as would use a whip on Flannery,' said Shenk.

'Here, are you trying to make me out a liar?' snarled Will Tavern, advancing menacingly on Shenk with fists clenched. Lucky for Shenk was the cry from the rim to the effect that Harry was at last in sight. Those in the Welsh section of the crowd grunted their relief as their champion appeared, and a few cheered and others cried 'Good old Harry' as he bounded down the slope to his corner.

'Where the hell do you reckon you've been?' Slasher wanted to know, pulling off Harry's shirt.

'That Shoni of ours stole eight shilling out of my pocket, so I had to deal with him before...'

'All right, you can tell us about that after you've dealt with Flannery, who's been bouncing quite a bit; reckoned you wasn't going to turn up, and that you was afraid of him, had the shites and...'

'Afraid of a bloody Irishman.' He spat out the mixture of vinegar and water, 'a rinser', which Slasher, on whose knee he was now seated, had given him to clean his mouth out. 'I could beat a boat-load of the bastards.'

'Don't we know it,' said Slasher, who called out: 'Well, are you Micks ready?'

'Sure, haven't we been ready this hour an' more,' joyfully cried Flannery, springing into the middle of the ring.

'So are we,' grunted Slasher, easing his man up and forward towards his opponent. There was no better second in the district than Slasher. Having himself been a principal in a score of hard-fought battles, none knew better than he the value of caution and restraint in the early stages of a fight; and he also knew the value of a second who knew the ropes as he did. Yes, Slasher knew all there was to know about the handling and nursing of a man through a fight. Flannery was by no means as well served as was Harry.

The number of spectators had grown until the bowl-shaped hollow was filled to overflowing by the time the men were sent up for the first round. What a contrast. Flannery tall, upright, fair, smiling, well proportioned. Harry nearly a head shorter than his opponent, dark, bulky, scowling. They at once got to work, watched by the large and silently excited crowd; but as the two men warmed to their work many in the crowd started grunting, squealing, cursing and fighting empty air. A few there were who yapped like dogs.

Flannery, who played to the gallery quite a lot for the first quarter of an hour, held himself like a guardsman; Harry crouched and moved – and at times looked – like a gorilla. For the best part of half an hour Flannery rushed Harry off his feet, pasted his face with a nasty left, and threw him several times.

'Isn't it time you had a drop of this?' Slasher asked the now rather worse-for-wear Harry, holding his bottle of 'the right stuff' up to his man's lips. Harry took a good swig, blew thick blood out of each nostril of his badly damaged nose. 'That's better,' he said.

'Ay, isn't it,' said Slasher, looking across to where the landlord of the Anchor was pushing his way about shouting odds of two to one against Harry. 'Hear that, Harry?' said Slasher.

'What's stopping me? But he won't be shouting two to one for long.'

Harry began to steady Flannery with pile-drivers to the body in the next round, and from that round he was relentless – terrible. Flannery couldn't keep him out, he closed in and delivered blows which left their mark on Flannery's fair-skinned body, blows that made the receiver gasp. For about twenty minutes Harry punished his opponent's body before stretching him out with a right under the heart. As Flannery's people were working on him,

Slasher gave Harry another swig of the 'stuff' and said: 'The bastard's not as tall as he was, Harry, now that he's trying to protect his body more. So what if you began plastering his mug a bit.'

'I think I will,' said Harry, and as soon as he was eased up and forward towards his now swaying opponent he went for his mug. And didn't he plaster it, plastered it until the almost senseless Flannery's nose, moustache and lips were pounded into one piece of blood-soaked hairy flesh.

Glyn bowed his head and closed his eyes long before the 'plastering' of Flannery's mug was completed; he had tried to force his way out of the crowd, but he was wedged in, so he closed his eyes, but he left his ears unstopped, and heard Shenk squeal: 'O, Christ.' Then it was that he raised his head and opened his eyes just as Flannery was being pushed forward by his second to receive the *coup de grâce*. *Smash*. He fell, and the blood-drunk crowd yelled before it broke when the Irish admitted defeat. What he had seen caused Glyn's innards to turn a somersault; he was suddenly and violently sick. He crawled up the slope and away as fast as he could until he came to a field in which there were some cows; he pushed through a gap in the hedge and sat there in the field watching the cows for a long time before getting up and starting for home. He hadn't gone far when he remembered that he had promised his father to go up as far as Mary's house that morning. So he turned again, crossing the slag-tips so as not to pass near where the fight had taken place.

To get to where his sister lived he took a short cut through the world's largest steelworks. As he hurried along between mile-long strings of low wagons loaded with steel rails for various distant parts of the world the thought that he was in a way embodied in the rails struck him for the first time. Funny he had never thought of that before. The rail-banks, furnaces – all that greatest of works would be useless but for the coal he and others hewed daily. How much coal have I during the fourteen years turned out? was what he was trying to calculate as he reached the railway line stretching for about eight miles from the steelworks to the ten pits which it served, pits owned by the same company that owned the steelworks which used up the total output of the two most productive pits.

Thinking more or less idly of coal and steel, Glyn walked for some distance, after he had walked through the works, along the railway line leading to the pits – though it wasn't a railway line in the ordinary sense. For it was the company's private line, over which only coal-trains and colliers' trains, or 'cwbs', as the morning and night trains which conveyed the miners to and from the pits were called, ran. Walking this line in an unusually observant mood, Glyn noted with surprise that it ran over the mountains parallel with the old trolley-line he had heard his father refer to many times, and also with the mountain road along which pack ponies had carried coal from the pits to the works and foundries long before the trolley-line was laid. And now the railway line. What next? he wondered.

He left the line just as a Sunday train of only one carriage was bearing down on him. He knew that train, colliery officials on their way out to inspect the pits.

'Well, I'd rather them be going than me today,' he murmured.

He went on his way, and soon he was looking down on the row of cottages threatened by an oncoming slag-tip which towered above them. His sister lived in the second of the six cottages, in front of which he could see his good-for-nothing brother-in-law sitting with a baby in his arms. He was singing joyfully.

'Yes, well you can sing, you lazy swine,' muttered Glyn, looking down on them.

Twm Steppwr was a red-headed, merry-looking chap, undersized, though. But he was a good-looker when seated. He looked up and stopped singing when Glyn began slithering down the slope towards him.

'Hullo, Glyn,' he cried heartily. 'See untle dyn?' he then went on to ask the baby he was holding. 'Dere 'im is tumin down de tip.' Next a loud shout: 'Mary, Mary, here's your Glyn. You're an early bird, ain't you, Glyn? But I can tell where you've been. You've been to see the fight.'

'What if I have?' said Glyn sourly. 'How was it that you wasn't there to encourage your drinking-chum?' he asked sneeringly.

'There's a difference between drinking and fighting that's next door to murder,' replied Twm. 'I knock about with Harry, I know, but when he puts his fists up I'm missing. Oh, here's Mary.'

She came out of the house smiling. 'Hullo, stranger,' she said.

'Hullo, you,' said Glyn. 'God, what a wreck,' he thought.

Though only twenty she looked at least ten years older. Waxen; hanging breasts. And in the family way again.

'How's dad down there?' she asked.

' 'Bout the same.'

'Oh. Won't you come in a minute to see the other two children, I'm washing them all over in the tub. You won't know 'em, for they've grown...'

'No, I won't come in, I'll stay out here and have a smoke and a talk with Twm.'

'Then I'll finish washing the children.' Into the house she went.

'Twm, I've got a bone to pick with you,' said Glyn.

'Oh.'

'Ay; about – about Mary.'

'What about her?'

'What about her, indeed. Well, in the first place, she's not looking up to scratch, is she?'

'I don't know,' indifferently replied Twm, dandling the baby. 'I haven't noticed anything wrong with her, neither have I heard her complain...'

'Stop playing with the damned baby whilst I'm talking to you, can't you. She complain? Not her, but it's to be seen with half an eye that she's going all to pieces; anybody can see that, and anyone that can't see it must be blind.'

'You mean me?'

'Ay, you, you that leaves her alone with the children in this hole for the best part of a week at a time.... Oh, I know all about your tricks.'

'Has Mary...?'

'No, you know damn well *she* wouldn't tell me; but can you deny that you were away best part of last week?'

'A couple of nights, that's all, picking up a few shillings

in the Rhondda and at Pontypridd. I can't afford to miss Pontypridd on market-day....'

'Market-day, be damned; you're enough to drive anybody mad. At a time like this, when there's any God's amount of work about, you're talking about market-days.... You'll never do any good playing that concertina of yours up and down the country. And you with three little children, an' all. Why don't you start work in the pit again?'

'Because the work don't agree with me, that's why. Another couple of months of it would about kill me.'

'Don't talk so damned dull, man. Has it killed me? And I've had fourteen years of it.'

'But we're not all built the same, see, Glyn.'

'Oh, for God's sake don't start...'

'Just a minute, Glyn. No, let me talk.' He clasped the baby closer to him. 'This isn't the first time you've got at me this way. All you can think and talk about is work, work, work, and you want me to think and talk the same...'

'Not think and talk, but work.'

'Well, I tried it, didn't I? And a week of it was all I could stand. On lovely mornings like this morning being flung down Cwm Pit...' He broke off and shuddered. 'No, never again. I like the daylight, the sunshine, and a bit of time to make up songs, to practise a new step, a new tune on the concertina...'

'Bloody laziness! But even if you can't stick the dark in the pit you can get plenty to do in the daylight and the sunshine, can't you? What's the matter with Dowlais or Cyfarthfa works? I know a chap as'll get you a job in either place any day. It's a wonder to me you're not ashamed to be seen tramping around with a concertina under your arm, playing tunes and poking your cap into people's faces like a blasted beggar.'

'Maybe my tunes and songs are worth what little I get for 'em.'

Glyn rose from where he had been sitting. 'I can see it's no use trying to talk sense into you. If Mary had any damned sense she'd leave you before you land her deeper in the mire than you have already. She's welcome to come back home any time – and she can bring the children with her.'

'Why don't you tell her that?'

'Because I know it's no use, for you've mesmerised her with that fine talk of yours. But she'll get to know you some day.'

'Some day,' repeated Twm. 'Yes, we'll all be known some day; me and my concertina; you and your work, work, work. No doubt you'll be a model husband.'

'I'll work to keep a wife when I take one; she won't have to depend on pennies begged in pubs.'

'Let's hope not,' said Twm pleasantly. 'Mary,' he called. 'Your Glyn's going.'

'Not so soon, surely,' cried Mary as she came out of the house with her second in her arms and the first holding on to her skirt. 'I was hoping you'd stay to dinner; we've got a lovely bullock's heart for dinner that Twm brought home last night.'

'Well, he can do with some heart, your Twm can,' muttered Glyn as he started up the slope. 'S'long, Mary.'

'S'long. Tell dad that I'll be down for the day tomorrow.'

'He's expecting you.'

'Oh; and tell him that these houses have been condemned and that we've got to be out by Christmas.'

'All right.'

From the top of the slope Glyn looked down at Twm and his sister, now in laughing dispute for possession of the baby, Benny.

'As though I'd never been anear 'em,' he murmured. 'What a place to live in; time they were condemned. Oh, what's the use.'

He walked fast back the way he had come to his sister's place, and was soon back on the road leading into the old, derelict Penydarren works, from where Trevithick had started off the first locomotive way back at the beginning of the century which was nearing its end. And Trevithick, Glyn reflected, now long dead, and the little works in which his once most revolutionary ideas on locomotion had been fostered now crumbling ruins which harboured each and every Sunday a score or more gambling schools. From early morning up to the time the pubs opened for the mid-day session, and during the hours between the midday and evening drinking sessions, hundreds congregated in and around the old works to try their luck at banker, all-fours, nap and pitch-and-toss, the latter being the favourite game of chance.

That morning Glyn walked past all the card schools, but he stopped near the largest of the pitch-and-toss schools in amazement at the sight of Saran's fair and firmly fat, cunning and dangerous brother Shoni, standing in the centre of a double circle of men who were betting on the toss of the coins which lay flat on the palm of Shoni's upturned right hand.

'I'll head for another sovereign,' he was shouting. He was soon accommodated.

'Where in the name of God did he, of all people, get sovereigns from?' Glyn asked himself as Shoni tossed the two pennies into the air. Down they came – two tails. Shoni had lost, and apparently his reason as well as his money, for he did a mad stamping dance on the innocent faces of the two pennies, swearing horribly as he danced. Never in the history of the game could a Queen's or King's image and superscription have been so vilely treated.

Glyn hurried away and left the gamblers to it, still wondering where the usually penniless Shoni had got the gold he had just lost.

The 'lost ones' were gathering near the pubs in readiness for opening-time and those who claimed that they had been 'saved' were on their way to church and chapel as Glyn turned out of the old Penydarren works on to the main street. This was the hour of church parade, though perhaps it would be more correct to call it chapel parade, for the chapel people were dominant in the district. True, there were a few Church of England buildings in which the upper ten of the district gathered to listen and take part in what the chapel people regarded as lifeless services; and there were also a couple of places where 'them old Irish' and a handful of Italian ice-cream barmen gathered to hear from their priests what the Pope wanted them to do whilst sojourning in what was a nonconformist stronghold; and it was also strongly rumoured that the growing Jewish community of the district were soon going to build a place in which to worship the God of their fathers. However, counting the Jewish intentions as a synagogue, for it eventually materialised, there were only six places of worship which Church of England, Catholics and Jews could boast of between them, and what were they against the scores of nonconformist chapels at a time when nonconformity was go-ahead and aggressive in the extreme. Having as good as won the battle for Sunday closing, and planning their campaign for Disestablishment of the Church in Wales, the nonconformists regarded with contempt all creeds and denominations which had no victories worth speaking of to their credit.

Yes, there they were, marching, those nonconformist Christian soldiers, to their chapels, 'marching on to war', as Glyn was returning home. If the boozers, bouncers, bullies, wife-beaters and children-starvers had had it all their own way the day previous, they certainly did not on the Sabbath, when the nonconformist battalions marched proudly into Nebo, Caersalem, Shiloh, Noddfa, Tabernacle, Beulah, Moriah and scores of other citadels. Even Glyn, son of a stalwart nonconformist though he was, was made to feel unworthy and he wilted as he walked with downcast eyes past his more righteous brethren; so what must 'them old Irish' and 'those old church people' have felt like as they slunk by on their way to sit at the feet of priests and clergymen who knew not how to preach. Talk, and recite flatly, oh, yes; but as for singing and preaching... no, they didn't know how to.

Glyn was glad to reach home that morning after having run the gauntlet, as one might say. As he reached the door he met his brother Dai coming out.

'Hullo, where have you been to?' asked Dai.

'Out walking – been up as far as Mary's. Where do you reckon you're off to?'

'Well, if you want to know, I'm going out to get myself a pint.'

'I thought so; can't you leave it alone on a Sunday? You know how dad...'

'Yes, I know; but, indeed to God, Glyn, I'm feeling all to rags. I'm only going to have one. You don't think I'm off to get drunk, do you?'

'I've known you get drunk twice on a Sunday before now, and then it was only going to be just one pint.'

'Yes, but I – look here. You come down with me, and if I take more than one, then...'

'Don't shout, do you want dad to hear you? Oh, go on, but if you come back here... well, you'll see.'

'And you'll see me back before you can say knife. Hell, I've got more respect for dad than to...'

Glyn pushed past him into the house; Dai hurried off to the pub.

'Has dad asked for me?' Glyn asked Marged, who was peeling potatoes for the Sunday dinner.

'Yes; I told him you'd gone up as far as Mary's.'

'Then you told him the truth,' said Glyn as he went upstairs, where he found his dad, with spectacles on, endeavouring to read the heavy old family Bible.

'Hullo, dad.'

After a bout of coughing his dad said: 'Trying to read – a little – but this big Bible is so heavy.'

'You know it's too much for you to hold on your chest like you do,' said Glyn, taking the Bible from him.

'I'm afraid it is, but the print in the little one is too small for me to see. And I like to read a little every day, and especially Sunday.'

'Shall I read it for you?'

'Yes, please.'

'Where shall I read from?'

'The Psalms I was reading – so read anywhere from the Psalms.'

Glyn started to read; he read haltingly at first, for the longer words held him up, but he got better as he went on. He hadn't been reading long when his brother Dai entered the house and came straight upstairs. 'Well, I kept my word, didn't I?' was what his eyes signalled to Glyn. Aloud he cried: 'Hullo, dad. Here, our Glyn reads the Bible nearly as good as Thomas, Zoar. He'll be a preacher if only he'll stick at it.'

His father smiled up at him fondly and said: 'What if you read to me for a change? Oh, Glyn. How did you find your sister Mary?'

'Er... oh, not so bad. She's coming down with the children to spend the day with you tomorrow. Told me that they've got to get out of that house soon.'

'If they're not out soon it'll be buried under the slag-tip, which is getting closer to the houses every day,' said Dai.

The father sighed. 'So I've been told; though where the people are to go to is hard to say, for there isn't a house to be had in the district for love or money. Marged was telling me only this morning that people are offering as much as two pounds for the key of a house of any sort. But you were talking about preachers, Dai. Well, if you want to hear the finest preacher in Wales then go to Zoar tonight – you're too late now for the morning service.'

'John Thomas, do you mean?' said Glyn.

'No, John is preaching away, and Sylvanus Price from Pontypridd is taking our big meetings. Oh, how I wish I was well enough to go to hear him. Why don't you boys go? You won't regret it.'

'I may go tonight,' said Glyn half-heartedly.

'And I'll stay home to keep you company if Glyn goes,' said Dai, 'for I expect Marged'll be going as usual.'

'All right, that's a bargain,' said Glyn. 'If you stay and read to dad I'll go to Zoar and let dad have a report of how things go.'

'He's asleep – look,' said Dai.

Glyn looked, and was not surprised to see that his dad was asleep. He had lately dropped off to sleep whilst talking, in the middle of a sentence sometimes.

'Weakness, I expect,' said Glyn. 'Come on, let's go down to dinner.'

After tea Glyn got himself ready to go to Zoar. As he was walking down the street in his Sunday best he thought of Saran and decided to go across to where she lived to invite her to accompany him to chapel. As he drew near to where she lived he could hear Harry roaring about something or other, so he stopped and asked one of the boys living in the row to go and ask Saran to come out to see him.

The boy went and returned to where Glyn was standing on the corner. 'She asks if you'll wait a minute till she's ready.'

'All right,' said Glyn, giving him a penny.

He must have stood there at least twenty minutes before Saran made her appearance. 'I've been waiting...'

'I know; come on, I'll tell you as we go. Our Shoni again...'

'What's he been up to again?'

'Plenty. Oh, he'll be the death of mam and dad, I'm sure he will. He... p'raps you heard that Harry fought Tim Flannery this morning?'

'I was... yes, I heard about it.'

'Well, Harry got three golden sovereigns for beating Flannery from them as backed him to win. He came home all covered with blood and took off his coat and waistcoat in the house before going out to the tap to wash himself. The three golden sovereigns was in his waistcoat pocket, but they wasn't there when he came back in after washing...'

'Shoni took 'em.'

'Who told you?'

'Nobody; but I seen Shoni this morning in the old works playing pitch-and-toss, at which he lost at least two pounds on one toss as I was passing.'

'So that's where he went, was it? Harry was searching the town for him. Oh,' she sighed, 'but that isn't all. The police have been to the house after him.'

'What for, name of God?'

'For stealing a new overcoat from Seidle's pawnshop,

where he went to pawn his shirt. And after he stole it he took and pawned it with Cohen's down the bottom of High Street.'

'Well of all...'

'I'd rather the police get hold of him than Harry, for if Harry... what chapel are we going to?'

'Zoar, dad asked me to go to Zoar tonight. Some grand preacher there, he reckons.'

Saran was scanning with anxious eyes the groups then gathering near the pubs in readiness for the evening drinking session, hoping to see Shoni so as to warn him to keep out of sight of the police and out of Harry's way. 'I expect Shoni's far enough away by this time,' she murmured. 'P'raps gone on tramp to work at that waterworks up England way same as he did before that time. Well, well, here are we going to chapel whilst all them there are waiting for the pubs to open.'

'Well, they'd better make the most of it, for they've only got two more Sundays before Sunday closing starts.'

'I expect they'll get beer somehow even then. Here we are.'

'Yes, and here we'll be by the look of things,' growled Glyn after he had been informed that there wasn't even standing room.

'Wait,' said Saran as he was turning away. 'Look, they're carrying forms and chairs from the vestry.' Saran intercepted old Evan Matthews as he was puffing his way from the vestry into the chapel with a chair in each hand. 'Let me have them, Mr Matthews,' she said, taking them from him and handing one to Glyn. 'There, now you can go and get two more, can't you? Zoar will have to have overflows tonight by the look of things, Mr Matthews. Come on, Glyn.'

Admiring her cheek, Glyn followed her down the centre aisle, at the pulpit end of which she placed her chair and sat down, motioning to Glyn to do likewise. Though it was a little after the usual time for commencing the evening service, there was no sign of the preacher, who was waiting in the little room behind the pulpit until the extra seating accommodation had been provided. Eventually every inch of space was occupied and the congregation waited for the preacher to come out and start the service. There was a lot of whispering going on, but it ceased as Sylvanus, the greatest of the giants of Welsh pulpits, made his appearance.

He entered quickly, with his eyes on the ground, from the little room and ascended the three steps leading to the roomy pulpit – he liked a roomy pulpit and something firm in front of him on which to emphasise his points with two-finger taps and blows of the fist.

'And so this is the famous Sylvanus,' murmured Glyn.

'A fine-looking man,' murmured Saran.

He was a man – well, a big, powerful man wearing side-whiskers on his pale face. After a word of silent prayer he stood up and announced the first hymn.

'My, what a weak voice,' whispered Saran.

Everybody was singing – all kneeling afterwards before God in Zoar – again all sang – then all listened to the reading of God's most comforting Word – and sang again – Sylvanus bowed his head in prayer as the collection was taken – *then*:

'Before I submit for your consideration my interpretation

of the message delivered by Isaiah to King Hezekiah, I want to say a word regarding the work of a social character still to be accomplished by nonconformity, which is the only militant religious body of our times. We have won, despite the Established Church, the battle for Sunday closing in Wales, and very soon now there will not be a single drinking-den open on the Sabbath. I said despite the Established Church, which in the fight we have for long waged and, God be thanked, have at last won, displayed indifference most ghastly. And we nonconformists are under the heel of this ally of the brewers, this... but I'll leave it at that, for soon we shall marshal our forces for the fight to free Wales of the chains that bind it, chains which were forged and clapped on us for the benefit of the Established Church.

'Wales today, with its great mineral wealth, is the foundation stone of the rapidly growing British Empire, which is expanding amazingly; and the most important factors in this expansion are the coal and steel of South Wales, and the men who produce them, of course. And if the British parliament thinks that it can keep us for ever under the heel of the Established Church, then we shall...'

Things were warming up in the Albion, one of the three pubs practically on the doorstep of Zoar Chapel. Those patronising the Albion on Sundays, and most week nights as well, were able to follow the services almost as well as those in the chapel itself, for not only could they hear the singing, but also what the preacher was saying once he reached peroration point. 'Being here's like having one's drop of beer in the chapel,' some of the chaps used to say, but there were others, especially the domino-players, who disliked the 'noise', as they called it, made by those in chapel when they were considering whether to play the double six or the six-four next. But none of her patrons felt as bitter against the chapel and its membership as did the landlady.

'Yes, they're satisfied now,' she was saying, 'now that they've robbed a poor widow of her living. A working man is not to have his drop of beer on Sunday, and all through them. What if I objected to them kicking up a row every week night and annoying my customers. Yes, every night they're at it, if it's not in the chapel it's in the vestry. And we mustn't say a word. Oh, no, let them have all the say. Soon we won't be able to breathe for 'em, the old hypocrites as they are. I know 'em. Don't I? I do. All day Sunday, then prayer meetings, band of hope and the rest of it all the week. I wonder they don't make us close altogether.'

'What are you worrying your guts about?' said Wat Ward to her. 'Let 'em close the pubs on Sunday – but there's back doors to pubs.'

'Yes, I know, but it's little I'll be able to do round the back with the peeping Toms from two chapels looking down on the place from morning to night of a Sunday. No, I think I'll leave....'

'A great preacher,' said Glyn as they left the chapel.

'Not so bad,' said Saran, 'once he began talking from the Bible, but when he was on about the drink I thought little of him. I see no harm in a man having a drop of beer if only he keeps himself tidy.'

Glyn turned on her: 'Then if that's the case why did you rush in and make me look such a damned fool in front of all those chaps in the Black Cock yesterday?'

'Oh, so you've still got that stuck in your gizzard, have you? I thought when you came and asked me to come to chapel with you that you'd forgotten all about that.'

'Well, I haven't, see.'

'Then the sooner you do the better. I said if a man keeps himself *tidy,* but he's not behaving tidy when he goes on guzzling and leaves a body waiting like you left me all that time outside the threeatre. And didn't you make me look a damned fool standing there?'

Glyn pushed on in silence until they got on to the road leading to Pontsarn, a favourite place with the young couples on Sunday evenings in the summertime. Saran broke the silence.

'P'raps I oughtn't to have done it.'

A hundred yards further on he said: 'You know damned well you oughtn't to have done it. It would just serve you right if I didn't take you anywhere tomorrow.'

'You can please yourself, my boy. Humph, I can enjoy myself as well without you as with you – and p'raps better.' She stopped. 'And being as you're talking that way, you can talk to yourself, see. S'long.'

CHAPTER 3

A HECTIC WEEKEND – MONDAY

August Monday, the greatest holiday of the year, thought the miners, steelworkers and their womenfolk. 'Yes, Easter Monday's all right, and so's Whitsun – and Christmas-time's jolly, but August Monday's *the* day.'

When Glyn and Dai went downstairs that morning they found their sister Mary and her children in the living room, where they were being 'stuffed' with the best of everything by Marged.

'Hullo, Mary,' cried Dai, 'you're down early, ain't you?'

'None too early, is she?' snapped Marged.

'Not a bit; but where's Steppwr?' asked Glyn.

'Oh, Twm was off early with his concertina,' replied Mary. 'He helped me with the children as far as Tom Hall's corner, then he went on down to the Black Cock, for Mrs Davies begged on him to come and play there for her today.

He promised to call for me on his way home tonight.'

'Yes, but he'll have been drunk at least twice before then,' laughed Dai, 'so...'

'Don't think everybody's like you are,' said Marged. 'Don't take any notice of him, Mary. Now, what do you want to eat?'

'I've had plenty, thank you, Marged. Now, let me put breakfast for the boys, I don't often get the chance.'

After they had breakfasted the brothers, Mary and her three children went upstairs and crowded the little bedroom where the father lay.

'Now, you'll be all right today with Mary here, won't you?' said Glyn. 'Me and Dai are off out now.'

'Yes, I shall be all right this day,' said the father, smiling up at his daughter whilst his wasted left hand rumpled the hair of the eldest of her three babies. 'And see that you boys keep yourselves tidy.'

'We will,' Glyn assured him, placing his hand over his dad's for a second. 'Come on, Dai. S'long, Mary; look after dad, remember.'

'Yes – and here's something for the children,' said Dai, pressing some silver into his sister's hand.

And off they went to enjoy themselves, feeling as though they had received in advance absolution for whatever the holiday spirit might lead them into. Dad would be happy with Mary and the children, of course he would. Then off down to the town of a hundred delights. All sorts of sport from cockfighting to bare-knuckle fighting in secret places, and foot, cycle and pony racing in the Big Field, where the sports were due to commence at 2.30 sharp, but the gates opened at noon for anyone who wanted to go and have a drink and a snack at either of the four big marquees erected for the day by the man who had the contract for the catering. Still, plenty of time before we go there, thought the brothers.

'What about a drink?' said Dai as they neared the Black Cock.

'Plenty of time for that too,' Glyn told him. 'Let's have a walk round town first.'

So they walked round, first to see the new sensations on the Iron Bridge fairground. Then back through narrow streets crowded with people going here, there and everywhere. To the Eisteddfod which had already started at the Temperance Hall; to singing festivals about to commence in two of the largest chapels; to the fairground; to the registry office to get married, and afterwards into one or other of the numerous pubs to drink the health of the young couples in good beer at twopence a pint.

The pubs, which had opened at five that morning, as they did most mornings, to supply liveners to those badly in need of same, were already discharging into the gutters their first batch of drunks, those up-and-doing chaps who boasted that they were able to get drunk three times every holiday and twice every Sunday. It took some doing, getting drunk twice on a Sunday, for time was so limited, and a man had to bolt his beer in order to get his two drunks in, but on a holiday, or any weekday when the pit happened to be on stop or the furnaces were not going, a man could get his three drunks in comfortable without having to bolt his beer, for he had eighteen hours to do it in from when the pubs opened at five in the morning to when they closed at eleven at night; and the man who couldn't get drunk three times in eighteen hours, 'well, he's not worth a damn'.

The brothers, having completed their tour of inspection, were back in Pontmorlais, where they stood to watch broken-nosed Tom Duke and his Louisa, better known as 'the Duchess', coaxing their weather-beaten old Aunt Sally outfit on to its feet with the aid of string and a borrowed hammer. The brothers were only two of many who enjoyed watching and listening to the notorious pair, Tom Duke and his 'Duchess', when they turned show-people only on two holidays of the year, Whitsun and August Mondays; Tom worked as a carter for the rest of the year.

He was an Englishman who had been left stranded in the district after the circus with which he had travelled around had left. He had been leading stake-driver and tent-packer; and whilst having an argument with one of the other circus workers he was hit in the face by a heavy stake swung carelessly by the other chap. He was in the infirmary when the circus packed up and moved on, and as nobody in that infirmary knew anything about nasal surgery Tom left there to talk through his nose with the minimum of intelligibility for the rest of his days. Being a strong fellow who was used to horses, he got himself a job as a carter and stayed on in the district where he met the loose and once lovely Louisa Westcott and married her. He was told enough, goodness knows, about Louisa, but marry her he did. There was only one black man in the district at the time, he came from God only knows where and got himself a job in the gasworks which few but he could or would do. Hard and dirty, it was, but the lone black man stuck it until it killed him. But that's not the point. The point is that Tom Duke knew before he married Louisa that she had been guilty of consoling the black man in his loneliness. 'Yes, a bloody black man,' chaps told Tom. And yet he went and married her, though she was no longer lovely. They lived together after a fashion.

And here they are cursing each other as they work on the erection of the Aunt Sally outfit, which eventually is declared open for business.

'Now, where's that box of cigars?' cried Tom.

Louisa handed him the box of three-a-penny cigars they had invested the last of their money in.

'Good, now we can make a start.' He and Louisa faced the world with three wooden balls in each hand. 'Three balls a penny, three balls a penny,' they shouted. 'Every time you knock one of the old ladies down you get a cigar such as you've never had the pleasure of smoking before. So let 'em have it, gentlemen, for they have no friends or relations – ah, there's another old lady on her back. Here you are, sir, the best cigar in town – give this gentleman fivepence change, Louisa....'

They soon had an enthusiastic band of Aunt Sally slayers, Glyn and Dai amongst them, demanding penn'orths of ammunition. The brothers got one cheap cigar apiece in return for the energy and the shilling expended. Puffing at the cigars they promenaded the main street.

'Well, what about that drink?' Dai asked.

'All right.'

Into the crowded Black Cock they turned. Glyn pulled back as Dai was leading the way into the long bar, at the end of which the battle-scarred Harry was seated in the midst of admirers listening to Twm Steppwr playing 'A Sailor Cut Down in his Prime' on the concertina.

'Here, let's not go in there amongst that lot.'

'Why not?' asked Dai.

'Because if I do Harry'll be bouncing pints out of me same as always. Come on, let's go into the little room behind the bar.'

'And miss the fun? Not I,' said Dai, pushing his way into the bar.

Glyn made his way along to the little room where he could sit and hear all that went on in the bar without being seen by Harry and the rest. And there he sat drinking 'special' at threepence a pint as he listened to Steppwr entertaining the company in the bar with those improvisations for which he was famous in a hundred townships of the five largest mining valleys. Glyn couldn't refrain from smiling as he listened to the singer in the bar rendering his scandalous song-portraits, after each of which the company in the bar roared laughingly the seemingly innocent refrain:

Did you ever see,
Did you ever see,
Did you ever see-ee
Such a thing before?

Then they listened for the next spicy verse; and how they relished his risky treatment of many absent and well-known characters; but there were many of those present who stopped laughing when this Welsh counterpart of François Villon completed his song-cycle dealing with absent ones and began looking around for subjects. By way of a start he fastened on the landlord's huge belly and his lady's spare frame and combined them in a manner so shocking as to cause even that hardboiled pair to protest and threaten to turn the singer out.

'So let's have less of that, please,' said the irate landlady.

'Oh, take your bloody gruel, woman,' Harry shouted at her. 'Take no bloody notice of her, Steppwr. Go on, let it rip.'

Well, it was holiday time and everyone was spending freely, so the landlord and his lady 'took their gruel' and Steppwr's jingling stream flowed on uninterrupted. There was a storm of applause when he at last sat down, and many there were who crowded towards him with tots, glasses, pints and quarts held out. 'Here, take a swig out of this.' And how sorry they all were when he announced that he was due to leave to keep his promise to play, sing and dance at the Blue Bell that afternoon.

'Well, half a minute while I take my cap round,' said Harry, glaring around. 'Damn it all, isn't he worth more than a sup of holiday beer? Of course he is; why, things would be as dead as mutton for us chaps as takes our drop of drink if it wasn't for Steppwr and his sort. Too true it would. Some goes to the theatre, and many more goes to chapels to listen to people as are not half as well worth listening to as Steppwr is, and them people got to pay salty for listening.' He placed a patronising hand on Steppwr's shoulder. 'Well, here's our jester and musician, so let's see what we can do for him. And none of your bloody ha'pennies, either.'

He pushed the cap over the bar into the face of the landlord, who tossed sixpence into it. Next he held it before the landlady.

'My husband's given sixpence, hasn't he?' she cried.

'But that's not you; come on, fork out.'

And fork out she had to before he would allow her to carry on serving the thirsty customers. Harry took the cap around, collecting, browbeating, and then returned to where Steppwr was seated.

'Here you are, Steppwr,' he said, emptying the money out of the cap into Steppwr's cupped hands. 'Mostly copper, worse luck, some of these chaps are afraid to part with a bit of silver.'

'I'm satisfied, Harry.'

'That's not the thing; some of the bastards would have seen you go out without a copper. You could play, sing and dance till you dropped for some of 'em, and all you'd get from 'em would be the bottoms of their pints. Don't I know thc bastards.'

'Yes, but we chaps got to work hard for our bits of silver,' up and said one whose wife and her fancy lodger Steppwr had linked in a song in a way as left but little to the imagination.

'And what the hell do you reckon Steppwr's been doing for us?' menacingly Harry askcd. 'Isn't it work? Of course it is, you bloody melt. Maybe you think it's easy? Right, I'll tell you what I'll do. If you can play anything as'll sound like a tune on his concertina, or make up two lines about anyone here in the bar, then I'll stand drinks all round – and best beer at that. Come on, what about it?' he growled, moving down on the chap with fists clenched.

Goodness only knows what he'd have done to that poor chap had not his attention been diverted by a row in the jug-and-bottle, in the direction of which all eyes now turned, so the chap in danger from Harry seized the opportunity to sneak out of the pub and out of danger.

'So this is where you are, you old cow, you,' flat-nosed Tom Duke was shouting at someone in the jug-and-bottle. 'Here, lapping it up as fast as I can shout it in, me out there shouting my lungs out. Get out to that stall, you drunken old sow, before I break…'

'You'll break nothing, you flat-nosed swine,' Louisa was shouting. 'If you dare raise your hand to me I'll split you from ear to ear with this quart…'

The landlord was on the spot shouting: 'Now, come on, you two, out of it before I throw you out. I wanted my head tied for serving you,' he told Louisa. 'And see that neither of you ever comes anear my house again, always the same you two are. Every time I see that blasted Aunt Sally outfit of yours going up I know I'm in for trouble. Come on, out you go.'

He had said sufficient to unite man and wife.

'The man must be mad, Tom,' in the refined manner she could put on when it suited her. 'Isn't our money as good as the next man's, and can't a man and his wife have a word to say to each other without such as you intruding? It's come to something, Tom.' Then she exploded. 'As if we didn't remember him coming to the place with the tail of his shirt hanging out through the arse of his trousers, and her, the big-sorted bugger as she is, without a shift to her back. And that's the sort as now tries to ride the high horse. Come, Tom, let's clear out of the damned hole to where we're welcome.'

She led the way out and back to the stall with head in air, and it was not until they had been back at the stall some time did Tom realise that he had been sidetracked from his grievance by becoming Louisa's silent ally during her handling of the landlord.

Glyn, having had by this time nearly as much three-penny 'special' as he could carry and stand up, was leaving the Black Cock when he ran into Steppwr in the passage-way, who was leaving to fulfil his afternoon engagement at the Blue Bell.

'Wait. Now listen, Steppwr,' Glyn began ponderously, 'I want a word with you. Mary – you know Mary's up at our house?'

'I do.'

'Yes, and the shildren. Nice little shildrens. Pity for them. Ay, indeed. But – but they're all right up our house.'

'Of course they are.'

'Yes; and remember you call for them on your way home tonight.... But tidy, remember. Tidy, like me.'

Steppwr laughed: 'Oh, like you.'

'What the hell are you laughing at?'

'Nothing, your worship. S'long, Glyn.'

Glyn stood swaying in the entrance watching Steppwr pushing along the street with his concertina under his arm. Lord, that 'special' must have been stronger than usual, stronger even than that Scotch ale he had been knocked over by that time. And all he'd had of it was three pints. Better take a walk to clear the head. But where? Then he thought of Saran. An awkward wench if ever there was one. Yet there were few smarter gels about. Still, she had walked off and left him standing like a fool in the middle of the road after he had taken her to chapel, which few chaps would have done after the way she had simpled him before those chaps in the taproom of the Black Cock on the Saturday evening. Yet... well, he'd give her another chance.

He started off to fetch her out. As he crossed the little bridge over the stinking brook, which was almost dry and stinking worse than ever, he saw her with the old woman her mother sitting on the low wall in front of the house.

'Oh, Glyn,' cried the old woman as soon as she saw him coming. 'Have you seen my John anywhere?'

'No. Seen Harry, in the Black Cock he is.'

'It's not Harry, but his brother John that I'm worrying about. He hasn't been home all night; and Sergeant Davies the bobby been here after him today again,' she concluded tearfully.

'Oh, stop snivelling,' snapped Saran, who hadn't as much as looked at Glyn standing within a few feet of her.

'Though it'll be just as bad if Harry finds him,' the old woman moaned.

'Well, he shouldn't have stolen Harry's money,' said Glyn judicially. 'Serve him right if...'

'It wasn't your money he took,' Saran flamed out. 'The best thing you can do is to keep your mouth shut and go back where you came from.'

'And I can, plenty of welcome there.'

'Then go.'

'Now, you two; isn't there enough old rows without you two rowing again?'

'Oh, let her alone,' said Glyn, trying to look dignified and hurt at the same time, but only succeeding in looking ridiculous. 'That's what a man gets when he comes tidy and with money in his pocket to ask her to go for a walk.'

'Go and put your hat on and go, Saran,' advised her mother.

'What for? To be left standing outside one pub after another whilst he slips in for bolters, and then have to lug him home, p'raps. Not I. Look at him, he's three parts drunk already.'

'I'm nothing of the kind.'

'Go and put your hat on and go when he asks you,' ordered the mother who had never known of a brickyard gel when 'fetched' by her young chap to refuse to go with him just because he had had a little drink.

Saran looked Glyn over and afterwards stipulated: 'Well, I don't mind going with him if he has a good sluish under the tap and a strong cup of tea after to...'

'I'll see you in hell before...'

'Now, Glyn bach, go on and swill your face under the tap – just to please her, that's all. Here's a towel – put your coat there on the wall. I'll have a cup of tea ready by the time you've swilled.'

'Well, being as you... but she needn't damned well think that she can bounce me into...'

'Certainly not, my boy. Go now,' said Saran's mother.

But it was Saran that picked up his coat and brushed it

long and lovingly whilst he was having a most sobering and refreshing sluish under the one water tap which served the twelve houses, and which was fastened to the wall somewhere about the middle of the row, opposite the one small ashpit and three closets which were shared by the twelve families.

On returning to the house Glyn was made by Saran to drink two large cups of strong tea before she helped him on with his coat. Then they went out to town together.

'Remember, if you see John, tell him whatever he does, to keep out of Harry's way,' Saran's mother called after them.

'Where are we going to?' asked Glyn, as the sound of what the famous Cyfarthfa Brass Band was playing up in the Park where the Sports were about to begin was heard by them.

'What say if we go to the Big Field Sports?'

'As you like.'

He bought tickets for the best part of the field, where he parked her on the grass to watch the sports whilst he dodged from one marquee to the other drinking beer and talking about how much work he could do and how much coal he had turned out in this working-place and that to chaps similarly disposed. Now and then he'd think of Saran sitting out there on the grass, and when he did he'd struggle with others for lemonade and sandwiches, thick ones, which Saran devoured with relish. Four sandwiches and two bottles of lemonade she had in all whilst watching the foot racing, pony racing and cycle racing, the latter by far the most exciting, Saran and the rest of those watching thought. There were world champions in the Penydarren Park riding cycles both single and tandem that day – and everybody said that the Cyfarthfa Band played lovely.

Glyn managed to get back to where she was seated as the final of the pony race was being run, and in an attempt to delude her into thinking that it was the sport he had mainly been interested in during the afternoon, he started shouting encouragement, to whom or what he knew not, as the ponies ridden by almost fleshless riders flashed by.

'It'll be time to go to the threeatre after we've had a cup of tea,' said Saran as they were leaving the sports-field.

'The theatre? Again?'

'Yes, can't miss tonight, for it's *Uncle Tom's Cabin* tonight, got real bloodhounds, the checker told me. And we'll have to be there early to get a seat tonight.'

'Oh, let's go down the fairground instead?'

'We could take a stroll down there after the threeatre, p'raps. Now, come on, be fair, Glyn. I sat up there all the afternoon by myself whilst you hopped from one marquee to the other meeting your pals and drinking with 'em. And if we don't go to the threeatre it'll be the same tonight, only it's from pub to pub you'll be hopping whilst I cool my heels on the pavement. Now, you know I'm not agen you having a drop of drink, but there's a limit, you know.'

'But I don't like old plays, gel; and you know none of the chaps ever go there. Women and kids, that's all.'

'Is it, indeed, then how was it that I seen dozens of chaps there on Saturday night?' she lied. 'In any case, it'll be better than sticking yourself in a pub all this night again.

And there's nothing to stop you going to get a drink between the acts.'

'Oh, all right.'

After more strong tea at Saran's place they walked across to the little wooden structure dignified by the name of theatre, before the entrance of which a crowd was gathered.

'There, didn't I tell you?' growled Glyn. 'All women and kids, not a man among 'em.'

'Oh, yes, there is,' insisted Saran, pointing to two youths about fourteen years old. 'Look at those two chaps. Where are you going?' she asked as he moved away from the theatre down to the corner where stood a shop, Tom Hall's, which was doing a roaring trade in nuts, oranges and sweets.

'What did you come here for – to get some nuts and oranges?'

'Well… ay, you can get some if you want; but I came here out of the way till them doors open and we can walk straight in.'

'But we won't get in if we don't join the crowd and push.'

'Then we won't get in at all, for I'm not going to stand there, let alone push.'

'There, the doors are opened; let's go.'

As he walked slowly towards the entrance with Saran, Glyn watched the desperate struggle for admission. There were scores of women with children in arms and others clinging to their skirts, and these children, as though trained for it, howled in chorus when the doors were opened and the rush started, and gave the cue to their mothers.

'Oh, my God, mind this child in my arms.... Stop your pushing there. If you... oh, my baby. No, that other little one of mine underfoot.' Others were more abusive. 'Blast your eyes, can't you see that child underfoot, you cheeky young slut, you. P'raps if you had children of your own you'd have more thought for other people's.' And so on.

'Nice damned place to bring babies,' muttered Glyn, standing with Saran at the rear of the crowd.

'What are they going to do? They've either got to bring them or stay at home to mind them.'

'I'd like to see a woman as b'longed to me bringing a child of mine into a place like this. I'd show her...'

'Yes, you'd show a lot. Now are you coming in or not?'

'Not until that lot are in out of the way.'

'And more coming along all the time. S'long.'

He grabbed her arm. 'Wait. I'm coming.'

She shook herself free. 'Then come,' she said, throwing herself into the crowd around the entrance, and she breasted a road along which he followed to the pay-box.

'I'll get the tickets.'

'I'll get my own,' she told him.

He pushed her out of his way and cried: 'Let's have two of your best seats.'

'Two shillings, please,' said the man in the pay-box.

'No, no,' protested Saran, who had never paid more than threepence.

'Get in there,' he told her, pushing her before him masterfully to where the two rows of shilling seats were situated.

'Whatever did you want to bring me in here for?' hissed

Saran as she gingerly seated herself on one of the rickety chairs backed with patched red cloth. 'This is where the tradespeople sit. I always sit back there in the three-pennies.' She looked back to the benches on which those who paid only threepence had to sit. 'Oh, lord,' she murmured.

'What's the matter now?'

'Some gels as works with me in the brickyard are back there, I'm sure they seen me, so I can look out. They'll be saying as I'm stuck up and... can't you change the tickets, Glyn?'

'Not likely. Damn it all, what's the matter with you? You're not satisfied now that you have got me here, and being as I am here I'm damned if I'm going to sit back there in the middle of a swarm of crying babies. So shut up, for if I once get up from here I know the seat I'm going to be in for the rest of the night.'

'Humph, so do I.'

'Then shut up! Huh, look at these,' he whispered, jerking his head in the direction of two drapers' assistants and their sweethearts as they came forward from the entrance to the shilling seats. 'We're as good as they are, any day.'

In a whisper Saran agreed and went on cracking nuts between her strong teeth and spitting out the shells on to the floor. The two shop assistants produced and lit the two cigars they had won at an Aunt Sally outfit earlier in the evening.

'Cigars,' whispered Saran to Glyn, who was smoking his pipe.

'Looks well, cigars,' she whispered again.

'Yes, them chaps look better than they'll be feeling soon,' Glyn said, 'for they look to me like two of old Tom Duke's cigars, fifty a shilling he buys 'em at. I'm damned sure it was one of them made me feel drunk before I came to fetch you, for I'd only had three pints of "special", and...'

'Hush,' hissed Saran as a man came out from behind the canvas flap left of the proscenium and seated himself before the badly out-of-tune piano, on which he pounded until the old thing gave expression to sounds which might have been recognised as plantation melodies by a keen student of same. Anyway, nobody listened to the overture. Everyone, with the exception of Glyn, waited almost breathlessly for the faded drop-curtain to roll itself creakily out of the way so that they could get their first look at the old Kentucky home. The 'Great Holiday Production' commenced, and Uncle Tom wearily led the way from the plantation on to the stage followed by four supers, his fellow slaves. 'Them's the supers,' said Saran. 'That's Dai Genteel, and the one behind him is Evan...'

'I don't want to know who they are.'

So she shut up. The play was rapturously received by all but Glyn, who slipped out for a drink not only between the acts, but at the end of each scene as well. Saran was much too interested in the play to notice his exits and entrances. She was cheering Eliza across the ice, hissing Simon Legree, laughing at Topsy, crying over little Eva and Uncle Tom. 'Oh, I cried my eyes out,' said Jane Jones to Saran as they met on the way out. 'And as for that old bugger – what's 'is name, now?'

'Simon Legree.'

'That's the bugger; I felt like going on to that stage and hitting him between the eyes.... Here, who're you pushing?'

'No' so bad, was it?' said Glyn thickly as he stumbled clear of the crowd with Saran at his side.

She caught him by the arm and steadied him. Now she was able to note the effect of the number of 'quick uns' he had taken whilst she was watching the play. 'Here, I'd better take you home,' she said.

'I'm not drunk.'

'Not far from it.'

He didn't argue. 'I feel bad,' he said presently.

'How bad?'

'In my stomach.'

'Then turn aside into the old works.'

'Better now?' she said when he returned to her.

'Ay; would you like to go down the fairground?'

'Not if you're feeling bad.'

'I'm feeling right as rain now. It's a bit late, but the fair'll be on till midnight, and as we shan't have another day's holiday till Christmas, we'd better make the most of this. Come on.'

It was long after midnight when they parted on Tom Hall's corner, both very tired, and he quite sober by this time. When she got home she found her mother seated on the three-legged stool looking down on Harry, who was asleep on the floor.

'Here he is tonight again,' sighed the mother. 'Your father was nearly as bad, but I managed to get him up to bed.... Here, where can you say you've been until this time of night?'

'Morning, you mean. Well, after coming out of the threeatre I went down as far as the fairground with Glyn.'

'Oh, as long as Glyn was with you. Did you see your brother Shoni anywhere?'

'No; it'll be a long time before Shoni shows his nose back here again. He's far enough by this time. Come on, let's go to bed.'

'What about him?' asked the mother, pointing down at Harry.

'Let him alone; the dog's here to see the rats don't get at him. Come on, or it'll be time for me to go to the brickyard before I know it.'

Sighing as though her heart were breaking, the old woman climbed the stairs; Saran waited until she got to the top of the stairs, then blew out the table lamp and followed her up.

Glyn was surprised to find Mary and her children still there when he got home. 'Hasn't Steppwr called then?'

'Not him,' answered Marged. 'Here, you'd better help Mary home with these babies.'

'Why couldn't our Dai...'

'Humph, Dai. Mary and I had to put him to bed. Come on, take two of these children.'

'No, I'm damned if I will; let Mary and them shift here for tonight.'

'No, I must go home to Twm, for you never know...'

'Oh, come on then.'

He picked up two sleeping children off the couch and started off, followed by his sister with little Benny in the shawl. Oh, what a jaunt it was. Several times he had to sit down to ease his aching arms. And then to find the man whose children he had humped for miles through the night sleeping on the floor... oh, he could have kicked him. But his sister, softie that she was: 'Oh, Twm bach,' she cried, putting little Benny in the armchair and then turning to take the folded tablecloth off the table and put it under her husband's head. 'Thank God he's home.'

'Never mind that lazy swine,' shouted Glyn, 'but take these children off me before I drop 'em.'

'Yes, Glyn, I will as soon as I've lit the candle. There, now give me them and I'll take them straight upstairs.'

Relieved of his burden, Glyn sank exhausted into a chair, from where he looked down bitterly on the face, the peaceful face, of the concertina man. How could he sleep peacefully when…?

'There,' said Mary as she came downstairs. 'Now, you must let me make you a cup of tea, Glyn; but before I do p'raps you'll help me to get Twm up to bed. Oh, look at the old silly,' she fondly exclaimed. 'His concertina safe as usual, and something for the children same as always,' she went on to say as she bent down to pick up the concertina and some bags containing fruit, sweets, and a larger bag than the others containing a pint of cockles, off the floor. 'Cockles, he's fond of cockles fried in bacon-fat. Now, Glyn, you take his feet, will you?'

'I'll see him in hell first,' Glyn exploded. 'Look out, you softie. I'll wake him.'

He took the kettle from the hob and emptied it over the sleeping man's head, almost wishing that it was boiling-hot water instead of cold. Then he violently shook him awake, and having done so rushed out of the house as Twm Steppwr was demanding to know what was the matter.

CHAPTER 4

CHRISTMAS IS HERE AGAIN – AND AGAIN

Yes, a lot can happen in five short months, in five short minutes for that matter, Glyn was thinking on the Saturday evening which that year also happened to be Christmas Eve, as he stood, pipe in mouth and his second pint of beer before him on the counter of the bar of the Star, a pub he rarely patronised; but as a pit-mate had sold him a couple of tickets for the big Christmas draw to be held there he had turned in just about the time when the draw was due to take place. What started him thinking of all that had happened during the five months previous is more than he would have been able to explain had anyone chanced to ask him to.

They had been months of hard work, and months without daylight other than the little on Sundays from

October onward to Christmas. Work-drunk returning from the pit night after night; turning into pubs on the way home for body-builders of the good beer that was food and drink to an exhausted man. Then a few extra hours of drinking on Saturday nights, but no longer any open drinking on Sundays, for Sunday closing was at last an established fact, was law. The doubtful pleasure of meeting Saran for a few hours each weekend was often spoilt by the intrusion of Harry between the young people.

Then the typhoid epidemic which came about corn harvest time and wiped out thousands who thought they were going to live for ever. But old Death mowed along the banks of the stinking Morlais Brook and along the banks of the polluted River Taff. No sooner had he reaped his harvest there than he started work in the mean streets until shrieking headlines in the London papers, 'Whole Families Wiped Out', appeared and seemed to satisfy him for the time; for soon after those headlines appeared the number of deaths fell back to normal. But not before all the graveyards in the district were filled and the huge new cemetery, which the council with great foresight laid out in a beautiful valley bought from the county authority of the next county, was started off well with a few hundred victims of the epidemic whose bodies were laid to rest in Breconshire after a life spent in Glamorganshire. Yes, and it was a terrible long way to have to carry a body, and most of them had to be carried.

Glyn's sister Mary and her children had been taken, but old Death, for reasons best known to himself, spared Twm Steppwr, who had since been as free as the air to go playing and singing and dancing around the pubs, but his freedom from responsibilities didn't seem to increase happiness, for, in his fashion, he had truly loved Mary and the children. He cried a lot at the funerals which Glyn and Dai had to pay for, and he afterwards went to lodge in the same common lodging house as Davies, MA, down in the notorious Iron Bridge district. He still went about the pubs, his constant companion and protector being Saran's blackguardish brother, Harry.

Saran's father, the old, unwanted puddler, was also taken after he had died to the new cemetery. There was hardly a family in the district left untouched, but the district seemed more crowded than ever for all that. There were many sad hearts after old Death had passed by, none sadder than Glyn's father, who didn't seem to care whether he lived or died after Mary and her children were taken.

And of these and other happenings Glyn was sadly thinking on Christmas Eve as he smoked his pipe and drank his beer in the bar of the Star; when who should walk in but Harry and Twm Steppwr.

'Ah, now we're right for a drink, Steppwr,' cried Harry as soon as he spotted Glyn. 'Come on, Harris, fill us a quart, my future brother-in-law'll pay for it.'

'Don't you draw that beer, Mr Harris,' said Glyn, 'for I'm not paying for it. If I'd been asked tidy I might have, but...'

'If you'd been asked tidy,' growled Harry as he advanced towards him. 'If I'd have gone down on my bloody knees, is that what you mean?'

'No, what I meant...'

'What you meant, you mingy swine...'

'Now, Harry, don't be a damned scamp,' cried Steppwr.

But it was too late, for Harry had let go viciously with his left, which travelled with deadly speed to a point between Glyn's two eyes and blackened and nearly closed them. As Steppwr afterwards said: 'Harry had the skin of his arse on his face that day, no doubt about it; and before we could say knife he let poor Glyn have it between the eyes. Bash. It was the dirtiest thing I've seen Harry do, and I've seen him do a few dirty tricks – and I up and told him it was a dirty trick. But what Harry gave him was nothing compared to the blow poor old Glyn had when he reached home and found his father dead. Thought a lot of his father, Glyn did. Oh, and when Saran heard about what Harry'd done to Glyn she said she was going down to the Star to brain Harry, but when she got there and tried to do it he gave her a backhander that knocked her flat. Man or woman, Harry's not particular...'

Frank, the mason, was buried in the new cemetery on the day after Boxing Day, and everyone said it was a grand funeral, though the feeling between the two sections that followed his body was none too good, but it was a grand funeral all the same. Glyn and Dai had scraped every penny they could to hire the only hearse in the district with glass windows, through which everyone could see the coffin with brass fittings and the two wreaths. They wouldn't have been able to get that hearse with the glass windows if they'd had to pay for a new grave, but as they only had to pay for the opening-up of Mary's grave they were able to pay the extra for the hearse with the glass windows.

All the chapel people and two choirs, the chapel choir and the Sunday-school choir – for Frank, the mason, had been a Sunday-school teacher for fifteen years before he took to his bed – turned out to show their respect for him, as did the three preachers dressed in tailcoats and top hats. Two of them prayed lovely over the body in the house until Mr Williams, the undertaker, coughed meaningly several times and afterwards said 'Right-o' to the men waiting to carry the body out of the house and into the hearse with the glass windows. But it was Frank's own preacher that did the praying and preaching over him at the graveside, and never has anyone preached better than he did over Frank that day.

First the Sunday-school choir sang in front of the house, and the chapel choir joined in as the body was carried out, but everybody combined to make Cwm Rhondda most thrilling at the graveside, even the three publicans sang, for there were publicans and sinners who turned out to the funeral partly out of respect for Frank, the mason, but chiefly because they knew Glyn and Dai as good customers. Anyway, the publicans felt they were entitled to a day out after the busy time they had had over the Christmas-time, and Boxing Day in particular. And, fair play to them, the three publicans were dressed up to the nines in finer tailcoats and more shiny top hats than those worn by the three preachers.

As soon as the body was deposited in the hearse, Mr Williams, as was his duty, began to marshal the following, but as soon as 'the family', Glyn and Dai, were in their places behind the hearse, the chapel people and the two choirs rushed to get all together so as not to be mixed up with 'those other old things', meaning the three publicans and the ragtag and bobtail who only attended funerals in the hope of getting soaked in drink on the way back. The chapel people wouldn't be seen walking with the likes of them, they had enough to put up with as it was. Just fancy having to walk behind one of 'the family' whose two eyes were nearly as black as his bowler hat. He had applied several beefsteaks and had bathed his eyes with vinegar several times, and still Glyn's eyes were black – well, as good as. He had wanted to wear a black cap which he could have pulled down over his eyes, but old Marged wouldn't hear of it. 'Who ever heard of a man wearing a cap at his father's funeral?' she indignantly asked. So he had to wear his bowler hat, and didn't he feel ill at ease.

Yet not more so than the three publicans who had been pushed to the rear of the procession by the chapel people, right to the rear where they had to walk side by side with such nobodies as Twm Steppwr, who had turned out in a borrowed black suit miles too big for him. But on the way back from the cemetery the three publicans showed them chapel people who was who, for they invited all and sundry into the hotel that had been erected for the convenience and solace of sorrowing ones and their friends just outside the gates of the cemetery. For the publicans, mean though they might be when behind their own bars, were as good as gold when on the way home from funerals. Thought nothing of throwing a gold sovereign on the counter and saying: 'Go on, lads, drink that between you.'

All three of them that day invited the sorrowing brothers in to have all they wanted to drink; and the three preachers, hoping for a couple of converts, offered to give the brothers a lift back to town in the one-horse brake that had been hired, but Glyn and Dai managed to please both saints and sinners by saying that they had to go back with Mr Williams, the undertaker, to settle up for the coffin and things. So they hurried off with him, and when the three of them got to the Lamb and Flag on the Brecon Road the undertaker stopped, looked back the way they had come, and said: 'I think we've shaken 'em off, let's slip in here for a couple.' When he and the brothers were comfortably seated with drinks before them he went on to explain: 'Got to be as cunning as a wagon-load of monkeys in my business – that's if you take a drink, for some that's been at this funeral today, if they once saw me turning in for a drink, would rather go to their graves in their shirts than in a coffin of my making. Drink up and have another.' They did. 'Well, boys, you gave him a grand funeral, and he deserved it, for if ever there was a good craftsman, it was your father. As good a mason as ever picked up hammer and trowel, best man as ever worked for me.'

'And he used to say that you was the best boss as ever he worked for,' said Dai.

'That's neither here nor there, but there can be no two opinions about your dad; and what licks me is that neither of you had sense enough to take to the trade.'

'And work years for next to nothing when we could be earning good money in the pits,' said Dai.

'As we have done,' said Glyn.

'Yes, but you haven't got a trade in your hands, have you?'

'Oh, I don't know.... What do you reckon getting coal is?' asked Glyn.

'Well, it's certainly not a trade. Drink up and have another.' They did. 'But what's the use talking, can't get boys to take to a trade these days, for no sooner are they breeched than down the pits they go. But, you mark my words, these pits and works will have their day, and then you'll wish you had a trade in your hands.'

Dai's third pint was making him argumentative. 'Nonsense,' he cried. 'Why, there's enough coal in the valleys of South Wales to keep us busy for hundreds of years; and do you think they'd be putting up all that new plant in Cyfarthfa and Dowlais works if they weren't going to last?'

'They were putting up new plant in the old Penydarren works when that closed down never to start again. Well, I must be off...'

'Not until we settle with you for the coffin,' said Glyn.

'The coffin's my present to your father.'

'No, thank you all the same; dad's not resting in anything but what's paid for,' Glyn told him.

'In that case – what about thirty shillings?'

Glyn paid him.

'What about a last drink? I shan't have another, but there's no need for you two boys to hurry off. What is it to be?'

They told him, and he ordered their drinks as he was passing through the bar on the way out.

'A good old sort,' said Dai.

'Not bad.'

'Well, and what are we going to do now, Glyn?'

'How do you mean?'

'Are we going to carry on the house same as before or...'

'Certainly we are. What made you ask that?'

'Well, I thought, now that dad is gone, that you and Saran...'

'Don't talk to me about her,' cried Glyn, blinking his still damaged and discoloured eyes. 'I'm not having anything to do with that lot.'

'Oh, you know your own business, but all the same I don't reckon you should have it in for Saran because of what Harry...'

'Shut up about them, I tell you, and don't you ever mention her name again to me. If you only knew how she sticks up for those brothers of hers, you'd... but what are we bothering about her for?'

'I've finished bothering; what about another drink?'

'No, we've already had more'n I intended we should have this night. Let's keep tidy this night, anyway. Come on, let's go home so as I can get into a cap as'll hide these eyes of mine a bit.'

Glyn hadn't spoken to Saran for twelve months, though he had seen her many times since the night Harry blackened his eyes; seen her standing in the crowd waiting for the theatre doors to open, seen her on the street, and once when he was later than usual going to the pit he had seen her on her way to her work in the brickyard. Once or twice, he thought, she had been on the point of speaking. So had he, but he wouldn't admit it even to himself.

'If she won't bend, then neither will I,' he used to mutter.

He was working harder than ever, not only in order to try

and forget about her, but in order to keep his end up and hold his own with other chaps in one of the stiffest places he had struck during the years he had worked in the mines. He and Dai, do what they would, weren't earning their salt in the place, and their pride and pocket were suffering. 'It's like the hobs of hell,' Dai remarked to old Joby the roadman one day when the latter came into their roadway to eat his bit of snap in company with the brothers.

Joby, now a roadman, had hewed coal before the brothers were born, and long before that: had hewed many a ton of the first cargo of Welsh coal to leave Cardiff, coal that had been sold at the pithead at four shillings a ton, and which he had had to hew for eightpence-ha'penny a ton. Now, nearing eighty, he crept about the Gethin Pit doing pretty much as he liked for the low wage he was paid to do what road-repairing he could.

'Yes, I expect it is, Dai bach,' he said in reply to Dai's description of the coal in that particular working-place, 'yet there's many as burns our coal that thinks we shovel it in like they have it shovelled into their coalhouses. Little they know about it, Dai bach.'

'If they only had to…'

'But they haven't, so what's the use bothering? Now, I worked coal like you've got in front of you on the pillar system sixty years ago, and I can tell you two boys how to make this place go. I admit that you've got a stiff place, and that you're doing your best, but for all that you can't get the place to go. It sticks like glue to the roof, and worse to the bottom, and as you said, Dai, it's like the hobs of hell. Well, what are you to do? You go on beating at it for hours and all you've got is a capful, it's breaking your hearts and you're thinking of chucking the damned place up. And still it might be made to go. Now, here are the two of you hammering side by side on the day shift, from morning till night you're slogging away, and on towards the end of the shift – when it's time to put the tools away and go home – you find that it's beginning to move a bit better. Isn't that so?'

'Ay, so it do, Joby,' the brothers said together.

'Don't I know it; and when you come back to it next morning it's...'

'Like the hobs of hell again,' said Dai.

'Ay, and I know that too, hasn't it had twelve hours to settle down, to get stoon again. Of course it has; you've got to keep the damned thing goin' once you've got it goin', keep at it round the clock. One of you worry it through the day, and the other through the night, that's the only way you'll get this place to go, boys.'

'Might be worth trying,' said Glyn.

'Don't I know it is,' said old Joby.

'But there's Sunday,' Dai reminded him. 'Suppose we do keep it going all the week bar Sunday, won't it stiffen up again over Sunday?'

'No, the devil jumps out of it on Sundays,' said the old man cryptically. 'Keep its arse warm every day and night 'cept Sunday and you'll get this place to go. I remember when...'

'Hoy, Joby,' called a haulier from the parting about twenty yards away.

'What do you want again?'

'There's a rail out of place on the heading; better come and fix it before it throws me off the road all-fours.'

'Some of these hauliers want carrying about,' grumbled the old man as he went out to fix the rail.

After he had gone the brothers considered his suggestion.

'What if we try it?' said Glyn.

'I'm game,' said Dai. 'Which of us works tonight?'

Glyn put the palm of his right hand to his mouth, then held it out palm downwards. 'Wet or dry?' he asked.

'Wet,' said Dai, and wet it was.

'So it's me for the doubler,' said Glyn. 'You'd better leave me what food and drink you've got left.'

So Glyn hammered away through the twenty-four-hour stretch; and wasn't he glad to be relieved by Dai at six o'clock the following morning.

'How's it been going, Glyn?' shouted Dai as he entered the working-place.

'I think old Joby's right; it's pouncing a bit already.'

'Good; off you go to get some sleep. 'Spect you can do with it.'

Glyn had to admit that he felt whacked as he walked back to the pit bottom, then there was the long walk home from the pithead. It was nearly eight o'clock when he reached the outskirts of the town, and he was much too tired to be interested in the fact that there were more people than usual about, and that they appeared excited over something or other. He turned into the Express and said: 'Give us a pint, Griffiths, for God's sake.'

The landlord filled him a pint and made a mark with the chalk behind the door, for Glyn had no money on him, but his name was good.

'And another,' he said. 'I hardly tasted that one.'

'I expect you've heard about the explosion?' said the landlord as he filled the empty pint.

'What explosion?'

'Down the Rhondda Valley, in the Naval colliery. They reckon there's hundreds killed, though it'll be a day or two before we know how many for certain.' He moved to the end of the bar to serve others.

Glyn lit his pipe and began to notice who was present in the bar, feeling but little shocked by what he had heard. Neither did any of the others in the bar seem to be shocked in the least, the news seemed to be taken as something sensational rather than shocking, for all present were familiar with the varieties of fatalities which were a daily occurrence in the pits.

'Still, it's high time something was done to prevent these explosions,' Ned Luke was saying. 'This is the second we've had around here in less than six months.'

'Man alive, it's more than six months since the Risca explosion,' said Ike Hughes.

'I know damned well it's not more than six months.'

'But I know damned well it is, see.'

'You do, do you? Then I'll bet you a quart it isn't.'

'Right, I'll bet you a quart it is. Why, it happened on the very day my sister's boy…'

'Never mind your sister's boy, Ike,' said the landlord, taking a memorial card from between two whisky bottles. 'This'll settle it. "Risca Explosion, July 18th." So fork out, Ike.'

'Ay, fill him a quart,' said Ike, tossing fourpence on to the bar.

'It isn't often I make a mistake,' chortled Ned Luke. 'And

as for this explosion... why, me and five other chaps went down to have a look at the pit the following Sunday in old Jim Hone's brake. What a spree we had, for the pubs were open on Sunday over in Risca...'

'And here at that time,' said Ike Hughes.

'Are you sure?'

'I'll bet you a quart they was.'

Ned considered for a few seconds: 'I think you're right, Ike. Anyway, we went over, six of us, and old Jim Hone got too drunk to drive us home, so I had to drive the old horse. Took us about twelve hours to get back, so none of us were in work on the Monday, so we...'

Glyn felt a powerful desire for sleep, so he shook himself and hurried out of the pub and home to get himself washed and into bed.

Not until after he had sunk so low as to go down to the notorious Iron Bridge district, where he was saved from making a beast of himself by old Davies, MA, did Glyn bend to speak to Saran again, though he had seen her many times since the night Harry had given him two lovely black eyes. But he often thought about her; he was thinking about her on this Saturday night in the Eagle singing room when Shenk, who had only that minute finished singing 'When Other Lips', suddenly said in a whisper: 'I bet you're not game, Glyn.'

'What for?'

'To go down to the Iron Bridge and get ourselves a Moll apiece.'

Of course, he would put it that way, Glyn thought. 'Not

game'; always putting the onus on him. Yet why not? Life had been nothing but bed to work, work to bed for nearly two years, with nothing more than a drop of drink now and then to cheer a chap up. 'I'm game,' he said.

And off they went to look for a Moll apiece, a thing Glyn had never done before, partly because he was afraid to go into such a rough district by night, and partly because when on the way to work on summer mornings he had met many of the Iron Bridge Molls coming away from the coke ovens where they had spent the night with 'easy marks' or with their bullies; and seeing them coming from the coke ovens Glyn didn't feel he could ever have anything to do with them. A man could have any of them for a drink and the price of her night's kip. But the district was most dangerous for anyone with money in his pocket. It was the common lodging house district on the banks of the River Taff, and near the terminus of the Glamorgan Canal, over which a considerable amount of the production of the district was still being carried by barge to the port of Cardiff, twenty-four miles away. The Iron Bridge district was the rendezvous for hawkers, travelling tinkers, subbing navvies, prostitutes and those who patronised them; it was also the hiding place of an occasional man of parts such as Davies, MA. When the lodging houses were full the overflow went to sleep at the nearby coke ovens, so did the penniless ones rest their weary and lousy heads there, and many a one who went to sleep there never woke, for they were overcome by the fumes from the ovens and passed away peacefully in their sleep.

And this was the place where Glyn went on a Saturday

night, when it was particularly dangerous for an outsider to be around there. There was only one policeman who dared walk that district alone at night, and, funnily enough, his name was Lamb, Jack Lamb. Yet toughs who boasted that it took at least a dozen bobbies to take them to the lock-up went quietly with PC Lamb, for he was long, tough and bony, and of a most tigerish nature. He was standing on the Square this Saturday night as Glyn and Shenk turned into the Patriot to pick up a Moll apiece.

As soon as they went in, Glyn was annoyed when he heard his name called by Twm Steppwr, who was sitting with old Davies, MA, in a corner by themselves.

'Why, Glyn; what can you say you're doing down this part of the world? Surely you're not...'

'Out for a bit of a stroll, that's all. How is it, Mr Davies?'

Davies, who had aged considerably since Glyn had last seen him, peered up at Glyn. 'Well, young man, I'm alive. How do you come to know my name? Have we...?'

'Oh, I've heard you recite many times. On the bank in front of the Lord Nelson; down near... will you have a drink with me?' invited Glyn, at the same time watching Shenk out of the corner of his eye establishing contact with a couple of Molls who were standing with glasses of spirits in their hands near the door leading out to the passage.

'I don't mind a drop of whisky, young man,' said Davies.

Glyn ordered the whisky, and some beer for himself. 'And being as you're here you may as well have a drink,' he said grudgingly to Steppwr.

'No time,' said Steppwr, rising. 'I promised to meet

Harry at the Owen Glyndwr – thanks all the same. S'long. S'long, Davies, see you at our hotel when I return later on.' And off he went.

'It isn't often he refuses a drink,' said Glyn, taking Steppwr's seat.

'Indeed, I've never, unfortunately, been in a position to find that out for myself,' said Davies. 'Do you come to this place often?'

'Pass here on my way to the pit, but I've never been down here before to – er, to...'

'Quite. Yet, glad though I am of the whisky, I'm sorry you did not pass on tonight. Is that your friend?' nodding his head in Shenk's direction.

'Ah, that's him that I came here with.'

'Really. Well, he appears to be fixing things.... You'll pardon me asking, I hope; have you ever been with women of that sort before?'

'Never been with a woman in my life,' Glyn confessed.

'You surprise me. How old are you?'

'I shall be twenty-five next August.'

'And never known a woman. Most remarkable.'

'Oh, I don't know; don't feel much like women after slogging away in the coalface for twelve hours a day, it's nourishment a man wants after that. A couple of pints, and a square meal afterwards...'

'But why are you down here tonight?'

'Well, Shenk said I wasn't game, so...'

'I understand. Young man, I'm going to offer something which you may or may not appreciate. Be advised by me and clear out of this place before that damned fool there links you up with one of those poor trollops he's speaking to. You'll get little satisfaction out of them. If you must get a woman, then get married. Haven't you fancied a girl who...?'

'Yes, for years, but she's got two brothers that...'

'Never mind her brothers. Marry her and stick to her. I've been hanging about this quarter some time now, and I've seen respectable married men, as they are called, come here and take those poor trollops up to the coke ovens or down along the canal bank as far as the arches. They seek a change, even as I did once...'

'Drink up and have another.'

'Thanks. Yes, same again. As I was saying, men come here and to such places elsewhere in the hope of finding something different in the way of sex...'

'Come on, Glyn,' said Shenk as he hurried across to where they were sitting, 'I've settled everything with them two standing over by the door...'

'... But they are disappointed,' old Davies droned on with his eyes on his empty glass, 'even as I was when I was seeking from the women for hire in the capitals of Europe that which I could have got from the wife I thought I had grown tired of. I sought Helen, Cleopatra, Baudelaire's negress in scores of assemblies and hundreds of brothels, sought them vainly; yet my wife could have been all of them, and still have been my wife. One's imagination...'

'Come on, I tell you,' impatiently cried Shenk, 'and don't sit there all night listening to that drunken old fool.'

'... Sought and experimented until at last I got what I deserved, the disease which is slowly rotting me, and which...'

'I'm not coming, Shenk,' said Glyn.

'... Fear of exposure drove me to quacks in distant places, and an even greater fear drove me from my wife and home...'

'... After I've paid for drinks for 'em, and given them the money for both of us,' Shenk was saying. 'Do you think you've got me on a string giving them a shilling apiece?'

'Then you've done them a good turn,' said Davies, rising and forcing the angry Shenk into a chair. 'Now do yourself a good turn by leaving them severely alone. If you value your health. Sit down, please. I know what I'm talking about, young man, for I've lived much too close to people of that sort this last few years. They are... but I can see that you have decided not to have anything more to do with them. Good. As for the shilling apiece that you gave them, well, that will pay for two nights – for on Saturday nights we who reside in the communal centres of this part of the town are called upon to pay two nights' bed-rent in advance – and will leave them with fourpence each in hand for food and drink. Speaking of drinks...'

'What are you having?' said Shenk, no longer interested in the women.

Davies had another whisky, with which and a shilling to pay his weekend bed-rent the two young men left him to return to the singing room of the Eagle a little – but not much – wiser than when leaving it.

Steppwr hurried away from Glyn and old Davies to keep his appointment with Harry at the Owen Glyndwr, for Harry was a bad one to keep waiting. As soon as Steppwr entered Harry rose from where he was playing dominoes with a chap and took Steppwr aside.

'How much money have you got?' he whispered.

'Not a cent. Why?'

'I've lost two games at a shilling a game, and a quart on each as well. If I only had enough to call for the beer I could make him play on until I got quits even if I had to force him to play all night.'

'Won't the landlord strap you another couple of quarts?'

'He'll bloody well have to,' said Harry as he moved towards the bar. 'Fill us a couple of quarts, Jenkins,' he said to the landlord.

'When I see the colour of your money, I will.'

Harry was desperate. 'You'd better, Jenkins,' he said menacingly.

'Now, look here, Harry, you owe me...'

'Will you fill me two quarts before I come behind that bar and fill them myself?'

The landlord was pale, but still firm. 'Now, don't be foolish, Harry,' he advised, 'for you'll only get yourself into trouble if you try that on. I'm not saying that I won't fill you a pint,' he hastened to say as Harry moved towards the counter-flap.

'Pint be damned,' roared Harry, and all present swallowed their drink and slunk out to avoid being mixed up in what looked like turning out to be a court case. 'Are you filling me two quarts?'

The landlord, with his bartender, and his wife who had hurried into the bar from the kitchen, were bunched together near the counter-flap. 'Slip out the back way and fetch a policeman,' said the landlord to his wife. And off she went.

Harry shouted: 'You mingy swine,' then kicked the counter-flap up. Steppwr rushed in from the street to shout: 'She's gone to fetch a policeman, Harry. Come on out of it, you damned fool.' The landlord and the bartender closed with Harry and forced him out from behind the bar to the door leading to the street, overturning in the struggle benches, chairs, tables, and smashing several of the pints, quarts and glasses that were on the tables. After about half a minute's swaying about, Harry managed to free his right arm, which he at once brought into play. A short hook to the chin poleaxed the unfortunate bartender. The landlord made for the door when he saw his man felled, but before he managed to get through it he had a terrific kick in the tail from Harry which landed him on all fours in the gutter outside. The field was clear, so Harry went behind the bar to get himself something to drink.

'Come on away out of it,' Steppwr poked his head through the door to say, but Harry went on drawing beer. 'What do you think of me as a landlord, Steppwr?' he asked with a smile as he came out from behind the bar with a quart measure filled with beer in one hand and a bottle of whisky in the other. Knocking the neck off the bottle against the bar he went on to pour the whisky into the beer until the mixture spilled over on to the floor. Then he took a long drink.

'Ah, something like a drink,' he cried. 'Try this, Steppwr, it'll warm the cockles of your heart, it will.'

Before Steppwr could say yes or no a strapping young

policeman came rushing in through the door, closely followed by the landlord and his wife. The policeman pluckily went for Harry, only to be met with a right and left that put him to sleep on the floor at the side of the bartender.

'That's for making me drop my drink,' said Harry, picking up the partly full whisky bottle he had dropped to meet the policeman as he charged.

'Well, you've gone and done it with a vengeance now, Harry,' said Steppwr, looking down on Harry's two victims.

'I wish that bloody landlord had followed him in as far as here,' said Harry after he had poured what whisky there was left in the bottle down his throat. 'Where did the bugger go to?'

'To look for more policemen, I expect, so it's time we went.'

'Just as well, I s'pose.'

They were far enough away by the time the landlord returned with Sergeant Davies and two other policemen, who found the young policeman who had taken the count seated in the sawdust mopping the blood off his tunic and face.

'H'm, gone, is he,' said Sergeant Davies as he helped the young policeman up. 'Well, come on, I know where he lives. You needn't come, Morris; you shall have the pleasure of paying your respects to him when we bring him to the station.'

'But I'd like to...'

'Yes, I know you would, but it'll keep, that which you've got in salt for him. Come on, lads. Hurry back to the station, Morris.' And away to where Harry lived they went, and almost frightened Harry's mother into her grave.

'He's not here, Sergeant bach,' said the old woman tearfully. 'What have he done now again?' she asked.

'Enough to get him six months. Tell him from me when he does come home that the sooner he surrenders himself the better it will be for him. Will you be sure to tell him that?'

'Indeed I will, Sergeant bach.'

'You'd better, for if we have to fetch him and he starts being funny... well, he'll see. Come on, lads.'

Saran found her mother crying piteously when she got home from the theatre. 'What in the name of God's the matter now again?' she asked.

The old woman told her what the sergeant had said, and begged on her to go out immediately to see if she could find Harry to warn him that the police were after him.

'I expect he knows that,' said Saran. 'I think I know where to find him, so make up his pack for him in case I'll manage to persuade him to clear right away out of the district until this blows over a bit.'

Saran drank a cup of tea, and then set off for the lodging house in the Iron Bridge district where Steppwr hung out. She avoided the main street so as not to give the police a chance to follow her, and she got to the lodging house as the town clock was striking midnight.

'What in the name of God do you want down this quarter at this time, Saran?' said Steppwr when he went to the door to see who it was that had asked to see 'the little chap that plays the concertina'.

'Where's Harry?' she asked.

'Inside playing all-fours with three navvy chaps.'

'Tell him I want to see him, and that I've got his pack for him to clear off from the place.'

'I'm afraid he won't come, for he's winning, and I know how he is when he thinks something'll break his luck...'

Saran pushed by him into the common room of the lodging house where she found Harry seated at cards with three navvies, from whom he had won a fair sum of money. When he saw her he cried: 'I knew damned well something or somebody would come and break my luck. What the hell do you want?'

'I want to see you about...'

'I'll see you up home in the morning; now, bugger off.'

'You'd better come out to hear what I've got to tell you.'

'Ay, come on, Harry,' appealed Steppwr. 'She won't keep you a minute.'

Harry gathered up the money he had on the table before him. 'I'll be back in a minute,' he told the navvies.

'He won't,' Saran told them as she followed Harry out. 'Now, listen, Mr fly-me,' she started as soon as she, Harry and Steppwr were outside the door. 'Oh, don't rise your fist, for I'm not afraid of that. The police, three of 'em, have been to the house after you, and the old woman is nearly off her head. I don't know what you've done, but Sergeant Davies told mam that you've done enough to get yourself at least six months; so she wants you to sling your hook to somewhere where they can't find you. And you're going. *Now. Tonight.*'

'I am like hell...'

'Here's your pack...'

'You will if you're wise, Harry,' said Steppwr.

'Do you think that I'm afraid of the bloody bobbies?'

'No more is Sergeant Davies afraid of you,' Saran told him. 'You've had to pay salty before now for the pleasure of knocking one of 'em about, haven't you?'

'She's right, Harry,' said Steppwr. 'They gave you a hell of a lacing when they got you into the cell after you'd... but there, you know all about that without me telling you. Now, take my tip and clear out as Saran says; go over the mountains and into the Rhondda Valley and stay there until this dies down a bit, and perhaps it'll be forgotten.'

'It will like hell; they'll have me if it's in ten years' time.'

'How do you know? The old woman knows Sergeant Davies since he was that high. But please yourself. All I know is that if they get you into that cell whilst they're feeling bitter they'll knock hell's bells of buggery out of you...'

'And give you six months on top of it, which will kill mam as sure as you're standing there,' Saran added.

Harry stared into the oily, dirty water of the River Taff on which the high-riding moon conferred a sheen, trying to make his mind up one way or the other. It hurt him to think at all times. 'I don't want to make things hard for mam,' he muttered. 'If she thinks it best for me to sling my hook...'

'Didn't she send me to tell you to at this hour of the morning?'

'All right, I'm going,' growled Harry. 'Give us that bloody pack.'

'I'll carry it for you as far as the top of the mountain.'

'You will like hell. 'Fraid I'll double back, are you?'

'Don't be silly, Harry,' said Steppwr. 'Humph, it's come to something if we can't send you and carry your pack as far as the top of the mountain, from where you'll have a bellyful of carrying before morning. Now, I'll walk ahead of you and Saran a hundred yards or so until we get out of town, and if I do happen to run into a bobby... but I don't suppose I will at this time of the morning. Wait until you see me over the bridge before you start from here.'

With Steppwr as advance guard, Saran and Harry trod lightly along moonlit streets until all three were clear of the town and climbing the steep mountain road towards Aberdare. Once clear of the town Steppwr waited for them and walked at Harry's side; Saran, knowing her place, fell back, and afterwards followed the two men up the mountain, keeping a half-dozen paces to their rear, from where she could hear Steppwr explaining to Harry the kind of place the Rhondda was, and where he was to go when he got there.

Right on top of the mountain they stopped, Steppwr and Saran looking ahead at the strange and silent valley below, Harry looking back down the valley from which they had just climbed. Impartially the moon shared its light between the two valleys and scornfully looked down to where the steelworks of a half-dozen townships threw patches of reddish light up into the night sky.

'No, I'm damned if I will,' groaned Harry, starting back the way he had come.

Saran planted herself in his way and Steppwr caught him by the arm and said: 'Now, don't be damned fool, Harry.'

'Here, take this pack,' said Saran.

'Ay, take it, Harry. Man, it isn't hell you're going to, but to the rich, roaring Rhondda valleys, where it's livelier than ever it was here, and where there's good beer to be had in a dozen towns for twopence a pint, and work. Ay, and plenty of easy jobs…'

'Work, who the hell wants…? Can't I get all the work I want here?'

'But it'll be work without pay this side for at least six months,' Saran reminded him.

After a last long look down into his home town Harry grabbed the pack from Saran, and with his head down started running down into the strange valley, into the unknown. Saran and Steppwr stood watching him go.

'Don't forget to go to them people I told you about,' Steppwr called after him. 'They'll put you up – tell 'em I sent you.'

Harry was by this time a blurred figure in a sheeny mist.

'Come on, Saran,' said Steppwr. 'We may as well go back home now.'

CHAPTER 5

A MARRIAGE HAS BEEN ARRANGED

On the Saturday evening following Harry's flight to the Rhondda, Saran had the surprise of her life when Glyn accosted her as she was on her way to the theatre.

'Hullo, Saran,' he said.

'Hullo,' was all she said in reply.

'Er... well, to cut it short... er... I've been thinking that it would be all right if us two got married.'

'Married?'

'Ay; what do you say?'

'Why, this is the first time you've up and spoke to me since a twelvemonth last Christmas.'

'Oh, all right, if that's how you're going to talk...'

'But I'm not saying I won't. Let's get off the middle of the road, we don't want everybody to hear our business.' She led the way round the corner of Tom Hall's shop.

'Now,' she began as she stopped and turned to face him, 'I'm ready to get married whenever you are; though to tell you the truth, I thought you'd finished with me for good.'

'Ay, but that was your Harry's fault. P'raps you don't know that he gave me two black eyes the night my father died?'

'Oh, yes I do. But let's not bother about him. Where are you off to tonight?'

'I was going to meet Shenk down the Eagle singing room, but if you want to I'll go for a walk with you instead,' he condescendingly said.

'I'm going to the threeatre. It's *The Octoroon* tonight, and I wouldn't miss that for... why not come with me?'

'You know that I'd as well go to hell as go there.'

'Ah, but wait till you've seen *The Octoroon*. And you can slip out for a drink between the acts if you want to.'

He allowed himself to be persuaded and feigned interest in the play in order to please her. There were four intervals which he spent in the nearest pub, so he was most talkative as he walked as far as the bridge with her after they had left the theatre.

They stood on the bridge and she let him talk for a long time about this, that and the other before she up and asked him: 'And where do you reckon we're going to live after we're married?'

'At our house, of course.'

She looked across to where she lived with her mother and thought for a minute: 'And my mother as well?' she asked.

'Oh, I don't know about your mother. Old Marged's with us, been with us ever since mother died. And there's only the two beds, Saran, and old Marged's been sleeping in the one dad used to sleep in. She'll have to start sleeping on the couch downstairs again when we're married, for Dai's bound to have a bed to sleep in after working hard the way he do. So I don't see how your mother...'

'Why can't we live with her instead of going to live in your house?'

'And have your Shoni and Harry bouncing me from morning to night? Humph, what do you think I am?'

'Now, listen, Glyn. Shoni's gone far enough, and we're not likely to see him ever again; and it'll be a long time before we see Harry, if at all. Anyway, we can be looking for a house of our own, and be in it long before either of 'em are likely to show their faces around these parts again. Harry...'

'I heard about the way he carried on in the Owen Glyndwr; and a chap told me that the police are after him.'

'Well, it's no odds to him, is it?'

'To who?'

'To the chap that told you; for it's Harry'll have to pay for what was done, not him, or you, or anyone else.'

'Oh, you drive me mad when you talk about Harry as though...'

'As though he was as good as you? He is, and p'raps better than many as talks about him.'

'He is like hell. Look here; did you ask me to walk across with you to have a row?'

'As you like about that.'

'If I hadn't asked you to get married...'

'Nobody heard you, so don't let that bother you. S'long.'

'Wait. Now, Saran, simmer down so as we can talk sense. You don't think Harry or Shoni will come back to this place again?'

'If ever they do, then it'll be after we've found a house of our own.'

'If only I was sure of that I'd chance it.'

'Oh, you'd *chance* it, would you? Here, if you're wanting to get married, then only if you're willing to live with my mother, who hasn't got a soul to look to but me. Yes, I'm laying the law down now. Chance it, indeed.'

'Now, don't get nasty, Saran, for I was only thinking... but never mind. When shall we get married?'

'As soon as you like if you're willing to live with mother.'

'Certainly I am. How about next Monday week?'

'Yes, I think Mrs Cheshire'll make me a dress ready by then; and I can give a week's notice at the brickyard on Monday, though I could go on working there, for mam is still able to look to the house.'

'When we're married you're not going anear the brickyard, for if I can't keep my wife...'

'All right, all right, I'm not all that struck on the brickyard.'

Glyn clasped her to him and whispered: 'Well, being as we're going to get married so soon, how about...'

'Stop it, can't you see my mother in the doorway looking straight across here?'

'Then let's...'

'And it would be just the same if she wasn't. If you could keep from talking to me for nearly two years, surely you can wait another week before... stop it, I tell you.'

He released her. 'I was only teasing you,' he said. 'Will you tell your mother about us or....'

'Yes, I'll tell her, everything will be all right. I'm off in now. See you tomorrow night. S'long, Glyn.'

'Good night.'

It was Saturday afternoon, and Glyn and his brother Dai were hurrying along the underground roadway towards the pit bottom when they saw the gaffer discussing a Sunday repairing job with the deputy on the double parting.

'Hadn't you better tell him?' said Dai.

'You tell him for me. Go on, Dai.'

'Hoy, gaffer,' called Dai.

'What do you want?'

'Me and Glyn won't be here Monday.'

'Why not?'

'He's getting married.'

'More damned fool him,' said the gaffer.

The brothers continued on their way towards the pit bottom.

About the time they were on their way to the pit bottom Saran was standing in the line moving up to the pay office of the brickyard, where she was to draw her last week's wages as a producer that day. When she got to the little window through which the eldest son of the boss was handing a pay envelope to each girl as she came up, she found that he had made up his mind to have his bit of fun before handing to her the pay envelope he held in his hand. He poked his head right through the little window-space and smiled up into her face.

'Not until I wish you joy properly, Saran,' said the young man, who often boasted that he had covered at least half the eighty girls his father employed.

'Let's have my money.'

'Don't be in a hurry, Saran, for this is our last goodbye, remember. I bet you're looking forward to Monday night.'

'Isn't he a cough-drop?' cried one of the girls, giggling.

'Aren't you looking forward to Monday night?' he persisted.

'And what if I am?' said Saran.

'Nothing; only this. If he happens to get too drunk to do his job properly, don't forget to send for me, and I'll be with you...'

'Give the gel her money so as she can go, you damned young scamp as you are,' shouted old Sophie Lewis from her place at the end of the line. 'And if you really are hard up for somebody to go to bed with on Monday night, then come up and see me.'

All the girls in the line laughed, for Sophie was the veteran brick handler, flat-footed, big-handed and ill-favoured generally, but the best friend to new hands as ever lived.

'There's your chance,' said Saran as she snatched her pay envelope out of the hand of the boss' son and moved off.

'I'd rather go to jail,' he laughed.

Saran stopped just outside the gates and looked back into the yard where she had worked from the time she was little more than a child. She took it all in, the stacked bricks, the kilns, the tip of fresh clay, the coal for heating, the barrows and the rest. She tossed her hand-leathers into one of the barrows and hurried off, and as she walked she untied her red cloth hair-cover to allow her hair to hang free almost down to her waist. People who saw her wondered, a few thought she was drunk, for it was not considered decent for a brickyard girl to walk home from her work with her hair hanging down her back.

The day of days, and Saran and her mother ready dressed waiting for Glyn and his brother Dai to call for them. The registry office was at the bottom end of the town, and Saran, in the dress made for her by Mrs Cheshire, the dressmaker, thought she was going to create a sensation as she walked down through the main street to get married, but when Glyn came with his brother Dai to fetch her and her mother he put paid to all that by insisting that they walk down along the old tramroad, because he was too bashful or not enough of a man to face the people to be met with on the street.

So along the mucky tramroad she had to follow him in her nice new dress, and Glyn was congratulating himself on having dodged those who lay in wait for young men on their way to be married when he was spotted by Ianto Roberts, who hurried to tell some other chaps, one of whom ran into the house to get a rope, with which they waited outside the registry office for Glyn and Dai and Saran and her mother to come out.

A sour old man who filled his nostrils with 'High Dry' snuff soon married them and afterwards hurried them out to face Ianto Roberts and the other chaps who were holding the rope across the entrance to the office. Ianto and the other chaps wished them joy before Ianto cried; 'Come on, fork out the price of some beer so as we can drink your health, Glyn.' So Glyn forked out. Five shillings he handed to Ianto, who invited the young couple, Dai and Saran's mother to come and have just one in the Three Salmon before proceeding home. Glyn's mouth was dry, and he was also anxious to get somewhere under cover.

'All right, just one.'

Once inside the little back room of the Three Salmon Glyn was a different man. Out there on the street he had felt, so he now said, as though he were part of 'a damned peeping-show'. Now...

'And what are the ladies going to have? What's the blushing bride and her mother going to have?' Ianto Roberts wanted to know.

A ginger beer apiece was all they would take, and they sat silent in a corner whilst the men settled down to business. How quick that first five shillings went on beer, but what was five shillingsworth when shared among so many? Not an eyeful apiece. So Glyn and Dai forked out another half-crown apiece for more beer, and that again was nearly all consumed when who should walk in but Twm Steppwr with his concertina.

'Ah, now we're right,' cried Ianto, 'now we can celebrate properly. Is there a drink left in that quart for Steppwr? No, I'm damned if there is. Here, what about some more beer, Glyn?'

'Certainly,' said the now most jolly Glyn, tossing a gold coin on to the counter. 'And we'll have a song now that Steppwr's with us.'

Steppwr was over in the far corner wishing Saran joy.

'I'd have been with you before this, but I've been over the Rhondda for the weekend, to see whether Harry was fixed up all right...'

'And is he?' asked the mother.

'As right as rain.'

'And what part of the Rhondda is he at?' asked Saran.

'He's... he's where he can be got at when he's wanted.'

'Is he working, and is he behaving himself down there?'

'Come on and drink this, and then let's have a tune and a song,' said Ianto Roberts as he crossed over to where Steppwr was talking to the two women of the party. Steppwr took the pint and emptied it down his throat. 'Damn, I wanted that,' he said as he pushed his hands under the concertina straps and fingered the keys lovingly. 'Well, what'll you have?' he asked. Anything, they weren't particular. So he played, sang and danced as the other men drank, joked and laughed.

'They're spending fine,' Saran whispered to her mother.

'Now, I'll sing you a song,' shouted Glyn. 'Can you play "Let Me Like a Soldier Fall", Steppwr?'

'He can play any damned thing,' said Ianto.

So Glyn sang that one for a start, and afterwards gave them 'I'll Take You Home Again, Kathleen' as an encore, and as he sang he looked straight across to where Saran was sitting with her mother in the corner.

'I wish to God he would take me home,' Saran said in a whisper to her mother. Dai was now about to sing. 'But by the look of things it's me as'll have to take him home.'

All the men were at least three parts drunk leaving the Three Salmon, and Saran suggested going back to the house the way they had come from there earlier in the day, along the old tramroad, but Glyn wanted to know what the hell was the matter with her, was she ashamed to let the whole town know that they were man and wife? She followed, walking arm in arm with her mother, her husband, as he swaggered through the main street with Dai on his left and Steppwr on his right, acknowledging congratulations and accepting invitations to wet the wedding, the bride and her mother waiting on the pavement outside the pubs they were pressed to enter. 'If we go in with them the chances are that they'll settle down again same as they did in the Three Salmon,' said Saran as she waited outside pub after pub with her mother. By the time they reached the Lord Nelson the old woman could stand about no longer, so she went on home, where Marged had been waiting hours to serve at the modest feast she had helped to prepare for the party and a few selected neighbours. So Saran was left alone to pilot her husband home.

He condescended to go home with her about two o'clock in the afternoon, at which time he was badly in need of her as helper. With an arm around her neck and his feet dragging he sang as she, smiling like a Cheshire cat to hide her annoyance, kept him on his feet along the short stretch from the Lord Nelson to the house.

'Here we are, Marged,' he cried.

'About time, too. Here, lower him into this armchair, Saran. There you are.... Where did you leave young Dai?'

'He's toshing like hell f'pints in the Nelson. Have to wash him, I will, or he'll lose all his money. He had two pounds – same as me – starting out this morning. Lose all...

but not if I know it. After him soon's I've had a bit of… here, what about a bit of food, Saran?'

'Come on, look after your husband, gel,' laughed a neighbour.

They all sat down to belly-pork and other delicacies, of which Glyn ate a bellyful before he went back to the Lord Nelson to see how his brother and the others whom he had left there were getting on, so Saran saw no more of him that day. After a quiet tea with her mother and old Marged she went for a walk down the street and bought a nice pipe for her Glyn. It was seven o'clock in the evening when she returned home.

'Hasn't he come yet?' she asked.

'Not yet,' said her mother.

'You won't see him until stop-tap,' said Marged.

'Then I think I may as well go to the threeatre. What about you two?'

No, felt too tired, did the two old women, so off Saran went on her own, and she enjoyed herself grand, for it was *The Moor of Venice* that night, in which her favourite actor, Mr Cavendish, played the man who kills his wife on the bed, and by the time he smote himself Saran had ceased to think of her brand-new husband. But when the play was quite over and she was pulling her shawl over her shoulders she happened to notice her wedding ring. 'Must be nearly stop-tap now,' she murmured.

She got home to find her mother alone.

'Where's Marged?' she asked.

'Gone this good bit.'

'Glyn hasn't come yet?'

‘No, but he can’t be long now, for it’s gone stop-tap,’ The old woman laughed. ‘P’raps he’s forgotten by now that he was married this morning, and gone to his old home as usual.’

‘Not him,’ said Saran confidently. ‘Any of those chitterlings left?’

‘In that plate on the shelf. There, right before your eyes, gel. Ah, well, I think I’ll go to my bed. Listen. Isn’t that him now?’

Saran went and stood in the doorway to listen to a singer who was staggering along towards where she stood.

I love my share of pleasure,
And I’ll have it while I can.
I love the honest woman
That loves an honest man,

he was singing.

‘Yes, that’s him,’ said Saran.

‘Seems happy enough.’

‘Yes.’

‘Not blackguardish in his drink like some are.’

‘No.’

‘Well, I’m off to bed.’

‘See that I don’t oversleep in the morning.’

‘I’ll watch that; and mind you don’t leave his working-clothes or boots about the floor in case the rats come up from the brook same as they did that time they ate the tops of Harry’s boots – or was it Shoni’s – one of ’em, I know. Hang his clothes and boots on the line above the fireplace. We’ll be bound to get another dog. Good night.’

Saran was watching the approaching singer, smiling fondly she was, as she stood framed in the doorway. When about ten yards distant from her the singer stopped and looked about as though trying to locate the house.

'Here you are, you old silly,' called Saran.

He saw her, stumbled forward into her arms and clung to her.

'Oh, my lovely gel,' he oozed wetly.

'Come on in so as I can shut the door,' she said.

The hooters had started blaring their message at five o'clock regardless of the feelings of the scores of thousands they were calling to their work in pit, works, foundry and brickyard. Caring nothing for the joys and sorrows of those whom they roused each morning, the hooters shrieked loud and long the call to work. It was the same call, though the notes varied from the powerful bass note of the Dowlais works hooter to the sweeter tenor note of the Field pit hooter. When they all startled the district for the first time each morning at five o'clock, thousands of women would swivel out of their beds, slip something on and hurry down to living rooms to make things nice and cosy, or as cosy as things could be made, before they went upstairs again to timidly shake their breadwinners awake. And from five to seven o'clock each morning the hooters kept blaring at intervals of fifteen minutes. 'Come on, hurry up, hurry up,' they kept on blaring.

For many years those hooters had hurried Saran to the brickyard, but their reign of tyranny was at last over as far as she was personally concerned, though they still had, through the man who had undertaken to be her bread-winner, a firm hold on her. So at five o'clock in the morning following her wedding day they made her rise from her place in the bed at Glyn's side, slip on a petticoat and hurry downstairs, where she soon got the place ready for her man.

'Glyn,' she called, standing at the side of the bed looking down on him. 'Come on, Glyn, it's nearly quarter past five. Come on, wake up.'

He opened his eyes and looked at her, at first as though he were looking at a complete stranger, and later resentfully. Then he looked up at the ceiling as he began moving his tongue about in his head and champing his jawbones in an effort to loosen his sticky mouth, and sat up in bed with his head in his hands.

'I don't think I'll go to the pit today,' he said after a while, lying back in the bed again.

Saran had expected him to say that. 'Oh, and after I've been down and got everything ready. Come on, Glyn; you know how people will talk a lot of old nonsense if you stay away from thc pit today. So come on downstairs and see how you feel after you've had a nice cup of tea.'

'Tea, be damned.' He sat up in bed again. 'Any beer in the house?'

'No; if I'd known…'

'Then is there any vinegar here?'

'What do you want vincgar for?'

'I'm asking if there's any here.'

'Yes, there's a pint of vinegar in the pantry, Saran,' her mother called from her bed.

Glyn got up and made a livener of vinegar and water. 'Ah, that's better,' he said after he had swallowed about a pint of the biting mixture. Then as he started to dress for work: 'In future, see that you have a drop of beer in ready for mornings after holidays, and never forget that I expect my pint of beer to be ready for me on the table every night when I get home from work.'

'All right,' said Saran, handing him his things. She had her own views about beer in the mornings, but she also had more sense than to argue the point with a man when getting him off to work. 'Remember, whatever he says, a man is always right – in the morning,' her mother had often told her. Saran remembered, and soon Glyn went off cheerfully to his work, and after he had gone Saran sat down and breakfasted in leisurely fashion, and whilst at breakfast she thought of those girls then on their way to the brickyard, and to think of them made her feel ever so happy. She took a cup of tea up to her mother as she was going back to her bed for a long sleep, a longer sleep than she had ever had on a working day. She lay in bed thinking of her Glyn earning ever so much money in the pit, and it was of that she was thinking when sleep overtook her.

But on that day Glyn earned not a penny for himself or his Saran. Not him, though he had descended the pit intending to work like blazes, as he usually did. When he got to the lamp-station below ground he was annoyed to find that his brother Dai was not among those assembled there awaiting the deputy's 'all clear'. Dai's absence caused him to suffer additional leg-pulling during the short wait for the deputy, and when he arrived and learnt that Dai had not turned up he managed to raise another laugh by saying: 'Let's see, was it you or Dai went and got married yesterday?' Glyn pushed by him with the laughter of his workmates ringing in his ears. 'This bloody getting married,' he was muttering as he turned into his working-place. Soon he was, but for a gauze-like singlet, stripped to the waist and shedding all discomfiture and a deal of sweat in the hard-end of his working-place, the end where the air was none too much or too good. He was hewing away when he heard a shout from the working-place above.

'Hoy, Glyn, stop anyone coming up through my face,' shouted Tom Ellis. 'I'm firing a shot in my roof.'

'Carry on.'

Glyn heard the shot go off, and soon afterwards heard the dull sound of a heavy fall of roof. Then a cry, and as Glyn hurried out of his roadway he met Tom Ellis' ten-year-old boy, Sammy. 'What's the matter?'

'My dad – he's fast – on in front of the tram where the fall caught him and his lamp...'

Glyn was no time getting to where Tom Ellis was somewhere, and in God only knew what state under the fall of roof. Glyn's experienced eye took in everything at a glance, and in less than ten seconds he had completed a mental reconstruction of how the accident had happened, one of those accidents which are so common, and which are, when they chance to be fatal, reported in papers short of copy. Glyn, thinking he heard a cry from under the fall, held up his hand for silence as some of the other chaps working on that heading, with the gaffer and the master haulier, all of whom had been startled by young Sammy's crying, came rushing into the roadway. They all stopped and looked at Glyn.

'What did you hear?' asked the gaffer.

Glyn went forward along the side of the loaded tram of coal standing on the rails close up to the fall to listen.

'Come back, you bloody fool,' cried Tom Rees, the master haulier. 'Can't you hear that roof working like yeast above your head?'

'Shut up,' the gaffer told him. They all listened, and, sure enough, they all heard a faint cry from under the fall. Glyn wriggled his way back along the side of the tram and said: 'Well, it haven't killed him. Judging by the sound of his cries from on there where I was I think that there's something, maybe an old post or something, holding the fall up off him...'

'Then what the hell are we standing here doing nothing for?' roared the master haulier, who was all shout when the gaffer was about. 'Let's get to work and get the man from there.'

'We can't rush things with the roof above like it is, and us not knowing what to touch for fear of letting the whole lot down on him,' Glyn said.

'Quite right, Glyn,' said the gaffer. 'Now, keep your big mouth shut,' he told the master haulier. 'Now, Glyn, what do you think best to do?'

'I think we'll have to work through to him along the right side of that tram of coal – but we daren't move the tram from where it is, for I think it's an old post, p'raps two, that have fallen from the side and against the tram that are keeping the fall from off him. So we'll have to be careful. We'll want some short props by the time we've worked to beyond the tram; and we shall have to work only with our hands. So if you chaps'll stand back a bit to give me a chance in case the roof begins giving again…'

The chaps moved back a little, and Glyn started working his way carefully along the side of the loaded tram, and all that could be heard was the sound of Glyn working with his hands at the fall, an occasional whimper from young Sammy who was with the other boys back out on the road-parting, and, after Glyn had been working for about an hour, the voice of the trapped man was heard distinctly by all.

Glyn shouted encouragements to the trapped man before he wriggled his way back out of the tunnel-like impression he had made on the fall with his bare hands.

'We'll have to be careful from now on,' he said after he had taken a drink out of the drinking-jack held out to him, 'for I've worked to the end of the tram, so from now on both Tom and the one working to get through to him haven't got the same protection, and it'll be domino on both if it starts moving…'

'Come on, which of you are going to spell Glyn?' said the gaffer.

The man with whiskers had already pushed his whiskers down inside his singlet, and before anyone else had a chance he was wriggling forward into the opening made by Glyn.

'Well, Jim knows what to do,' said the gaffer quietly. 'Go and shut the damned boy up,' he hissed as the whimpering of young Sammy from out on the road-parting came forward to disturb the silence. One of the men tiptoed back to silence the boy.

They all stood looking at old Jim Jones' feet, which was all they could by this time see of him, as he worked his way carefully forward, scooping the debris he unloosed out of the mass ahead of him with his hands back along the sides of his legs. Maddening slow work. Soon old Jim had to wriggle out for some short props to prop up some dangerous huge stones he had worked partly under. Man after man took his turn in the hole of death, where there is no day, until about noon. A doctor had been sent for and was waiting in case.... Then, when the man with the whiskers was doing his second turn in the hole, he wriggled his way out to the others and warned them to be ready for the pull-out, as everything was clear for the pulling out of Tom Ellis. Then back he went, and Glyn laid down in the hole behind the one with the whiskers, and Shenk at the mouth of the hole took hold of Glyn's legs, and a man behind him took hold... well, like a tug-of-war team they were, and they got Tom Ellis out all right without a scratch on him, for, as Glyn thought, a couple of old posts leaning out from the side, and a big stone across them again, had kept the mass of debris from falling on him and crushing him to death.

After they had given Tom a drink out of one of the tea-jacks the gaffer went to show the doctor back as far as the main roadway leading to the pit bottom, after which he returned to find Tom and all the other chaps with the exception of the whiskered one still gathered in Tom Ellis' roadway.

'Here, why aren't you chaps back at your work?' he shouted.

'Tom's not feeling so well after all, gaffer,' said Shenk,

who had during the gaffer's absence persuaded Tom to pretend that he was badly shaken up.

'He told the doctor he was all right,' said the gaffer.

'I didn't feel so bad when the doctor was here, but as soon...'

'He went all shaky when he tried to make a start clearing this muck,' Shenk supplied.

'Then perhaps you'd better go home, Tom,' said the gaffer.

'That's what I was telling him, gaffer, as you was walking into the road,' up and said Will Hamont, who was also in the plot. 'Take the rest of the day to get over the shock, I told him. So me, Shenk and Glyn'll slip and put our things on and take him home safe, see, gaffer.'

'Surely he's not so bad as to want three of you to see him home.'

'Gaffer, do you remember what happened when Ness Edwards went out of this pit and tried to get home hisself?' said Shenk gravely. 'And he looked all right when he left this heading; and I'm sure you don't want anything like that to happen to Tom.'

The gaffer searched their faces, but was unable to detect anything other than what he thought was concern for their recently entombed comrade. Anyway, they were all pieceworkers, so the loss would be theirs. 'All right, then,' he said, taking out a pocket-book from which he ripped a leaf to write something thereon. 'Here you are,' he said, handing what he had written to Shenk. 'Give this to the hitcher at the pit bottom; mind you don't lose it, for he won't let you up unless you produce that.'

'But what about that other note, gaffer?' said Will Hamont.

'What other note are you talking about?'

'As if you didn't know. Why, the note which will get us chaps a drop of beer after we've seen Tom safe home. Honour bright, now, don't you think we're entitled to a drink after the way we worked to get Tom out?'

The gaffer looked at them suspiciously, but Tom looked as sickish as ever, and the other three looked back at him seriously. 'Well, I'm sure I don't know. I gave those Black Vein hauliers a note for beer last Thursday, and there wasn't one of 'em in work next day.'

'I've always said that those Black Vein hauliers…'

'And maybe you're no different,' the gaffer told Shenk. 'Still, you did work well.' He ripped another leaf out of his book and wrote something on it and handed it to Glyn. 'But if any of you are absent from work tomorrow…'

'We'll be here, gaffer. For God's sake put that beer-note safe, Glyn,' cried Shenk, who hadn't worried much about the safety of the note to be handed to the hitcher.

'Well, I must be off on my rounds,' said the gaffer as he hurried away from them. The three other chaps rushed to have a look at the note Glyn held in his hand.

'A lousy ten pints,' growled Shenk and Will.

'Hardly worth pretending to be bad for,' said Tom.

'If it wasn't that the best part of the day is gone,' said Glyn, 'I go to hell if I'd go out for this mouthful. Ten pints between four of us.'

'Still, you never know your luck,' said Will Hamont. 'We may run into some good Samaritan, and if the worst comes to the worst we can always strap a couple of pints apiece. Come on, let's go.'

Soon they were up out of the pit and on their way to the Collier's Arms, the place at which the colliery company ran an account for 'allowance beer', which on production of the company's note was served to hauliers who drove all day through water-swamps below ground, and to all grades of workmen who were prepared to do extra work for liquid payment.

Glyn and the other three chaps were almost at the Collier's Arms when Will Hamont suddenly stopped and cried: 'I've got it, I've got the bloody open sesame, boys.' The others looked at him. 'Let's see that note,' continued Will. Glyn handed it to him. 'Now, see that figure one?' asked Will.

'What's to stop us seeing it?'

'Well, there's room for a little stroke down that way, and another little stroke across that way, and that would be?' He paused for a reply.

'Then it would be a four,' said Shenk.

'But we've got ten pints as it is, so why change it to four?' said Tom, who was as dull as a bat where jiggery-pokery was concerned.

Will Hamont looked at him pityingly. 'I think you must be shaky in the head, Tom, if you can't see what I'm driving at. Look here, this is what it says: "Please supply ten pints of beer to bearer." Right, I makes the one into a four, and then it'll be: "Please supply forty pints to bearer." '

The others gasped.

'That'd be a tidy drink apiece for us,' said Shenk.

'And maybe a summons at the end of it,' said Tom.

Will Hamont had gone into a nearby grocer's shop to

borrow a pencil, with which he added the two strokes necessary to enable chaps to have a tidy drink. Then into the Collier's Arms they went. The landlord thought the note a bit high and unusual for so small a number, and said so, but when Will Hamont threatened to take the note for translation into beer at another of the pubs patronised by the colliery company, the landlord hastened to serve them with the first four pints of the forty.

'You keep tally, Glyn,' said Will Hamont, 'for I don't think this bloody landlord's above cheating us out of our rights.'

So Glyn kept tally, and they settled down. After the second pint apiece they opened their food-boxes and ate the food that loving wives had that morning placed so nicely in the food-boxes, food which their wives thought would sustain them whilst they earned a good day's wage in the pit, and there they were, eating it in a pub before they had earned as much as a penny between them. The afternoon passed, and with the approach of evening the necessity of 'strapping' more beer became obvious, for no good Samaritans had been met with. So they 'strapped' through the night up to stop-tap, whilst their wives at home were…

Well, Saran felt certain that her Glyn was working overtime for her. She had been waiting and watching from seven o'clock, the hour at which she had expected him to reach home from the pit. She had his pint of beer ready on the table in a bottle, and a lovely plate of taters and meat which she was keeping nice and warm in the oven. A lovely pork chop off the loin she had got for him, remembering how partial he was to pork chops off the loin. Yes, he'd like that. At eight o'clock she found it necessary to pour a little boiling water into the plate from the kettle to prevent the taters and meat from drying up. At nine more boiling water, for how could she keep his bit of taters and meat warm without the gravy drying up? By ten o'clock the lovely plate of taters and meat was as good as spoilt, by eleven o'clock it was spoilt, so she took it, such as it was by this time, out of the oven and put it away on the pantry shelf. It was most annoying. Still, if he was working overtime...

She grunted angrily as she heard from somewhere outside the same song as she had heard at about the same time the night previous.

'I love my share of pleasure,' etc etc.

'Humph, and me thinking he was working overtime, and sticking myself in here all night waiting for him when I could have been in the threeatre enjoying myself,' she said to her mother. 'Well, he sounds as though he's had plenty without this,' she added as she picked up the bottle of beer off the table and hid it behind the earthenware breadpan in the pantry. 'I expect he'll be wanting that in the morning.'

'Yes, no doubt he'll be glad of it in the morning,' said her mother.

And he was glad of it in the morning.

CHAPTER 6

IN BORROWED PLUMES

'Yes, you're a lucky young woman if ever there was one,' said old Granny Rees the midwife as she placed the newborn babe into Saran's arms. 'Two boys for a start, and there's poor Lizzie Ann Ward next door down who's had seven and not one boy. Poor thing, let's hope the one she's in the way with now'll be a boy. Well, you didn't have such a bad time with this one, though I was a bit afraid for you after that bit of trouble we had with your first. But you'll be all right from now on, you'll have no trouble bringing 'em. Unless, of course, you're foolish enough to let one of them slips of gels they sends out from the hospital mess you about, like they messed up Mrs Harris the shop, the stuck-up old thing as she is. She asked for all she got, but it was a pity to have to cut the little baby about. But she had to have somebody with a stificate to handle her, my gel, but, as I told Lizzie Ann Ward next door down, it isn't stificates brings the babies alive and kicking. Oh, there's that other chap of yours that I put over on your mother's bed crying, I forgot about him. Wants the breast, I expect.'

'Yes, let me have him,' said Saran.

'Wait till I move this chap to your other side first. That's it. Oh, shut your row,' cried the old woman as she picked up Saran's hungry firstborn off the bed of Saran's mother, where he had been deposited for a short time whilst his brother was being brought into the world. 'Hungry-gutted little bugger this,' observed the old midwife as she placed him to Saran's breast. 'Not a twel'month yet, is he?'

'Not until the twenty-fourth of the month.'

'I thought so. Time your mother was back, isn't it?'

'She won't be long now.'

'I hope not,' said the old midwife, who was beginning to feel like the 'drop of short' which she expected, and usually got, as a sort of perquisite from all her clients after the safe delivery of a baby or the laying-out of a body, and as soon as Saran's second had been safely delivered, the old midwife had reminded the old woman, Saran's mother, of what she referred to as 'the usual', and Saran's mother was out getting it. 'Your mother's none too gay these days, either, Saran,' the midwife continued as she went on putting things to rights. 'I wouldn't be surprised to hear of her going off any day now, though she's not as old as I am by a good bit. But your mother's one of these God-help-me sort, Saran, one o' them as is always worrying their guts out. She was the same as a young gel. Don't you ever worry your guts out, Saran, for when you've got no guts... oh, I shall have to get some more snuff when I go through the street.' After snuffing she went on to tell Saran of the women near their time on whom she was keeping an eye. 'All of 'em my customers, same as that Mrs Harris was till she got it into her head about them old stificates. Humph, after me bringing her into the world before stificates was thought of, and before ever they thought of building that hospital. Now, there was a nice woman, Saran.'

'Who do you mean?'

'Mrs Harris' mother.... Oh, here's your mother at last. Will you take a drop – just a drop – in some hot water, Saran?'

'No, thank you.'

'No, p'raps you'd better not. What about you?'

'No, none for me,' said Saran's mother.

The midwife didn't press her. 'I expect your husband will be surprised when he comes home and finds that the baby's here before him,' she said as she sipped her 'drop of short'. 'Is he fond of children?'

'I've never asked him,' Saran replied shortly, for she felt like having a sleep now it was over. The midwife understood.

'Well, I'll be off now. I'll look in to see you in the morning, Saran. Not that there's anything to worry about, for between us we've made a good job of it, a better job than them with their stificates could ever do. Humph, stificates, indeed.'

'She don't talk any less than she used to,' said Saran's mother.

No reply from Saran, who was sleeping as sweetly as the children, so the mother went downstairs to get things ready by the time Glyn reached home, but she wasn't able to get things ready, after all, for she died; and she must have died quietly, for she didn't wake Saran, who slept until Glyn got home from work to find the old woman dead in a heap on the stone floor she had evidently been trying to scrub when her life came to an end. Poor old Glyn hardly knew what to do, so he sent a boy up to tell old Marged to come down at once, for Saran was talking foolishly about getting up, but Marged when she got down there soon put a stop to that nonsense.

'Are you mad?' she said to Saran. 'Get up, indeed, and you like you are, hardly closed up after the baby. You'll stay where you are, my gel. I've sent for Granny Rees, and after I've made your husband a bit of something to put in his belly, she and I will tend to your mother, God help her.'

So Saran had to stay where she was in bed, and soon her mother was brought upstairs and laid out tidy on the next bed, only a couple of inches away from Saran's.

'Well, well,' said the most businesslike Granny Rees, 'little did I think when I left you, Saran, that I'd be here again before the day was out.... But wasn't I telling you? Didn't I say that I wouldn't be surprised to hear of her going off? And here she is...'

'Don't cover her face up, please,' said Saran. 'Leave her face uncovered so as I can look at her now and again.'

'Certainly, my gel,' said Granny Rees, turning back the sheet. 'She looks peaceful enough, God help her. There, there, don't cry and make yourself bad after your confinement,' she said as the bitter tears began to run from Saran's eyes. 'That's the way things are, my gel. One comes, another goes. Your boy's come, your mother's gone. And that's how it'll be with you – and me. Here, let me have that baby – give me the two of 'em, and I'll wash and change 'em before I go, for I don't expect I shall be with you very early in the morning after this jaunt.'

After she had washed and changed the two babies she placed them back in the bed with Saran. 'There, they're all right for the night now. I've told Marged to make you a drop of gruel, and after you take that you'll be all right for the night, too. Now, is there anything else you want?'

'Yes; I'd like if you'd ask Mrs Ward's gel, Gwen, to go and ask Twm Steppwr to come up to see me tonight for certain. Gwen knows where he stays.'

'Ay; and so do I, and a nice place it is, though it's plenty good enough for the likes of him. Smith's lodging house, down by the Iron Bridge, isn't it?'

'Yes; and tell the gel to mind to ask for the man as plays the concertina, for that's how they know him best down that way.'

In less than an hour Steppwr, with his concertina under his arm as always, was standing at the side of Saran's bed.

'I want you to go down to the Rhondda to let Harry know about mother,' she said. 'But tell him he needn't come up here and risk getting six months in jail, for we'll see that she's buried tidy. I don't want him to come up here and be nabbed, yet I feel that he'd never forgive me if I didn't let him know.'

Steppwr started off early the following morning on foot, and by nightfall he was in that part of the Rhondda Valley where Harry by this time had made a bad name for himself. He had met and defeated the ten best bare-knuckle bruisers in the valley, had run up a score behind the scoring-doors of all the pubs he had patronised, and he was a fancy lodger in the house of a childless couple, a house in which what the French are said to call a *ménage à trois* was the order of things.

But when he got to the place Steppwr didn't go to the house for the reason that he was almost certain that Harry at that time in the evening was settling himself down in some pub or other. He first tried the Welsh Harp. Not there, but he found him in the Adam and Eve playing dominoes. As soon as Harry saw Steppwr with his concertina under his arm walking into the bar of the Adam and Eve he jumped up with his pint in his hand. 'Here's Steppwr,' he cried joyfully, bounding towards him. 'Here, drink that up whilst they're filling you a pint,' he said, holding out his pint to Steppwr.

'But...'

'Drink that up, I tell you.'

Steppwr drank it up.

'Now sit there. Fill two pints, missus. When did you have grub last, Steppwr?'

'I had a bit when resting on top of the Aberdare mountain about middle day.'

'And some bread and cheese as well, missus,' roared Harry as though he owned the place. 'Damn, Steppwr, but you're a sight for sore eyes...'

'But, listen...'

'Shut your mouth until you've been stuffed. Ah, here's the two pints for a start. Drink up, I'll go to the kitchen to hurry up that grub.'

The bar was full to overflowing in less than five minutes

after the word had gone round that the little chap from Merthyr who played so well on the concertina was in the Adam and Eve. So 'drink up' it was. The landlord and his wife were very glad to see Steppwr any time, for he could draw the crowd with his playing, singing, and dancing, and that's why the landlady hurried to execute the orders Harry gave to provide the wandering minstrel with all he required in the way of food and drink.

After Steppwr had drunk two and a half pints of beer and eaten some of the bread and cheese set before him, he was ready to commence his one-man show, which Harry produced with pride, but without trimmings.

'Now, order, everybody. I'm not calling on Steppwr to oblige until I get the best of order; and once he starts playing there's to be no drinks called for or served until he's finished the item. I hope I've made myself quite clear, for if anybody makes a sound whilst he's playing, then they'll get this under the ear,' he threatened, exhibiting his leg-of-mutton-like right fist. 'It isn't every day we get the chance of listening to him. Now, *order*.' And there was order. 'Right, Steppwr.'

Steppwr led off with 'Alice, Where Art Thou?' with variations, which brought the place down, and which he followed with a number of other items before he got too drunk to play, sing or dance. Then the landlord took up a collection for him, just before chucking-out time. When the money collected was handed to him Steppwr took it and in a lordly manner dropped it carelessly into his right-hand coat pocket without counting it.

'Come on home wi' me,' said Harry, who had a quart

bottle of beer in two of his coat pockets. 'You're sleeping wi' me tonight.'

When the woman of the house called Harry to go to work in the pit at five o'clock next morning she was told by him to 'go to hell out of here', and she went out. Harry went back to sleep until nine o'clock, at which hour he sat up in bed and began to groan: 'Oh, my bloody head.' He looked sourly at Steppwr, who was snoring like anything. 'Hoy, Steppwr. Come on, wake up, and let's go out for a livener.' He got out of bed and began to dress himself. 'Oh, I've got a head like a bucket.'

'What time is it?' asked Steppwr, sitting up in the bed.

'Time we had a livener. Here's your trousers,' he said, picking them up off the floor and tossing them on to the bed. 'Your coat and waistcoat's on the bed.'

'Ay, and there's some money on the bed as well,' said Steppwr. 'And silver as well as copper. Oh, damn, I remember now. The collection. Why, we're in God's pocket, Harry, we're right for a spree today. But half a minute. Didn't I tell you last night, Harry?'

'Tell me what?'

'About the old woman, your mother.'

'Damned if I remember. What about her?'

'Well, she's – she's – well, dead.'

Harry lowered himself on to the side of the bed. 'Mam – dead?'

'Ay, died day before... was it? Ay, day before yesterday. I expect they'll bury her tomorrow. Saran it was that told me to tell you; but she said it was no good you getting yourself nabbed...'

'And so mam is gone,' Harry was murmuring as he looked straight at nothing at all. 'She's gone.'

'Ay, she's gone.' Steppwr went on dressing himself, but he hadn't finished when Harry rose from where he had been sitting on the edge of the bed and cried: 'Come on, for God's sake let's get out somewhere,' and downstairs and out of the house he rushed, but he didn't make a beeline for a pub to get the livener he was saying he so badly wanted but a short while before. No, he passed pub after pub and, crossing the square, he started to climb to the top of Rhondda's highest mountain. And there on top of the mountain Steppwr for the first time saw Harry shedding tears. He let him cry on whilst he had a smoke and watched trucks of coal being marshalled into trains near the pit-heads down in the valley below, trains which would soon be on their way to Cardiff Docks to make up cargoes of 'Best Welsh' for various parts of the world.

Harry had stopped crying. 'When did you say they were buryin'?' he asked.

'Tomorrow, in the new Cefn cemetery.'

'I'd give anything to be able to go to Merthyr to walk behind her for the last time, but I'd like to go tidy all the same. This thing's the only suit to my name, and this....' He shook his head.

Steppwr glanced at the suit, then he, too, shook his head. 'No, you can't walk behind her in that thing. It's not black for a start, neither is it...'

'You don't need to tell me. So she'll have to go on her last journey without a man b'longing to her follering.'

'Glyn, Saran's husband will be there.'

'What was he to mother? Nothing; I'm thinking of the

old man and we three boys. The old man gone, and our Ike went before him out in Zululand. Shoni – swine as he is – God knows where. He may be dead too. So there's only me to follow her, and the only suit I've got in rags.'

'P'raps it's just as well you can't go, for if you went and the police spotted you – and they'll sure as hell spot you – it would mean at least six months, and maybe a hiding from them into the bargain.'

'If I had a decent suit I'd go even if it meant six years and a dozen hidings.'

'Well, if that's how you feel, we'd better see what we can do. What about that man of the house where you lodge? Has he got a suit to lend you to go to the funeral?'

'No, he's worse off for clothes than I am.'

They sat there in silence looking down into the valley for some time.

'Come on,' commanded Steppwr, rising to his feet.

'Where to?'

'You'll soon know.'

Steppwr led the way down the mountainside, and soon they were back down in thc township and in the main street opposite the pub where Steppwr had entertained the patrons on the evening previous. As he was about to turn in Harry caught him by the arm, stopped him and said: 'No, no drink for me this day, Steppwr.'

'Who's asking you to drink? I've a bit of business to talk over with the landlord, so come on in for a minute and wait.'

Harry followed him into the bar and seated himself in a corner as Steppwr went forward to where the landlord was smiling a welcome from behind the bar.

'Two pints – or would you prefer a quart?' he asked. 'Have whichever you like, for you're having this with me.'

'Then two pints,' said Steppwr, one of which he took across to where Harry was seated moping in the corner, and left the pint on the table for him to drink it or not, just as *he* liked, but Harry managed to drink it all right as soon as Steppwr went off and stood breasting the bar whilst he talked with the landlord, who started by saying: 'Boy, we had a great time last night, and it's a thousand pities you are not staying here in the Rhondda with us. But what's the matter with Harry today? Looks like a summons.'

'Ay, he's had a knock-out blow; the old woman, his mother, is dead.'

'Ah, pity, pity. Well, such is life. You'll excuse me for...'

'I was wanting to have a talk with you in private – important.'

'Well, I'm sure I don't know; the wife is busy in the kitchen...'

'Come on, we'll go into the kitchen to talk, and she can come and look after the bar. Won't keep you a minute. But fill this pint and bring it to me in the kitchen.'

Steppwr walked out of the bar to the passage and along to the kitchen with the air of one about to confer a signal favour on somebody, and the way he carried it off so impressed the landlord that he took a pint into the kitchen and told his wife to go and look after the bar whilst he talked to Steppwr.

'Your very good health,' said Steppwr. 'A drop of good beer, that. Now, I want you to do me a favour.'

'Certainly, if it's any way possible.'

'It is, and I'll do you one in return. Now, Harry wants to go to his old mother's funeral.'

'Naturally.'

'As you say; but he hasn't got a rag of clothes other than that old suit he's now wearing; and I'm sure you wouldn't like to be seen in your mother's funeral in a suit like that, would you?'

'Good God, no.'

'No more would I. Yet poor old Harry's breaking his heart to go, so if you'd only...'

'Here, just a minute. If you're going to ask me to lend him the money to get a suit, then you can save your breath. My oath you can. Why, do you know how much that chap owes me for beer?'

'Beer. Now, who's talking about beer? Or money? I'm not going to ask you to strap him beer or lend him money. But you're about his size; and what I'm asking you to do is to lend him your suit of black just for one day to...'

'What, *my* suit of black that cost me seven guineas money down to Evans the tailor for him to go and get drunk in? Why, I'd see him...'

'Now, hold your horses; he'll not get drunk in it, for there'll be somebody in Merthyr as'll stop him getting drunk in your clothes or in any other clothes. And won't I be there? Now, if you'll lend him the suit so as he can look a bit decent at the old woman's funeral – and I'll guarantee that it comes back as good as when he gets it – I'll stay and entertain your customers tonight again, and I'll do so for a couple of nights when we bring you the suit back, and without charge or asking for a collection.'

'I tell you that I'm not lending my black suit that I paid seven...'

'Oh, never mind the price. If you won't, then you won't, and that's the end of it. Maybe the landlord of the Black Lion'll oblige me, for he's as near as damn it Harry's size. Thank you for the couple of pints, and...'

'Wait a minute,' cried the landlord, who was as anxious as any man in the booze business to quickly gather a pile of money so as he and his wife could go and live retired on it at some nice seaside place where he and his wife could be respected members of a chapel again. And to attain that desirable end the help of men like Steppwr was not to be sneezed at, for as a pub entertainer Steppwr was undoubtedly the greatest draw in South Wales and Monmouthshire, and if he was in the Black Lion just across the road, then it would be there that the majority of the good spenders would be listening to him and drinking Black Lion beer, which he often heard from customers was nothing better than cats' piss. But the chaps would put up with that stuff to have the pleasure of being entertained by Steppwr. 'Now, if it was you wanted the suit...'

'It is me that wants it – for Harry, but it's me that's willing to hold myself responsible for it. Well, what about it?'

After he had considered the matter for a while, the landlord said: 'I must have a word with the wife... no, no, you stay where you are and finish your pint.'

'I've finished it.'

'Then I'll bring you one back with me after I've talked this matter over with the wife. Smoke your pipe, here's some 'bacco.' In less than a minute the landlord was back in the kitchen. 'Can I rely on you bringing my suit as I paid seven guineas for back to me as good as I give it you?'

'As sure as my name's Twm Steppwr.'

He looked rather doubtful when he said: 'Very well, then.'

'Good; we'll have Harry in here to try it on, just the coat and waistcoat, that's all.'

The landlord called his wife from the bar to get the clothes.

'There's nobody looking after the bar,' she reminded him.

'I'm going into the bar, and I'll send Harry in here to you.'

The suit fitted Harry like a glove.

'I thought it would,' said Steppwr airily to the landlord.

'Did you?' said the landlord grudgingly.

'Yes. Look, Harry's brighter already; and you'll be after the business you'll do tonight if only you'll send the word round that I'm to be here at six o'clock sharp; and long before stop-tap you'll be able to sell 'em the wife's water – and your own – as Harrap's XXX, for they won't know the difference. We're off up to Harry's lodging to get some grub and a couple of hours' doss, but we'll be with you at six sharp.'

And they were. As they were on their way to the pub Steppwr said to the now much brighter Harry: 'If we sweeten the old miser a bit, and business turns out to be as good as I expect, then p'raps I may be able to persuade him to lend you his 'lastic-sided boots and bowler hat to go with the suit. Then you'll look grand, Harry.'

Harry's face saddened again. 'I haven't got much stomach for sitting in a pub all night, and her in her coffin.'

'Well, if she knew, I don't think the old woman would mind us working in a pub to get the lend of a suit and things for you.'

'Think she wouldn't, Steppwr?'

'No fear she wouldn't. Here we are.'

The place was heaving with night workers who would soon be leaving for their work, but not before they were relieved by the day workers, who would hurry along in their pit clothes and with their breath in their fist when they saw the notice that the landlord had stuck up on a post near the point where the workers from four pits passed on their way home, just a simple notice which read: 'Twm Steppwr will be obliging at the Adam and Eve from six to eleven tonight.' That was quite enough. Steppwr worked through those five hours without the assistance of Harry as compere. He played and played again and again; he sang and sang again and again; danced and danced again; drank... and when eleven o'clock came his audience still called for more. But the landlord and his wife and helpers for the evening were all shouting in chorus that it was time, and they hurried the chaps out to face the night and their wives, for the landlord had had the wire that Sergeant Daniels was watching his place in the shadow of the Black Lion, which had been practically empty all the evening.

'And I know who put Sergeant Daniels to watch my place,' said the landlord after everybody with the exception of Harry and Steppwr had been cleared out of the place. 'It's that Lewis, the Black Lion, the... oh, there's a dirty hound of a man, if ever there was one. And do you know what, Steppwr? I've known that place full on a Sunday –

chapel-time at that – and I've never as much as opened my mouth to a soul. But he...'

'Never mind him now,' said his wife. 'Let Harry and Steppwr and these helpers have a bit to eat so as they can go home to their beds.'

'Ay, come on, boys. They can't summon me for giving my friends and helpers a bit to eat. Now, eat hearty, Steppwr, for if ever a man earned a good meal, then you did tonight. Oh, there's the suit; the wife brought it down to air, for I haven't worn it since we buried the landlord of the Rose and Crown. And there's one of my best shirts and collars to go with it. Yes, we'll turn you out like a gentleman, Harry.'

'Yes, he'll be all right,' said Steppwr. 'All right except at the top and at the bottom.'

'What do you mean?' asked the landlord.

'Well, look at those old slaps he's wearing on his feet – and look at this cap. Spoil the look of your good clothes, they will.'

'Of course they will,' cried the landlord, rejoicing inwardly as he thought of the night's takings, and disposed to be generous. 'But we'll soon fix him up. Where's those 'lastic-side boots I had done up a week ago, missus; and that bowler hat of mine? Bring the two, the old one and the new one, and let's see which fits him best.' The new one fitted him best.

Williams the undertaker was screwing the lid of the coffin down and the four chaps who were entrusted with the ticklish task of carrying it down that narrow awkward stairway under Glyn's supervision were standing by in readiness; and it was a bit of a mess, for what with the two beds in the one room, and now the coffin, and Saran and her two babies still in the biggest of the two beds... Glyn wanted the coffin left downstairs, and then carry the old woman down into it, but Saran wouldn't have that. Had the upstairs window been a bit bigger – oh, more than a bit – one of the chaps was thinking when suddenly a well-dressed man appeared in their midst.

'Harry,' cried Saran.

'Wait a minute, Williams, before you screw her down. Just one look, if you please.'

Williams let him have a look, after which he went to sit on the side of Saran's bed near the head, where he buried his face in his hands and cried, but not loud. Saran was crying a little too. The four chaps waiting to carry the body downstairs took stock of Harry's fine clothes and wondered where he had got them from before they started up-ending the coffin to get it downstairs. Saran didn't look once the coffin passed her bed, neither did Harry, but if they had they would have seen their mother's body up-ended, turned on its side and goodness knows what all before the chaps managed to get it downstairs and out of the house.

'These houses weren't built for people to die in,' remarked Williams the undertaker to Glyn as he wiped his brow. 'Neither are they fit for people to live in,' he added. Glyn didn't answer, for the reason that he could hardly trust himself to speak now that Harry had turned up. Fancy having to walk right through the town and all the way to Cefn – for he hadn't been able to hire a hearse, much as

Saran had pressed – right behind the body with Harry, of all people, at his side; and not knowing the minute the police would stop the funeral and take Harry *right from his side*. Where had he got that suit from? It was a better suit than he, Glyn, ever hoped to be able to wear, he was thinking as he and Harry fell in behind the body and four of the hundred and odd chaps as had turned up to the funeral took the first turn at carrying the old woman to her last resting-place, nearly four miles away. Anyway, she was only a handful. Glyn and Harry, being chief mourners, didn't carry, just walked behind the coffin. A nice little funeral it was, though not what the neighbours considered was 'a lovely funeral', for as there was neither hearse nor wreaths of flowers it could not properly be described as 'a lovely funeral'; besides, there was no choir of any sort to sing her on her way, and that again reduced it in importance as an event. Still, it was a nice little funeral for an old woman who was hardly known beyond the row in which she had lived.

As she was being carried through Pontmorlais Square Harry happened to raise his head – and who do you think? Standing in the middle of the square was Sergeant Davies and the young policeman whom Harry had flattened out in the Owen Glyndwr that time.

'That chap walking next to the coffin looks something like that Harry,' said the young policeman to his superior. 'But it can't be him, dressed as well as that.'

'It's Harry right enough,' said Sergeant Davies quietly, looking after the procession. The young policeman closed his mouth with a snap, put his chin-strap tidy and was about to make a dash for Harry. 'Wait, don't be in a hurry,' said the sergeant. 'We'll have him, but not before he's on his way back. Let the funeral go on some little distance, then we'll follow on.'

And that's how it was, and Harry knew that it was so as he walked the miles to Cefn behind his mother. Anyway, he was allowed by Sergeant Davies to pay his respects properly to his old mother before Sergeant Davies and the young policeman who had it in for Harry stopped him as he was coming back out through the cemetery gates. And even then they didn't make an old show of him, for Sergeant Davies was a decent man who had known Harry's mother since he was a boy, so he just said: 'Hullo, Harry. Come on in the Cefn Hotel and have a drink, will you?' And in Harry went, into a back room with the two policemen. 'Well?' he said. Sergeant Davies called drinks, but the landlord wouldn't let him pay for them. 'No, you're having them with me,' he said. After they had finished their drinks Harry said to the two policemen: 'Well, I've had the sugar, eh, Sergeant, and I'm to have the shite when you get me into the cell, I suppose. Well, you can do what you bloody well like with me now that I've been let follow the old woman without shaming her.'

'You needn't be afraid of that, Harry.'

'I'm not afraid. No bloody fear; if I'm to have a poultice in the cell, then I can take it.'

'Well, you'll be spared that if you go quietly with us. I suppose you know that we could have had you without walking these miles for you, know that we could have taken you out of the funeral as it was passing through Pontmorlais Square?'

'Yes, I thought you saw me; I won't forget you for that, Sergeant. Well, I'm ready.... Oh, these clothes don't belong to me, so if you'll let me change into my old ones as we're passing by where Steppwr lodges he'll be able to take them back to the Rhondda to the man as was good enough to lend me them.'

The sergeant was agreeable, and after he had changed into his old clothes Harry was taken to the police station, and the following day he was committed to the Assizes, and everybody said that he was lucky to get off with only twelve months' hard labour; most people expected that he would have had more than that for flattening out a bobby and a bartender, and robbing the beer and whisky, to say nothing of the breakages and the flying kick in the arse he gave the landlord. Anyway, twelve months was all he got.

CHAPTER 7

A NICE BROTHER-IN-LAW HE IS

Though she was still washing her latest baby every morning, it was only on Sunday mornings that Saran washed her three babies in the tub before the fire. She had at last succeeded in weaning the eldest, and it was high time she did, for he was walking as straight as a line by now, and when he sucked at her he certainly made her supply of milk, and she had a good supply of splendid milk, but he made it look small, so it was time she weaned him. And by the look of him on the Sunday morning it was high time she bathed him as well. But there, he was running and crawling about all over the place....

Glyn was dressing to go up as far as his old home to see his brother Dai, as he did most Sunday mornings.

'About time our Harry was out of jail, isn't it?' said Saran as she lifted a dripping baby out of the tub and proceeded to dry it.

'He is out – this good while,' snapped Glyn, who hadn't by a long way got over Saturday night's booze-up.

'Who told you?'

'Steppwr.'

'Hm, the time's not gone; p'raps he got time off for good conduct.'

'Good conduct? Him?' Glyn laughed sneeringly.

'You never know... keep still,' she told the squirming baby on her lap. Then to Glyn: 'Anyway, you might have told me that he was out.'

'Why should I bother my head about the swine?'

'Well, he's my brother; and your brother-in-law, isn't he?'

'Ay, worse luck, and a nice brother-in-law he is.'

'He's as good as your brother-in-law, that Steppwr, any day.'

'Well, I didn't have to pay to bury Steppwr's mother.'

'No; but you had to pay to bury Steppwr's wife and children.'

'Is that any bloody business of yours?'

'It is when you talk about burying my mother; though you didn't go short of beer to pay for her coffin. It was me and the children had to go short to pay that off.... And let me tell you now. If you play the same trick another Saturday that you did yesterday again, then you'll find me over at the Nelson, or whatever pub you're in, showing you up before everybody...'

'Just you bloody well try it on, that's all.'

'All right, we'll see. If you don't come home next Saturday with a bit of money for me so as I can go and do my bit of shopping like other women, you'll find me there at your side. What's good...'

'Oh, go to hell.'

'Go to hell yourself.'

Glyn stood over her with his fists clenched. 'Here, do you want what Tommy Ward next door gave that mouthy bitch of his yesterday for coming to fetch him away from the Black Cock?'

'I'd like to see you try it on.'

'I will if you don't shut up.'

'I'll shut up when you take to come home decent on a Saturday with the money that you give to the landlady of the Black Cock – Fanny fine-talk – and to Watkins the Nelson, the fat swine as he is. You go to them before you wash the dirt of the pit off yourself. Oh, you must pay off your score there; but as for me and the children...'

'Shut up.'

'I won't shut up.'

'Won't you.' He let go at her and knocked her off the three-cornered stool on to the floor, and she with a baby on her lap at the time, but she managed when falling to save the baby from being hurt, though that one and the other two started crying like anything. 'Hush, will you?' she screamed at them as she came up with the poker out of the fender in her right hand. 'Glyn, would you like to see me hanged?' she said in a tone that reminded him of Harry. But he had a thick head, and she had not got him a drink of beer in as she should have done, and the damned kids were enough to...

'Ay, hanged, or drowned, or any damned thing, you mouthy...'

'Then hit me again. Come on, hit me again; I haven't got

the baby in my arms now. So why don't you hit me?' she screamed, raising the poker to strike.

He fled, and lucky it was for him, and her, that he did, for if ever she was her brother Harry's sister, then it was that Sunday morning. After he had run out of the house she went on to finish washing the babies, and whilst she was doing so she thought of the first cause of the row which had almost had serious consequences. Why couldn't he come on a Saturday with his money and give her her share of it so as she could get the few things and afterwards have her little bit of pleasure? No, he must go and sit in his pit clothes drinking until she was forced to go across to the pub and as good as beg for what was her due. Well, whatever the consequences, she'd have no more of it. Any other night he could stay in the pub undisturbed by her, but in future, on Saturdays, pay days, he'd come home with his pay and wash himself and then, if he wanted to, go and get drunk decent in his evening clothes – but not before she had had what was her due. And if ever he as much raised his hand to her again – well, it would be God help him.

'Ann Thomas; but she's off her head, I tell you,' Glyn was saying to Dai, his brother, who had declared that he was going to marry old Thomas Thomas' only child. 'By God, you're running into trouble with a vengeance.'

'Nothing of the kind. Ann's all right; it's only when she has those old fits. Dr Biddle reckons she'll be as right as rain once she's married.'

'Like hell she will. Still, you know your own business

best. Humph, married. I wouldn't care who had two wives as long as I didn't have one.'

'Oh, another row, eh? Well, I told you to go home and wash…'

'Huh, you're a nice one to talk.'

'Am I? Anyway, when I'm married I'll take my pay and share it with my wife before paying best part of it away to publicans.'

'We'll see. What do you think?'

'What?'

'She got the poker to brain me this morning.'

'Oh; but what had you done to her?'

'Gave her a bit of a flip, that's all.'

'Hm, it won't pay you to flip her, Glyn. Come on, let's go back down to her.'

'If you think I'm going to knuckle under to her…'

'Who's talking about knuckling under? I'm going down to invite her to my wedding, Ann's anxious for her to be there. And Ann's father wants Steppwr there with his concertina. Yes, Ann's father's lashing out, I tell you. There'll be plenty of everything there.'

'Well, he can afford it.'

'Come on, let's go and put things right with Saran.'

Steppwr was trying to persuade Harry to accompany him back to their native place from the Rhondda Valley, where Harry had gone directly he was released from prison after doing his twelve months. 'Come on back with me for a few days, man,' Steppwr was urging.

'I tell you, no; I've finished with that damned place for

good. A man can't move up there for p'licemen and chapel people. No, give me the Rhondda before it any day, for here in the Rhondda a man can have a bit of fun now and then without being sent to jail by the p'lice or to hell by the preachers. This place is rougher, livelier than ever our town was, Steppwr. Here you've got two strings of growing townships in which there's any God's amount of money being earned – not by me, for I don't hold with too much work – and spent, and it can be picked up easier here than in any place I know. I get twice as much for licking a man here as I used to get in the old...'

'And still you're always like myself, without two ha'pennies to rub together. All right, Harry, you can have the Rhondda, I'm off back to Merthyr; and it'll be a long time before you see me over this way again.'

'Oh, damn, don't say that, Steppwr, for you know how much I banks on seeing you now and then.'

'Yes; but you don't think that p'raps there's somebody in Merthyr as would like to have a squint at you now and then.'

'Who the hell wants to see me?'

'Your Saran for one; she was asking about you the day before I left Merthyr to come down here; said I was to remember her to you.'

'Then why the hell didn't you?'

'Because you stops a man's mouth with beer before he can speak, and you see that it's kept stopped and – well, then it's forgotten.'

'Saran's not so bad. How many kids did you say she had?'

'Three, or is it four? It's either three or four.'

'I wouldn't mind a look at our Saran again, for she's...'

'Then come. Listen; her Glyn's brother Dai is getting married tomorrow to Thomas Thomas the joiner's daughter...'

'What, Ann Fits, as we used to call her?'

'That's her, but she don't have fits like she used to. There'll be plenty to go at the wedding, for old Thomas Thomas isn't without money. So we'll have a good spree and you'll see all the old pals, and...'

So they went up to Merthyr to the wedding, to which nobody other than Steppwr had invited Harry, but Harry wasn't in the habit of waiting for invitations. As soon as they arrived in Merthyr, by train this time, they made a point of calling to see Saran before going on to where the wedding feast was prepared. They found Saran helping her Glyn, who was to act as best man for his brother, to get a stiff collar fixed around his neck, for Thomas Thomas had insisted that the wedding should be solemnised in the chapel, and that being so Glyn wanted to look his best walking into the chapel with his brother, and in order to look his best a man had to have a stiff collar and a sham front on.

And that's what he with Saran's help was trying to get on when Harry and Steppwr, dressed little better than tramps, burst in upon them.

'Mind you don't bloody well choke him, Saran,' roared Harry in a way that frightened the babies and started them off crying. 'Lord, how many have you got?' he went on to ask as Saran ran to greet him, leaving the end of Glyn's collar to fly back as far away from the stud as ever. 'Well,' said Harry as he looked with a savage sort of pride on his sister, 'I must say that married life seems to be agreeing with you. But what in the name of God have you been doing to this chap of yours? Like a razor, isn't he, Steppwr?'

'Never mind what I'm like,' snapped Glyn, struggling with the collar. 'Saran, are you going to give me a hand with this or...'

'Ay, go and dress him, Saran,' Harry told her. 'We're going as far as the Nelson to see a few of the chaps, but we'll be seeing you at the wedding. S'long for now.'

'Who asked him to the wedding, I should like to know?' Glyn cried.

'I did,' lied Saran, succeeding in bringing the collar and stud together.

'Then you had no business to; ten chances to one he'll be wanting to fight us all before...'

'Hadn't you better go before they have to send up for you?'

He snatched the bowler hat she was holding out to him and rushed away to the chapel; as soon as he had gone Saran got herself and the babies ready to go up to where Glyn had lived up to the time he had married her, for this was where the wedding feast was laid out. And, in fairness to old Thomas Thomas, it must be admitted that the feast which he provided on the day his daughter was married was something like a feast. Plenty of everything for everyone present. There was – let's see, now. First there were two nine-gallon casks of Harrap's XXX and two pint-and-half bottles of rum for the men; and there was a bottle of whisky and a bottle of gin for those of the women who liked their drop of drink, and lashings of tea for those who didn't, and as much food as you could want, and good food at that.

Old Marged, who was in charge at the feast, for the bride had lost her mother years previous, warmly welcomed Saran, but the welcome she extended to Harry when he hurried in shortly after his sister, was icy, though that didn't worry him in the least. As soon as he arrived he at once took charge of what he called 'the drinkables', and he had one of the casks running freely before the bride and bridegroom got back to the house from the chapel; and he had pocketed one of the bottles of rum, but Thomas Thomas, who had paid for it and who was not blind, made him put it back on the table to be consumed by everyone. After all had eaten well – some too well – and oiled their throats, Steppwr was called upon to liven things up when they began to drag, as they usually do after people have stuffed themselves. Steppwr livened them up, and kept them very much alive until all the drink had been lapped up. Then Harry, after he had up-ended the cask to get the last drop out of it, sighed and said: 'Well, it's no use us staying here any longer, is it?' All the men present agreed that it certainly was not. 'Then what if we go as a body across to the Lord Nelson?' said Harry, who hadn't the price of a pint to his name. But there were others who had, and Harry knew it. So across to the Lord Nelson all the men went as a most friendly body to finish up the day properly, and again old Thomas Thomas had to pay for most of what the male members of the wedding party drank whilst standing in line breasting the bar. Then Harry went over to play Dai Genteel dominoes on the table in the corner, and when Dai Genteel had beaten him for a quart which Harry had no money to pay for it looked as though a row was brewing, but Thomas Thomas, determined that there should be no display of bad feeling on this day and night at least, stepped in between Harry and Dai Genteel as they were squaring up to each other and said: 'Now, now, what are you having, the pair of you?' and so restored peace, which was maintained up to chucking-out time. The women, the bride included, who had been left to do what they liked with the evening, all went to the theatre to cry through *East Lynne*, and as the theatre closed before the Lord Nelson did, they were all back in their homes in time to get everything ready for the homecoming of their lords and masters.

Up to the time the hauliers struck work throughout the district Saran had had, all things considered, a fairly comfortable seven years of married life. Then things began to happen which made life difficult. The hauliers, always the storm section of the South Wales army of miners, brought the coalfield to a standstill by striking again. Thousands of coal-hewers were idle in consequence, for hewers cannot go on hewing coal unless there are hauliers to drive the horses which take the trams filled with coal away from the hewers' working-places.

And so Saran's Glyn was idle and cantankerous, and soon there wasn't a penny to get anything with. Glyn was away from the house most of the time except mealtimes and bedtime, and Saran was left alone with her babies and her thoughts. She would sit giving the baby the breast and time after time ask herself what was the use of strikes which put her and her like in the fix they were. Still, she thought, it wasn't fair to expect hauliers to go on driving horses, whose greasy heels stank enough to knock a man down, through the dark, the sludge and the water, for twelve hours a day, and for a wage of about a pound a week at most. No, Saran readily admitted to herself, the hauliers were not altogether to blame. If only the bosses… but there, it was none of her business, as Glyn sharply reminded her when she had pressed to know the reason why it was that he would not want calling to go to the pit in the morning following the night the hauliers decided to strike at their meeting in the skittle alley of the Morlais Castle. 'Nothing to do with you women,' Glyn had told her. Wasn't it, indeed, she often thought. If she had nothing for him when he came home ravenous after a long walk into the country with the other chaps he might think differently.

And she had been hoping soon to move to a bigger house, with the key-money of which she had up to the time the hauliers struck been saving sixpence a week, and which she had been forced to spend the first weekend that Glyn had no wages to draw. Now, when he started work again, she would have to start saving key-money again. Not that she herself had anything against the little house in which she had spent her married life up to then, and where she had lived with her parents and brothers before her marriage. But now that she had a houseful of children, for she realised by now that six children were more than enough in such a house, she must start saving as soon as possible….

No back, that was the worst thing about the house, the back wall of which was serving as the foundation wall for the house above, one of 'the Top Houses', as the row of cottages built on the bottom row in which she lived was called. Then – pouf, smelling as strong as ever, she thought – running by her doorstep, was the stinking Morlais Brook, the near left bank of which was surfaced with human and animal excrement for about a foot above the original bank. Ashes and other refuse had for years been emptied over the bowel refuse and had hardened it into layers of dung cakes which were by now capable of bearing the weight of all who hurried to the left bank to ease themselves when the three earth closets which the twelve families living in the twelve houses in the 'Bottom Row' shared, were found to be engaged, as they usually were from morning to night. Men would sit in them at their leisure, and with the doors open, smoking, and continuing the conversation with those in the house, which the call of nature had interrupted. So Saran and her little ones often, and sometimes in broad daylight, had to go and 'do their business' on the left bank owing to the closets being unavailable when nature called. And Saran often, in the night especially, had to accompany her children, who feared the rats, to the left bank.

Oh, the rats, as big as they were brazen. In broad daylight, hundreds of 'em, playing about and sometimes feeding off the high – very – and dry bodies of the drowned cats and dogs which during dry seasons stood high out of the little water dribbling along towards the River Taff and the sea. Why, if it hadn't been for the chaps who liked a bit of ratting on a Sunday those rats would have done goodness only knows what. The left bank, the bank nearest and within a dozen feet of the doorsteps of the houses, was the rats' playground; there was no right bank they could play on, for on the right rose the high wall of the back yards of the houses, pubs and shops of the main street, and in this wall the rats had their sleeping apartments. There was no need for them to work through the wall and up to the backs of the houses in the main street, because why trouble to do so when the tradespeople in the main street threw over their back wall into the brook every mortal thing a rat could possibly want. Butchers and fishmongers, once anything began to niff a bit, would fling it over the back wall into the brook. Splosh, and out the rats would rush to investigate. A long drop it was, and the children of the Bottom Row delighted to watch things fall – *splosh* – into the brook; and they also used to stand and wonder at the way the chemicals from the works changed the colour of the water of the brook. One day the rats after they had swam from their sleeping apartments in the right wall to the playing grounds on the left bank, would come out of the water brick red, and maybe the next day a shiny green – all the colours of the rainbow in turn.

And there were other drawbacks such as periodical fever and smallpox epidemics. But living there, Saran thought, had its compensations; for less than a hundred yards from her doorstep there was a good stretch of the main street open to view, to her an unending source of interest and entertainment. There was something worth seeing to be seen there all the time from morn to midnight, and she could see it all from her doorstep. People and traffic – she always watched for the passing of the new Merthyr-Dowlais bus which was drawn by four of the finest horses she had ever seen. And she laughed as men were seen falling off their high penny-farthing bicycles. As good as a play, she thought it was, as she rested from her work to watch the stretch of main street over the head of one or other of the babies which was drawing life from her bounteous breast.

By this time she could tell by listening alone what was going on there. It started about five each morning, when the 'early birds' of the thousands of miners and steel-workers and brickyard girls commenced the overture to toil which is played by heavy boots on metal roads. It began quietly, and Saran would note the way it worked up until it sounded like an army corps hurriedly retreating, and then die down and away when at seven o'clock a mocking chorus of hooters would hoot their 'Too-oo-ooo-oooo late now' into the ears of those who had been too fond of their beds to get up in time to get to the pit before it started winding coal or to the works before the gates were closed, or had stayed too long in the pub into which they had turned for a livener. 'Too-oo-ooo-oooo late now.'

Then peace until eight o'clock, at which hour the chorus of hooters that had hurried men to work was repeated to hurry the growing army of children through breakfast and away to school. And if there was anything Saran hated, then it was the eight o'clock hooter. She didn't mind it at five or any time up to seven, for those early hootings had to do with sending men to work. But to have to get up at eight again, just when she was enjoying the carefree sleep which came with the consciousness that she had not overslept, and that her man was at the pit, just to send children to school – she'd had no schooling, and was none the worse for that, she insisted savagely in reply to the hooters. It was true she could neither read nor write, but what time did the likes of her have for reading and writing, anyway. She could work, had a good pair of hands, could put a bit of food when it was there to put, could knit and sew, and was well able to see to it that none of the other women living in the Row, bouncers though some of them were, should in any way 'put upon' her or her children. And though she couldn't read she was able to follow the plays put on in the 'threeatre' as well as them that could. School, why, if she had her way...

But the man she called 'that blasted Bobby Greencoat' saw to it that she did not have her way. He saw to it that she and the other women in the Row sent their children to school, and because of that was regarded, and even told to his face that he was nothing short of a 'damned nuisance'. Morning, noon and night he was around telling them that they had to send their children to school, and, said Marged Jones, 'unless we do, he says we'll be summoned and God knows what all. And him an old Englishman who makes us get up in the morning to send the children to school where they don't hear a word of Welsh, and where the teachers beat them for the least thing. Didn't Mary Jane Hughes go... I don't know. I'm up half the night drying Jim's clothes and watching the time; and no sooner than I've got him off to work and am in bed to rest my bones in peace, I'm up again to send the children to school.'

So they grumbled when meeting each other at the one

water tap that served the Row, and many of them wondered at Saran sending her two eldest of six to St David's School, which they said was 'an old Church school', but Saran said, 'Let 'em go to the nearest place.' Nothing but schools, she thought. The British School, and then that Higher Grade school where people who intended making preachers or lawyers out of their children sent them – but not her boys. As soon as they were twelve she'd have them out of the old school and down the pit with their father, have them where they would do something to help to keep the others. And she would look forward to the day when her boys would be earning good money in the pit.

Meantime, there were the sights to be seen out on the main road. Like watching the myriorama in the Temperance Hall, she used to think, as she sat and looked, sometimes forgetful of the fact that the baby in her arms had ceased to draw at her breast, and that it was exposed to view outside her bodice. Traffic, and people passing on their way to do their shopping, on their way to get a drink, on their way to buy, sell, beg, borrow, steal, on their way... well, to do all the things that human beings have done and will go on doing to the end of time.

And occasionally an evening on the threepenny benches at the back of the wooden theatre where John Lawson and his company were by this time playing. Four of her six children with her, the two eldest waiting their dad home from the pub. 'If he's home before I'm back, here's his supper in the oven.'

Even on Sundays there was plenty to see. The large-scale rat-hunts along the left bank. Men with sticks who arrived with terriers at their heels and ferrets in their pockets. Rats were slaughtered by the score. Great sport, and the chaps enjoyed it until the 'saved' came marching by on their way to or from chapel, and then the sporting and damned lowered their voices, and many of them slunk away with their terriers at their heels and the ferrets in their pockets. For the procession of the black-garbed Roundheads of that industrial community was an awe-inspiring sight to all but the most hardened, such as Saran's brother, Harry. But to most others the sight of the nonconformist legions on the march to where they were to meet their God was a sight which inspired awe even where it failed to compel respect. Saran always went in from the doorstep to watch the chapel parade through the window. Once – but only once – shortly after the birth of her first baby, she had brazenly sat out on the doorstep giving the baby the breast as the 'saved' passed on their way to chapel, and the eyes of those who looked as they passed seemed to burn Saran's breast.

CHAPTER 8

The patagonian panther

Saran, as time went on, wondered what had become of her brothers, for she had not heard anything about Shoni from the day he had cleared out after robbing Harry of the three golden sovereigns he had got for licking Flannery. Neither had she seen or heard anything of Harry from his sudden appearance on the day he had come up from the Rhondda with Steppwr to eat and drink at the marriage feast. The following day, without even calling to say goodbye or anything else to Saran, he had disappeared from the town, taking Steppwr with him. Saran was trying to think how long ago that was, when who should walk in just after the children had arrived home from school to their dinners, but Harry and Steppwr. It was the very day the navvies started breaking up the road along the main street, and Saran's eldest boy was saying as she was putting the dinners:

'Hundreds of men, our mam. Making room for the tramlines for buses without horses in 'em to run from here up to Dowlais and back...'

'And to Cefn and back,' cried another. Then all the children were frightened when someone roared: 'Hullo, Saran.'

It was Harry, and with him was Steppwr, both looking well but not prosperous.

'Hullo, what's brought you back home?' said Saran coolly. 'Get up so as your uncle can sit there, boy. Sit down, Harry... sit over there in the armchair, Steppwr. So the Rhondda's got too hot for you, Harry?'

Harry was looking around at the children incredulously. 'Good God, whose are all these?'

'Whose do you think they are? They're mine, of course.'

'Seven – and another on the way,' he added after a glance at his sister's pregnant figure. 'You have been busy. The Rhondda too hot for me, was that what you said? Not it; but there hasn't been much doing for me and Steppwr down that way lately, so we thought we'd run up here for a spell, and before I'd been here an hour I'm on a job.'

'What, with the navvies laying the tramlines?'

'Navvies be damned. No, the job I've got is in Billy Samuels' booth tonight; a pound for doing six rounds with a big black feller; I've got orders to let him hop about a bit before I give him a fetcher under the ear and put him to sleep. It'll be easy...'

'Say you don't know,' Steppwr said.

'Steppwr, I've beaten the best they could find to put before me in the Rhondda, so do you think a bloody nigger...'

'Ay, but this is with them gloves on, remember.'

'I know, but it would be all the same if it was with pillows on, Mr Sambo'll go down just the same.'

'Never mind Mr Sambo,' said Saran. 'Draw up to the table, the pair of you, and have a bit – such as it is.'

'Not before I have a drink,' said Harry, rising. 'I came straight across to see you before I'd had a drop. I tell you what you can do, though. Let's have that small loaf and some of that cheese to take with us to where we can have a drop of drink to wash it down. And if you could lend us a shilling until I draw that pound tonight...'

'Save your breath, Harry, for I've no shillings to lend you, but you're welcome to the bread and cheese.'

'Let's have it then,' he growled. And off to the pub he and Steppwr went.

'I seen the notice outside the booth, mam,' Saran's eldest bubbled, 'but I didn't think it was our uncle Harry. For ten pound a side, it said.'

'Eat your food.'

She knew that there was no ten pound a side at stake, for having lived with Harry she knew the way proprietors of boxing booths aroused interest as a preliminary to drawing the crowd. She believed as firmly as Harry did that the nigger was an easy mark for him, for Harry was the unbeaten champion at his weight, and stones over his weight, of the five mining valleys.

Still, whatever he was or had been, the nigger played Hamlet with him that very night. Before they went into the ring Billy Samuels had both the men, one on his right and the other on his left, on the raised platform outside the booth, where he exhibited them under the gory, glazed, crudely painted ring-fight scenes with which the front of the booth was covered.

'Gentlemen,' Billy Samuels was saying as Saran's eldest boy, who was nursing Saran's youngest of seven capably, hurried towards the crowd gathered before the booth. 'Tonight I am proud to be able to inform you that I have managed to arrange a six-round boxing contest for a purse of ten pounds, with side-stakes of ten pound a side, between the redoubtable Joe Wills, better known as the black panther of Patagonia, and one of the best and gamest lads this town has ever bred, Harry…' (cheers for the local lad cut him off) '… and I myself have consented to take charge of this important contest, so you can rely on everything being carried on in a sportsmanlike manner. In this pavilion of mine I have from time to time presented in turn all the present champions of Great Britain at their respective weights; and I think I am justified in claiming that the present holder of the middle-weight title learnt all he knows in this pavilion of mine when a member of my troupe. And he's far from being the only one.' Here he paused and rapidly calculated what the number of men in the crowd before him at sixpence a head would amount to. Yes, he decided, they'll about make it. 'But that's well known to most of you,' he continued. 'Gentlemen, whatever contests you may have been privileged to witness in my pavilion and elsewhere, I can promise you that nothing you have previously witnessed will bear comparison with what you will have the pleasure of witnessing this evening. Look at them – just look at them. Two remarkable specimens of manhood, gentlemen. On my left, Joe Wills, the black panther of Patagonia. On my right – but you know this lad and his record as well as I do. They are now going inside to get themselves ready for a bout which will be long remembered in this town of yours; and the price of admission is only sixpence. Take your time, gentlemen, please. Oblige that lady at the entrance by having your money ready as you come up. Thank you, gentlemen.'

Billy went on barking until the booth was crowded. Then he went inside and climbed into the ring, where he at once called the smiling negro and the scowling Harry from their corners to give them the final word.

'Marquis of Queensberry rules, remember. Time.'

'I'll knock that bloody smile off your chops,' muttered Harry as he went for the nigger bald-headed. But when he got to where the nigger had been a split second before the nigger wasn't there. But he soon learnt where he was when a stinging left came from somewhere to almost flatten his nose. 'Damn you,' he muttered, turning and charging in the direction the blow had come from, only to receive a stinger from another direction. And so it went on throughout the round, a round during which Harry saw but little of the coloured man who smiled, and who looked like an ash-grey ghost when outside the circle of light from the naphtha-flare lamp hanging from the wooden crossbar under the Pavilion's canvas roof.

At the end of round one Harry went to his corner bleeding from the nose and from an old wound above his left eye, and mad with rage because he had not once during the round got within striking distance of the negro who was now smiling across at him from the other corner. Harry blew his nose into his right glove and waited impatiently for the call of '*Time*'.

'Let him have it this time, Harry,' roared the crowd, and Harry went all out to oblige. The negro slipped him, then hit – hard; sidestepped and hit – harder; ducked, then delivered rocking uppercuts; countered, then brought smashing rights across.

'Science, that is,' murmured Billy Samuels proudly as the smiling untouched negro returned to his corner at the end of the second round, by which time Harry was in a very bad way indeed. The old wound above his right eye was now gashed open, and his lower lip was split enough to hang to below the gum. 'Give it best, Harry,' Steppwr whispered loudly from where he stood outside the ropes below and behind Harry's corner. But Harry heard not, for there was a sound as of the sea in his ears, and mad rage blinded him to all else but the smiling negro at whom he glared with damaged peepers. From his heaving chest there issued a horrible sound that reminded Steppwr of the snore of a water pump when in action. 'Why don't he chuck it?' moaned Steppwr. *Time.*

Still groggy, Harry went for the nigger gamely, only to meet with the same treatment as before, treatment quite in accordance with the Marquis of Queensberry's rules. No one present other than Billy Samuels had ever dreamt that one man could do to another what the nigger did to Harry by the end of the third round. A terrible state he was in, yet he hadn't been knocked down once. At the end of the third round he wouldn't go to his corner to receive the attention he was so badly in need of, but remained swaying in the centre of the ring with blood streaming from his face on to his heaving chest and from there to the floor of the arena. And as he stood there he kept on saying, or rather groaning: 'Fight me – toe to toe – you black – bastard, you. Here – I am – toe to…' Before he could say any more he fell senseless.

He was carried to his corner, where he was washed and brought to his senses, and after that was done Billy Samuels shook him by the hand and said that never had he seen a gamer chap than Harry had that night proved himself, and the negro boxer also shook Harry by the hand and said that he was the stiffest proposition he had met in any part of the United States of America or here in this country, and Billy Samuels after giving him his pound and his own white handkerchief out of his breast pocket to bandage the wounds over his eyes took the hat around so that the crowd could show its appreciation of the gamest chap Billy Samuels had ever known. The collection amounted to eight shillings and sevenpence ha'penny, so Harry had in all one pound eight shillings and sevenpence ha'penny in his pocket when Steppwr led him out of the boxing booth and down to the Morlais Castle pub to have a drink. Harry did not go back to the Rhondda after that, neither did Steppwr. They stayed in their home town, but in the worst part of it, down the Iron Bridge district in a common lodging house, and Harry carried on something awful, and Steppwr went round the pubs playing.… Ay, a pretty pair.

'I thought I was getting on too well,' sighed Saran as she stood in the little front garden of the cottage she had recently moved into, and from where she watched the thousands of men coming away from the mass meeting. She had got on, no doubt about that. Her eldest boy was by this time working with his dad in the pit, and her second boy was being got ready to go to the pit the following Monday. And she had at last managed to find another and bigger cottage to live in, a cottage with a back door, a tiny back yard, and a strip of garden in front. Better still, a closet which she and her family shared only with the family living next door, a closet which she and her children could expect to find empty and ready for use nearly every time they required the use of it. And there, in her roomy – compared with the one she had moved out of – cottage high up on the rise above the town and far away from the stinking brook and the rats, she was settling down nicely when, all of sudden, it happened.

There had been rumblings, but what with the Jubilee, and moving, and another baby, she had no time to listen to the talk that was flying about, or to bother her head about the meetings that were called from time to time. Glyn, but only when under the influence of drink, had talked about what the new miners' union was going to do for the miners, and Saran comforted herself with the thought that it was only the drink talking. But when the talk of a 'big strike' began to grow she began making tentative enquiries of her eldest boy, Benny, knowing that if she asked Glyn any questions she would only be told to mind her own business.

So it was Benny that told her about the huge gathering at which the decision to strike was unanimous. The meeting was held in the huge, bowl-shaped hollow where

Harry had fought Flannery in the days now long gone. There must have been thousands at the meeting; Benny told his mother that there were 'millions' there. From all over the district they came. Dowlais, Merthyr, Pentrebach, Abercanaid, Troedyrhiw and from other outlying places they came to hear the great Mabon, MP, and other miners' leaders speak. Mabon spoke first, in Welsh, and he had not spoken for more than a minute, Benny told his mother, before somebody in the crowd shouted: 'Let's have it in English, Mabon,' and this looked like starting a row, for the natives were not partial to the English who had come from everywhere into the district, where by now they were strong enough to crowd, on Sundays, the Church of England edifices and the three chapels inside which no Welsh was spoken.

Mabon saved the situation by replying in English to the English section of the audience. 'At least two of the speakers who are to follow me will address you in English, so with your kind permission I'll conclude what I have to say in my native tongue,' and the Welsh majority cheered this, and the English minority had to wait in patience until Billy Brace started talking in English. Before the end of the meeting there was enough talking in both English and Welsh to satisfy the veriest glutton. Even Mabon, MP, and the other moderate leaders said that things had reached a stage when it was no longer possible for men to put up with what they had had to put up with from the owners for so long, and that unless the owners showed signs of a more just spirit than they had up to then shown, then it would be necessary to consider...

Consider, consider, consider, sneered the younger miners' leaders. The time for consideration was ended, the time for action had arrived. When had the South Wales owners showed signs that they were prepared to concede to the miners what they were entitled to? At no time in the history of the coalfield. Then why this talk of consideration? It was high time for Mabon, with all due respect to him, to realise...

The South Wales miners are organised as they never before have been, so why waste time talking and talking whilst the owners are preparing? I say let's put the question to the vote. And after the vote is taken – and there's not the slightest doubt in my mind as to how you'll vote – let the Executive get down to a discussion of ways and means of carrying on the struggle in a way that will ensure victory for our cause. Whilst we are dilly-dallying, the owners...

Benny told his mother that Mabon, MP, warned all present to behave themselves whilst on strike, and then led them in the singing of a hymn before dismissing them. Saran listened to all Benny had to say, and afterwards asked him: 'Did Mabon say anything about us having strike pay?'

'I didn't hear him say anything about strike pay, p'raps dad can tell you about that.'

So that night she asked Glyn: 'Will we get any strike pay?'

'A bit, maybe. But our Federation haven't got much to give as yet.'

Saran sighed. 'Well, we'll want something from somewhere if it lasts any time, for there's ten of us to be fed and...'

'You talk as though you'd like us to go on working for nothing.'

'Nothing of the kind. All the same, I don't see why things can't be settled without knocking us flat like this. What's the use of all the schoolin' people are getting these days if they don't learn enough to settle things?'

'What's schoolin' got to do with it, woman?'

'Not much, by the look of things, for if it did we shouldn't be having these strikes and lockouts...'

'Oh, shut up, for God's sake,' said Glyn, as he went out.

The weather was glorious, so for a week or two it was like being on holiday. Plenty to eat, a tidy drop of drink for the men, and a bit of excitement most days when blacklegs were waylaid, had white shirts put on them and with them on were marched through the streets to be ducked in the canal. But there were very few blacklegs. The holiday feeling died down before the end of the fourth week of the stoppage, for there was but little money coming in to help feed the miners and their families. True, the English miners were sending all they could, and a man who was afterwards elected to Parliament organised the first of the male choirs to go singing through Britain in order to raise funds to support the miners in their struggle.

Saran's Glyn, and his brother Dai, whose childless wife had died on the Monday of the third week of the stoppage, went out with the first choir, with which they were away from home a month, a month during which Saran was forced to beg for food to keep herself and the children alive. And to get it she had to go outside the district where she lived to towns in which steelworks were working on coal from the English coalfields. Three days a week she went begging accompanied by one, sometimes two, of the eldest of her eight children. She carried the food she begged on her head in a clothes basket over mountain roads from distant places, and the boy or boys with her carried smaller supplies of food, sometimes old clothes or boots that could be made to do, in parcels under their arms. And whilst she and the 'chosen' one or two boys were away on begging expeditions the biggest of the boys left at home had to see to the baby and scrat a little coal from the nearest pit-refuse mountain to sell to Morgan's the butcher for a bit of meat, the article of food most difficult to beg. So they managed to keep things going; and she was away begging the day Glyn returned home after his month on tour with the choir.

'Where's your mother?' he asked nine-year-old Jane, their only girl, who was nursing the baby and looking after the house whilst the boys were away scratting for coal.

'Away after food,' replied the child. 'She didn't think you'd...'

'Gone to the shop, is she?'

'No, dad, to Rhymney she's gone today.'

'Here, are you daft? Gone to Rhymney, seven miles away, to buy...'

'No, not to buy, dad, but to go round the houses asking. And some days she goes farther than Rhymney, too. To Blaenavon and...'

'Bloody well begging,' muttered Glyn. 'Well, tell her when you see her that I'm home.... But I'll tell her.' Then he went out again.

It was late that night, after all the children had gone to bed, when he went back home to find Saran waiting for him with the air of one who has cleared the decks for action.

'You're a nice one, you are,' he shouted as soon as he saw her.

'Why, what have I done?'

'What have you… no sooner do I turn my back and go roughing it up England way with the choir to get money to send home to you…'

'What home are you talking about? It's little money I've had.'

'You've had your share same as every other woman, I expect. But that's not the point. Oh, I'll never be able to lift my head for shame,' he cried melodramatically. 'Hell, woman, you're as bad as that Steppwr, if not worse. Begging from door to door like a common…'

'Do you want any supper before I go to bed?' interrupted Saran.

'Some of the food you've mooched? No, I'd starve first.' She began clearing the food off the table. 'To think that a wife of mine…'

She turned on him with a butter-dish in one hand and a newly started loaf in the other. 'Oh, for God's sake, shut up. You and your fine talk… all right, being as you're talking so big after enjoying yourself up and down the country for a month, p'raps you'll give me the money to buy food, so as I won't have to go tramping over the mountains to get it. Come on, let's have the money.'

'You know damned well that all the money we got by

singing was sent to the fund, and that you've had your share of it same as others.'

'I've had one five shillings – a fat lot on which to keep myself and eight children for a month, isn't it? I think I'll go away singing next month and leave you to look after 'em; then we'll see how you'll go about it to fill their bellies. You make me sick when you stand there up to the neck in beer and...'

'I've had three pints whilst waiting for you to come home.'

'Then you've had three pints more than I've had. And now, if you don't mind, I'll go to bed; and don't waste your breath talking as you have been, for I shall be taking one of the boys with me and going off somewhere to look for food in the morning again. Ashamed, indeed. No; but I would be if one of 'em had gone to bed hungry tonight.'

'Saran, as sure as God's in heaven, if you go out begging tomorrow again, I'll go straight back to where I came from today, and you'll...'

'Oh, go where the hell you like.' She went to her bed. Glyn sat at the table, scowling down on the piece of greasy and crumb-strewed newspaper which had served as tablecloth, and something caught his eye, for he blew the crumbs away and bent over to read:

'... and with South Wales and Monmouthshire at a standstill owing to this regrettable and disastrous dispute, the men will be well advised to consider this latest and, in our opinion, generous offer of the owners without regard to anything that their short-sighted socialist leaders may recommend. It is high time for the miners of South Wales and Monmouthshire to realise how much the welfare and future of our great and growing Empire depends on them. Our supremacy at sea also largely depends on them, for without a constant and plentiful supply of Welsh coal, our Navy is handicapped to the nation's detriment. Has the word patriotism no longer any meaning? We continue firm in our belief that it has, and that the word socialism will not now or ever obscure the meaning of patriotism in the minds of the miners of South Wales and Monmouthshire. To repeat what we stressed in yesterday's leading article, coal is our nation's only sure foundation, and if...'

Glyn snorted as he rose to his feet to blow out the lamp before going up to bed.

Although Saran was as good as her word and went off begging with young Benny next morning, Glyn did not go straight back to where he had come from as he had threatened to the night previous. No, he got out of bed late in the day, and after he had eaten what little Jane placed before him he went with about two thousand other men to the mass meeting, where he heard one of the leaders putting it in a nutshell: 'I am as much for peace as the next man – but not peace at any price. I love my wife and children, I'd die for them if need be, but I'd see them eat grass before I would recommend acceptance of such terms. Men, stand firm. And if only you will, then the owners will soon see the advisability of offering much better terms than these which I have just explained to you. We've got public opinion behind us; and the English and Scottish miners are rallying to our aid, by levying themselves to support us in this fight, a fight which is as much theirs as it is ours. For, make no mistake about it, if we are defeated now...'

Someone had shouted 'Vote, vote', and the vote was taken. Fight on, and they fought on day after day, week after week, Saran begging her way through, though daily having to go farther for less, for there was a limit to charity, it seemed. One Sunday evening she went to chapel, taking with her the four youngest, for the four eldest had nothing in which to go out on a Sunday. And she heard the preacher say: 'This dreadful struggle has now been going on for four months, and the suffering, particularly of the women and children, is increasing as the days go by. And still, as far as we are able to see, no signs of an early settlement. Today, throughout South Wales, nonconformists are everywhere praying for the coming of the Spirit of Peace, praying that He will be able at last to influence the contending forces in this costly and terrible industrial struggle. And may the settlement, when it is arrived at, be a lasting one, that is what we hope and pray for. As announced last Sunday, today's collections are for the fund out of which the soup kitchens, which have been the means of lessening the suffering of the many necessitous children of this area, are maintained. So please...'

Saran's baby started crying, so she had to take him out.

CHAPTER 9

RECONSTRUCTION

Twenty-five wageless weeks is a lot to make up for, as Saran was to find out during the two years following the six months' mining stoppage of '98. But with the help of two more of her boys in the pit, making three in all, she managed it, and also managed to move house again, and this time to one of the new houses in which there was a bath, which the old-fashioned Glyn referred to as 'the swimming-bath', and which he for long refused to avail himself of, preferring to cleanse himself of pit dirt in the tub as he had from his boyhood days. But his boys were delighted with the bath.

And there was also a water closet, the first that Saran had in her life been privileged to have the say and use of, at the back of the house. And the new conveniences, three bedrooms, front room, kitchen and back kitchen, transformed

Saran from an illiterate, rough-tongued woman into a quiet-spoken and remarkably self-possessed – almost ladylike person. True, she was still unable to read, but she no longer went out of the house and to town to do her shopping dressed in a flannel skirt and a shawl covering her upper part. No, as soon as she moved into the house with a bath she was a hat-and-coat woman, and a tailor-made coat at that. She had five beds in the three bedrooms, two, two and one; the room with one bed in was her room. The three boys working in the pit had a new Rover cycle apiece, latest model, paid for 'money down' by Saran, who hated the instalment way of getting things. Her children attending school were dressed as well as they were fed, for now, as she was fond of saying, 'I'm able to see to their backs as well as their bellies.' 'And well she can, with her man and three boys working regular and earning good money,' envious neighbours sometimes said.

Yes, she was getting on, as the town was. Such changes, she was thinking as Benny, who worked with his father as butty, hurried in from work, late as usual, with a discontented expression on his face.

'Look here,' he shouted as he tossed his drinking-jack and food-box on to the kitchen table, 'if the old man thinks he can work me from six in the morning until after seven every night, then he's mistaken. Let our Sam or Hugh go and work with him for a change, and see how they'll like it. They're washed and out every night before I get home, but if I want to get out early to go anywhere I'm...'

'I'll talk to him about it again. You see, he's used to working...'

'I don't care what he's been used to, he's not going to make a blasted slave of me; I'll go to the war first.'

'Don't talk so soft, boy. Remember, your uncle Ike, my brother, was killed out there in Zululand.'

'Might as well get killed there as be worked to death.... Clean towels in the bathroom?'

'Yes; and your clean shirt's behind the bathroom door. Where did you leave your father?'

'Where did he leave me, you mean. At the door of the Express, same as usual. And that's where I expect he'll stay gutsing beer until chucking-out time. Beer and work, that's all he thinks about.'

With that he went upstairs to the bathroom, and Saran told Jane to shine his shoes ready by the time he came down. Fancy him talking about going to the war, she thought, as she prepared a meal for him. And him not eighteen until November. Still, he was nearly as good a man as ever he'd be, one of the new men, one of the scores of thousands in the district who had had their seven years of schooling up to the age of twelve before starting in the pits or steelworks, and who were now almost, if not quite, as good workmen as their fathers. But they thought differently, and talked differently, in the English tongue. And they read books and papers – couldn't live without the *Merthyr Express* and the *Echo* – and shouting themselves hoarse and in English at the football matches on Saturday afternoons, and running about the country on their bikes on Sundays and summer evenings. Not so keen as they might be about going to chapel, yet that was balanced by the fact that they seldom were to be found in a pub. Glyn had smoked his pipe and drunk his beer long before he was as old as Benny.

And the town... electric trams travelling like lightning, all these bikes, and those new motor things. New houses, shops, huge new public offices with a clock tower, all being rushed up, and people flocking into the district from everywhere. Then the new Theatre Royal and Opera House, as big – well, the biggest she had ever been in.

Benny hurried down and sat in his underwear at the table to eat, but he hadn't been eating long before he pushed the plate away, saying: 'My suit, mam.'

'Finish your supper, boy,' said Saran.

'No time. This suit's beginning to go, too, mam. When am I getting another so as I can take to wearing my best in the evenings?'

'When I can afford to get you one.'

'Afford it... when did I have a suit last?'

'I thought you was in a hurry to get to the threeatre?'

'So I am, and I'm in a hurry for a suit as well.'

That was another thing, she thought after he had rushed out to get to the theatre in time to see the last two acts of the play he had so badly wanted to see, the play of Shakespeare's which Saran thought least of. *Macbeth* was not in her opinion a good play. The suit he said he wanted. May as well get it him first as last, for Benny would give her no rest until she did. Particular about clothes, he was, as all the young chaps were getting. Glyn had never been so particular about his clothes as Benny was, but there, anything would do to wear sitting in a pub. Glyn stuck it in the pub most nights until chucking-out time in his pit clothes, a thing she could never see the fastidious Benny doing.

'Come on, Jane, give these children what they want to eat so as we can get them upstairs to bed before your father rolls in. Come on, all of you.'

In the Express Glyn was getting well on when the conversation worked round to politics. Reynolds the baker's son was also getting well on, and it was he switched the conversation from the way the trams were making people too lazy to walk to politics.

'Yes, it's come to something at last,' he shouted so that all in the bar should hear him. 'And who is this feller, this socialist? I think it's an insult to ask us to as much as listen to a socialist, and a Scotch one at that...'

'A Johnny-fortnight, is he?' asked someone.

'I don't know what he was when he was working, if he ever did work,' replied Reynolds. 'But what I do know is that it's come to something when we as Welsh people are asked to send a Scotchman, and a socialist at that, to represent us up in St Stephen's.'

'An atheist, isn't he?' said the landlord as he drew more beer.

'Of course he is, and the funny thing about it is that a bunch of young chaps as are members of Tabernacle are mainly responsible for getting him down here. And members of Tabernacle, of all places, to bring a man of that sort... when I first heard that it was they who were getting him down here, why, you could have knocked me down with a feather. I said to the wife... fill me a pint, please, Mr Harris. I said to the wife...'

'It's bound to lead to trouble, such as strikes,' said the

landlord as he placed the pint of beer asked for before Reynolds, who drank most of it before going on to say: 'Of course it'll mean strikes, ay, and revolution. For that's what the feller is, a revolutionist, one of them as is against everything. Now most of you know what I am. I've been a conservative all my life, and there's not a man in this town as worked harder for Pritchard Morgan than I did. Most of you are liberals – all but Mr Harris and myself. We've fought, but we fought clean, and we're none the worse friends. But when it comes to these people sending up to Scotland for a red-hot revolutionary and an atheist to come down here to ruin our town, then I think we should unite to fight these socialists.... What the hell's up in the taproom?'

Several of those in the bar rushed out into the passage to see what was up in the taproom on the other side of the passage from the bar, to find when they got there that Billy Walters, who used to drive the Merthyr-Dowlais bus which had been driven off the road by the trams, was having a fight with a navvy chap whom no one knew. They fought their way out of the taproom and into the passage, where the landlord and a couple of willing hands got hold of the pair of them and rushed them out through the back way into the Castle Lane, where they left them to fight it out.

Glyn left and went home after that, for a fight always upset him; but it was time he went home, anyway, for he had had enough, more than enough, in fact.

Whenever Saran heard people talking about the war, or saw beefy, long-moustached soldiers wearing slouch hats swaggering along the main street when she was out shopping, and also during the mainly drunken celebrations for which the news of the relief of one place or another was the excuse, she hugged the thought that 'none of mine are old enough to go to the old war, anyway'. Not that she had anything against 'the old war' that she could think of, or speak about in the way her live-wire countryman, Lloyd George, was engaged in doing at the risk of his life and limb, as some said. She heard in the home the boys saying something about Lloyd George having to run for his life from places, and about him having to dodge away in disguise in bobby's clothes. Well, let him. As long as my boys, now that they're beginning to earn good money and help the way they are....

But she spoke too soon, after all, for one of her boys went to the 'old war' at the tail end, and she blamed the man who recited on the stage of the theatre for his going. She was there herself that night and heard the man; in the gallery, as usual, she was, but Benny was with some of his pals in the stalls, for he was earning as much as his dad by this time, and as he got a half-sovereign a week pocket money he could swank in the stalls, where a seat cost two shillings, as well as the shop assistants who filled the stalls on Thursday evenings could. The house was packed that night, for it was the end of the week during which somewhere or other in Africa had been relieved, and one of the members of the company playing the theatre that week was reciting each night Kipling's 'Absent-Minded Beggar' in honour of the event.

It was a brilliant as well as a full house that night when

Saran went to see the play and hear the man recite during one of the intervals. From her place in the front row of the gallery, with four of her youngest, two on either side, with her, Saran looked down on the 'big people' of the district in the circle plush seats immediately below, and the few front rows of the stalls nearest the stage. The circle was filled with the professional men of the district and their families, which in some cases included a khaki-clad son who was serving his Queen and country with the Yeomanry, and all in the circle applauded when Dr Wade and his brave son who had been wounded so badly when trying to save the flag were being shown to their places in the front row of the circle. Saran had seen the wounded soldier son in his place in the circle many a score of times before he went to the war with the Yeomanry, he never missed a night during the pantomime season, and there were some who said... but they're all applauding him now, anyway. Then there was the handsome son of the widow of the man who had kept a pack of hounds until the sinking of pits and the driving of coal-levels into the sides of the mountains made hunting impossible. Well, his son, who had been left all that money, had gone to the old war and was wounded and had been sent home, and here he was, leaning heavily on a stick as he followed his proud widow mother into their reserved seats in the circle. He, too, Saran remembered as she looked down on him and the others who were making way for him and his mother to get to their places, had been a most regular attendant during the pantomime seasons before the war. And there were others present in the circle that night whom Saran had from her point of vantage been able to keep under observation as they moved often from their places to the circle bar, and back to their places again to feast their eyes on the lovely ones who in tights and little more from the stage below...

Yes, Saran knew most of them by sight, and she had heard... but that was all over now. Duke's son, cook's son, son of a hundred kings. What applause. Patriotic songs followed the rendering of Kipling's poem. Then an appeal to the audience to contribute generously to the comforts fund. Showers of money from all parts of the house on to the stage, the pennies of the galleryites flying through the air above the heads of the richer circle patrons. Pass the hat for your credit's sake, and pay, pay, pay. All the members of the company busy gathering up the money off the stage. 'On behalf of those who are at this moment serving Queen and country in our fight against the most treacherous, most...' But it was little one could hear of what the man was saying as some of those present kept on finding from somewhere more silver coins to throw on to the stage, and the people standing up cheering as the coins landed. So it was much later than usual when the orchestra played 'God Save Our Gracious Queen', which was played twice through with all present singing as they stood to attention as best they could in the narrow space between the rows. Wonderful enthusiasm, yet Saran had forgotten most of what she had that night seen and heard in the theatre before she and the children were halfway up the hill road which she had to climb to get from where the theatre was situated on the right bank of the stinking brook to the house in which she now lived with her family.

But the scene in the theatre evidently deeply impressed her eldest boy, Benny, for instead of going to the pit next morning, as he should have done, he went in his pit clothes down the street to the recruiting office, where he waited for the recruiting-sergeant, to whom he said lies about his age in order to get himself into the Army. Off he was packed in his pit clothes to the depot at Cardiff, from where he wrote to Saran. 'So he's gone,' was all Saran could find to say after having had the letter read to her, first by Glyn, and then by the boy, Sam. 'For fear your father might have made a mistake in reading,' she said to Sam. It was the first letter that Saran could remember having from anyone or anywhere, but she had plenty after that, for Benny kept writing, first from Cardiff, and later from Raglan Barracks, Plymouth, from where he came to spend a few days' leave at home before leaving for the war in Africa. And that was the last Saran saw of him for a long time, for after the war in Africa was over he went with a draft to join the 2nd Battalion of his regiment, which was stationed at some place on the north-west frontier of India, from where he sent his photo home to his mother, who had it framed and hung on the wall in the kitchen on the right of the Roll of Honour which included the name of her brother Ike, who had been killed by the Zulus in Zululand when she was a girl; and when she used to look at the Roll of Honour and her Benny's photo she was glad that the Boers had not done that to her boy Benny which would have put his name in a Roll of Honour same as his uncle Ike's was. 'Well, well, we won't know Benny when he comes home,' she murmured as she stood back to view the photo of her boy after it was hung on the wall in its nice frame.

'What the hell's to stop us knowing him?' said his father.

Harry was knocked down and run over early one morning when on his way back into town from the coke ovens, where he had spent the night drinking and worse with Gypsy Nell, who people said was the biggest old whore down the Iron Bridge way. Judging by what Steppwr, who was one of the first to arrive on the scene after the accident, said to Saran, Harry must have still been under the influence of all the drink he had necked during the night when the engine ran over him in the morning; for Gypsy Nell told Steppwr when she came to the lodging house to fetch him that Harry had shouted from the top of the coke ovens' tip: 'Come on, Nell, I'll race you down the tip,' then ran headlong down, and he was near the bottom, along which the Cyfarthfa Company's line ran, when the little shunting engine, running light to fetch a short train of coal from Gethin Pit to the steelworks, came round the corner at a fair speed, and before Harry could stop himself he was in front of the engine. By the time she got to the bottom of the tip the engine had pulled up, and the driver and his mate, who was shunter and fireman, being as it was only a little engine, were doing what they could for Harry.

'No, it's his leg that's the worse,' said the driver. 'Here, help me to tie this around it before you run for the doctor.'

'Let him go for the doctor,' said Gypsy Nell, whipping off her shawl to make some sort of a pillow for the unconscious Harry's head.

The driver looked up at her in a way that clearly revealed what he thought about her and her sort, whom he had seen hundreds of times on their way down from the coke ovens with the different chaps they had spent the nights with there. Still, in a case like this it was no use being finicky. 'All right, you run and fetch the doctor, Jim,' he said to his mate. 'Dr Webster's surgery's nearest.... And tell him he'd better be quick. Never mind messing about with his head,' he shouted at Nell as his mate ran off to fetch the doctor. 'Let's have that shawl of yours to tie tight this end of his leg, my scarf'll be long enough to go round the lower end. Now, pull. What the hell's the matter with you? Pull, can't you?'

By the time they had done all they could for Harry the driver was a little less harsh in his manner and speech to Nell.

'Who is he?' he asked her.

'Harry... I don't know his other name.'

'Where do he live?'

'Where I stays, over Smith's lodging house.'

'Ay; but where's his home?'

'I don't know.'

'Do you know if he's got anybody b'longing to him?'

'I've heard him talk about his sister.... But I know who can tell you. The little chap as plays the concertina, he stays over Smith's lodging house, too.'

'I wish that doctor was here,' murmured the driver as Harry moaned. 'Here, how long will you be, fetching that concertina chap?'

'Not long,' said Nell as she started off.

She was back with Steppwr before the doctor arrived on

the scene, and Steppwr told the anxious driver who Harry was.

'Here's your mate coming with the doctor,' cried Nell.

It wasn't Dr Webster or his chief assistant, but the young assistant. Some swore that he was better with the knife than any of the other doctors in the district.

'The sooner we get him to the hospital the better,' he said after he had examined Harry and expertly stopped the bleeding. 'I'm going back to the surgery to report to Dr Webster and to get some things. Let me see, now. How can we get him there?'

From where they stood grouped around the prostrate Harry, Steppwr saw Jack Gray's pony and float being driven by Jack himself over the canal bridge towards the market for the day's stock of fruit, fish and vegetables, which Jack hawked for a living. 'There's Jack Gray in his flat cart,' cried Steppwr, pointing. 'I think he'll run him up, for Harry's sister, Saran, is one of Jack's best customers.'

'After him, then,' cried the doctor.

And off Steppwr raced. After a little grumbling about the likelihood of all the best stuff being sold by the wholesalers before he could get back to the market from the hospital, Jack Gray turned his pony round and drove to where Harry was waiting in an unconscious state to be picked up.

'Lord, I'll have to scrub my bloody float after I've unloaded him,' cried Jack Gray.

'Go on, take the bloody man to the hospital,' said the engine-driver, who was anxious to get away for the coal they were waiting for at the steelworks.

Jack drove off with Harry on board, with Steppwr

trotting alongside. Gypsy Nell accompanied them as far as the Patriot, where she turned in for the drink she felt so badly in need of, leaving her now blood-stained shawl under Harry's head to keep it up off the wooden bottom of the float, which, driven along the main street by Jack with Steppwr trotting alongside, attracted considerable attention. But neither the pony, Jack nor Steppwr had time to answer any of the many inquiries which were shouted after them, such as: 'What's happened? Who is it?' and so on.

Jack was driving past the Theatre Royal and Opera House when Harry came to himself and cried: 'Where the hell am I?' probably thinking he was in heaven when he opened his eyes to see the beautiful morning sky above him. Then he turned his head sideways to find Steppwr, now almost winded, for Jack trotted the pony most of the way, running alongside. 'Steppwr; what's up… oh, my bloody leg.'

'Lie quiet, Harry.'

'Where are they taking me to, Steppwr?'

'Up to the hospital – very near there,' gasped Steppwr.

'Stop. *Stop,* I tell you,' roared Harry, and Jack pulled up as passers-by left the pavements to step into the road to see who it was that was shouting.

'Now, see here, I've got to get back to the market for my day's stock,' Jack explained. 'And before doing that I shall have to scrub the bottom…'

'Turn your horse round,' said Harry, who by now was able to grasp the situation.

'Yes, when I've dropped you at the hospital, and not…'

'Do as I tell you before I throw myself out of this cart of yours. I tell you I'm not going to any hospital, so…'

'But your leg's damned near off, man,' Jack told him. 'And the doctor said...'

'Never mind what he said; I'm going to no hospital.'

'Talk sense, Harry. What the hell am I to do with you.'

There was a crowd around the cart by this time, and one of the crowd, who lost patience as Jack Gray had, cried out: 'Take the bastard to Bolton's, the horse-slaughterer, Jack.'

'Jack, please, Jack,' faintly and humbly now Harry cried. 'Don't take me to that hospital, please. Tell him not to take me to that place, Steppwr. Tell him to take me to our Saran's, will you, Steppwr? She'll look after me. Will you take me to my sister's house, Jack, please? Oh, this leg.'

Touched more than he outwardly showed, Jack tried to hide his feeling by shouting to those around the float: 'Get out of the bloody way so as a chap can turn round.' The crowd made way and away Jack drove in the direction of Saran's house. First to the left after passing the new Theatre Royal and Opera House, where *The Grip of Iron* was drawing crowded houses that week, then to the left again as soon as he had crossed the bridge over the stinking brook, then right up the hill, leaving the magnificent cathedral-like brewery building on the right.

'Hullo, Steppwr,' said Saran with a smile as soon as she opened the door and saw who was standing on her doorstep. Then looking past him to where the cart stood in the road before the house: 'What in the name of God have you got there?'

'It's Harry, and...'

'Drunk, is he?'

'No, his leg's damned near off, Saran. Knocked down by

the engine, and the doctor said he was to be taken to the hospital, but Harry says he'll go to hell first...'

'Give me a hand to get him into the house and upstairs.'

'I've had a bloody time of it with this brother of yours, Saran,' said Jack Gray as she approached the cart to superintend the unloading of Harry.

'You'll lose nothing by it,' she assured him. Neither did he.

When the old doctor, who was Saran's family doctor, and a well-paid family doctor at that, for he drew twopence out of every pound of the earnings of all Saran's pit-workers for as long as he lived... well, when he arrived with the young assistant carrying the tools in the bag, he shouted at Saran like anything.

'What kind of a game do you call this, Saran?' he wanted to know. 'When I and my assistant got to the hospital...'

'But I sent Steppwr over to the hospital to tell them there to let you know where he was, doctor.'

'I know; and I've come here to tell you that he's to go back there at once. We can't do anything with him here.'

'Then you're not likely to do anything with him ever, for he won't let you take him to the hospital – I wish he would, for I know he'd get better tendance there than I can give him here with all these children to look after. But he's like my Glyn and a many more, doctor; swears he'll die before he'll go there.'

'Of all the... do you think it's any use me talking to him, Saran?'

'Not a bit, doctor. He'd have been in the hospital ready for you if talking could have got him there. For you know I'm for the hospital, doctor.'

The old doctor stood scratching his head. Then he sent his assistant over to the hospital to get a few things, and when the assistant came back to Saran's house with the few things they worked on Harry with Saran as co-opted assistant and took his leg off just above the knee-joint. There wasn't much the matter with his head, though he had to have a couple of stitches in his head, too. After the two doctors had gone off in the doctor's high-wheeled trap Saran returned to where Steppwr was sitting in the kitchen and said: 'You'd better go up and sit by his side ready to talk to him when he comes to hisself, for I can't stay up there with him with the children coming home for their dinners, and things to get for Glyn's and the boys' suppers by the time they come home from the pit. I expect Glyn'll be mad when he hears that Harry's upstairs, for he and Harry was never the best of friends, but whatever Glyn says he's staying until he's able to get about again, and after that if only he'll behave hisself. You'd better have a cup of tea and a bit to eat before you go up to sit with him; I don't suppose he'll want more than a cup of tea to drink when he comes to himself.'

That night, Glyn, who about that time was working in a wet place in the pit, a place where water dropped from the roof on to his back most of the time, hurried home to get his wet things off; he walked all the way home with Sam, the boy then working with him.

'You're early, ain't you?' said Saran as he entered.

Glyn looked up at the kitchen ceiling and listened for a few seconds before asking: 'Who's upstairs?'

'Our Harry, and Steppwr, your brother-in-law,' she replied.

‘Harry and… what the hell can you say they’re doing upstairs in my house, woman?’

She explained briefly.

‘But couldn’t they have taken him to the hospital?’

‘They could if he let ’em, which he wouldn’t, for he don’t like that hospital any better than you do. Take those wet clothes off; I’ve got the hot water ready for you to wash. Hurry up.’

‘Well, this is a damned fine lookout,’ grumbled Glyn as he began undressing. Then as he started to wash himself kneeling over the tub of hot water. ‘A nice feller he is to have in the house…. And he’ll be here for months,’ he cried out in alarm at the prospect.

‘P’raps you’d like me to send him to the workhouse?’ said Saran.

‘There’s better bloody men than him there.’

‘Then if that’s the case there’s the hell of a sight better bloody men than you there.’

‘Am I a scamp? A blackguard? A whore-master? And…’

Saran stopped his mouth with the washing flannel. ‘Now, simmer down, Glyn, my boy; for if he heard you talking as you are he’d get up and hop on one leg out of this house in the shape he is, and that would be the death of him. Don’t worry, you won’t have to go short of anything because he’s with us.’

‘Well, if Steppwr’s going to be here as his…’

‘You know damned well that Steppwr would rather starve than…’

‘I know damned well that you’ll talk white black…’

The rest was lost as he buried his coal-dusty head under

the water in the tub. Saran went on laying supper, for by now the other two boys were home from the pit and shouting up to Sam to hurry out of the bathroom so as they could get there to bath. For the next hour Saran and her Jane were busy feeding and waiting on the pit-men, all of whom were in a hurry to get out to somewhere or other where the hard, wet and dangerous labour of the day could be forgotten for a short time. The boys had hurried out before their father, who complained that they got far more attention from Saran than ever he did.

'Don't tell your lies,' Saran said as she handed him his bowler hat after brushing it. Then as he was about to walk out of the house: 'You wouldn't be mean enough to walk out without as much as going up to say how-do to him, would you?' Oh, the way she said it.

'Oh, I forgot,' he said.

'I thought so,' she said as he went upstairs to where Harry lay. 'Tell Steppwr to come back down with you, for I shall be going to sit with my brother for the rest of the time before bedtime.'

Having thrown Harry the bare bone of an invitation to stay until he was able to get about again, Glyn turned to Steppwr as he was going out of the room and said: 'Saran wants you downstairs.' And off down and out of the house he went, thinking: 'I'm a workman, they're a pair of rodneys as have always dodged work. So why should I be nice to them?'

'Here,' Saran was saying as she handed Steppwr a shilling. 'Go on, take it. I want you to run up here most days now that Harry is with us, for it's little time I'll have to sit and talk to him, and both of us know how he gets when he's got to lie by himself for any time. So you'll be doing me a favour by coming up every day. Don't take any notice of Glyn's sour looks, and tell Harry not to, either. S'long, Steppwr.'

And that's how it was for the best part of six months. Each day the concertina man would play a little and talk a lot to keep Harry from moping; and as soon as Glyn arrived home from the pit each night Steppwr would take his leave with the usual shilling from Saran to pay for his bed and a couple of pints and a bit of food. And during Harry's convalescence Saran rigged Steppwr out in a barely worn suit that her Benny had left behind when he went and joined the Army, and also a good flannel shirt and a good pair of boots. But that was nothing to what she insisted on doing for Harry when he, as soon as he could bear the weight of his body on the stump of his leg when strapped to the wooden peg leg which was now his from the left knee down, said he wasn't going to stay any longer where he wasn't wanted.

'Glyn don't mind you staying, it's only his old way, that's all,' said Saran.

'It may be, but though I might take a drink with him some time again, I go to hell if I live under the same roof any longer. I know it's his house, and... ah, well, we never have liked each other much.'

'That's not his fault.'

'I'm not saying it is, Saran. I suppose that I'm one of these awkward buggers as don't know how to...' He bent down to adjust one of the straps fastened around the stump of his leg. 'Bit tight for a start,' he explained. Then he stumped experimentally to where Saran stood watching him. Steppwr watched from the foot of the stairs. 'Not so bad for a start, Steppwr, is it? In about a week I'll be able to hop about just as well as I used to.' Then seriously, as he placed a big hand on Saran's shoulder. 'I'm off, then, Saran bach. You've been – well, what I knew you'd be to me. If I was any bloody good at all I'd know how to tell you... come on, Steppwr, let's push off.' And he stumped out of the house with his eyes full of tears; and Saran followed him to the doorstep, where she stood watching him gingerly stumping his way down the road leading into town. There were tears in her eyes, too, but before they came out she shook her head impatiently and went back into the house, where there was a bellyful of work awaiting her, for it was washing-day, and she was going to try and do the bedclothes of the bed on which Harry had been lying for nearly six months, for it was a lovely drying-day, and if she left them she might not get such another drying-day for a long time. So she started on her big wash about the time Harry and Steppwr were finishing their second pint in the Bird in Hand, where Harry was demonstrating the qualities of the peg leg. 'Damn near as good as the other leg,' he swore it was.

CHAPTER 10
BREAKAWAYS

Benny returned to civilian life to play his part in the breaking up of the family which his leaving for the Army had started. He returned to find that Hugh had had to get married in a hurry, and that he had gone to work and live at Senghenydd, his wife's home town. 'Time some of us got married or something,' grumbled Benny after he had been back a week in the overcrowded home. True, they were one less than when he had left for the Army, but they had all grown so, he hardly knew his brothers when he returned home to them, and having grown so they took up more room. What with their bikes and clothes... And the rows. Boys three in a bed, for Jane by now had to have a room of her own. And Benny wanted a room of his own, but his mother said: 'Don't be silly, boy; you're not a young woman like Jane is. So tumble in with the rest.'

Big-sorted, that's what Benny was, thought the other brothers as soon as the close contact with him had like a late frost killed the hero-worship that had developed during his absence abroad. And Benny shouted at the little boys, and was thrashing one for refusing to go and get him cigarettes, when Meurig rose from the table and said: 'Let the kid alone, our Benny.' Then there was a fight, and the next day Meurig went off to the Rhondda to work, said he'd had enough of Benny's domineering ways.

'I don't know what's coming over 'em,' Saran would sigh.

'They're all getting too damned big for their boots, especially that chap back from India,' said Glyn, one night after Meurig's departure when they were alone in the house. 'To hear him talk – "Told the gaffer the other day" – but there, they're all alike. Now, Lewis, there's a mouthy little swine if you like. Last night, puts his things on, and off away and up the pit, leaving me to finish off the tram myself, said he was off to see a fight between that Ike Bradley and somebody. If only we had as much sense as sparrows, and drove 'em out as soon as they're able to take care of themselves. I shan't be sorry when some of the others follow Meurig to the Rhondda, or Hugh to Senghen...'

'Yes, no doubt you'd be glad to see 'em all go.'

'I shouldn't worry, for it's work I'll have to...'

'Mam, mam,' cried young Mervyn as he ran into the kitchen. 'Uncle Steppwr wants that crutch Uncle Harry used before his peg leg was...'

'Now, take a breath. Now, who wants the crutch?'

'Uncle Harry, of course. He's been fighting – I seen him

fighting with his back 'gainst the wall and his peg drove into the ground. We boys were playing fire across the road when Uncle Harry rushed out of the Tanyard Inn, threw his coat in the air; and when he was fixing hisself against the wall Uncle Steppwr came out of the Tanyard Inn and said, "Don't be a damned fool, Harry," but Uncle Harry kept shouting for that Wat Morris to come out of the Tanyard Inn...'

'Bloody scamp,' muttered Glyn.

'Yes?' said Saran, putting her coat on.

'Wat Morris came out and said: "I don't want to bother with you, Harry," and he was going away when Uncle Harry called him dirty names. Then Wat Morris turned back to where Uncle Harry was standing against the wall, and told him that it was lucky for him that he only had one leg, and with that Uncle Harry up fist and hit him. Then they started fighting like anything, with the men all round 'em, and some men was telling Wat Morris to leave our uncle Harry alone; and Mrs Lewis of the Tanyard Inn gave a boy a penny to fetch a policeman. And soon our uncle Harry was down and his face was bleeding, and some of the men took that Wat Morris away. Then I went up close to see, and Uncle Steppwr was trying to do something with uncle Harry's peg leg, but he couldn't, for half of it was sticking on uncle Harry's leg and half of it sticking up out of the ground, and Uncle Steppwr when he seen me told me...'

'Here, mind you don't bring that bloody scamp back here,' shouted Glyn as Saran got the old crutch from where it had lain for years in the lumber cupboard under the stairs. But she was off like the wind, with the crutch at the trail, and young Mervyn running alongside her. She fixed

Harry up with the crutch and in decent lodgings with a widow woman until she could get him fitted with another peg leg and in less than a month after she had bought him the new peg leg she managed to persuade one of the under-managers at the Dowlais steelworks to work Harry into the vacancy caused by the death of the old gatekeeper of the upper level crossing. She had less trouble persuading the manager to get Harry the job than she had to get Harry to take it. 'Just the job for you Harry. Don't be a fool now; take it.' He did. All he had to do was sit in the shanty near the gates until the engines from the steelworks blew their whistles to let him know that they wanted to travel along where the line crossed the main road. Then he was expected to get up and stump out of the shanty to man the wheel which, when turned to the right, would send the two long gates right across the road and stop all traffic until the engine and whatever it had behind it were safely by. Then he would turn the wheel to the left so that traffic along the road could continue flowing... then he could go back to the shanty to sit down and smoke his pipe. 'A bobby's job,' Steppwr said it was. Not a big wage, it's true. Still...

Anyway, he stuck it, and Saran was much relieved to know that he was working at something, for she had her hands pretty full with one thing and another, so she didn't want him on her hands as well.

She was beginning to find that it wasn't all honey having her Glyn and five of her boys working, though there were only three of them at home with her after Hugh had married and had gone to live with his wife at Senghenydd, and after Meurig had gone to live and work at Tonypandy in the Rhondda. And now her eldest, Benny, was talking about getting married to the girl who was a servant at Colonel Lewis'. And the other two working in the pit and still at home were getting to be a bit of a handful as well. Wanting this, and wanting that. Off somewhere or other every night of the week, though never to the pubs. To dances, boxing matches, the theatre or the Temperance Hall, which was the district's leading variety house; to one of the new billiard saloons that were being rushed up. Spending far more money than ever their dad had on drink. And they dressed up to the nines to go spending it. And neither of her boys at work in the pit would hesitate to tell the gaffer to keep his work if they thought they were being exploited more than they thought they should be.

And the way they talked about this, that and the other. It was from their talk that Saran learnt that the first socialist member that Wales had ever had, had been elected by them and their sort in that district. A socialist representative, and the Miners' Federation daily growing stronger in readiness to fight the owners; not the old-style individual owners that their dad had even called by their Christian names, for all those had been wiped out by the companies which had been formed, even as the companies were also in their turn being wiped out by the combines which were coming into being. Saran couldn't make head nor tail of it all. It was a restless and fairly prosperous time. Liberalism was conceding to the workers many things that they had long clamoured for, and the new socialist movement was promising more than it would ever be able to give. The sad-faced socialist member and his young colleague, Ramsay MacDonald, were predicting the collapse of Capitalism, and the rising out of its ruins of the glorious Socialist Commonwealth; and there was much besides that Saran heard at second hand, without comprehending, from her boys and her husband's talk in the home.

She also heard from the chapel people that it was a sinful age, that the people were puffed up, work-proud, wage-proud, and that they had turned away from God, Who would soon punish them, and so on.

And then, suddenly, out of the west, came the Welsh John the Baptist of the twentieth century, and like wildfire the great revival spread through Wales. A pale-faced young collier armed with power from God started on his task of saving Wales from the wrath to come. Baptisms in brooks, prayers in pits, sermons in streets. Singing. Pregnant silences, during which the young collier whom God had chosen as the bearer of His message of warning stood in pulpits looking accusingly at and through his congregations, the members of which broke down and confessed aloud their sins over and over again. Pandemonium. Lo, he speaks. Hush. Listen. Strange, moving, stirring are his utterances. Time passes. He falls silent again, and remains silent for long, his hands clasped, his soul pouring upwards – and outwards.

He, his work, his helpers, the numerous conversions, all are reported at great length in all the leading papers of Great Britain, and across the Atlantic the Welsh community at Scranton, PA, USA are inspired by the news from the old country. For months the newspapers sent out to them from the old country featured the revival, and Welshmen the world over rejoiced to think that Wales was leading the peoples of the earth back to God.

Then, just as suddenly as they had flared and spread, the cleansing fires died down, though not quite out. The young collier-revivalist broke down under the strain, and many of his converts returned to their vomits. But not Harry.

Whilst sitting in his little shanty on the right of the level crossing, smoking his pipe, Harry was several times tackled by one of the most enthusiastic of the revival workers, who earned his living as a fireman on the biggest of the steelworks' engines which Harry opened the gates for. Spent the major portion of his mealtimes wrestling with the devil which had for so long lodged in Harry's soul. Called Harry 'brother', did this earnest young man. 'Listen, brother.' The first time or two he called Harry 'brother', the devil in Harry's soul prompted him to tell the young man to 'get to hell out of here'. But the young man stayed until the hooter blew him back to his work, and all the time he was with Harry in the little shanty he went on revealing to Harry the horrors of the Hell he, Harry, was bound for. He read to him passages from the Book; knelt down and prayed for Harry's salvation; and each time as he was going after the hooter blew, he would invite Harry to come with him to hear the revivalist who was doing such wonderful work in the district.

'Please come,' he begged one evening after he had been fighting the devil in Harry for about a fortnight. 'He's leaving the district for the Rhondda tomorrow, and you may never have the chance of hearing him again. So do come with me tonight, brother.'

'Oh, all right,' said Harry, now curious to see the man about whom there was such a lot of talk, and who, Harry made no bones in saying, was 'driving people off their bloody heads'. So he went to Calfaria Chapel with the earnest young fireman just to see what the man was like.

It happened to be one of the revivalist's silent evenings; had he preached the chances are that Harry would never have been moved in the least. But by standing silent and anguished before Harry for hours whilst the huge congregation sang, prayed, confessed, gave thanks, wept, and rejoiced, he somehow did something to Harry. Harry wept, and as he wept cleansing tears he thought of his mother, his father, his brothers Shoni and Ike, his sister Saran, of Steppwr, of men he had stood up to, of women he had laid down with, and he wished them all there so as he could beg their forgiveness. He couldn't kneel down because of his peg leg, so he sat on the floor of the aisle between the seats, where he wept and mumbled spasmodic prayers. The only tears he had shed up to then were the bitter tears, but now his tears were sweet, and healing. 'O God, help me. Help an old blackguard, please, God.'

Saran, though she hated the thought of handing over her wage-earners to other women, was relieved when her first-born, Benny, informed her that he and Annie had decided to get married on the Saturday before Whitsun Monday. And she was glad, for after that terrible fight which he and Meurig... made her feel faint when she thought of it. One as bad as the other.... Meurig had come up from the Rhondda to spend a weekend at home, where he had become notorious, even as his uncle Harry was before him, for fighting and all sorts of rough-housing. On the Sunday he went playing pitch-and-toss and lost all the money he had come home from the Rhondda with, and after he had lost it he tried to borrow money from his mother to go on playing.

'You'll have no money of mine to throw away after your own,' Saran told him. 'I'll see you all right to go back to the Rhondda tomorrow...'

'Only five shillings; and if I get my own back...'

Then Mister Benny had to interfere. 'Don't you be a fool, mam, to give hard-earned money to a waster who hasn't sent you home a penny all the time's he been in the Rhondda.'

'Shut your mouth, Benny,' said his mother.

'He'd better, before I shut it for him,' said Meurig.

One word led to another, and on they went from words to blows. Then they went at it hammer and tongs, fighting their way out of the living room into the scullery, and from there out into the backyard, where Meurig gave his eldest brother the finest pasting a man ever had before Saran and Jane managed to part them. 'You damned little blackguard,' said Saran to Meurig. And that was only one of many rows and fights, so no wonder Saran was not sorry to hear of Benny's marriage.

It was a classy wedding, in the chapel, with a best man and two of the girls who were in service with Annie at Colonel Lewis' acting as bridesmaids. Annie had a veil and all, and Benny had on a new double-breasted blue suit, a high choker collar, and a buttonhole in his coat. And the young couple hurried away from the feast Saran had prepared to enjoy their honeymoon, which was 'something', said Saran in reply to a question Steppwr had asked, 'as I never had – or wanted'.

'But I thought you said there was going to be a wedding,' said the mystified Steppwr, who had turned up with his concertina under his arm.

'God only knows what a bloody nuisance he was when he was boozing, but he's ten times more of a nuisance now that he's "saved", as he reckons he is,' grumbled the landlord of the New Inn as he and his chucker-out came back into the bar from the front after having seen Harry off the premises in a rather forcible manner. 'Damn it all,' he continued as he ducked under the bar-flap to resume duty behind the bar, 'he's worse than them Salvation Army chaps as walks in every now and then. Give them a copper, or buy a *War Cry* off 'em, and they'll bugger off tidy; but this Harry... two quarts, did you say? Certainly.' He soon forgot all about Harry as he went on serving the Saturday night crowd.

Harry, muttering: 'Forgive them, God,' was picking himself out of the gutter into which he had been deposited by the landlord and his chucker-out. Passers-by laughed at the old man that but few of them knew as he struggled up on to his one foot and the peg, for Harry had altered in appearancc so much that he was unrecognisable to all but the few still interested in him sufficiently to have noted the alteration taking place. He had allowed a circular rim of grey whiskers to grow around his swarthy, battle-scarred face, and this alone was enough to prevent him from being recognised by those who had known him but slightly in the days before he was 'saved'. And now he bore himself meekly, his one-time swaggering manner and gait had vanished.

By this time he was getting used to being forcibly ejected from pubs; two ejections a night bar Sundays was about his average. And still he persisted in the hope of 'saving' some of those who, in his opinion, were hell-bound. When on his nightly visits to the pubs, he carried in his hand a little Bible of which he could not read a word, but he had memorised certain passages which he had made the fireman who had turned him to God repeat until he knew them off by heart. He also got the fireman to turn down the pages on which the selected and memorised passages could be read by all who wanted to read them, though it was seldom that he was allowed to remain on licensed premises long enough to recite one of the selected passages, for the landlords and their chuckers-out gave him but little time to recite before they scruffed him out through the nearest exit. 'Come, on, out you go.'

Having brushed a little of the mud off his clothes with his hands, he stood leaning against one of the windows of the premises he had so recently been ejected from, trying to make up his mind where he should go next. The sound of the organ as it was borne to him on the wind from the Iron Bridge fairground decided him. Yes, he'd go across to one of the pubs in the Iron Bridge district, where he thought he was most needed. So off he stumped through Victoria Street. As he stumped along he thought with shame of the years he had spent as pimp, bully, bouncer, gambler, whoremaster and so on in the Iron Bridge district. Thought of the navvies and flats he had rooked and beaten, of the women... how was Gypsy Nell these days he wondered? Was she in prison? The workhouse? Or was she still carrying on with other men as she had once with him? Poor Nell. His first duty was to find her and warn her... though not until he had begged her forgiveness.

He looked into two of the pubs in the district, looked in the bars and in all the rooms, without being able to find her. Then he tried the Patriot, which was crowded, for in addition to 'the usuals' there were scores of navvies in for the weekend from the big waterworks job which was in progress about seven miles out of town. The navvies who worked double time on this job lived in huts on the job, miles from anywhere the place was. Bed to work, work to bed, that's what it was, they said. So after a few weeks they'd draw their back time and make for the delights of the Iron Bridge district of Merthyr, where they would soak themselves in drink, get a woman – and some got themselves a dose of the pox into the bargain.

And the navvies were there in force on the night Harry went down there to look for his old flame, Gypsy Nell, whom he found in the Patriot, seated between two drunken navvies who had their arms around her neck as they sang 'Sweet Rosie O'Grady'. And there were other navvies sitting with other willing women of the district. Unnoticed in the crowd which packed the smoke-filled bar, Harry made his way from the outer door across to where Gypsy Nell was seated between the two navvies. As he drew near to them he heard one of the navvies say: 'I'm going to get a bottle of rum to take with us up the coke ovens. Won't be a minute.' As he rose to move up to the bar to get the bottle of rum the other navvy also rose and said: 'And I'll get a couple of quart bottles of beer. Rum an' beer – can't beat it.' He winked at Gypsy Nell. 'Best horn mixture going.' And he moved up to the bar, where his mates were then lined up two-deep calling for drink. Harry went and sat at Nell's side.

'Here, what the hell...?'

'Hush, Nell. Don't swear, please.'

She looked at him closely, and after she had scanned his face, looked down at the peg leg. 'Good God, Harry,' she gasped.

'Yes; I came down tonight... what are you laughing at?'

'Those bloody whiskers of yours. Ha, ha, ha, they make you look like... but I go to hell if I know what they make you look like. Ha, ha.'

'Be quiet, Nell, and listen to me, please. Listen, before those two chaps...'

'Half a minute, Harry. Tell me one thing. Why didn't you bring my shawl back that time?'

'Shawl?'

'Now, don't act strange. You pawned it, I expect.'

'Indeed, I didn't. What shawl are you talking about?'

'The same shawl as I told you about when you was down this way last, before you grew them whiskers, that was. The shawl I put under your napper when they put you on that cart of Jack Gray's to take you to hospital. Now do you remember?'

'I think I do; it must be at my sister's house. I'll... oh, here they are coming. Nell, don't go up to the coke ovens with these two chaps, I beg you. Think what you're doing,

Nell. Listen to what it says here, Nell.' Hurriedly he recited: 'Let us walk honestly, as in the day; not in rioting and drunkenness, not in chambering and wan...'

'Here, who the hell is this?' cried the navvy with the two quart bottles of beer, one in each hand.

'For if you lie in sin with these men...'

'Here, you bug-whiskered old bastard,' cried the one with a pint-and-a-half bottle of rum in his left hand, 'get to hell out of this before I wipe the floor with you.' Then he palmed Harry's face from his chin to his eyebrows with the palm of a hand as rough as sandpaper through working in cement and mixing concrete, and as he palmed Harry he pushed him backwards towards the door.

Harry had, so to speak, been turning the other cheek for the two years which had elapsed since his conversion, though on many occasions he had found it most difficult to do so when he was suffering indignities and being roughly handled. But not once had he been 'palmed' by anyone, let alone such a rough-handed chap as this navvy. So, on this occasion, before he could force him back, the old Harry escaped from his prison and used the new Harry's right fist with terrible effect on the navvy who had the pint-and-a-half bottle of rum in his left hand. He went down with a crash, for as he fell he brought a nearby table and glasses and pints down with him.

'Oh, God forgive me,' murmured Harry.

'What the hell,' cried the landlord, Tim Crowley, rushing from behind the bar. 'Oh, it's you, is it?' he cried on seeing Harry. 'Didn't I tell you...'

'Sorry, Mr Crowley...'

'Sorry, be damned. Here, Mike, throw this bastard out...'

'Mr Crowley, I promise I'll go out quietly if only you'll let me stay until this poor man comes to himself so as I can ask his forgiveness. You see...'

The landlord and Mike hustled him out of the place. 'You're damned lucky I'm letting you go without paying for the breakages,' said the landlord. 'See him right away from the place, Mike, for I've got to get back behind the bar.'

Mike stood in the doorway looking after Harry until he had stumped his way along the Glebeland. Then he went back to his duties in the bar.

As he stumped along the Glebeland Harry considered various places where sinners were plentiful and convertible. He passed the Beehive, the Belle Vue, the Wyndham, and other pubs. He stopped outside the Lamb, and was about to go in when he remembered Gypsy Nell's shawl, then he decided that he would straightway go up to Saran's house and ask about the shawl.

'Well, well, and what can you say you've been up to again?' cried Saran as he appeared before her in the living room of her house. 'You're muck from head to foot. Sit there in the armchair, and take off that coat so as I can brush it.'

'It's nothing; what I...'

'Let me have that coat,' she insisted. He let her have it. 'What were you going to say?'

'Oh, it's about a shawl.'

'Shawl?'

'Yes, Gypsy Nell's...'

'Oh, I remember; that shawl that was under your head the day you were brought here on the cart after the engine knocked you down. Yes, I washed it and put it away. So it belongs to that old creature.'

'Now, Saran, don't be nasty. We're none of us so good as all that; and she, poor gel... well, let her alone, that's all. She wants her shawl back, so if you'll let me have it...'

'I will, but not tonight. You're not going down that place with any shawl at this time of night when it's not safe for a regiment of soldiers to be there, let alone a man with only one leg. You shall have it to take down in the morning when it's daylight and a bit safer to be about there. I shan't forget, not if I live to be a hundred, that night when I had to go down there to tell you that the p'lice were after you, that night when you walked the mountains into the Rhondda.'

Harry smiled sadly. 'That was a long time ago, Saran.'

'Oh, not so long. It's them old whiskers of yours makes you think that. Why don't you have 'em off?'

'Why... well... oh, I don't know. They – they helps to stop me thinking about women like – like I used to. No woman would look twice at me with these on. They laugh, and that's what I'd rather 'em do. For there are times now... I haven't got rid of the devil yet, Saran. I up and hit a poor man tonight, a poor man as was in his drink. I don't know what God'll think of me.' He wept freely.

'Here, have this cup of tea and a bit to eat.'

He supped tea out of the saucer and went on tearfully bewailing his shortcomings. 'Yes, I hit the poor chap for nothing, same as I hit your Glyn once. And I haven't asked Glyn's forgiveness for that, either. Where is Glyn?'

'Away down the stone-coal district burying his brother

Dai. Killed last Wednesday in the pit down there, he was. Didn't you hear?'

'Not a word. But that's how it is, Saran. Today we're...'

'Come on, drink that cup of tea; and eat something as well.'

CHAPTER 11

'ISN'T HE LOVELY, GRANNY?'

She had barely finished getting her own supply of children before they began getting theirs. 'Isn't he lovely, Granny?' was a question she had by now heard more than once from daughters-in-law who, she thought, made a lot more fuss than they should about bringing their babies into the world. Her Hugh's wife was bad enough, but Annie, her Benny's wife, was enough to make a person swear. And Benny himself was almost as bad. Messing about the house instead of going to his work as he should have done. What did he want there? What could he do, anyway? There was the midwife – district nurse or something of the sort she called herself, Saran, who thought she was as good as any midwife, and then Benny insisted on having the doctor as well. And every time she went down into the kitchen to fetch something, Saran would find Benny out on the landing, or at the foot of the stairs, or walking from one corner to the other of the kitchen looking just like some of the men she had seen playing Hamlet and other nerve-racked parts in the theatre. 'How is she now?' he kept on asking. 'Oh, she's all right. Why don't you go out for a walk?'

Not he; and when it was over, there he was acting soft enough to shame any mother, though his old softness seemed to please Annie, but there, she was as soft as he was.

Three boys married already, and her only girl, Jane, wanting to get married to her Ossie. On and on about it. Wouldn't listen to what Saran tried to tell her about all the work there was to do with all them boys about the house, half of whom were going to the pit and the other half to school. 'So it's a lot of work, Jane.'

'Well, it isn't as if I was going to live away; I'll be near enough to help, won't I? And Ossie's sick of lodgings. If his mother hadn't gone and got married again he wouldn't have minded waiting a bit longer, but now...'

'Oh, all right, we'll see.'

It wasn't the work Saran minded, but the loss of Jane, whom she thought more of than she did of any of her boys. Still, being as she was set on getting married – and there was many a worse chap than Ossie, that she knew – then let her. She'd find her a little house close by, near enough to keep an eye on her, and also near enough to call her in on washing-days, and on Fridays to do the upstairs rooms. So the date of the wedding was fixed, and Saran saw to it that her Jane had as fine a wedding as either of the three boys had had. She rounded up every member of the family, and the only one outside the family honoured with an invitation to attend was old Marged, who had kept house for Glyn's father, and then for Glyn and Dai. So Marged, who was now living on the parish and the few shillings she got going about doing a bit of washing, white-liming or papering for one or the other, was the only one outside the family invited by Saran to the wedding of her daughter Jane.

All the family – well, except Saran's brother Shoni, for nobody knew where he was, or whether he was alive or dead, though the navvy chap did say... but the navvy chap was drunk. Anyway, Shoni wasn't at the wedding, but all the other members of the family were. The two uncles, Uncle Harry and Uncle Steppwr, were there, and only Saran knew the job she had to persuade Harry to be present. But she managed it. Then there was Glyn, of course, he gave his daughter away, for it was a proper wedding in the chapel.

Then there were Benny, Annie, and their two children; and Hugh and his wife and their three children up from Senghenydd; then Sam and Kate and their baby – Kate was looking none too well, either. Then there was Saran's favourite boy, Meurig, 'Mad Meurig', up from the Rhondda, where, so people whose business sometimes took them into the Rhondda said, he was carrying on fine, 'same as that old uncle of his used to'. But Saran didn't care what they said about him, she was as proud as could be to have him up for Jane's wedding. Then there was Lewis, as mouthy as they're made, still, not a bad boy to his mother when it came to the push; and Mervyn, and Idris, and Jim – she'd have to watch that cough of his, have to get another bottle of Scott's Emulsion. Then the two youngest boys, Tom and

Charlie; Tom worked carrying out for Davies the butcher in the evenings after school and all day Saturdays, and he was as proud of his ability to earn a shilling and a pound of sausage – which he only got when there was sausage left at closing-time – each week as were the boys in the pit of their ability to earn wages. So Tom and Charlie were allowed to stay home from school on the day of Jane's wedding.

Saran saw to it that everything was done in style. Cabs to take the party to the chapel, and cabs to bring them back to the house again after the ceremony – and everyone wearing flowers from Gray's the florist, who specialised in wreaths. And when they all got back from the chapel Saran made them all sit down whilst she and old Marged waited on them hand and foot. It so happened that the wedding took place on the very day that the Eight Hours Act for miners became operative, and it came up in conversation because Glyn told young Lewis that he was lucky to have a day off from the pit to attend his sister's wedding.

'Oh, I am, am I?' said young Lewis to his father as cheeky as you like, and speaking with his mouth full of bread and roast pork. 'Well, I shall be having a lot more time off now that the Eight Hours is law. And about time, too; time we had our share of daylight.'

'You won't get fat on daylight,' said his father, who believed every word that the owners' spokesmen had said and written about the effect the shorter working day would have on the industry. 'More daylight – less wages,' Glyn prophesied.

'No fear,' Lewis said, 'they can't pay us less than they're paying.... Oh, and you'll have to watch yourself, too, from now on, our dad, for anyone staying in the pit after time will be summoned…'

'Here,' cried Meurig from where he sat near to where his mother stood carving off the leg of pork, 'did I come up here all the way from the Rhondda to hear you chaps talk about work?'

'Certainly not,' said Saran. 'Now, shut up, Lewis.'

'Then let's have some more of that pork,' said Lewis.

'I will after I've given everybody their first bit. Here's yours, Harry; I know you like the fat.'

It was a fine spread, and everyone did justice to it; even Harry, who might easily have turned out to be the wet blanket it was feared he would be, ate as hearty as anyone present, and did his best to appear jolly on tea out of respect for Saran; and, though with the air of a martyr, he even went into the front room with the men after the meal was over.

'Glyn, you and Steppwr and the boys – but not you little ones – had better go into the front room for a bit whilst me and Marged and the gels clears up,' said Saran. 'You know where it is in there. But p'raps you'd better stay in here with us, Harry?'

'No, I'll go on into the front room with 'em out of the way,' said Harry, though knowing quite well what Saran meant by 'it', for 'it' meant drink.

So the men adjourned to the front room, and the younger boys were given coppers and sent out of the house to play whilst their elders drank the health of the young couple, and whilst the women cleared up in the kitchen. In all there were seven men in the front room, but only three were fond of their drop of drink. The bridegroom was one, Glyn, his father-in-law, another, and Steppwr, of course. Harry, of course, strict TT; whilst the boys, Benny, Hugh, Sam and Meurig – which makes eight in all, not seven – were not any too keen on drink, though they were not averse to taking a drink when in company.

'Sit down,' Glyn told them as he went to the cupboard and brought to view a couple of bottles of port wine. 'There's beer for all as wants it, and there's port for them as don't; and for them as don't want either, there's a bottle of herb beer of your mother's make. Now, what'll you have?' Some had beer, some had port, but Harry wouldn't even touch the herb beer. Some smoked pipes, others cigarettes, Harry nothing at all.

'So you and Jane are not going away anywhere?' said Benny to the bridegroom.

'No, he's not so daft as you was,' said Glyn. 'What's he want to go 'way for? Can't he get everything in comfort here? Of course he can. Drink up, Ossie. Now, Steppwr, let's hear from you.' Steppwr played, with one eye on the sad-looking Harry, and when he had finished his selection of popular airs, Glyn wanted to know who was going to oblige with a song. 'Well, if nobody cares to oblige, I'll sing you one for a start.' He sang. 'Now, who's going to oblige with the next song?'

Meurig, who was beginning to feel bored, was fingering the pack of cards he always carried about with him: 'What about a game of penny nap?'

'Not damned likely,' cried his father. 'No gambling in my house. If I take a drop of drink I draws the line.... How is it that every time you come up home from the Rhondda you want to start gambling as soon as you come, Meurig?'

'Well, I like a little gamble.'

'Then you're not having it here. Come on, you fellers, drink up. There's plenty here. Come on, Ossie.'

'Thanks. Now, I'll sing a song if you like, but it's only comic songs I know,' said the bridegroom, who was warming up rapidly.

'Order for a song,' cried Glyn. Meurig sighed and went on fingering the pack of cards in his pockets as the bridegroom went on singing a song entitled 'I Only Came Down for Nails'. Really funny, he was.

'Not at all bad,' said Benny patronisingly, and then went on to tell his uncle Steppwr that it was a pity he hadn't learnt to play the concertina as well as Perci Honri, who had played in the theatre the week previous.

'Your uncle can play better than Perci Honri or any other you ever heard,' said Harry to the surprise of all present.

'And what about Ossie's singing?' Glyn wanted to know. 'I never thought I'd have a son-in-law as could sing a comic song as well as Ossie sang that last song. Know any more, Ossie?'

'I can do as well in the Carmarthen Stores as ever you'll do in your shop, my gel,' Saran was telling Benny's wife, whose youngest she was nursing now that the clearing up was done. 'It's all very well for these shops b'longing to these old companies to come here and sell their old muck that isn't...'

'Well, what I buy there isn't muck,' Annie, Benny's wife, up and said – for she wasn't afraid of Saran if Sam's wife was. 'I get better butter from my shop than ever I got from the Carmarthen Stores.'

'Yes, but what about their bacon?' said Sam's wife, supporting her mother-in-law. 'I tried a pound the week before last, but Sam wouldn't touch it, yet he enjoyed the bacon I got him from the Carmarthen Stores.'

'Of course he would,' said Saran. 'All these multiply shops...'

'You mean multiple,' corrected Annie in a superior way.

'Well, whatever they are they're not worth dealing with, whether it's food, clothes or anything else. Just because things are a little cheaper with 'em people rush there. And what do they get in the long run? Shoddy stuff, that's what they get. Lizzie Jane Warde's husband bought a suit of black cheap in that big new tailor's shop next door to the post office, and in less than a year it was off his back. Now, Glyn bought a suit of black to follow his father in, long before we was married, that was. Paid four guineas to Evans the tailor for it, and he's wearing the coat for work – wearing it now, after twenty years. Twenty years – what am I talking about? Why, Benny is...'

'What about a song from one of you boys?' Glyn cried. No response. 'Well, what a damned lot of boys I've got. Then will one of you recite something? Oh, talking about reciting... come on, drink up. More like a funeral than a wedding. Yes, there was a reciter if you like. Wasn't he, Steppwr?'

'Who do you mean?'

'Old Davies, MA, who else? What if these boys had heard him recite that piece about the man and his dagger?'

'*Macbeth*, was it?' asked Benny.

'P'raps it was; all I know is... where is the old chap now, Steppwr?'

'He died in the workhouse.'

'I closed his poor eyes for him,' Harry roused himself to say. 'It was shortly after I began visiting the poor chaps in the workhouse. He was lying next to poor Charlie Rowlands in the...'

'Well I'll have to be going,' said Benny, rising to his feet.

'What's your hurry?' his father wanted to know.

'Who do you think I met the other day in the Rhondda, Uncle Harry?' said Meurig. Benny sat down again.

'I'm sure I don't know, my boy.'

'Ned James.'

'Ned James?'

'Ay; him they used to call the Tylorstown Tiger.'

'Oh, I think I know the man.'

'Well, you should do. He was telling me about the time you and he fought on a Sunday morning on that piece of flat near the Rocking Stone on the mountain above Pontypridd. Said you was a hard nut to crack about that time, and that he had his work cut out to lick you...'

'He never licked me, nor did any other...'

'Well, that's what he said.'

'Then he's a liar,' roared Harry. 'I licked every man they put up before me, as your uncle Steppwr that's sitting there can tell you... but what am I talking about?' he broke off to ask wildly, looking into the faces of each in turn. 'No, it wasn't me that fought him, or the others. It was the devil – the...'

He turned and stumped his way out of the room and out of the house without as much as a word to Saran or any of the other women out in the kitchen.

'Of course, you would put the fat in the fire,' Glyn said to Meurig. 'And after all the trouble your mother had to get him to come...'

'And to tell lies,' said Steppwr. 'Harry was never once beaten by anybody all the time he was living down the Rhondda, so how could you say...'

'Well, he was sitting there like a man in a trance, so I thought I'd try and wake him up. And I shall be in a trance if I stay here with you lot much longer, so I'll clear out down as far as the Lucania for a game of snooker.' He picked up his cap and walked out.

'Oh, let him go,' said Glyn. 'Now, Ossie, what about another?'

'Yes, and I'm going tonight again,' concluded Saran.

'And so am I,' said Jane.

'Well,' said Annie, 'I don't know how you can sit to see the same play for the fourth time.'

'I could sit and watch Leonard Boyne in *Raffles* every night for the rest of my life,' said Saran.

'Oh, I wouldn't go as far as to say that,' said Jane.

'It's *The Manxman* I liked,' said Marged.

'All right go, and be damned to you,' said Glyn, as Benny, Hugh and Sam walked out of the front room to, so they said, have a look to see how the women were getting on in the kitchen. 'But me, Steppwr and Ossie are going to make ourselves comfortable where we are. Tell your mother to send one of them gels in with what's left of that roast pork and a small loaf,' he shouted after them. 'Now, Steppwr, and you, Ossie, draw up to the fire. We're all right where we are. Too true we are. Better than going off some place into lodgings like that damned fool of a Benny did when he got married, isn't it, Ossie?'

'It is that,' said Ossie thickly. 'Any more por' wine left?'

'Nearly a bottle full, and plenty of beer as well.'

'Then less have some, and I'll sing another...'

Steppwr never told Harry, and he made Saran promise never to tell him, that he was indirectly the cause of what resulted in Steppwr's death. Before Harry lost his leg he and Steppwr went year after year to the great annual Neath Fair, Steppwr to pick up a few shillings playing his concertina in various pubs, and Harry to earn a pound or two putting up a show in one or other of the boxing booths against men introduced to the open-mouthed crowds as champions of this place and that. It was the spree of the year for Harry, and after he had earned a pound or two in the booths he used to let it fly in the pubs. It was one long glorious drunk for as long as the money lasted, and then more often than not the pair of them had to walk home, unless they happened to be fortunate enough to get a lift.

'Come on, let's get back to Merthyr,' Steppwr each year had to plead when all their money was spent and their credit exhausted, a state of affairs which made Harry an awkward and dangerous chap to meet. And this was the position they found themselves in after the Fair of the year before Harry lost his leg. Penniless and reluctant to start on the long tramp home, Harry made a last round of the pubs with Steppwr in forced attendance, in the hope of begging, borrowing or stealing the money necessary to pay their train fare home to Merthyr. After many failures they at last found a landlord out of whom Harry was able to bounce two pints, and it was whilst they were making the two pints last out until the something Harry was hoping for turned up that the two young chaps from Resolven entered and called for drinks. Harry at once livened up when he saw the eldest and biggest of the two young men push a golden sovereign along the bar to the landlord when the latter came with the drinks ordered. Then Harry set to work, and when Harry laid himself out to be nice to anyone, he could be really nice. Without a penny in his pocket he suggested a game of dominoes for stakes of a half-crown a game, and a half-gallon of beer on each game as well so as to make things pleasant. The landlord, knowing that Harry was broke, was about to open his mouth to tell the young chaps from Resolven what he thought they were entitled to know, when Harry moved up to the bar like a tiger and shouted as he moved: 'The dominoes, please, landlord.' Then he whispered fiercely: 'It'll pay you to keep your bloody mouth shut.'

The landlord handed the box of dominoes over the bar with a trembling hand, and kept his mouth shut. Harry and the young man, with the change left out of the golden sovereign in his pocket, started to play for the stakes suggested, and the beer, to make things pleasant. Harry won three games in succession, and the young man paid up like a gentleman. Then he won a game. 'Good play,' complimented Harry. 'You played damned well to win that. Go on, double or quits. Come on, bring that half-gallon across, landlord.' Harry paid for the half-gallon of beer.

The young man from Resolven won the next game also, and Harry was even more complimentary than before. 'I'm afraid you're too good for me,' said Harry. 'You play better than Bat Hickey, and he's the champion of Merthyr. What about the beer, landlord?' shouted Harry as he went on shuffling the dominoes. 'Yes, you play like a champion, and if I had any bloody sense I'd give you best... never mind, double or quits.'

The young man opened his mouth to point out that the stakes of the two games he had won had not been handed across the table by Harry, when Harry stopped his mouth with the drink he had poured out for him. 'Yes, if you beat me this time for ten shilling or nothing, then I'll give you best; and when I get back home to Merthyr I'll back you to beat Bat Hickey, the champion, for as much money as they can find. Come on, pick for dap.'

Steppwr was shifting about uneasily in his seat as he sat watching the game. 'Double or quits.' He hoped, for the Resolven young man's sake, that Harry would win, for he knew what was likely to happen if the young man won and demanded payment. And that's how it turned out. Harry rose to his feet and accused the young man of cheating, and in less than a minute from the time the game finished the young man from Resolven was stretched unconscious in the sawdust, and his friend was kneeling over him, trying to bring him round.

‘That’ll teach him to cheat,’ said Harry, picking up the half-gallon measure and pouring himself some beer. ‘Come on, Steppwr, drink; no sense in leaving for others the beer I’ve paid for.’

‘I don’t want any more of it…’

‘We’ll have you – if it’s in ten years’ time, we’ll have you for this,’ screamed the young man who knelt over his bleeding, unconscious friend. ‘This haven’t finished today, you dirty blackguard, you.’

‘Get out of the bloody way,’ said Harry, giving him a backhander that knocked him into a sitting position as he went out. ‘Come on, Steppwr, let’s go and catch the puff-puff back to dear old Merthyr.’

Steppwr followed him out, the young man on his behind in the sawdust shouting after them: ‘We’ll have you; have you if we have to wait…’

Well, they had to wait a long time, and they’re still, that’s if they’re alive, waiting for Harry to show up at Neath Fair; for after Harry had lost his leg, and him being ‘saved’ afterwards – ‘Lost his leg and saved his soul’, was how Tommy Rees used to start ’em laughing in the Anchor taproom – Harry thought no more of the great annual Neath Fair, which at one time he reckoned he wouldn’t miss, no, not for a gold watch. But as for Steppwr: well, Steppwr didn’t go to the great Fair, either, for five years following the year Harry lost his leg. Then Jack Taylor, who was taking his Aunt Sally and ‘Three Rings a Penny’ outfits to the great Fair, offered Steppwr a lift over and back in return for a little help in fitting the outfits up and taking them down after the Fair.

'And whilst the Fair is on you can be doing your eye good playing your concertina in the pubs, see, Steppwr,' said Jack Taylor.

And that's how it was. Leaving Jack Taylor barking before his 'Three Rings a Penny' outfit, and Jack's wife doing her best in charge of the Aunt Sally outfit, Steppwr started off to work the pubs. It was close on stop-tap that night when he was spotted by the two young men from Resolven who had been waiting so long to get their own back on Harry. In the bar of the Salutation, it was.

'There's the chap that was with him,' whispered one of the young chaps to the other, pointing to where Steppwr stood with his concertina under his arm and a drink on the bar before him.

'So it is. Where's the other swine, I wonder?'

'We'll soon find out... he's off out. Come.'

But Steppwr was only going to the urinal at the back, and a stinking hole it was by this time. No water to flush the place; vomits and excrement and goodness knows what altogether. Steppwr was opening his trousers when he saw the two young men from Resolven standing menacingly near.

'Pouf, isn't this a hell of a place,' said Steppwr pleasantly.

'Where's that swine that was with you that time?' snarled the most powerful of the two.

'With me? Who do you mean?'

The young man roughly gripped him by the coat and jerked him inwards until Steppwr could see the two nasty scars the young man proceeded to direct his attention to. 'The swine who left me these marks. Where is he? You'd better tell me before I...'

'Oh, it's you, is it?' gasped Steppwr, recognising the young men.

'Yes, it's us,' said the young man.

'Well, please let me button up and I'll tell you...'

'Where is he?'

Steppwr was telling them about Harry's conversion when one of the young men said to the other: 'Well, he was with him, wasn't he? And had share of your money, I expect. So take that – and that, you swine. And that,' they kept saying as they went on using their feet on him after they had knocked him down into the filth. And after they had given him what one called 'a double dose' they both danced on his concertina. Then they left him to hurry back to the bar to get another drink before chucking-out time. 'And that's what we'll give that other swine whenever he shows his face here next,' said one as they went back into the pub. But Steppwr didn't hear him, for he was out to the world, and he stayed out for two hours after chucking-out time, when he scrambled to his feet a broken man in more senses than one. But what hurt him more than the injuries to his face and body was the smashing of his concertina. He crawled about in the filth trying to pick up the pieces but was unable to retrieve more than the two hand-straps and a bit of wood that was still hanging to one of them. He cried soundlessly in the moonlight over the loss of his beloved instrument until his broken ribs compelled him to breathe as lightly as possible.

Through the silent street he painfully made his way to the fairground, where Jack Taylor, his outfits packed up, was on the point of starting for home. 'You're a nice feller,' he cried, 'leaving me and the missus to do the bloody lot after you promised... what's the matter?'

Steppwr couldn't tell him then, so Jack and his missus helped him into the back of the van and put him to lie down with the Aunt Sallies and other things. It was morning, and the children were on their way to school when Jack's old horse pulled the van and its load across Pontmorlais Square, at the far end of which Jack pulled up to ask: 'Where do you want me to drop you, Steppwr?'

'I'd like... oh. I'd like if you'd drop me as passing Saran's – you know, Glyn my brother-in-law's wife. She'll give me a drop of something as'll...' he groaned in pain.

Jack stopped the van in front of Saran's house and shouted: 'Here we are, Steppwr,' but Steppwr couldn't move from where he was lying, so Saran and Jack and Jack's wife and a man who happened to be passing had to lift him out of the van and carry him in and up the stairs and into the bed that Harry had been carried into years before on the day when he refused to go to the hospital to have his leg taken off properly.

And now Steppwr is groaning in the bed as Saran washes him clean and puts one of Glyn's clean shirts on him to make him look as tidy as possible by the time the doctor Jane has gone to fetch comes to have a look to see what is the matter with Steppwr altogether. After she had washed him and put the clean shirt on him she warmed him a drop of milk, and it was whilst he was supping as she held him up in a sitting position that he told her something of what had happened to him over Neath way the night previous. He also, in reply to her inquiries, told her how it was the two young men had set about him, after which he begged on her not, on any account, to say anything to Harry beyond what he himself intended saying when Harry called. 'That's if he calls at all before I'm able to get up and about. I expect I'll be all right again tomorrow or the next day.' 'I expect you will,' she said, but she knew different. Then the doctor came and said that the best thing she could do was to have Steppwr taken to the new infirmary, for they wouldn't take him into the hospital, he said, for the reason that Steppwr was not a contributor to the hospital either privately or through the scheme which the workers of the district supported by allowing so much per week towards the hospital to be deducted from their pay.

'No, I'll let him stay on here,' Saran said to the old doctor as he was packing up his things out on the landing in readiness to go.

'Well, I don't think he'll stay long with you,' said the old doctor.

When Glyn arrived home from the pit later than usual, though he was sober enough that night for a wonder, Saran followed him into the back kitchen, where he had gone to wash his hands before sitting down to his supper, and said: 'Steppwr's upstairs.'

'What's *he* doing upstairs?'

'Dying. But you needn't tell him that.'

'What in the name of God's happened to him?'

She told him as much as she thought he ought to know as he sat eating his supper, of which he hadn't eaten half when he pushed it away.

'Don't want any more. I'm glad you took him in, Saran,

for, after all, he's… he's… Mary thought the world of him.'

'Why shouldn't she? There, come and get yourself washed, and when you go up to see him try to be a bit jollier than you're looking now.'

'Have you let Harry know?'

'No, but I'm going to. He's not home from his work yet, though I expect he will be by the time young Tom gets to where he lodges.'

Harry stumped up to Saran's in his working clothes as soon as the message was delivered to him by his young nephew.

'What about your supper?' the woman at whose house he lodged cried after him. 'Supper, indeed,' muttered Harry more to himself than to young Tom, who was trotting along at his side, and the boy had to trot, for Harry was taking extremely long steps with his good leg, and then swinging the peg leg in half-moon sweeps outward and forward in the second or so he stood on his good leg; so they were at Saran's in no time.

'Where is he?'

'In the same room that you were in,' Saran told him. 'Wait. Now, remember, no preaching or any of your hellfire talk, for that's the one thing he don't want. You'll find Glyn up there with him.'

Glyn rose to give his seat to Harry when the latter entered the bedroom where Steppwr was. 'I'll slip down for a smoke now,' said Glyn, who had been warned not on any account to smoke whilst with Steppwr, for the doctor had told her that Steppwr had all he could do to get his breath in and out his broken ribs without having more difficulty in doing so when coughing from tobacco smoke being where it could go down his throat. So Glyn went down to the kitchen to smoke and Harry sat in the chair at the bedside, where he smiled like an angel down on his old boozing pal.

'Well, you're a nice chap. What can you say you've been up to now?'

'Oh, the drop of drink...' Pain twisted his features as a bout of coughing tortured his broken body.

'You mustn't talk any more,' Harry told him. 'Now, lie still, and I won't say another word.'

'No, no – no dumb band,' gasped Steppwr. 'You talk. And I will, too. As I was saying – the drop of drink. Fell under a cart... wish it didn't smash my con – concertina. Look...' He lifted his hand up a little off the counterpane and showed Harry the hand-strap with the little piece of polished wood hanging from it. 'All – that's left – of it.'

'Never mind, I'll soon get you another.'

'Not 'nother like – like him.' Tears welled up and ran down his face. 'Not 'nother like him, Harry.'

'Yes, and better,' insisted Harry. 'So don't worry your head any more about it. Why, now that I'm working reg'lar and saving like I've been, I can buy you one better than any of them that chap they said was playing on the stage of the theatre had. I will, so don't worry. Besides, it's wrong to worry over things that God in his wisdom takes from us, Steppwr,' he said, forgetting what Saran at the foot of the stairs had said to him about preaching; but there was that plainly written on Steppwr's face which impelled Harry to speak as he then went on to speak. 'God takes things from us for our good. If He hadn't taken this leg of mine where would I have been, and what would I have been today? I used to be proud of the way I used to stand up on my two legs in front of chaps to batter 'em, then God took a leg away from me and made me a laughing stock for a while before taking me back into the fold. And now He's gone and took away from you the thing you thought most of in this world, and He's brought you down same as He brought me down, Steppwr, for everybody must be brought down in some way or other before they shall see God. He used a cart to bring you down...'

'And He had – had to use an – an engine to – bring you down, Harry....' Another bout of coughing twisted him into knots.

'You shouldn't make fun, Steppwr bach, for I'm trying to make you see how God works to get us all back after we've been straying here, there and everywhere. Big bouncers like me, big men of money like old Crawshay in his big stone castle, men who plays music like you, and them as knows more'n is good for 'em like old Davies, MA. And poor women like Gypsy Nell,' he added, closing his eyes for a moment as though in prayer. 'We're all His children, Steppwr, and stray – where we will, we've got to come back to Him like children. But p'raps you want to sleep a bit?'

'No – it's the candle – my eyes. You – you tell me Harry.'

'There's not much to tell, Steppwr bach. Just that we're all God's children, that's all. Oh, it's wonderful when you come to think of it, Steppwr. First, we're little children, looking up to our earthly fathers. Then we grow up, and some of us bring our fathers' heads down in sorrow, same as I did mine. Boozing, fighting, gambling, whoring. Yes, I was the big bouncer who could hold my own with anyone, the big bouncer who could fight his way through life without help from anyone. Oh, what fools we are. How we cling to the things of this world long after we should have let go of 'em. Even after I lost my leg I wanted to show the world what a bouncer I was, and we're nearly all the same. Them as makes money burden themselves with it right to the end, and them as have learnt a lot won't forget it and get back like little children to God, Who only gives money and knowledge and power to be used for a short time here on earth, not to... am I right, Steppwr?'

'Yes – qui' ri' – Harry. You – tell me.'

'What is there to tell? God is waiting for us, you know that. Not waiting for bouncers, men with money, men as can play music grand and them as can stand up and talk a lot and make people clap 'em. Nor for women as rides in their carriage and pair or them as goes up the coke ovens with men. No, Steppwr bach, God is waiting for His children, and no matter whether we lie down to sleep in Cyfarthfa Castle or in the Cyfarthfa works' coke ovens, it's God's little and wilful children we all are. Am I right, Steppwr? Steppwr. *Steppwr.* Oh, Saran, Saran. Come quick, Saran.'

CHAPTER 12

SARAN RENDERS FIRST AID TO A RIOTER

'Well, let's hope they're satisfied now that they've got the soldiers there,' said Glyn as he came in from the back kitchen wiping his hands, for he always washed his hands before sitting down to his supper, which was more than some of the boys did.

'Soldiers?' said Saran, placing his taters and meat on the table.

'Ay, soldiers, regiments of 'em, so a chap in the Nelson just told me.'

'Yes, but where?'

'Down the Rhondda, woman, I tell you.'

'You told me no such thing. Anywhere near where our Meurig is?'

'Well, if he's in the Rhondda...'

'You know quite well he's in the Rhondda.'

'Then you should know quite well he's where these soldiers now are.'

'But what do they want soldiers in the Rhondda for?'

Glyn stopped chewing and sighed. 'Woman, don't you know any damned thing? Don't you know that the Combine strike's on in the Rhondda, and that the men have been playing hell there? Bursting shops open and stealing things, and knocking policemen about...'

'Yes, I heard somebody say something about it. I hope our Meurig keeps out of it.'

'He'd better; for now that they've got soldiers on horseback as well as them on foot down there it'll be God help anybody as tries to act the goat. Where are you off to?'

'To the threeatre with Jane.'

'Why don't you go and live in the damned theatre?'

'I would if they'd let me. Here's your clean things; the water's ready on the hob. I've shined your boots in case you're going out...'

'How can I go out without a penny in my pocket?'

'You'll find a shilling on the mantelpiece.'

'What's the good of a shilling?'

'It's sixpence more than I'll pay to get into the gallery of the threeatre.' And she was gone to laugh at the two brothers who were so funny in *The Swiss Express*.

As usual, she was down in the kitchen lighting the fire and getting everything ready for them, before calling Glyn and the boys to go to work next morning, before the five o'clock hooters began their chorus. She was oiling the heavy and hard pit boots when she heard a tapping on the kitchen window which startled her a little, but she was soon herself again. Again the tapping, so she went into the back kitchen and opened the back door and fearlessly asked: 'Who's there?'

Out of the dark into the light of the kitchen walked her Meurig, wearing a blood-soaked bandage under his cap and round his forehead.

'What in the name of God's happened to you?' she gasped as he walked past her to seat himself in the armchair near the fire.

'Nothing much; been in a bit of a row, that's all. Give us a cup of tea, mam, for God's sake.' He drank the cup of tea she poured him in three almost scalding saucerfuls. 'Another?' she asked. 'Yes.' 'A bit to eat?' 'Later.' 'Let's have a look at that head of yours.'

'H'm. What was it that hit you?'

'Er, I don't know quite. Something that was used in the row.'

'And who was it put this rag and plaster on you?'

'One of the chaps...'

'Never mind; bend your head.' She cleaned and dressed the wound. 'Well, whoever hit, and whatever he hit you with, it's a good job he didn't hit a bit harder.'

'He won't hit anyone else for some time.'

'Well, I'll have to call your father and the boys soon...'

'They mustn't see me.'

'Why not, name of...'

'I'll tell you after they've left for work. Now, where can I go to until they've left?'

'Go into the front room, nobody goes in there of a morning. Here, have this other cup of tea to take in with you.'

After Glyn and the boys had left for work, Meurig returned to the kitchen from the front room. 'Dad grouses as much as ever, I noticed.'

'Never mind talking about your father. Now, sit down and have something to eat.'

'Draw that blind.'

'What are you afraid of?'

'I'll tell you after I've eaten.' He ate hearty, and lit a cigarette. 'This is a wallop a policeman gave me with his truncheon,' he informed his mother, pointing to his head.

'A policeman's... but how did he come to hit you?'

'Oh, they charged a gang of us and well – we stood up to the swines. They had their truncheons, so we let 'em have it with stones – and whatever else we could lay our hands on.'

'Haven't I always told you never to mess with p'licmen? Your uncle Harry paid dear for messing with...'

'Yes, I know, but this wasn't a public-house affair; and when hundreds of blasted policemen start ordering and pushing chaps about just because we were standing up for our rights. Yes, hundreds of 'em; from London, Bristol, and all over the shop. What did they want there, in the first place?'

'It's too late to ask that; you should have kept out of their way.'

'Couldn't, I tell you. They were chasing us all over the damned place. Chasing us off the street, off...'

'Then why didn't you come home?'

'What do you think I am?'

'A bit of a fool to stay long enough to get that.'

'The one that gave it me got worse.'

She looked at him without speaking for a minute or so. 'So you had to run for it over the mountains, like your uncle Harry did years ago, before you was thought of. But it was into the Rhondda he had to run. Do you think the police know now that you were in the tussle in which you got that?'

'I don't think so, yet I'm not quite sure. That's why I want to lie low here for a while, until it all blows over.'

So he did lie low; he sneaked out for a stroll most nights after everyone was in bed, and the wound healed up. Though nobody came to the house to inquire about him, he didn't risk returning to the Rhondda after the strike was settled for fear that he would be picked up and given a long term of imprisonment. Others, who had been far less troublesome than he, had been arrested and sentenced to heavy terms of imprisonment. So he decided to stay away from the Rhondda for good, and got himself a job at home again. 'Old Merthyr's going to be good enough for me from now on,' he told Saran. 'Too good for him, I think,' she used to say as he went on making things hot for himself and other members of the family. 'Mad Meurig he is,' said Jane after she had paid the ten shillings and costs which her Ossie was fined for a prank he had been led into by Meurig. And now that he was home Benny and his wife would not come near the house to pay their respects occasionally to Saran.

'No, not while he's there,' Benny told his mother one night when they met coming out of the theatre. 'You're always welcome to my home, mother, and if he were not…'

'Yes, you told me before. What did you think of the singing tonight?'

'Really fine, I thought, though, of course, not to be compared with the Carl Rosa production of the same opera.'

'I don't care much for op'ra. Good night, Benny.'

She had to admit to herself as she walked home with her almost inseparable companion, Jane, that Meurig was most difficult to get on with – well, for his brothers to get on with, for she could put up with him at his worst, for she was soft about him, yet not so soft, either. He gambled as long as he had a penny to gamble with, gambled at cards, at billiards in one or other of the many large billiard saloons a company claimed to have blessed the district with; at pitch-and-toss – gambled in any and every way possible. And he was always fighting somebody or other over something or other. He owed sums of money to all his brothers, with the exception of Benny, who kept him at a distance, and Hugh, who was too far away to 'touch'. He worried his younger brother Idris for loans until Idris decided to leave home and go down to lodge and work with his brother Hugh at Senghenydd. 'Sick of it', he told Saran he was. 'But why do you lend him money all the time?' asked Saran.

'If I've got it I can't refuse him,' said Idris. 'So if I'm not here he can't ask me, can he? Anyway, work around here's none too good nowadays, and Hugh told me he'd find me a job down there with him when he was up home last Bank Holiday.' So off to Senghenydd went Idris. Saran didn't mind, for she knew he'd be all right with Hugh, and she had plenty left to look after without him – and all working at last. Lord, there was something to do with them all. Glyn and six boys to get off to work every morning, and with this eight-hours business they were back home again before a woman could look around. Then there was the nightly rush for the use of the bath, the quarrels as to who owned this tie and that shirt. Meurig, who seldom bought himself a tie or a cap, made no bones about taking and wearing anything belonging to the others that he fancied, and so caused endless rows, which Saran had to patch up somehow or the other. By pleasing one she was sure to offend another; and there was Glyn always sneering to the effect that there should never be more than one fully grown man in any home, and that, as she insisted on having a houseful of sons, now men, around her, she must put up with their squabbling and fighting. But he'd go to hell before he'd put up with it much longer. She could do as she liked, but his mind was made up. If a man worked as hard as he did, then he wanted a little peace in his home. Yet what did he get? Yes, what? A lot of cheek, that's what he got from blasted boys who didn't know what hard work was. And what was more, he had to be damned careful to avoid getting a dab in the eye every now and again from one or other of the three oldest, and he had no doubt – not the slightest – that the three youngest would talk and act just as big when the time came. Now, when he ought to be taking things easy – as he had a right to after having slaved to rear 'em all – what did he find? Found that he had to work harder than ever.

'Give me my things, woman, so as I can get out of it.'

And out he'd go to where everybody smiled at a man and deferred to his opinion for as long as he had the price of a pint left.

And the boys would in their turn shout: 'Give me my things, mam, so as I can get out' – but not to the pub like their dad. Dances, to look the girls over. Billiard saloons, to play black pool and snooker. The theatre, music hall, Eisteddfod to hear the champion solo competition only, the new swimming baths on long summer evenings and Sunday afternoons as well, and occasionally chapel to listen in a rather critical mood to the cream of visiting preachers. Yes, a lively lot, Saran thought. Too lively, thought others.

'Work, work, work and be contented' evidently was not the song which appealed to Glyn and the boys and the rest of the miners of South Wales during the period the Liberal Government was in office, for the Minimum Wage Stoppage overtook Saran before she was quite aware of its coming, and before she had made any preparations to meet it.

'And what is it over now?' she asked Glyn.

'Well, of all the damned women... if your head wasn't so full of that theatre...'

'Of work, more like.'

'And the theatre. Didn't I tell you what was likely to happen that night after me and Ossie had been to hear that Frank Hodges speaking?'

'Who is Frank Hodges?'

'I suppose you know who Louis Calvert is?'

'What's to stop me? But who is this Frank Hodges?'

'He's one of the best,' Meurig informed her. 'He's the boy that's making the pace for the old leaders in our fight for the minimum wage.'

'Minimum?'

'Well, of all the blasted women I ever heard...'

'Shut up, wise man,' Meurig told his father. 'This is it,

mam. We're demanding that if we're working in a place where we can't earn a decent wage when we work honest, then the bosses must make up our money to a certain figure, and that certain figure is the minimum.'

'Well, I don't see that that's asking too much. But can't it be got without a strike?'

'Don't seem like it,' said Meurig. 'Never get much out of the bosses without a strike.'

'Well, it isn't much that we get out of them or anybody by striking, either,' said Saran. 'I remember the first long strike when you lot was small, and it was little we got out of that.'

'This won't be as bad as '98,' Mervyn assured her. 'We'll all have strike pay from the Federation this time.'

'A fat lot that'll be,' she sighed.

She smiled and paid her way through a stoppage which lasted six weeks, a stoppage which resulted in the miners being granted the minimum wage, and which made the reputation of a young miners' leader named Frank Hodges, who had been but little heard of before the stoppage.

'That's the sort of leader to have,' cried Meurig in the house on the evening when the news of the settlement came through. 'Different to Mabon and the old gang, the old gang would never have got this for us.'

'Here, you've no call to run Mabon and the other old leaders down,' Glyn told the boys that night in the home. 'Mabon got us many things before Hodges was born.'

'A fat lot he got you,' sneered Lewis. 'Got you the Mabon's Monday holiday, and that's about all.'

'What are you talking about?' cried Glyn, as he glared from one to the other of his six sons still at home. 'Who was it fought for us to get you your eight-hour day? If it wasn't for Mabon and his sort you'd be working twelve hours a day like I had to... I'm not saying anything against Hodges or Cook or any of the other young fellers our Federation has paid to keep for years in a college – which was more than Mabon ever had, remember. They got us things without any college training to do it with, so don't be too ready to run 'em down. Where could you get a better man than Tom Richards?'

'Who is Tom Richards?' Saran asked.

'Well, of all the women...'

Bang – and what a *bang* it was. It shook Wales, shook Britain, so the newspapers said, and shocked the civilised world, so the papers also said, on the very same day on which Jane's second baby was born – and a fine boy it was. Saran was as proud as proud could be, and she wondered why it was that Ossie looked at her so sadly when she went down to the kitchen to tell him that he could go up to the bedroom to have a look at Jane and his fine new boy.

'Well, ain't you going up?' she asked him as he stood looking at her with a face as long as a fiddle.

'Ay, just now. But there's something... now, don't, for God's sake, go up and tell Jane yet.'

'Tell her what? What are you trying to say?'

'There's been an explosion – down in – Senghenydd.'

'Seng – hen – ydd,' she slowly repeated syllable after syllable. Then she sank slowly into a chair and began to age before Ossie's very eyes. 'Seng – hen – ydd,' she again whispered. 'Oh, my lovely boys. But p'raps...'

She jumped up out of the chair and ran out of the house and on to her own house, hoping. Hoping, as others were, in vain. Hugh and Idris were two of close on five hundred of the explosion's victims. She went with Glyn to what the papers called 'the scene of the greatest disaster in mining history', and spent most of the time she was there trying to comfort Hugh's young widow, who was inconsolable then, though she was married again, to a North Welshman this time, in less than twelve months from the date of the disaster. But, as Saran said when she heard of her approaching marriage to the North Welshman, she was only a young woman, after all, and it wasn't to be expected that she would wear black and mourn Hugh all her life. Besides, there were the children to think of, and if only she was lucky enough to find a good man, then it would be a godsend to the children as well. But that was later; she cried in a way that would move the hardest-hearted person in the world throughout the day Saran and Glyn spent with her.

When Saran got back home she found her brother Harry, looking old enough to be her father with those whiskers of his, waiting to comfort her. Brushing Glyn aside he led his sister into the front room and sat silent holding her hand during the time she was crying the bitter tears. Then, after she had recovered a little, all he said was: 'They are with God, Saran bach,' but that didn't seem to comfort her much. So the next thing he said was: 'Come into the kitchen to Glyn, for he must be feeling it, too.' So into the kitchen they went, where all her boys, married and unmarried, stood silent looking on their father, who was sitting in a heap in the armchair near the fire, looking ever so much older than he had looked a week before. Ossie was there as well, and when she saw him Saran asked: 'And how is Jane up there?'

'Fine,' he said.

'And the baby?'

'A 1.'

'I'll come up with you to see her as soon as I've put a bit of food for… Glyn bach, don't cry. Tell him not to cry, Harry,' she begged for fear of breaking down in front of them all there in the kitchen, and the way Glyn sat hunched up made her feel as weak as water. Harry stumped quietly across the kitchen and placed his hand over Glyn's and said: 'You go on putting the bit of food, Saran. Glyn will be all right in a minute.'

And she went into the pantry under the stairs and got the foodstuff and started to lay the table for a meal and her boys shed their love about her as she moved about laying the table; and though none of them were able to eat much the sitting down together helped to steady them. As they were getting up from the table old Marged, who had been looking after Jane whilst Saran had been down in Senghenydd, walked in and said: 'I'll see to everything here if you'll run up as far as Jane's, Saran. She's worrying her heart out up there.'

'Come on, Ossie,' said Saran. 'Stay with Glyn a bit, Harry.'

They all got over it in time, and after people had given what they could to the different funds to aid the dependants of the victims, and after boxers had boxed in aid of the fund, and singers had sung, and the chapels had collected, and the Lord Mayor had declared that his fund was now closed, people began to forget, even as Hugh's widow managed to forget; and Saran said to Jane, the night they were told about Hugh's widow getting ready to get married again: 'It's wonderful how we do get over things.' It is.

One grandchild after another came to make up for the loss in family strength through the deaths of Hugh and Idris in the explosion. Saran was not so excited over the new arrivals in Benny's house and in Sam's house as she had been over the new arrival in Jane's house; but she was there to help them into the world. Grandchildren are all right, providing there aren't too many of them, she was beginning to think. And so were married sons and their wives, if only they weren't so often running in to ask: 'You don't happen to have this, that and the other you could let me have, mother, do you?' The married boys came to beg their father's tools, even his boring-machine for which he had paid four pounds ten, and their wives came to beg – well, everything. And Saran was beginning to get tired of her in-laws and their children, and was beginning to dread the day when Meurig and Lewis, who were both courting strong, would be married and running in to see whether there was anything they could relieve their parents of.

That was how her thoughts were running when, all of a sudden, the talk of a war started; and before she knew anything for certain her Benny was at the house asking her to go with him down to his house, where he said Annie was crying her eyes out.

'What for?'

'Well, haven't I been called up?' he asked impatiently.

'Oh, have you? I thought you'd finished your time on the reserve.'

'No; lost a bit of time over that Jo'burg business I told you about.'

'Oh.'

'Don't sit there saying "Oh" all the time. Come on down to Annie.'

'You go down and fetch her and the children up here.'

'But I've got to be off by the first available train, I tell you.'

'An hour or so won't make any difference, as long as you get there before night.'

'All right, I'll chance it.' And off he ran to fetch them.

Half an hour later he left his tearful Annie and his children with his mother, and off he went to the railway station accompanied by his father, brothers, and Ossie, for it was Bank Holiday, so they were all free to give Benny a good send-off.

CHAPTER 13

OH, OH, OH, IT'S A LUV-ER-LY WAR

'Sam's gone and joined up,' cried Sam's wife as she ran in with the baby in her arms and her breast in her fist, interrupting the reading aloud by Glyn of the account of how the linc was saved at Ypres by the cooks and orderlies and sick men being rushed into the line when the position was grave in the extreme. 'Granny, didn't you tell me that they were not going to allow any more colliers to join up?'

'I only told you what I heard,' replied Saran. 'But they were saying that before the last of our boys went. Never mind, gel, you'll have a ring-paper now same as Annie. Sit down and listen to Glyn reading how the line was saved at Yprcs. Go on, read on, Glyn.'

'I will when I have quiet, and not before,' said Glyn, with an air of importance.

'Oh, give the paper to one of these gels to read. You're not the only one that can read.'

'All right, take the bloody paper,' he said, tossing it across to Annie, who was sitting in the corner nearest the door giving her baby the breast.

'Go on, read for us, Annie,' said Saran. 'Your father-in-law's going out to get drunk on the 'lotment money our Lewis signed for him to have – more fool him.'

'And I s'pose Meurig wasn't a fool to sign his hand for twelve shilling a week for you?' roared Glyn from the doorway.

'Well, he knows I won't drink it. Go on, Annie, read for us.'

Glyn grunted and walked out of the house as Annie started reading the account of the battle from where Glyn had left off.

'H'm, must have been a near thing,' said Saran. 'I wonder if our Benny was in it.'

'I expect he was,' sighed Annie. 'And when I hear people wailing and worrying before their husbands are in uniform, it makes me...'

'I don't suppose your Benny would have been in uniform were it not that he was called up,' sniffed Sam's wife.

'My Benny...'

'Now, shut up, the pair of you,' cried Saran. 'Whether he would have gone or not is not worth arguin' about now he's there. And, now that Sam's gone and done it, another four of mine'll be there before long; though Glyn was reading in the paper... was it last night, Jane?'

'He reads most nights. About what were you thinking?'

'Of that he read to us about some big man saying that it would most likely be over by Christmas now that we've stopped retreating.'

'I hope it is,' said Jane, sighing. 'I expect Ossie'll start bothering about joining up now Sam's gone and done it.'

'Then if he goes that'll be all the war can take from us – this one, anyway – for my three youngest won't be ready for this one.'

'Don't be so sure, mam,' said Jane. 'If it lasts...'

'Over by Christmas the man said in the paper; anyway, we'll know for sure when the boys come home for Christmas. Let's have a cup of tea.'

'No, nor will it be over by next Christmas,' said Meurig.

'Never mind the war – get on with your dinners,' cried Saran as she bustled about serving; and glad she was to have old Marged's help that day, for all the boys with the exception of Benny were home for Christmas. What a crowd. Take the soldiers first. Meurig, a corporal; Sam, a private; Lewis, a trooper; Mervyn, a driver. Ossie, the one civilian of military age present, felt out of it as he sat in the midst of khaki-clad brothers-in-law. Then there was Benny's wife and children; Sam's wife and children; and Jane and her two children. Then there were Glyn and Uncle Harry. Lastly, old Marged and Saran herself. How many is that all told? Well, counting the children... still, we won't trouble to count them.

There was a turkey, a leg of pork, a ham, puddings, mince pies and jellies. And taters and cabbage and swedes, of course; and also a drop of drink for Glyn and his son-in-law, Ossie, and for any of the boys who might happen to want it – but not the three youngest boys, the soldier-boys, that's all. And, to Saran's great surprise, her four soldier sons started lowering the drink as though they had been drinking all their lives.

'Hullo,' cried Glyn, as Meurig refilled with beer the pint glass he had emptied without pausing for breath, 'I can see you fellers have learnt one thing in the Army. You've learnt to neck it as well...'

'Yes; why don't you leave it all for your father, my boys,' Saran sweetly interrupted him to say.

' "Your father" don't want it all; and don't try to be so bloody fly, woman.'

'Get on with your dinner. Marged, take the biggest of the three puddings out there to the children.'

All the children were seated along the trestle table fixed up for the occasion out in the back kitchen, where old Marged, under Saran's direction, served them. And what a feed they were having. In the living room the women were waiting for the men to finish so that they could sit down to their dinners.

The house seemed to be full of khaki clothing. Khaki overcoats, tunics, breeches and slacks, putties and caps. All the boys were tucking into their dinner with only their cardigans over their greyback shirts. Meurig had brought a cardigan home for his dad, who was wearing it under his waistcoat. 'Splendid cardigan – keep me warm,' said Glyn. 'Gave a chap two bob for it,' said Meurig. 'It's worth all that,' said Saran.

'Now, clear off into the front room out of the way whilst me and Marged and the gels have our bit of dinner,' cried Saran.

As the men were rising, Meurig shouted: 'Wait a minute.

Now, whilst we're all together, let's drink the health and good fortune of our Benny.'

'Ay, and all that's out there with him,' said Saran.

'The bloody Germans are out there with him, woman,' said Glyn.

'I didn't mean the Germans,' said Saran.

'Why not the Germans?' said Harry.

'What a question to ask,' said Glyn.

'Here's to our Benny and the boys out there,' cried Meurig.

'Benny and the boys out there.'

And they all drank, the children out in the back kitchen as well, even Uncle Harry supped a drop of water out of the glass in his hand.

Then the men went off into the front room and soon filled it with smoke and talk. The men out of the way, the women sat down to their dinners. 'I sometimes wonder how we'd manage if we didn't have a front room,' said Saran. 'Lord, what if we still lived in that little house near the bridge. Yet I s'pose we'd manage somehow.'

'One of our instructors is the champion of the British Army,' Sam was saying. 'Champion what?' asked his father. 'Boxer.' 'At what weight?' asked Meurig. 'Middleweight.' 'I knew it wasn't welterweight,' said Meurig, 'for the Army champion welterweight is in our lot. He's in the cookhouse; and if he's a champion... I had the gloves on with him one night, and do you know what?' 'What?' 'I planted lefts and rights just as I liked; so after we'd taken the gloves off I said...' 'We've got a swine of a troop-sergeant, if you like,' said Lewis. 'We were showing kit one day, and he...' 'Here, steady on with that beer, Meurig,' cried his father. 'Maybe others'll want a drink as well as you.' 'Why, I've only had...' 'Do you go to chapel on Sundays, Mervyn bach?' Uncle Harry was asking. 'Got to go unless we're on guard, of course.' 'Always go to chapel, Mervyn bach. And keep away from the old canteen, for...' 'Yes, talk to him, Uncle Harry,' said Meurig, 'for he spends on beer and hot suppers all his pay.' 'How do you know?' 'Well, you don't send anything home.' 'Oh, you needn't swank because you've allotted twelve bob a week to mam, for you get's that and more back by flogging the troops' food to the woman you're in billets with...' 'Damn you, are you trying to say that your brother's a thief?' cried Glyn. 'He told me himself that he was in the quartermaster's stores and that he...' 'Shut up.... What about a song, Ossie?' 'We've got a comic singer in our lot – been on the stage for years before he joined up – who is great.' 'I bet you he's not near as good as a chap we've got in our lot.' 'Oh, to hell with your lots,' Glyn shouted. 'We're going to have a song from Ossie.' 'You'll excuse me now, won't you?' said Uncle Harry. 'I'm off up to the workhouse to help to hand round the presents that are to be given out after the concert and tea.' 'S'long, Uncle Harry.' 'S'long, my boys, and may God watch over you all.' 'Now that he's gone let's have another drink apiece before Ossie gives us a song,' said Glyn. 'Why, the damned thing's empty. Lewis, ask your mother if there's any more beer to be had. I hope to God there is, for it won't be open-tap for another hour or more.' 'Are the picture houses open tonight?' asked young Mervyn. 'Of course they are – only one house, though,' Lewis informed him. 'Why don't you go and ask your mother if she's got any more beer in the house, Lewis?' 'Oh, go and ask her yourself if you want it.'

The ten days' Christmas leave were soon over, and Lewis and Mervyn, who had arrived home on leave a day before Meurig and Sam, stayed a day over their time so that they could all start back together. The railway station was crowded with the happy soldiers of the borough who were returning to their units, and with jolly parties of friends and relations who were seeing them off on that first Saturday morning of the New Year. Saran didn't go to the station to see the boys off, for she hated what she called 'a lot of old show', but Glyn and Ossie stayed home from the pit that day to see the four happy soldiers of the family 'as far as the station, anyway'. Meurig was travelling to Rhyl, North Wales; Sam to Bordon Camp; Lewis to somewhere in Ireland; and Mervyn to some place on the East Coast of England. Trains crowded with soldiers, singing and shouting as their trains started off from one or other of the four platforms. Kitbags, parcels of food, bottles of beer, cigarettes. Glyn and Ossie first went to number one platform with the four soldiers of the family; then across to number two with three soldiers, and from there back to number one with two soldiers, and lastly to number three with only one soldier.

'Well, they're gone, Ossie,' sighed Glyn.

'Ay; and Jane can say what she damn well likes, I'm joining up.'

‘There’s plenty there without you; let’s go and have a drink.’

After they’d had a decent drink they went home to their dinners, and the first thing they heard was that Benny had been wounded.

‘Here’s the letter,’ said Jane, who had been reading it to Saran.

Glyn took the letter. ‘Stop your snivelling,’ he shouted at Annie, ‘he says here that it’s nothin’ much.’

‘He might be saying that to...’

‘Now I *will* join up,’ muttered Ossie.

‘You’ll do no such thing,’ said Jane. ‘Come on up to the house to your dinner.’

‘Call in about an hour’s time, and we’ll go for a bit of a stroll, Ossie,’ Glyn shouted after him. ‘But why not have a bit of dinner here?’

‘Here, I’ve had enough to feed this last fortnight,’ said Saran. ‘You go home with Jane to your dinner, Ossie.’ And he went, and Annie and Sam’s wife took the hint, collected their children, and went also.

Ossie was back down to call Glyn out in less than an hour. ‘I’ve had a hell of a row with Jane,’ he told Glyn as they turned into the Tiger.

‘What over, now again? Two pints, Mrs Lewis.’

‘About joining up. As I told her, she goes with her mother to the recruiting meetings...’

‘Here, drink. Damn, that’s a drop of good stuff. Yes, Saran takes ’em all to the recruiting meetings, I know. It’s as good as going to the theatre for ’em.’

‘That’s right.... And as I told Jane...’

Through the afternoon and well on into the evening they went on drinking in various places where nothing but war was talked about, and it must have been nine o'clock when they both staggered into the non-stop recruiting office in High Street.

'Me an' my sonilaw wan' join up – *now*,' Glyn told Sergeant Knight.

'Well, I don't know what about your son-in-law; but you're like myself, a bit on the old side, I'm afraid.'

'Not a damn bit; the buggers have wounded my Benny, haven't they?'

'Yes, and a good many more. So...'

'So we're going, sonilaw an' me. Isn't that right, Ossie?'

'Quite right, old man.'

Sergeant Knight carefully attended to Ossie first, then he went through the motions with Glyn before asking him to sign a blank sheet of paper. 'That's all. Call here Monday morning and I'll have you both sworn in.'

'What about our 'listing money?' Glyn wanted to know.

'You'll have that Monday morning.'

On Monday Ossie was sworn in, and Glyn was sworn at and told to get to hell out of the recruiting office, where men had plenty to do without wasting time on such bald-headed, drunken old...

Bottomley was late, hours late, and the crowd which had been packed into the huge skating rink was getting restive, but not near as restive and troublesome to the elderly policemen of the borough – who were being called upon to do an awful lot of work now that all the young policemen and the reservists in the force had gone off to war – as was the surging crowd of about five thousand which was swirling around the outside of the rink and trying to force a way in.

'Lord, I'm melting,' said Jane, who with Saran had waited hours to get into the building and into the seats they were now occupying near the platform which had only that morning been knocked up. 'I'm glad I didn't bring any of the children with me. Oh, hear that lot outside.'

'Hullo, what's Mr Chairman trying to say again?' said Saran as a man rose from where he had been seated behind a small table in the centre of the most representative and distinguished platform party. The chairman himself – a brewer brave was he. There were three doctors, two lawyers, a vicar and a couple of curates, one of whom was in uniform, a couple of nonconformist ministers and a staff captain of the Salvation Army. Then there were three of the greatest ladies of the borough and – well, several more of the cream of the district. Saran knew most of them, but only by name, of course, she had never been privileged to speak to them. Oh, yes, of course, she had many times spoken to one of them, the old doctor, the one who had cut off Harry's leg that time. But Saran couldn't, not for the life of her, tell Jane who the man was that stood up at the side of the chairman to lead the singing of 'Keep the Home Fires Burning' and other suitable numbers whilst waiting for Mr Bottomley to arrive.

'... pleased to say, and I'm sure you'll all be glad to hear – for you've been most patient – that Captain Ellis, recruiting officer for our borough, has just informed me that Mr Bottomley (cheers) is now on his way (loud cheers) here from Dowlais, where he addressed one of the largest and most enthusiastic...' He was cut off by the loud roar of the crowd outside the building as it hailed the appearance of the Chief Inspirer, from whom they were demanding a speech as he was being escorted into the rink by a picked shock-squad of policemen. But the policemen surrounding him, the Chief Inspirer, forced a way for him through the crowd and into the crowded rink, where he was received with musical honours and with cheers loud and long.

'Lord, isn't he fat, Jane?' said Saran. 'No wonder he's sweating,' she remarked as the Chief Inspirer, now seated on the chairman's right, mopped his brow as his belly, which rested in his lap, strained the buttons of his trousers and the lower buttons of his waistcoat as he went on breathing heavily whilst the chairman introduced him as:

'... one whose name future generations will revere – I wish the friends outside would restrain themselves long enough to enable us...'

The double line of policemen at the entrance were swept forward as the crowd from outside, in its desire to hear the man who was rousing Britain as it had never before been roused, stormed its way in as far as was possible, which wasn't far. Women screamed and children cried, men shouted, and the recruiting officer left the platform to aid the police in restoring order near the entrance, where the crush was critical.

'Now that order is restored – and I do hope that our friends who are unfortunately unable for obvious reasons to get in to enjoy with us the privilege... it may be possible for Mr Bottomley to address an overflow – to address our friends outside after...' The Chief Inspirer shook his head and grunted a negative. 'Well, when next he honours our borough with a visit. And now, ladies and gentlemen, it gives me the greatest pleasure to call upon...' Loud and prolonged cheers as the Chief Inspirer hoisted himself up into the standing position. Inside the huge rink there was silence as he went on to tell the audience that was eating out of his hand, as the saying is, of the magnificent response to the call for service and self-sacrifice he was making throughout the length and breadth of the land; but outside the disappointed crowd kept roaring for a sight of him, for a word from him, roared in vain as the Chief Inspirer went on to tell the audience, the privileged audience within, of how the treacherous Germans had done this, that and the other, and he shot his hands high above his head, and as he did so his hanging belly was hoisted up a few inches, and he called upon his God, *our* God, the God of Britain and her allies, to avenge the bayoneted babies, the raped women and the old men with long whiskers who had been made to dig their own graves before being shot down into them by the devilish – and so on – Germans. And when he sat down, and his belly was once more in his lap, the audience rose and cheered him again and again, and the staff captain of the Salvation Army rose from where he was sitting behind Mr Bottomley on the platform and thanked his God, *our* God, the God of Britain and her allies, for having given us such a man as Mr Bottomley in our hour of need; and after the staff captain of the Salvation Army had thanked God for Mr Bottomley, others of those who were seated on the platform rose also to thank God and Mr Bottomley for the magnificent response the call for service and self-sacrifice was meeting with throughout the length and breadth of the land. Then one of the ladies on the platform stood up and said that it was all very well to cheer and thank God, but God helped them who helped themselves; and there were many present who might well have interviewed Captain Ellis or Sergeant Knight in the recruiting office long before.

'I see before me many young men,' she shrieked. 'Young men whose presence here this evening is nothing less than an insult to Mr Bottomley and the brave ones who in France and Belgium have defended, and still are defending, all that we hold dear....' And a lot more she said. Then the recruiting officer for the borough made an appeal for recruits, and he caused a sensation and aroused great enthusiasm when he called on to the platform a brave fellow who had been wounded during the retreat from Mons, one who 'had done his bit'. And no doubt there would have been even more enthusiasm and more recruits roped in after the meeting were it not that the brave fellow who had 'done his bit' was three parts slewed when exhibited, and therefore was not as impressive or as helpful as he otherwise might have been. But it was a wonderful meeting, all the same, and it would have been better still had Mr Bottomley been able to address the thousands outside who hadn't been able to get inside to hear him. 'Speech, speech,' they kept shouting as he was being escorted away from the building while those within went on cheering. But he wouldn't, perhaps the poor man couldn't after all the meetings he had addressed earlier in the week, and those he had addressed that very day; anyway, he didn't speak in the open air. No, he got into his car and told the driver, well, the recruiting officer told the driver, to drive away to the Castle Hotel, where Mr Bottomley had the few double whiskies which he felt badly in need of, and which no man can say he wasn't entitled to after all he had done for Britain that day.

'Well, what do you think of him?' Jane asked her mother on the way home.

'The man's all right, no doubt, and p'raps he's doing good,' was all Saran was prepared to say just then. 'But isn't he fat?' she added after they had walked a little farther towards home.

What Saran called ''cruiting meetings' were, if nothing else, the favourite form of entertainment as far as the women were concerned during the first year of the war. She herself had no more boys available for service, though her Jim would before it was over be old enough to serve, that is if it lasts as long as some people are now beginning to say it will. So she went on attending recruiting meetings with her daughter Jane and her daughters-in-law, 'ring-paper women' all. Saran took two ring-papers to the post office every Monday morning when she went to draw the twelve shillings per week dependants' allowance Meurig had signed for her to get, and the twelve shillings a week Lewis had signed his hand for his father to get, but unlike Jane and her daughters-in-law, she never carried a penny of the allowances out of the post office, just drew it and immediately deposited the full amount each week in the post office savings bank, into which she also deposited a pound or two of her own money fairly often, for she could well manage it with Glyn and the three youngest boys working and earning fairly good money in the pit. Things were getting dearer, it's true, but she managed to put a good bit away in the post office, all the same. 'It'll come in handy for the boys when they come home,' she told Jane, whom she also helped, as she did her daughters-in-law, whose separation allowances were little enough for them and the children to live on. But Saran saw to it that they didn't go short of much.

So she went on saving and working and attending recruiting meetings and going to the pictures and the theatre. The last recruiting meeting she attended was held at the Drill Hall on a night when there was a host of speakers; chief among whom were a Mrs Flora Drummond and a Mrs Pankhurst. Flora was fiery in the extreme; Mrs Pankhurst spoke quietly and sadly. We were in it. No time to discuss the why and wherefore. She hoped and prayed for an early, satisfactory and lasting peace, of which she saw little sign. So force of arms seemed to be necessary to bring the Germans down to where they would be glad to sue for peace. If that was the case, then everyone should do everything possible to shorten the terrible struggle. So she appealed to all present to...

'I liked that woman.... What was her name, now?' Saran asked on the way home with Jane and her daughters-in-law.

'Do you mean the fat one?' asked Sam's wife.

'No, not her.... What was her name?'

'Mrs Drummond,' supplied Annie, Benny's wife.

'H'm. Why is it that all fat people are so bloodthirsty?'

'You can't say that I'm bloodthirsty,' said Jane.

'No, that's true,' admitted Saran, 'though you're fat enough, goodness knows. But what was the other woman's name, the one with the grey hair and nice face?'

'Do you mean Mrs Pankhurst?' said Annie.

'That's the name; I liked her. She talked sense, or as near to sense as anybody can talk these days. Well, I don't think I'll go to any more 'cruiting meetings. Politics is bad enough, but some of the stuff as is turned out at 'cruiting meetings is...'

'What do you know about politics?' asked Sam's wife.

'Not much, though I went a couple of times to hear that Keir Hardie. They say he's awful bad these days, poor fellow.'

'They say this war has broken his heart,' said Annie, one of whose brothers was a worshipper of Hardie, and who had sworn that if ever conscription came he would be a conscientious objector.

'They say there's a lovely picture in the 'Lectric,' said Jane.

'Then we'll go tomorrow night,' Saran decided for all, knowing full well that she would have to fork out for all four and those of the children that they would fail to get by without payment.

After the meeting in the Drill Hall which was addressed by Mrs Pankhurst, Mrs Drummond and others, the attendances at recruiting meetings became disappointing in the extreme, so the recruiting authorities decided to go out into the open more, and to take the populace by surprise. They arranged with the Electric and Tramway company for the use of a double-decker tram, on the top deck of which they sat a brass band which played martial airs as the tram was driven along from one end of the district to the other from morn to midnight, except for the short breaks for refreshments – which were long enough to enable several of the bandsmen and two recruiting-office orderlies, one of whom was the wounded soldier who was exhibited at Bottomley's meeting, to get drunk before the night was out. The lower deck of the tram was plastered with the most appealing of the many recruiting posters then available. Lovely little homes worth fighting for; grey-haired mothers worth dying for; gallant little Belgium; your King and Country; Humanity, and ever so much more, all strong appeals to those who with Saran and her daughter Jane and her daughters-in-law and their children lined the main street and cheered as the tram with the band playing on the top deck was driven slowly by; and they placed coppers, some placed silver, in the collecting-boxes held out to them by those who ran alongside the tram collecting towards the fund for providing cigarettes and other comforts for the brave boys 'out there'. Finding the results of all the display and noise – all right, music – disappointing, the authorities had another conference, at which it was decided to arrange with all theatre and picture-house owners and managers to sandwich a recruiting speaker in the middle of the show, when the audience least expected to hear an appeal for more service and more self-sacrifice made to them. And Saran and the other 'ring-women' of her family would be sitting sucking oranges, supping sweets or cracking nuts in theatre or picture house, when all of a sudden the orchestra would give one loud long startling warning, and out would walk from the wings to the centre of the stage a parson, a lady member of the recruiting committee, or sometimes a soldier who had got his 'blighty' out in France or Belgium or one of the other places where 'blightys' were to be had for the asking and without, and who was now attached for duty as speaker to the recruiting office, where he hoped to stay for the duration. Such would walk from the wings on to the centre of stages and harrow the feelings of those who had paid to be entertained with such talk as: 'Whilst you are sitting safely and in comfort here, men are crouching in waterlogged trenches facing the enemy. Or in an advanced post, hungry and weak, yet holding on. Or, harder still, lying wounded and helpless out in no-man's-land, hoping against hope for help. They need help. Listen. As you sit here, over hundreds of miles of our long battle-front, the word is being passed along from left to right. "Keep a sharp lookout on the right." And men who have had no sleep for nights, men whom it has not been found possible to relieve, are keeping a sharp lookout on the right. Some of them your sons, your brothers, your husbands. And if there are any here...'

Of course he'd start the women off crying, and with their eyes filled with tears they'd look around to see how many young and middle-aged men there were present, and if there were any the women would sniff contemptuously in their direction, unless it happened to be their own men, of course; in that case the women who had serviceable men with them in theatre or picture house would look straight to their front as the other women whose men had gone ‘over there’ looked accusingly in their direction. Some of them blushed and got up and walked out, couldn’t stand the strain.

‘Well, if this goes on, I’ll have to stop going to the threeatre or the pitchers,’ said Saran on leaving the Palace one night after the performance had been interrupted to allow an appeal to be made, first by a lady who had just returned to the borough after serving buns and tea to soldiers from a YMCA handout on the docks at Southampton for a few months, and secondly by the only wounded soldier attached to the recruiting office who was sober enough for duty that night. ‘Let people alone, I say. If my boys hadn’t wanted to go, I’d have seen all the ’cruiting speakers in hell before I’d drive ’em into the Army. It’s high time this nonsense finished, and for ’em to take what they want to finish the damned thing off.’

‘They’ve taken all I had,’ said Jane.

‘Same here,’ said Sam’s wife.

‘They took Benny first,’ said Annie.

‘Took, took, took,’ cried Saran impatiently. ‘No, they was never took. Them boys of mine would have gone if... they’re same nature as my brother Ike as was killed out in Zululand; Meurig is his uncle Ike to a T. Then Benny, Sam, Lewis and Mervyn, more or less the same. Want to be going to somewhere. Didn’t Benny leave home to join up the time of the Boer War, joined in October, and him not eighteen till the November? That’s the way my boys are, I don’t know why; and I bet you our young Jim goes if it lasts until he’s old enough. You watch now. Let them go as wants to, I say, and let them as don’t want to go...’

'Well, if we have conscription they'll have to go whether they want to or not,' said Sam's wife.

'My brother swears that he'll never go,' said Annie, Benny's wife.

'We'll see,' said Saran. In less than a month conscription was in force, and the poor old wounded soldiers attached to the recruiting office were returned to their units, and the recruiting officer too was sent off to some place, and in his stead there came a little man with a pot belly who had been a Lord Mayor of some place and was now an honorary colonel or something of the sort. Anyway, the little man looked a rum 'un with the Sam Browne belt around his pot belly and his spectacles on. Still, he could be as regimental as the next man when he wanted to be regimental.

Saran was surprised when she saw her picture in the paper – well, when she saw them all, though she needn't have been, for she herself had given the photos to the man when Glyn brought him straight from the Market Tavern up to the house after chucking-out time one night the week previous. He was a hollow-faced, narrow-chested journalist who had just been released from a sanatorium to work as reporter-in-chief of the *Merthyr Express*, on which there was only a boy of sixteen as cub reporter, for all the other fellers had gone to the war. So this consumptive chap got a job reporting for the *Merthyr Express* and also doing lineage for one Cardiff and one London paper. So he had a decent job, and he coughed his way around all the pubs of the district in search of stories. He was well-on the night he ran into Glyn in the Market Tavern, and Glyn was well-on, too.

Bouncing, he was, about him having more boys in the Army than any other man in town. So the reporter asked him to have one with him. Certainly.

'Six boys, did you say?'

'Well, as good as six, for Ossie, the boy as is married to my only daughter, is as good as a son to me – thinks more of me than some of my own boys do.'

'Quite. I suppose you've got photos of them all?'

'Any God's amount, for they're always having their photos took to send home to the old woman.'

'And photos of yourself and wife as well?'

'Ay, I think there's one there as was taken years ago – but there's some of the children on that, if I'm not mistaken.'

'It'll do.'

'Do for what?'

The reporter explained, and Glyn was delighted, and after chucking-out time he took the reporter along with him to the house. 'Saran. Saran. Where are you, Saran?'

'In my bed, of course. Where did you think I'd be at this time of night?'

'Come on down a minute.'

'What for? Your supper's on the table.'

'Yes, but I've got a gentleman here as wants the boys' photos to put 'em in the paper.'

'Nice time of night for anybody to come to fetch photos or anything else,' grumbled Saran as she got out of bed and slipped a petticoat on over her nightdress. 'Now, what is it?' she asked as she walked into the living room in bare feet.

The journalist was coughing terribly. 'You'd better watch that cough, young man,' she said.

'I have been watching it for years,' he said; then he went on to explain what he wanted, namely, the particulars and photos that would enable him to work up a most acceptable story under some such heading as 'Merthyr's Most Patriotic Family', or 'Noble Parents' Great Contribution'. He soon got all he wanted, and Saran went back to her bed, but Glyn insisted on the journalist staying to share the bottle of beer Saran had got in for him as a livener in the morning.

Oh, and didn't he make a fine story of it. Really great, it was, and all the photos reproduced, Ossie's put in as one of six sons. And, above the six sons, Glyn and Saran, as they had appeared when they were photographed over twenty years before with the only three children they had been blessed with up to then.

'What the hell odds,' cried Glyn, when Saran pointed out that they both looked as young as their eldest boy, Benny, as shown in the papers which had printed the story and the photographs. 'There's only a few around here where we live as'll notice it, but there'll be thousands as won't. And them thousands will be proud of us...'

'Like hell they will.'

'Woman, if I happen to forget myself and swear once in a while, that's no reason why you should.'

'Now, get yourself washed, for I'm off out to the pitchers with Jane.'

'Pitchers, pitchers, pitchers...'

'Pints, pints, pints.'

'Don't try to be funny, woman.'

'I'm a fool for losing sleep to argue with you,' said Saran, as she rose from where she had been sitting arguing with Glyn for about half an hour after the rest of the household had retired to bed, well, been sent to bed. Arguing about the strike which Lloyd George had travelled to Cardiff to settle face to face with the miners. 'And you three sheets in the wind. I should have had more sense. But I'll still have it that your leaders were wrong to threaten a strike at a time...'

'Here, what are you two arguing about?' cried a voice from the passage.

'Who in the name of God...'

'It's – it's our Benny,' cried Saran joyfully, as she ran to meet one wearing his military greatcoat cloak-fashion, buttoned at the neck, the empty sleeves hanging down at the sides. 'Benny, Benny bach,' said Saran, embracing him.

'Mam.' He bent his head to touch her hair with his lips.

'Let – let my boy come and sit down, woman,' tremulously cried the now quite sober Glyn, timidly placing a hand on his boy's shoulder.

'Yes, but let me take this big old coat off him first.... No, mam'll do it. Oh, my God!'

Glyn dropped back into the armchair and burst out crying. They were all crying. Benny it was who recovered himself first.

'Now, let's all stop snivelling,' he said firmly. 'An arm is nothing to what some of my pals have lost. What about a cup of tea, mam?'

'Certainly, my boy – and there's some bakestone cake I made this morning... Lord, Benny, you're getting grey.'

'Never mind his hair, give the boy some food, woman.'

'I will. Empty the teapot, Glyn – there on the ashes for now. Put the small kettle on the gas while I lay the table, and get them eggs out of the pantry.'

'No, no eggs, mam; they've been stuffing me in that hospital until I can hardly button my tunic. Just the bakestone bread and butter and a cup of tea, that's all.'

They sat and watched him, their firstborn, adoringly, as he went on eating, and telling them where he had 'got it' whilst on duty at an observation point.

'But how is it that Annie and the children didn't come up with you?' his father asked, under the impression that he had been home before slipping up to see his parents.

'Well, I'll tell you...'

'Eat a bellyful first, and tell us after,' said Saran.

'I've had plenty, thanks. Now, it's this way, mam. Knowing that I wouldn't get here from Brighton until late; and as Annie knows no more about me losing my arm than you did up to a few minutes ago, I decided to come to you first, so that you, mam...'

'I know, my boy. You want me to go down to prepare her for – for that,' she said, pointing to where his arm used to be.

'You've got it first time.'

'I'll go straight down.'

'And I'll follow in about five minutes.'

'You'll do no such thing,' said his father. 'You'll stay here with me until your mother brings Annie and the kids back up.'

'But it's so late, dad, and the children are all asleep...'

'Late, be damned, what odds about time this night. I bet

she'll be glad to wake the kids and bring 'em up to see you. Off you go, woman.'

Away Saran went. Benny lit a fag, and his father lit his pipe, and as he smoked he kept looking at Benny in a way that made Benny feel more tender towards his father than ever before.

'I'm glad of this couple of minutes with you before anyone else comes between us,' said Glyn.

'Yes.'

'Yes…' And before he could say any more Glyn burst into tears, and before he recovered himself Annie rushed in half dressed, and she started to cry too; and then Saran came in with the children, and the children started yowping as well. Saran stood back and let them have their cry out. The noise they all made woke Saran's three youngest boys, who came down to see what the row was about. Then Saran told them to dress, and after they had said how-do to their one-armed soldier brother she sent Jim up to fetch Jane and her children down, and she sent Tom down to fetch Sam's wife and her children up. 'There's no one going to the pit from this house tomorrow,' she said.

'Today, you mean,' laughed Glyn, who had recovered himself by now.

CHAPTER 14

'STREWTH, WHAT A BLOODY GAME THIS IS

The one-armed Benny was knocking about in regimentals for about five months before he was finally discharged, and during those five months his four brothers and Ossie, his brother-in-law, had been home on leave, from which they returned to join drafts leaving for France.

'Well, they're all there now,' said Saran one day to Benny.

'Yes. Mam?'

'What?'

'I want to talk to you.'

'Well, here I am.'

'I want to talk to you in private.'

'Then wait until I get your father and these boys their things to go out. Shan't be long.'

'Well?' she said about twenty minutes later, Glyn and the

boys having gone out for the evening. 'Quick about it, Benny, for Jane'll be here soon to go to the pitchers with me.'

'Right. There's an insurance agent I know called up, and he's trying to sell his book, and a good book it is. I'm not much good for underground work any more, supposing I could get any; but I could collect insurance all right.'

'Certainly you could.'

'Yes, but where's the money coming from to buy a book?'

'Oh, that's it, is it? How much does that chap want for his book?'

He told her.

'H'm, that's a lot of money, Benny. Still, it'll be a living for you. And how much have you got towards it?'

'I've got nothing. Annie and the children had to have...'

'I know. All right, you can come over to the post office with me in the morning. But will they let me draw all that off at once?'

'I don't think they will, but you can get it through in a few days.'

'Will it do then?'

'Yes, as long as I get it by next Monday. And I'll pay it back to you every penny, and before very long.'

So she found him the money to buy the book, and she also helped him to get some new business before he'd been long at the game; and he himself picked up a lot of new business too, for few of his own friends or their people liked saying no to a man with an empty sleeve, so he soon had one of the best books in the district, and he paid back the money his mother had let him have to buy the book in the first place, and he gave her a pound extra for the lend of it; and before very long Annie, his wife, was turning her nose up at Jane and Sam's wife, and Saran up and told her about it one day, it was the day before the old telegram came: Saran's boy, Mervyn, who had looked so smart in his breeches, putties and spurs when on leave, 'Killed in action'.

Benny, calling in to report to his mother how what he called his 'body-snatching business' was getting on, found her sitting alone in the living room with the old telegram in her hand. Glyn and her own boys being in work, she had asked the boy who had brought the old thing to read it to her, and after the boy had read it she said: 'All right, my boy, here's a threepenny bit,' and then she went into the house to sit down. And sitting down she was when Benny walked in. What could he say? What could anyone say?

'Our Mervyn,' she said, handing Benny the telegram to read.

He placed the telegram on the mantelpiece after he had read it.

'I thought he was the safest of the lot,' she said with a sigh. 'Try to be here tonight when your father gets home from the pit, Benny, will you?'

'I'll be here – I'll hurry up and finish my round – I'll send Annie up...'

'No, don't bother. I'd rather be alone for a bit; but if you happen to be passing where your uncle Harry lodges... do you go anywhere near there today?'

'Well, I've got to call at two houses in Cambrian Street, which is not so far away from where he lodges.'

'Then you can call in and tell the woman of the house to

tell my brother about Mervyn when he gets in from his work. Go now, Benny.'

'Are you sure…?'

'Go, I tell you, Benny.' Off he went.

When he got back to his mother's house in the evening he found that his uncle Harry was there before him; seated in the armchair near the fire, he was, from where he watched Saran moving about preparing a meal for Glyn and the boys.

'And Keir Hardie is dead, Saran,' said Harry.

'Poor man.'

'That means a by-election,' said Benny.

'A fine man,' said Harry.

'Here's the boys, but their father isn't with them,' said Saran, as she heard footsteps.

'How do you know he's not?' asked Benny.

'I know. Where's your father?' she asked the first of the three boys to enter the house.

'He turned into the Morlais Castle.'

'Go and fetch him home, Benny, but leave me to tell him about Mervyn…'

'What about Mervyn?' cried Jim.

'Yes, what about him?' cried the other two boys.

'Go and fetch your father, Benny. He's killed, Mervyn is, my boys.'

Benny ran off down to the Morlais Castle to fetch his dad, who was halfway down his third pint of war beer when his eldest son went in to him and told him that he was wanted at once at home.

'What's up, Benny?'

'Mam wants you at once about something.'

It was a miserable business altogether, but there were a lot of people who were having to go through it about that time, and so had little time in which to sympathise with others. And the food regulations made people suspicious one of the other, and the jollity of the first year of the war changed into a sour stoicism. Instead of the boisterous and smartly dressed crowds of soldiers who had made the streets of the town ring with laughter and song there were only quiet groups of soldiers who looked as though they realised what they were in for when they went 'over there', and there were a few couples in muddy uniforms home on leave from the front who from twisted mouths sneeringly gave utterance to jokes about the first five years being the worst, and so on. And the number of wounded on the streets increased as the days went by, and conscientious objectors increased also. Saran saw two being taken from the police station to the railway station under escort to entrain for Wormwood Scrubs. Then there was all the standing about in queues to get a bit of food. Saran and Jane were standing in the queue outside the Home and Colonial shop on the very day when the two conscientious objectors were marched by under escort. The people standing about jeered at them, and there were some boys running after them who kept on shouting: 'They've got no guts, they've got no guts,' and one of the boys shouted a dirty name as well. Saran felt rather embarrassed as the objectors under escort marched past where she stood with Jane in the queue, for she was as good as related to one of the objectors. Not quite, but as good as, for one of the objectors was a teacher, and he was Annie's brother, and as Annie was married to her Benny, Saran felt that she was as good as related to Annie's too conscientious brother. But nobody else seemed to notice her connection with him.

'Well,' said a man who was standing in the queue because his wife was bad in bed and couldn't stand there in the rain for the bit of food, 'they'll get their bit of food reg'lar where they're going to, anyway – and they won't have to stand about hours to get it, same as we have to, either.'

'Where do you reckon they're being taken to?' a woman asked.

'Wormwood Scrubs is where most of 'em goes, I'm told.'

'But surely they can't all get into Wormwood Scrubs.'

'What the hell odds where they go to?' snapped the man, who was getting to feel fed up with long standing on the pavement in the midst of a lot of cackling women.

'All right, keep your hair on,' the woman told him; and as the man went on grumbling she up and told him that he should thank his lucky stars that he wasn't a German, for in Germany the people – and serve 'em right, too – had to wait longer for much less than he was going to have.

'Then God help the Germans,' muttered the man.

'May God blast 'em, I say,' said the woman.

Saran, with her food-cards in her hand, listened and watched her chance to get ahead of her turn, as she had done more than once before. But the other women were marking her too closely now, so she had to wait her turn, and it was night before she got what bit she did get, and by the time she got home and made the most of what she had got for supper for Glyn and the boys it was too late to go to the pictures with Jane.

The family was a proud one that day, the day when, after he had read the letter to Saran and the boys in the home, Glyn had sent the boys flying off to fetch Benny and his Annie and their children, Jane and her children, and Sam's wife and her children.

'And, whatever you do, don't forget to let your uncle Harry know that I want him up, Jim,' Saran shouted after the boy as he ran out.

'Now, are we all here?' asked Glyn as he fixed his glasses on. Yes, they were all there, Harry as well. 'Then listen.' Then he slowly read aloud the letter from Meurig, by this time a company sergeant major. Oh, great news it was. He had been awarded the DCM, for capturing a German bombing and sniping post, and in doing so had killed a number of Germans, and, what was more, he had rescued under heavy fire a wounded Scottish officer. All he said in his letter was that he had been awarded the DCM, what he had done to get it the family learnt later when the certificate signed by a general arrived long after. 'But that's not all,' cried Glyn. 'He's on his way home for a course of something at the Guards' Barracks, Chelsea, and he'll be with us for a couple of days before the course starts, and we'll have him with us for another ten days after the course is finished....'

'And where's he going after?' asked young Charlie.

'Where do you think? Back to France, of course. I'll see that chap tonight.'

'What chap are you talking about?' Saran asked Glyn.

'The chap that put all that in the paper about us before.

He's busy now with this damned old by-election, but when I show him this letter...'

'You're not taking Meurig's letter round the pubs to lose it.'

'Woman, before he puts about Meurig in the paper this chap'll want to see for himself...'

'Then let him come up here and see it,' said Saran, taking the letter from him.

'Well, of all the women... here, that letter's addressed to me.'

'Yes, but it's meant for me. The boys only addresses 'em to you because they know I can't read.'

'Then what the hell good is the letter to you? You can't eat it.'

'How do you know I can't?'

'Well, you should be thankful to know that he's still alive and well, Saran bach,' was all Harry said, but nobody took much notice of him sitting back there in the corner with them old whiskers of his almost hiding his features. What Saran wanted to bother sending down for him was more than Glyn could understand.

Meurig came in on the seven o'clock train in the evening of the day that both the candidates appeared in the open air on the rising ground near the Public Offices, the borough's civic centre. Glyn, Benny and his three under-age brothers met him at the station, but all the women of thc family waited with Uncle Harry, old Marged and the children at home for him.

'But where's the medal, where's the DCM?' young Charlie wanted to know.

Meurig smiled down on him and quietly said: 'Haven't had it yet.'

'Have you killed any Germans?' young Tom wanted to know.

'What's up here?' Meurig asked as he and his admiring escort drew near the crowd assembled on the rising ground near the Public Offices.

'Oh, an election meeting,' supplied Benny.

'That Keir Hardie died whilst you were in France,' his father said, 'and now they've got to 'lect a man in his place – and there'll be hell to pay before it's over.'

'How's mam?' Meurig asked.

'Up to the mark,' said his father. 'How about a drink before we go on up to the house, Meurig?' pausing outside the door of the Anchor.

'No thanks,' shortly returned Meurig, continuing on his way.

'As you like,' said his father, hurrying to catch up with him again.

A few minutes later they were in the home, where Meurig did not, as was expected by all present, play the part of the hero he was. After he had had a bit to eat he asked his mother to get him a suit of civvies to knock about in.

'But I'm taking you out to meet a chap as'll put a piece in the paper about you,' said his father.

'You are not. You've still got that old suit of mine, mam?'

'Of course I have, my boy. Did you think I'd pawned it?'

Then he laughed for the first time since his arrival. 'I wouldn't be surprised,' he said. 'Is it too late for you and I

– just you and I, that's all – to go to the pictures? Some place where they're showing...'

'Pictures,' sneered his father. 'Boy, what...?'

'Bit late for the pitchers,' said Saran. 'But we could manage to catch the second house at the threeatre, for it's v'riety there this week. But I'd like for us all to go, if you don't mind, Meurig.'

'You're right, mam. Come on, then, fall in, and be ready to march off from here right into the grand circle of the theatre by the time I get into civvies.'

'I don't want to go to the theatre,' said his father.

'Dad, as company sergeant major, I'm taking charge. So be ready. I don't suppose you'll come with us, Uncle Harry?'

'I think I will this once,' Harry surprised them all by saying. 'That is if none of you minds me coming like this?'

'What is there for anybody to mind, I'd like to know,' said Saran, glaring around into the faces of all present.

'Nothing,' said Meurig. 'Come on, get me those civvies, mam.'

The suit had shrunk a bit, and it was creased a little as well, but Meurig, who looked grand in anything, Saran thought, was more comfortable in it than he would have been in regimentals. And off they all went leaving old Marged, who said her legs were too stiff to go trapesing about at that time of night, to look after the place and prepare supper by the time they returned. And everyone, with the possible exception of Glyn, who said he couldn't stomach the beer sold in the bars of the theatre – though he bolted about five big glasses of it during the one interval

– enjoyed themselves immensely, for it was a good bill that week, the third week of the theatre's variety season. One turn, a stout woman she was, was great, they all thought. She sang a song – and a wonderful voice she had – with a touching chorus that Saran long remembered. What was it, now? Oh, yes:

Sunshine and shadow
You promised to love alway.
Now that the shadow hangs over me
Your dear face I never see,
Not that I would reproach you.
I trust that you'll happy be,
But you've taken away the sunshine,
The shadow remains with me.

Then there was a doleful comedian who made everyone laugh until their sides ached when he went on to tell the audience of how his wife treated him now that he had sold his food-cards to get money which he had gone and lost on a horse which a pal said was a cert. Then there was – well, it was a good bill, and by the end of the show Meurig was more like his old self than he had been from the time he had arrived up to then. He refused to hurry off from the party to get the one his father urgently whispered that there was just time for; and he insisted on escorting his uncle Harry every step of the way down to the place where he lodged. His uncle Harry said: 'God bless you, my boy, and may He watch over you, now and always'; and Meurig said: 'Thank you, Uncle Harry.' Then his uncle Harry went into the house of the woman with whom he lodged, and Meurig walked back to his mother's house, where all the rest and a grand supper awaited him.

After but one more day at home Meurig left to go through the short course at the Guards' Barracks in Chelsea, and all at home counted the days until he came back home again, for ten days this time, before returning to his unit in France. He arrived home the second time on the eve of the poll of the by-election, one of the most exciting days and nights in the history of the borough, for there were meetings on every street corner. More in the nature of unholy rows than meetings, they were. Meurig stood with his father and Benny on the fringe of the huge crowd assembled on the rising ground near the Public Offices, where the Independent Labour Party candidate was getting a very rough time indeed from the win-the-war crowd. He was trying for the umpteenth time to make himself heard when Meurig and Benny and his father arrived, on their way home from the station, at the place where the crowd was assembled. 'Just a minute,' said Meurig, stopping.

'Come on, that feller isn't worth listening to, even though he is one of our miners' leaders,' said his father. Meurig stood and his face darkened as he watched and listened. 'If he'd come out on the official labour ticket,' his father went on, 'and supported the war, we'd have supported him to a man; but...'

'Shut up; let's hear what he's got to say,' said Meurig.

'They won't let him say much.' Neither did they.

'Friends. In coming before you...'

'Are you in favour of the war? Answer that, yes – or no.'

'Ay, answer that,' roared the crowd.

'My friends, I...'

'Answer.'

'Well, my answer to that question, a question which I've already...'

'Yes or no is all we want. Are you prepared to support the Government in its efforts to win the war for us?'

'Well, I...'

'Are you?'

'No, I'm not...'

'Then neither are we prepared to support you.'

'Or bloody well listen to him.'

'That's how it's been at all his meetings,' Glyn informed Meurig as the crowd let itself go and the Independent Labour candidate and his handful of supporters again bowed to the storm of hooting and abuse and walked away up the hill towards the workhouse. Meurig and his father and brother continued their way along the main street towards home until they reached the Pontmorlais Square, just off which, on the patch of ground where the boxing booths had in the old days been erected, another meeting was in progress, and a most enthusiastic meeting it was, the chief speaker at which was the win-the-war candidate, who was saying as Meurig and his father and his one-armed brother drew near:

'If I am returned as your member...'

'You will be, Charlie.'

'... Mr Lloyd George (cheers). Yes, and we should thank God for having placed Mr Lloyd George at the helm of...' (Loud cheers.) 'And I shall support him through...'

‘Good old Charlie.’

‘... his efforts to secure victory; and to see that our boys in France and in...’

‘Come on, for Christ’s sake,’ muttered Meurig as he continued his way home, followed by his father and his one-armed brother.

‘By the time you come home next Benny’ll have had his false arm fixed,’ said his father.

‘Oh, what a bloody lot you are,’ muttered Meurig as they turned the corner by Tom Hall’s shop.

‘Boy, what’s the matter with you?’ said his father. ‘You talk as though you didn’t belong to us any more.’

‘If it wasn’t for mam...’

‘What?’

‘Nothing.’

‘Well, I’m damned if I know what’s come over you,’ grumbled his father.

‘Let him alone, can’t you?’ said Benny.

Meurig almost ran up the hill towards home and his mother, who soon put him in a good mood. For ten days and nights she left everything to old Marged, and what old Marged couldn’t manage was left to stand over until her Meurig’s leave was over. Meurig had any God’s amount of money, and it was family parties all the way: in a party to the theatre, where Saran sat with the borough’s best at the side of her DCM son in the three-shilling circle, the rest of the family party almost filling the front row of the circle on both sides of Meurig and his mother. Harry never went with them to any place of entertainment after that once to the theatre, but he was up at the house quite a lot during the ten days Meurig was home; and not once did he open his mouth against them going to the theatre and the pictures and to watch people skating in the roller-skating rink.

'Went like winking, the time did,' sighed Saran, as she sat in the house with Jane and the other women of the family and old Marged after Meurig, in his regimentals that morning, had left the house accompanied by his father and brothers to return to France. 'Oh, I don't feel a bit like work,' she said.

'Then what say if we all go down town for a walk?' suggested Jane.

'And with all the washing as I've been leaving and leaving waiting to be done?' said Saran, rising to her feet. 'No; must get on with it, and if any of you gels got nothing particular...'

'I've got a fine old dollop of my own as wants doing,' said Jane.

'So have I,' said Annie.

'And so have I,' said Sam's wife.

'Then you'd all better go and do it,' Saran told them, 'for you're not likely to get a better drying-day than today. Marged and I will soon have all I've got drying on the line.'

'But isn't it butter-day today?' said Jane.

'Damn, so it is. And you gels owe me nearly all those coupons of yours after the way you and the children been stuffin' yourselves up here all the time Meurig was home. Oh, look at Annie bridling. Some day you'll get to know me, Annie. Then we'll leave the washing today again, Marged, so as to go on parade with our food-tickets – though you can rub a few towels through whilst I'm out, for there isn't a clean towel in the house. How long will you gels be before you're ready?'

'I'm ready now,' said Jane.

'I'll slip down to wipe baby's face and put his best coat and hat on, then meet you on Tom Hall's corner,' said Annie. Off she dashed.

'If you'll lend me your white shawl to carry baby in, then I needn't go all the way down to the house for my best shawl,' said Sam's wife.

'What, my best shawl again,' cried Saran. 'You'll do, Mrs Sam. Go and get it out of the drawer. Sure there's nothing that you want to borrow, Jane?'

'Well, I could do...'

'You couldn't, not from me, my gel. Come, let's hurry. Mustn't keep lady Annie waiting.'

'It's more likely that we'll have to wait for her,' said Jane.

Ossie, Jane's husband, was home on leave from the front, but it was little Jane, Saran – or anyone other than Glyn, his father-in-law – saw of him during the fortnight he was home. It was booze, booze, booze all the time.

'That husband of yours had better not come home too often or he'll have us all in the workhouse,' said Saran to Jane as they walked towards where Sam's wife lived, for they had promised Sam's wife to call for her on the way to town to try and wangle a bit of extra meat from one of the butchers. 'This is the second day this week that your father has stayed home from the pit to go boozing with him; and...' She nearly let out about Ossie's borrowings from her.

'Well, after Saturday he'll be gone to where...

'Jane, gel, don't snivel here on the road where people... Come on, pull yourself together, gel. I was only joking about Ossie. Why, the boy's as good as gold; and it won't trouble me if your father don't go to the pit any more this week. Now, now. That's better. I expect we'll have to pay through the nose for the bit of meat old Hoskin promised to put on one side for me. But that's the way it is, if you want a bit extra, then you've got to pay for it.'

Then long months of working, saving – Saran only, who kept on adding part of the fairly good wages Glyn and her boys were earning in the pit to the two allowances which her boys in France were making to Glyn and herself – wangling, drinking, theatre and picture-going, and letter-writing – and ever so much more that helped the long and anxious months along. Then the second blow, a blow Saran felt more than she ever let on to anyone. Meurig, regimental sergeant major at the last, died leading an attack on a German position in Mametz Wood, though Saran didn't know where he had been killed until Sam came home about a month afterwards and told her. All she got was the usual notification and her share of His Majesty's sympathy, which wasn't much when shared amongst so many. Meurig gone. 'My God... humph, God indeed. My boy – my boys – and who the hell cares? Leave me alone, I tell you. Glyn, if you don't shut up... my Meurig. Leave me alone, Benny. Go on and attend to your work. No, I don't want Annie or anyone else. Meurig. I'm all right, Harry, thank you. My Meurig. Do you remember the night you were in the theatre with him and all of us, Harry? That was decent of you, Harry. Decent of you not to be too – well, what you might have been that night. And then he went on down to your lodging with you, Harry. My Meurig. I've often wondered what you two talked about that night, Harry. You and my Meurig. Did he talk about me at all, Harry? I'm all right now, thank you, Harry. I'm getting grey, Harry. Well, so was Lloyd George when I saw him on the pitchers in the Palace that night we all went with Meurig. With Meurig. Meurig.'

'Well, mam,' was all Sam could find to say when he presented himself to his mother before going to see his wife and children the night he came home for his first leave from the battle-front.

'Sam, bach, you've been away a long time. But you have come back, thank God. Meurig...'

'Ay; I came home as far as Pontypridd with a chap as was with him when – when...'

'Yes. Tell me, Sam. What did the man say?'

'Not much, man. Just said how Meurig copped out – all over in a second, he said it was. No pain, mam. In the head he said it was.'

'Where – where was it?'

'In the head, mam.'

'The place, I mean.'

'Oh, Mametz Wood.'

'What sort of a place is that, Sam?'

'Oh, a proper bloody slaughterhouse, mam. Regiment after reg...'

'Yes, but what sort of a looking place is it, Sam?'

'Well, something like Cyfarthfa Wood, only with all the trees shot in half and big shell holes everywhere.'

'Not much of a place, then, Sam.'

'No, mam.'

She sighed as she placed her hand on his head and rumpled his hair affectionately. 'Have you been home?'

'No; came straight up.'

'Then go straight back down to your wife and children, my boy. They're lovely and they're dying to see you. So is your father and the boys and Jane. Did you meet her Ossie out there, Sam?'

'No; we never ran into his mob.'

'Off you go, now; but bring Kate and the children back up after – well, by the time your father and the boys get back home from wherever they're gone to this night. I'll get Mrs Owen's boy to run around and tell the rest. Why didn't you write to let us know you were coming, Sam bach?'

'I...'

'Tell me when you come back up with Kate and the children. Off you go, now. Oh, I forgot to ask you about your brother Lewis. Don't you think it's time he was let come home to see us?'

'I should think it is...'

'Did you happen to meet him out there at all?'

'Not once, though I heard that his mob was within...'

'Yes, remember to tell me about that when you come back up to see your father and the boys. Don't forget now. Off you go.'

As soon as he had gone she gave Mrs Owen's boy sixpence to round up all the members of the family, and old Marged as well, for she knew that she'd want a bit of help to do things in style for Sam, as she had when her Meurig was home. But this time she would have to foot the bill for food and entertainment, for she knew that it was little enough Sam had to spend, whereas Meurig... well, he was a sergeant major, and an unmarried one at that.

And no sooner had she given Sam a good time and sent him back to the front with a tidy few shillings in his pocket... the letter came in the morning when she was alone in the house, and she was undecided whether to send for Mrs Owen's gel who had come home from service to read the letter for her, or to wait in the hope of Benny calling in, when who should walk in but Benny himself.

'Here's a letter,' she said, holding it out to him. 'I know it's our Lewis' writing, so there can't be much wrong. Maybe it's to tell us that he's coming home on leave.'

'He is home, for this is posted in London,' said Benny tearing open the envelope. 'He's wounded – slightly.'

'Read the letter out to me, Benny. Every word, remember.'

After he had read it to her she took the letter from him. 'Now it's Lewis,' she said as she sat down with his letter in her hand, looking up into Benny's face. Then after a while she said: 'I'm going up to London to him, Benny. I'm going to see him at that hospital – and your father shall go with me.'

'I don't see any need for going to such expense when he says in that letter that it isn't much, and that...'

'That's what you wrote to tell us when you had an arm blown off, Benny, and p'raps it's the same, if not worse, with him.'

'Not it. If you like I'll wire the hospital...'

'What need to when me and your father are going there?'

'Do you know that London is no place just now, now that these raids are on so often, for an old coup… well, for people who've never been there before?'

'Benny.' She rose to her feet and faced him. 'Do you know that I've lost four – two in the pit and two out there in France – without as much as a sight of one of 'em? If I'd only… but it's no use you or anyone else bothering. I'm going to London to see my Lewis.'

'Then I'll arrange…'

'Nothing, Benny. I'll do all the arranging as wants to be done.'

Every available man in the depot at the time – and that meant several hundred recruits under canvas in the field outside the barracks wall as well – was ordered by the officer commanding the depot to turn out on parade to honour the hero's parents, who were to receive the DCM their son had won on the field of battle shortly before he was killed in Mametz Wood. Benny wanted to accompany his parents to Cardiff, but Saran said: 'Never mind; your father and me will be all right. You've got to c'lect the insurance, and if you're not there on the day, then people may not have the money to pay two weeks the next time you call. So you look after your work, my boy; and your father and me will go for the medal.' And they went.

When stopped at the gates by the military policeman with the MP armlet on his arm and a stick under his other arm, Glyn nervously began to explain.

'Show the man the letter,' Saran suggested. And as the

military policeman was reading the letter she said: 'I'm his mother – and this is my husband – his father.'

'Come this way, please,' said the military policeman after he had read the letter and handed it back to Glyn. They followed him under the archway and around the corner and into the orderly room, where they were received by the adjutant, who was as nice as could be to them, though some of the old sweats who were trying to swing the lead at the depot reckoned that he was – well, you know. Anyway, he was as nice as anyone could be to Saran and Glyn, and so was the officer commanding the depot as well. Had tea in a silver teapot which was carried on a silver tray brought in to them, and it *was* silver, for Saran showed Glyn the stamp at the bottom of the teapot. And there were little cakes on a silver plate as well, but they couldn't eat any of them, though they were thankful for the cup of tea. The adjutant, just before he went out to the parade ground to inspect the parade, pulled out his silver cigarette case and opened it with a click and held it out to Glyn. 'Like a cigarette?' he asked.

'I smokes a pipe, thank you, sir,' said Glyn. 'But I don't want a smoke now,' he added nervously.

'Well, if you'll just wait here for a few minutes, I'll send the sergeant major to fetch you.' So they waited.

After the sergeant major had saluted the adjutant, and the adjutant had saluted the CO, and had given him the little case with the DCM medal in it that the orderly room sergeant had given the adjutant to give to the CO, the sergeant major, who had a game leg and a sandy walrus moustache, fetched Glyn and Saran from where they were sitting in the orderly room out on to the parade ground. And when they got to where he put them to stand in front of all them soldiers, the CO shouted: 'Slo-o-ope arms,' and all the soldiers sloped arms, and the adjutant and the two young officers he was getting ready to send out to the front sloped their naked and shining swords. They all stood like a rock for a couple of seconds, and then the CO shouted louder than before: 'Pr-r-resent arms.' And present arms they all did. Then, after he had told all the soldiers of the brave things Meurig had done, he walked up to Glyn and pinned Meurig's DCM medal on his breast, where it shone like anything in the April sunlight; and he shook hands warmly with Glyn and Saran and told them that they had reason to be proud – very proud indeed – of their brave boy who was no more. The regiment was proud of him – and of them. Then he ordered all the soldiers to slope arms again, and after he had dismissed them he walked across the barracks square as far as the gates with Glyn and Saran, asking them questions about their boys who had served and were still serving. And he offered them more tea, but they didn't want any more, so the CO shook hands with them again; and the military policeman saluted them as they walked past him on their way out of the barracks square. But before they left the CO Glyn unpinned the medal and put it back in the little box which the CO said he might as well have, and as soon as they were out of sight and hearing of the military policeman at the gates Saran said to Glyn: 'Give me that medal.' And he gave it to her, and she put it away safe; and as soon as she got home she had it put in the frame in which was the certificate on which it is written of all the brave deeds performed by her Meurig, and he did perform them, for the general signed the certificate, and his signature is on it for anyone to see. And Saran hung the frame with the certificate and the medal in it under the Roll of Honour on which is the name of her brother Ike, who was killed long before her Meurig was born out in Zululand where he was fighting the Zulus that time when the good old 24th was wiped out.

There was only one more trial in store for Saran before the old war was to end in victory glorious and complete for Britain and her allies. She lost no more of her boys, neither were there any more wounded – though her Jim – the young fool as he was to enlist after knowing what his brothers had had to go through – was vaccinated and everything ready to go out to France when the Armistice came and ended the damned thing, thank God. Pity it hadn't ended before her Jane's Ossie was blinded, though. Saran couldn't then, no more than she can now, understand how he came to be blinded without being marked at all. He told her and Jane in the train on the day they went to fetch him home from the place where the blinded soldiers were that a big shell burst close by him and killed several of his pals without touching him. But after it went off and he went to look around he found that he couldn't see. Anyway, that's what he told Saran and Jane. But however he had it, it was domino on him for the rest of his life, though he'd have his bit of pension, of course.

Soon after Ossie had started going to the place in Thomas Street where the blinded soldiers were being taught to make mats and baskets and other things – THE ARMISTICE. Saran could hardly believe, but it was right enough, for all the hooters started hooting, and kept on hooting, and in the streets people were behaving – well, anyhow. And in the pubs – well, there again... Glyn, Benny, Ossie, all of them gathered at her house, even Harry stumped up to see her, to rejoice with her. And they rejoiced. In the evening they all, except Harry, wanted her to come into town with them to see the people of the borough rejoicing victoriously, but somehow she didn't feel like going with them, so she stayed at home with her brother Harry, who didn't feel like stumping about the town either. After the others had gone down into the town Saran sat talking about many things with her brother. Then she went out to the coal-house at the back to get some coal for the fire, for it was cold enough that night. And as she lifted her head after filling the bucket with coal, she noticed the night sky, which that night was like an arctic ice field on the break. Pearly white it was, and the breaks were of a luminous blue. And there she stood for long looking at it and thinking. Silly, she afterwards thought, that just then she seemed to see the lost legions of war-taken ones – just their heavily shod feet and muddy putties through the luminous blue breaks in the pearly-white night sky – as they marched along the sky and into heaven to meet their God. And from the town below came the sound of voices singing 'It's a long, long trail....' And laughter, followed by cheers. 'Keep the Home Fires Burning', was also borne upwards to her on the wind from where the people of the borough were rejoicing.

Sighing, she picked up the bucket she had filled with coal and walked with it hanging from her strong right arm along the path leading to the house. She stopped outside the window of the living room when she saw her brother on his one knee praying with his eyes fast closed. Funny he looked on his one knee, and his kneeless portion of leg and the peg leg at the end of it stuck out straight almost at a right angle from his body.

He was kneeling close to the wall on which the Roll of Honour on which his brother Ike's name was inscribed was hanging, just above the frame in which were enclosed Meurig's DCM and the certificate that had been signed by the general. Standing there outside the window, with the bucket filled with coal all the time hanging from her hand, she could distinctly hear every word he was addressing to God. For he prayed loudly and rhythmically, and in their own lovely nativc language. After he had commended her and hers to God, he went on to thank Him for having at long last brought the so-long-mad world to its senses. He asked God to comfort all the bereaved ones, and to fortify all the suffering ones. Long he prayed, and the bucket filled with coal which Saran held grew heavier, and she was about to lower it to the ground when her brother humbly concluded by saying that he had asked in the Name of his Saviour all the things he had asked God that night to do. He rose from off his one knee and swivelled his stump and pcg around as Saran entered the living room carrying the bucket of coal.

'I was saying a few words,' he said, apologetically.

'Yes, I heard you,' she said as she began putting the coal

on the fire. 'It's cold enough tonight. You'd make a fine preacher, Harry, if only you could preach as lovely as you prayed just now. But there, you didn't have any schoolin', did you? And without schoolin'... and yet I don't know, I don't know what's up with me tonight, but out there... Harry.'

'What, my gel?'

'Do you think... are you sure my boys have gone to God?'

'To who else, my gel? Certainly they have. All who...'

'I don't see why not, even though they were not members of the chapel – or saved in the revival like you.'

'But they're saved all the same, Saran. He died for them, remember; and they died for – for – well, for something they thought was right, and worth dying for.'

'Ay, I expect most of 'em thought that. And now we've got to take stock, Harry. Well, that's easy for me to do now, no matter how hard it was to bear having two of 'em taken, and another two – well, three counting poor Ossie – battered and blinded. Sam's the only one of mine to come through scot-free.'

'Nobody's come out of this scot-free, Saran. Everybody's...'

'Oh, it's no use us keeping on about it, anyway. Let's have a quiet cup of tea together before all the others get back here.' She started laying the table. 'And do you know what I've been thinking, Harry?'

'What?'

'That it's time you came to live here with me. You're getting on, and I hate to think of you in lodgings with strangers all the time.'

'I'm all right, Saran.'

'I don't know so much. Still, p'raps you know best; but if ever you fall out of work you'll have to come to live with me. Try a bit of this roast pork. It's lovely.'

What Saran called 'the proper family reunion' was out of the question until her Lewis came home from the convalescent place he had been sent to after the third operation he underwent. So whilst she was waiting him home Saran and the rest of the family tried their hand at settling down after more than four years of upside-down life, but it was hard to settle down, for things were still at sixes and sevens, even though the war was over. There was the pat-us-on-the-back coupon election, and the setting up of the Sankey Commission, the formation of the Triple Alliance, and ever so many other things. And there wasn't any too much work about, either.

'Well, you'd think that after so many men had been killed out of the way, that there'd be plenty of work for them as is left,' said Saran.

But there wasn't; for her Sam for months after he had been demobbed was unable to get a place back in the pit, and if it hadn't been for his father he'd have been longer still before getting back.

'If another bloody war broke out tomorrow, I'd be off to it like a shot,' cried her disgusted Sam one day.

'Hush, Sam.'

'I would, indeed to God, mam. Humph, got to beg for a job after having been for the best part of four bloody years... and now the owners want the mines decontrolled so as they can do what they like with us and charge what they like for coal. But if Sankey's Report is once accepted, the owners'll...'

'What's the Sankey Report?'

'Nationalisation...'

'Oh, shut up, Sam,' cried young Jim. 'You're always talking about work.'

'And so would you if you had a wife and three kids to keep.'

'What's going to happen when this reparations coal starts going to France and Italy and...'

'What's reparations coal?' Saran asked.

'Damn, don't you know anything, woman?' Glyn wanted to know from her.

'How can I when you knows all?'

'I know what reparations coal is, anyway.'

'And so would I had I been to where your leaders gab about it as often as you have. Now, what is it?'

'It's what Lloyd George...'

'Now, be fair, dad,' cried Charlie, who, young as he was, was a great admirer of Lloyd George.

'Shut up, you young... reparations coal is what Lloyd George...'

'Oh, don't make a long story of it by bothering about Lloyd George,' interrupted Sam. 'Reparations coal, mam, is the coal that Germany's got to supply from now on to people as used to have to buy coal from us. Now they're going to get coal for nothing.'

'Who said they're to get it for nothing?'

'Lloyd George and his bloody clique, woman.'

‘I asked Sam, not you. Anyway, you can’t blame people for taking what’s to be had for nothing. I only wish I could…’

‘You’ll alter your tune when the damned lot of us are without a day’s work, woman.’

‘What’s the odds as long as we can draw unemployment pay?’ young Jim said.

‘It’s not certain that the Government are going to let us miners draw unemployment pay,’ said Charlie.

‘Certainly we are, it’s been decided to bring miners into the scheme,’ said Sam.

‘What, pay for bein’ idle?’ said Saran.

‘Certainly, being as they can’t find us work, woman.’

‘Oh, there’ll be plenty of work soon,’ said Saran.

But there wasn’t, she found as time went on, and her man and boys had to be satisfied with what they could earn by working half-time. And it was now she found the benefit of her saving throughout the years of the war. Not that she drew much of it out of the post office, where she had a sum saved which would have surprised her man and her boys had she been fool enough to let them know. But although she rarely withdrew any of her savings, it nevertheless gave her a feeling of security, to know that it was there to tap as a last resource, and it helped her through the long period of short time which preceded the first great miners’ strike of the post war period, a strike during which soldiers and sailors were drafted into many of the mining areas.

‘That’s your bloody Lloyd George, that is,’ said Glyn. ‘Him as betrayed us over the Sankey Report.’

‘Well,’ said Saran, ‘if Lloyd George has done all the things you say he has…’

'He hasn't,' up and said young Charlie.

'What do you know?' asked his father.

'I know more about the Sankey Report than you do.'

'Then keep it to yourself,' Lewis, who hadn't been home long from the convalescent place, told him. 'I've heard nothing but Sankey and Reparations ever since I arrived home. What's the...'

'P'raps you'd rather us talk about horse racing?' growled his father.

'Much.'

'Well, it's a good job we're not all like you.'

'You're right,' said Saran, 'for if you'd all been cut about like him it isn't work you'd be talking about.'

'In any case,' said Sam, 'I don't think any of us will work for the next few months. We won't give in, that's certain; and the owners seem as determined as we are; so unless the Government steps in and does something...'

'Humph, Lloyd George and his clique. A fat lot they'll do, and if they do do anything, it'll be for the owners.'

'Your father's got Lloyd George on the brain,' said Saran. 'Now suppose you all go out so as I can get on with my work. Go on, Sam. And you others. Lord, to think of all you lot running in and out of the house whilst this stoppage is on. I've had enough of it in this first fortnight, so if it's going to last months, as you say, Sam...'

'Why worry?' laughed Lewis; 'isn't our Benny still doing well at the body-snatching game?'

'Well, he's the only one of the family working,' said Saran.

'What about Ossie slogging away making baskets in the institution? Isn't he working?' said Lewis.

'Come on, get out of my way, the lot of you,' cried Saran. 'Tell Kate that me and Jane are going to the pitchers tonight, Sam.'

CHAPTER 15
SHOUTING THROUGH

They were all there with her to dinner this Christmas again, but there was nobody in khaki present, though there were them as had wore khaki there. First there was Glyn, who thought himself head of the household, and who by this time had been over three years on the retired list. Yes, the first long stoppage of the pre-war years in the mining industry had definitely placed Glyn and most of the miners of his generation, the used-up generation, on the retired list.

'Finished – done with – scrapped,' Lewis was fond of reminding his father in that sour way in which he had taken to talk after his return home from the old war with his inside none too good. 'You and your like kept the home fires burning until we came home...'

'Yes, I was good enough for them then, but as soon...'

'And so was Lloyd George good enough for you during

the war,' said Charlie to his father more than once when he used to grouse about being out of work. 'But no sooner was the war over than you and your sort helped to vote him out of his job.'

'Certainly, after the way he done us over the Sankey business. But I'm not talking about Lloyd George now. What I'm saying is that after more'n fifty years underground, I'm without a day's work, and nothing but the workhouse in front of me.'

'Don't talk so damned dull,' Saran used to tell him when he mentioned the workhouse, she knowing that he knew full well that there was but little danger of his ending his days there, and it made her swear to hear him referring to it as a probability.

'Fifty years', Lewis said, 'would have got you a decent pension had you been a policeman, a teacher...'

'Ay, anything but a miner,' said his father.

'Well, why didn't your Labour Government...?'

'Now, woman, leave it at that. I've heard enough of your sneers against the Labour Government.'

And with such talk the family marched along under the arches of the years when Britain was shouting its way through the first half-dozen years of the peace. 'Nothing but chopping and changing, shouting and old disturbances ever since the boys came back from the old war,' said Saran. 'First it was Lloyd George, then it was Baldwin; and after him MacDonald – and now Baldwin again. And none of 'em seems to make the slightest difference. No matter what they say, the men are still without work; the pits go on working half-time – our Sam didn't do more than three shifts a week last year, three shifts for which he drew twenty-six shillings. Isn't that right, Sam?'

'As if we all didn't know what he worked and how much he earned,' growled Glyn.

'I was talking to Sam, not to you.'

'But you talk so damned soft, woman. I've told you until I'm sick of telling you that there'll be no hope for us until we get a Labour Government with power, with a clear majority.'

'Well, things are no better in this district now that you've got this Wallhead.'

'He's only one, woman.'

'Yes, and so am I only one. See what those children out in the back kitchen want, Jane. I miss old Marged to look after the children. Still, she's where she can't be worried with 'lections and strikes and pits closing...'

'Here, if you're going to talk about where old Marged...'

'No, it's all right, Lewis, my boy. It was just those children out in the back kitchen shouting for tendance that made me think of the poor old soul, for she was ever so good with the children. Why don't you try and eat a bit of something, Lewis?'

'Because I don't feel like anything.'

'Here, try this bit of white meat off the breast.'

'I tell you I don't want anything.'

'Leave the chap alone, mam,' cried Sam. 'I'll have the bit off the breast being as he don't want it.'

'Indeed you won't after gutsing a leg that was nearly as big as your own. Will you have this bit of breast, Harry?'

'If nobody else wants it...'

'It's all the same if they do. Go on, eat it. Where are you going, Lewis?'

'Up to have a lie down on the bed.'

'But I haven't made the beds today yet. Wait until...'

'You stay and look after these people; the bed's good enough for me. Have a good time, you people. Here, share this among the kids.'

'Well,' said Saran to the remainder of the family after Lewis had gone upstairs, 'after all their operations, that boy's inside is far from right. Terrible pains he gets, and he don't eat enough to keep a robin alive. Only last night – and not only last night, either, I found him leaning out of the window groaning and gasping for breath. You could hear him a mile away...'

'I never heard him,' said Glyn.

'You wouldn't after all the Christmas beer you'd necked; but he was bad last night again all the same. And he won't let anyone do anything for him – not even me. No, he just looks at me as though I'd – well, as if it was my fault. You haven't finished, Benny?'

'Yes, thanks, mam.'

'And so have I, thank you,' said Annie, rising. 'And you'll excuse us now, for we've got some friends coming to our place to spend the evening.' Jane sniffed loudly. 'I expect the boys are ready, too,' she said as she walked to the door of the back kitchen, into which Saran had crowded all her grandchildren. 'Come along, Ronald, dear. And you, Eric. Oh, dear me, look at that mess on your trousers.'

'Yes, ma, but Cousin David threw a potato...'

'Where the hell did you dig them names for 'em, Benny?'

his father wanted to know. 'I don't remember any Erics or Ronalds in our family.'

'But there were in mine,' Annie told him as she wiped her son's trousers more or less clean of the greasy marks left by the potatoes his cousin, Jane's boy, had bombarded him with. 'Sorry to have to rush away,' she said to Saran, 'but our new maid is not as careful with the children as our old maid was…'

'Then why didn't you bring them up with you?' said Saran.

'Oh, I wouldn't think of bringing the three little ones out in this weather. Are you ready, Ben?'

'That woman makes me sick,' exploded Jane as soon as they were over the door. 'Ever since our Benny was made super'…'

'Now, Jane, don't start,' said her mother.

'Mam, that woman's as false as Benny's false arm. And did you hear the way she talked about her maids? Maids; and it isn't so long ago…'

'Don't start, I tell you,' said Saran. 'Annie's all right in her way…'

'Humph, in her way.'

'Yes; and she'll see that Benny and the boys get every chance to get on. Her two eldest have both won scholarships to go to the higher-grade school…'

'And Benny's won himself a bad name chasing the agents under him off their legs so that she can play the la-di-da.'

Glyn belched before he said angrily: 'How is it, gel, that every time Benny and his wife come up here you're talking about 'em as soon as their backs are turned? I think you must be jealous of 'em; but if you only had half as much brain as our Benny...'

'And if you had quarter as much,' interjected Saran, 'you'd be...'

'Come on, Tom, let's go out for a stroll?' said Jim.

'Where are you two going in this rain?' Saran wanted to know.

'Ask no questions and you'll be told no lies,' replied Jim.

'I can tell you where they're going to, mam,' said Charlie.

'Hullo, mouthy,' said Tom.

'Going to play solo again in the same place as they were at last night,' said Charlie.

'And now you know,' said Jim as he went out with Tom.

'Not a bad Christmas,' said Saran. 'We've all had a belly-ful, and there's still a bit of enjoyment to come.' She sighed. 'But I'm worried about our Lewis, about his inside. And he won't have the doctor up to see him. Had enough of doctors, he says when I want to fetch the doctor to have a look at him.'

'He drinks too much, that's what it is,' said Jane.

'Bookies must drink some,' said Saran.

'And some bookies drinks a lot,' said Jane, 'and our Lewis is one of them as drinks a lot. Spends more on drink each week than Ossie gets pension, so no wonder his inside is troubling him. And he does more than drink, too. He's out till the early hours of the morning with that...'

'Hush, your uncle Harry'll hear you. Jane.'

'What?'

'I'm going to make your uncle Harry come to live here with us.'

'But he won't, for him and dad...'

'Your dad had better not open his mouth. I can't bear to think of your uncle Harry trying to live in lodgings on what little the parish allows him. Whilst he had that little job...'

'How did he come to lose that job?' asked Sam's wife.

'He didn't lose it, it was took off him and given to a young feller back from the war with only one leg...'

'Oh,' cried Jane as she dropped and smashed one of her mother's best dinner plates.

'Oh, you careless article, you. It would have paid me to wash the things up myself.'

'Then why didn't you?' snapped Jane.

'Because I didn't, butterfingers. There, there, I didn't mean it, fathead. When is Ossie going to bring me that shopping basket he promised to make me?'

'He finished it on Saturday, but he forgot to bring it home from the institution. I'll remind him about it. When are you having Uncle Harry here?'

'He is here, isn't he?' replied Saran in a whisper. 'And when he rises from that chair he's sitting in and thinks about going, then I'm going to tell him that he is home. Charlie shall go down for his things as soon as he gets back from the pitchers. Now, you two see if you can put those plates and dishes away without breaking any, for I'm going to make a nice cup of tea.' Into the living room she went from the back kitchen. 'Hullo, Harry. Did you think we'd all gone out?'

'No, my gel; but I was thinking about going.'

'Going where?'

'Back down home, of course.'

'You are home, Harry. Now, listen a minute. There's a spare bed here – well, there will be, for I can put Charlie in with Lewis, he won't mind Charlie. So the four boys'll be in that double-bedded room, then the little back room will be free for you.'

'But I've told you before, Saran…'

'Yes, and I've told you before, Harry, that you needn't think that Glyn'll be against you coming to live with us; and as for the boys, the boys'll be glad to have you here,' she lied. 'And if ever they object to you living here, then they can go and look for a place elsewhere. You needn't bother with any of them though, Harry. I want you to come to me. You'll be a comfort to me now that that…'

'Will I indeed, Saran?'

'Of course you will, Uncle Harry,' said Jane. 'I thought you were going to make us all a cup of tea, mam.'

'So I will. You'll have a cup, Harry?'

'Please, Saran.'

'And you're staying here with me?'

'I'll let you know before the night's out, after I've had a talk to you alone.'

'Then that'll be as soon as we've had this cup of tea,' Jane assured him. 'S'long, mam.'

'S'long – it was a lovely dinner,' said Sam's wife.

'Now, Saran,' Harry began as soon as they were alone.

'Now what?'

'What you said about me stopping here always with you.'

'There's no need to bother any more about that.'

'But there is, Saran; better now than after I've caused an old bother by coming here.'

'There'll be no bother, I tell you.'

'Are you sure?'

'Of course I am; that is if you won't bother the boys about – well, you know, Harry. They're not bad boys, but they don't like anyone to bother 'em about their souls, or about their way of carryin' on. So if you'll only leave them to me, Harry.... As for Glyn – but there, you know Glyn. Grouse, grouse, yet as harmless as a child. He'll be all right...'

'But haven't you got all you can do to keep your own without having me to keep again? All I get from the parish is...'

'Who wants to know what you get from the parish? To hell with the parish, say I. And keep my own, did you say? Who is more my own than you are? Ain't you the only one I've got left of our side of the family? And don't you worry about how I'm going to keep you. I'll tell you, Harry – though I wouldn't tell anyone else, and you mustn't tell anybody, either. I've got a tidy bit put by, for I've never touched a penny of my Meurig's 'lotment, nor what I used to put to it. Then Lewis is very good, and me an' him... but never mind that. All you need know is that I'll be able to manage without troubling the parish or anyone else for as long as we'll... and you've got to come to us, Harry, for you're getting on, you know.'

'Well, if you think...'

'I know everything will be all right.'

And that's how it was.

When Glyn, all merry and bright he was, landed home from the Full Moon with his son, Sam, and his blind and merry son-in-law, Ossie, the first thing Saran told him was: 'Our Harry's going to stay here with us from now on.'

'Eh?'

'You heard.'

'Well, you needn't bite a bloody man's head off.'

'Where is Uncle Harry, then?' Sam wanted to know.

'Upstairs in his room having a lie down. And you look as if you could do with a lie down, too, Sam.'

'I'm all right.'

'Of course he's all right,' said Glyn. 'Sit down, Sam.'

'Yes, but not here,' said Saran. 'Off home you go, and you, Ossie. Home to your wives, the pair of you.'

'Driven from home, are we?' laughed Ossie, his sightless eyes alone without laughter.

'I'll meet the pair of you in the Full Moon about opening-time,' Glyn called after them.

'Yes, and mind that you're there sharp at opening-time to meet your father, Sam.'

'Don't try to be funny, woman,' growled Glyn. 'If me and the boys do any harm by taking a drink or two together once a year...'

'Once a year? Now you're trying to be funny.'

It was to please Harry that Saran first went to the Sisterhood, but she afterwards kept on going twice each week because she liked going, and because she felt she could be of service to the underpaid and overworked young minister as a sort of compulsory arbitrator in the continual disputes which made the Sisterhood meetings so real and entertaining to her, she being one who believed, rightly or wrongly, that a row to clear the air every once in a while was most necessary. She took Jane and Sam's wife along to the Sisterhood with her to see how she was 'managing 'em' one night, and that one night was enough for Sam's wife and Jane, who were of the generation following that to which nearly all the Sisters of the Sisterhood belonged. So from that night onwards Saran went on 'managing' the Sisterhood without whatever support the presence of members of her own family might lend her.

So her week was now full right up. Two evenings to the Sisterhood, two evenings with Jane and Sam's wife and their children to the 'pitchers' – admission to which she invariably paid for all, as she also did on the one evening of the week they almost filled the front row of the gallery of the 'threeatre'. Then she spared one evening of the week to sit with Harry, for he was getting on – 'and I mightn't have him for long'. Sundays, of course, there was always plenty to do. Getting dinner ready, and seeing to this, that and the other; and it was on Sundays that her grandchildren mostly were running in to pay their respects, in return for which they hoped she would hand out some coppers; failing her, there was always the dry-spoken Uncle Lewis with the twisted smile, who was a street-bookie to whom a sixpence was nothing at the end of a good week. So when 'Granny' failed them they could always hopefully turn to Uncle Lewis, though their other three uncles, Jim, Tom and Charlie, hardly ever forked out. But where were *they* to get it, for they weren't street-bookies. No, Jim was on the dole, Tom was working half-time and talking about going away up to some place near Oxford where a pal of his had got a job at a motorworks. Charlie was luckier than Tom, for there were some weeks when the pit worked as many as five shifts.

But even though there was little or no prospect of copper or silver, the grandchildren – even Benny's stuck-up boys, though Annie was a lot more to blame for their being stuck up than Benny was – thought it well worth while going up to Granny's, if only to see old Uncle Harry, whose face was covered with whiskers, but whose eyes were bright and twinkling, sitting in the low armchair near the fire. All the grandchildren liked him, for he used to tell them stories about the days when people thought it wonderful to ride from Merthyr to Dowlais on top of the bus, the days when never a word of English was spoken by anyone – 'except the old Irish that came over to work in the works, of course'. And the children laughed to think that people in those days thought it grand to have a ride on top of a bus.

'And didn't you use to fight bare-fist, Uncle Harry?' the eldest of the grandchildren, who had heard their fathers talk about Uncle Harry's fighting days, would sometimes ask.

Then Uncle Harry would look at them with sadness dimming the twinkling eyes that looked out on them from the matted whiskers, and Granny would cut in with: 'Now, off you go to play, all of you. What do you want to know about fights for?' But Jane and Ossie's eldest boy, who was pretty smart with the gloves for a boy of thirteen, was always pestering old Uncle Harry to talk about his fights. And their uncle Lewis, the generous street-bookie, was every bit as bad in that respect. On his bad evenings, evenings when his inside that had been cut about so was giving him gyp, he'd sit opposite old Uncle Harry and start talking about boxing to him. And sometimes when he felt more evil still he would start talking about the angels of

Mons and religion and God in a way, to say the least of it, that wasn't to his old Uncle Harry's liking. One night – Lewis was sitting on the low three-legged stool all hunched up with pain, and old Uncle Harry was seated in the low armchair which stood at that side of the fireplace where the oven which Saran said was not much good for cooking in was – it was after Saran had left for the Sisterhood, it was, and Glyn and Jim and Tom and Charlie had gone off somewhere, and there was only them two, Lewis and his uncle Harry, left in the house. Lewis lit another cigarette after he had finished poking the fire and said: 'Great fight at the Drill Hall last night, Uncle Harry.'

'Indeed.'

'Yes; for the Welsh middleweight championship. Went all the way, it did, and every round full of thrills. I backed the winner for a tenner. Wouldn't you like to see a real good scrap once again, Uncle Harry?'

'No, my boy.'

'Say you don't know. If you saw one... our Sam's kid's pretty useful, you know, Uncle Harry. You know that eldest boy of Sam's?'

'But he hasn't left school.'

'Soon will, though; and now's the time he should be taken in hand. I think I'll send him to Danny Jones' stable as soon as I can get him out of school.'

'You talk about the boy just as if he was a colt; and as if you was his father,' said old Uncle Harry with more heat than usual.

'Sam'll be damned glad to let me start the boy in Danny's stable, for it's different to the time when you used to scrap with the raw ’uns, Uncle Harry; for if a boy’s class these days he can make big dough. Anyway, what would he get down the pit with Sam? – that’s if Sam did manage to get him a job there. Shice, that’s what he’d get in the pit. But after Danny’s worked on him for a couple of years, and we get him matched the way that’ll bring him on, he’ll be in the running for a championship, which’ll mean thousands – yes, thousands – when he gets there. And there’s no reason why he shouldn’t if only he’s handled the right way. Look at the dough little Jimmy Wilde made; and our Sam’s boy’s more useful than Jimmy was at his age and got a bigger wallop.’

‘Wallop – dough – championship,’ muttered old Uncle Harry. ‘And with them all he’s got nothing. Them things don’t count with God, my boy.’

‘Oh, I forgot, you believe in God and His angels, don’t you, Uncle Harry?’

‘Of course I do, my boy.’

‘Perhaps you believe that there was angels at Mons that time?’

‘Why shouldn’t I? We know for sure that the devils was there, so why not angels to help those the devils was making kill each other?’

Lewis laughed. ‘Well, our Benny was at Mons, and the only angels he saw had bombs under their wings, which they dropped on the wounded on their way to hos...’

‘Please, Lewis.’

‘Some angels they were. And God – I never saw God out there either.’

‘Did you ever look for Him, my boy?’

Lewis waited until the pain which was twisting him up had subsided, then he said: 'I did like hell. Had all I could do to look out for them – devils did you say they were? – that poked their bayonets into my guts.' He groaned, then cried aloud: 'And if there is a God, and Him there to stop 'em, I hope He now gets the same bloody pains in His guts as I'm getting.'

'Lewis bach...'

'Here, what are you sitting in the dark for, Harry?' cried Saran as she bustled in from the passage. 'I put plenty of coppers in the meter before I went out, so let's have some light. There... oh, you're here, Lewis. I thought you'd have been gone out by now. How are you feeling now, anyway?'

'Eighteen carat.'

'Then what about taking a bit to eat? I won't be a minute...'

'I'll just have a Bombay oyster.'

'One or two eggs?'

'Two.'

'Right. Nothing but talk about this general strike that's supposed to be coming off up at the Sisterhood tonight. What's a *general* strike?'

Lewis explained briefly.

'Oh, so that's it. Well, we don't want general or any other strikes to knock us flat in this district, for we've been knocked flat enough already,' she said as she broke two eggs into a tumbler.

'This district will be knocked flatter yet,' Lewis prophesied.

'Can't be knocked much flatter than it is, for there's only

a few pits going out of twenty pits and scores of levels and drifts that was going before the war. And only one of the steelworks going, and that's not going half its time. And you say that this general strike is going to stop that, too. Here you are, Lewis,' she said as she handed him the tumbler into which she had broken the two eggs. 'Here's the pepper and vinegar. During the strikes we had when all you children were small we used to depend mostly on the places where the steelworks was, for the steelworks kept on working, and I used to go to them places – didn't I, Harry? To beg food to keep going.... Are you going out, Lewis?'

'Yes, may as well,' said Lewis wearily. 'I ought to shave, but... no. I think I'll wear that pinstripe suit.'

'Suppose you finish that Bombay oyster you asked for,' said Saran. 'And suppose you come home in decent time for a change tonight. You know how your father...'

'Oh, give it a rest, mam.'

'It's you wants rest, and at the proper time. And you want to put less of what you do put down that neck and into that belly of yours.'

'Will you bloody well shut up and go and get me that suit I've asked for? You make me... I'm sorry, mam. I'm feeling all...'

'I know, my boy. Sit down. But you've got to wash. Which shoes are you wearing?'

'Black, of course, with the pinstripe.'

'Of course. And your bowler hat?'

'Of course.'

The general strike started and was soon over, but the miners' strike went on and on, and Tom got fed up and went to where a pal of his was working in a motorworks near Oxford, and he was lucky enough to get a job there, and there he is to this day, married now and the father of four children; and it costs 'em quite a bit to come back home every Christmas like they do to have the Christmas with Saran, who manages to push them in somehow for the few days they are with her. Tom's wife is the only Englishwoman in the family up to now, but Saran says she's none the worse for being English, judging by what little she has seen of her. She knows how to look after her children, anyway.

And it was whilst the general strike was on that Saran saw and heard A. J. Cook, whose name was in everyone's mouth, and whose photo was in all the papers. She had heard in her time of many miners' leaders, but none of them had ever caused such a stir as this man was causing. So when she heard that he was coming to speak from the bandstand which stands in the hollow in the centre of the new Park – not the Cyfarthfa Park nor the Penydarren Park, but the one on the height above the town, the one where they fixed the first war memorial – she said to Jane and Sam's wife: 'I wonder whether there'll be any women there?'

Jane laughed at her and said: 'Of course there will. One would think to hear you talk that we hadn't had the vote. Didn't you hear what the town crier said. Women specially invited was what he said.'

'Then we'll go,' said Saran.

And the weather was beautiful on the day when the great

A. J. Cook came down from the north of England where he had been rallying the miners of an area in which there was danger of a breakaway, and being as it was such a lovely day Saran suggested to Harry that he too should go across as far as the new Park to hear the great A. J. Cook, but it happened to be Harry's day for visiting the workhouse, and he said that nothing on earth would make him miss his weekly visit to the workhouse, where there were those who waited hopefully and not in vain for his coming. So Saran said: 'All right, Harry,' and off she went across to the new Park with Jane, who was carrying the third baby she had had by Ossie during his sightlessness; and as they walked across the top to the new Park Saran noted that her Jane was getting fatter than ever, and she also noted that Sam's wife, who was on her left with a baby in her arms, too, was getting skinnier than ever.

'A lovely day if ever there was one,' said Saran. 'I expect all the district will turn out to hear this Cook today...'

'It said in the paper that he addressed a crowd of fifty thousand somewhere in England,' Sam's wife said.

'I seen a picture of him speaking somewhere with his coat off, and there was a terrible lot of people there, too,' said Jane.

'And so there will be here today,' said Saran, pointing to where people were pouring through the gateway into the new Park. 'Look, there's many going in there as are not miners or anything to do with miners. I expect it's because there's been so much talk about the man. That's why I wanted your uncle Harry to come, but he wouldn't miss his day at the workhouse for anything.'

'No more than he misses us to beg something to take to the workhouse for them old...'

'God help 'em,' said Saran. 'Them as are all right are let out a day or two a week to beg a bit of 'bacco and whatever else they can get, but there's them as can't be trusted out because they can't walk, or because they're a bit soft in the head or – or have got anything the matter that stops 'em coming out into the town. And it's them that Harry begs for. He gets a halfcrown every week from Lewis alone, and then he gets money and things from others; and so he goes loaded up every Thursday to see his friends, as he calls them. Takes 'bacco for one, snuff for another, a stick of Spanish for another; poor old Charlie Rowlands would die if he didn't have his stick of Spanish...'

'And after he's handed the things out I expect Uncle Harry makes 'em have some preaching and prayers.'

'And what if he do? I could listen to your uncle Harry praying any day, that's if I had time. Prays lovely, he do.... Oh, look at that crowd. We'd better go up there where those trees are.'

'But shall we be able to hear there?' asked Sam's wife.

'Yes, if the speakers've got any sort of voices. Oh, look, there's our Lewis. Well, this is the first meeting I've known him attend since he's home from the war.'

'Humph, he's got another new suit,' said Sam's wife enviously.

'Yes, a bookie like him got to dress tidy, my gel,' Saran told her. 'When he's dressed well he gets the bets of those that puts it on thick and heavy, for they think that a man with a good suit on is good for whatever they're likely to win. But I'll ask Lewis to let Sam have that old grey suit of his, though it's not what you can call old, either. Here we are. Well, we'll be able to see, but whether we'll be able to hear or not is more'n I can say. Well, well, I've never in all my life seen so many people at one time in one place. There must be millions here.'

'Don't talk so soft, mam,' said Jane. 'Would you like to hold the baby for me a minute?'

'Why, are you going somewhere?' asked Saran, meaning by 'somewhere' one of the two ladies' lavatories around which the park superintendent had made to grow a beautiful double screen of flowering trees.

'No, I'm not going anywhere,' replied Jane. 'I only thought that you might like to nurse him a bit.'

'No, I don't want to nurse him,' said Saran. 'I've nursed enough of you.... Who is that man they're making way for? Is that Cook?'

'No, that's Willie Paul, the communist – fine speaker he is,' said a man standing near to where Saran, Jane and Sam's wife had seated themselves under the spreading tree. 'You'll soon know when Cook's coming,' the man went on. 'You'll hear such a cheer... here he comes. Yes, that's him. Good old Cook,' the man shouted as a roar of welcome went up from the crowd to frighten the birds out of all the trees in the Park.

'Yes, I can tell him from the photo of him I seen,' said Saran. 'Seems to be a tidy little man,' she added as those already gathered on the bandstand rushed to shake hands with the man who was front-page stuff all the time.

Before he was introduced the chairman called upon the

noted Willie Paul to say a few words, but not before he had assured the crowd that he, the chairman, was not a communist. Then he went on to say that he agreed with the united front of all sections of the Labour Movement for achieving victory for the miners. Then he stepped back and the noted communist let go at the General Council of the TUC for all he was worth, and said that but for Cook the miners of the country would have been left at the mercy of the bosses, and that the miners could go on fighting knowing that their Russian comrades were behind them to a man. 'Great speaker, isn't he?' admiringly murmured the man standing behind Saran to no one in particular.

Then after the noted communist had finished and stepped backwards, people crowded together on the bandstand around Cook. The chairman, to show the working of the united front, called first on an ILP'er to speak, and after him on the chairman of the Trades and Labour Council, an official Labour man was he, and lastly on the great Cook himself. And what a welcome he had as he took off his coat to speak. The press-men stood with pencils at the ready, and the two policemen who had learnt shorthand and had been told off to 'take him down' that day also stood with pencils at the ready. And the police who stood off some little distance cocked their ears. And the runner stood ready near the PA man to rush away to the post office with the telegram which might or might not be flashed over the wires and under the seas to all parts of the world. 'Order. Keep quiet.'

And what a welcome Harry had from those hopefully waiting him when he stumped out into the backyard of the workhouse, the yard where all the wood was sawn and afterwards chopped and tied into bundles by the fittest of the inmates.

'Here's Hally, here's Hally, here's Hally,' old Charlie Rowlands, who wasn't half there, kept shouting as he danced around Harry. 'My Spanish, my Spanish,' he kept on demanding, driveling spittle all down the front of his clothes. He had been let out to do his own begging for 'bacco and black Spanish until the day when he forgot himself and started to piss on the pavement right in front of St David's School just as the girls of standards four and five were coming out of school. So the schoolmistress complained and Charlie was not allowed out after that. And there were many others like him who had offended in some way the people of the district, and were stopped from coming out into the town. Some of them were not even allowed to pull the firewood trolly through our town. Then there were others who shook too bad, smelt too bad, looked too bad to be allowed out in the town; and it was little they were able to get in the way of tobacco, snuff, cakes, sweets and so on until Harry started visiting the workhouse some time before old Davies, MA, died there. From that time on Harry took it upon himself to collect, for those who could not collect for themselves, the little luxuries which the workhouse authorities left it to others to provide or not to provide.

They all danced around Harry until he sat down in their midst with his peg leg pointing north and the bundle of good things on his lap.

'Quiet, my brothers,' he said, and there was quiet, for, daft though some of them were, they knew that the share-out would not begin until they were all silent and ready to take part in the little ceremony for which the handing out of each little gift was the occasion. Nothing much, though. Each recipient kneeled in front of Harry on one knee only, and as he took his gift said: 'Thank God for sending Harry with my bit of 'bacco' – or whatever it was that they received. And after they had all received their gifts they would all, in the summer when fine, seat themselves in a circle on the floor around Harry, smoking, snuffing or eating sweets, and listen to a report from him of what he had observed out in the world during the week that had elapsed since his previous visit. In the winter he submitted his report to them in the small mess room, the cleaning of which Harry superintended at the close of the gathering. And he also, as Jane suspected, prayed and said a few words which might be described as a short sermon.

'Now, brothers,' he was telling them, 'there's another day after today, remember, and I can't get here until next Thursday.' Charlie Rowlands pocketed what remained of his stick of Spanish and went on licking the black, sticky and sweet spittle which he had allowed to drivel into the bristles on his chin. The others pocketed pipes and packets of snuff and settled themselves to listen to their newsman. 'The world outside is upside down, my brothers,' he went on to tell them. 'Masters and men and the Government are at sixes and sevens more than ever they've been, and little heed is being paid to the will of God the Father, or to the message of Christ our Saviour. Men out there in the world are being made even more useless than we who are finishing our days here together. The men back from the big war are growing more bitter, and their children are growing up with none of the things everybody thought their fathers fought for, to look forward to. Men are no longer looking to God for guidance, but to this man and that man. Today, up there in the new Park...'

'... men are now solid again in the areas that looked liked letting us down. After a solidarity campaign in which I am pleased to say that I have been supported by all the Labour MPs with the exception of a reactionary handful – and we shall deal with them when the time comes – I am now in a position to report that our men everywhere are as solid as ever they were. And I am also pleased to be able to inform you that we are winning the sympathy of the British public. Men of standing; dignitaries of the Church; ay, and some of the most fair-minded of the owners, are now prepared to admit...'

'... a man who was selling needles and cotton. I seen him, brothers, going from door to door in the rain as I was sheltering with my sister in the doorway of the Royal Stores. Wet through he must have been, and still the people who answered the knock slammed the doors in his face. As one door opened to him the music of the wireless or a gramophone came out loud, and the woman who opened the door shouted loud enough for me to hear her: "*No,*" and slammed the door. It's a terrible thing, brothers, to have to go from door to door, trying to sell needles and cotton when it's raining hard. And do you know what I thought, brothers? What if Jesus came selling needles and cotton to our doors, and none of us knew Him, and we slammed the door in His face? Wouldn't we be sorry when we got to know Who it was we had turned away without as much as a kind word? Then, next day – but it wasn't raining that day – I seen men singing as they walked along in the gutter. Singing lovely they was, but people passed by without as much as looking at 'em. And that's how it is. The world is gone hard, brothers. No man should have to go from door to door selling needles and cotton in the rain, or sing in the gutter, either. But when they're forced to do it, don't you think, brothers, that people should be kinder to 'em? Of course they should, for we never know...'

'... stand by this resolution in which you've pledged yourselves to remain firm and loyal. Whilst doing all in our power to effect a settlement, we shall...'

'Come on, let's go,' said Saran.

'Wait until Cook finishes,' said Jane.

'I've heard all I want to hear,' said Saran, moving off.

'So have I,' said Sam's wife, following her.

So Jane followed her mother through the crowd and out of the Park to where she stopped for a minute to look at the War Memorial outside the gates.

'Our Meurig's name – and our Mervyn's name – is on there,' she said before moving on. 'They're...'

'What?' said Jane. 'Oh, nothing,' said Saran.

CHAPTER 16

ALL THE WORLD'S A STAGE

'Who do you think's coming to the theatre shortly, mam?' said Benny one day when he stopped his car outside his mother's house and ran in to see her for a minute.

'Hullo, stranger,' she said, for his visits were few and far between since he had gone to live up The Walk and had bought a secondhand car in which to drive about after his agents, and also to take his stuck-up Annie – who was more stuck-up than ever since she had moved to The Walk, and since her two eldest boys had won entrance exams into the University College at Cardiff – and her youngest children for a run on Sundays. Fair play to him, Benny had more than once offered to take his mother for a run, but she said: 'No, thank you.'

'Stranger?' he repeated. 'Why, I called in to see you last week, didn't I, Uncle Harry?'

'Yes, and I forgot to tell your mother, my boy.'

'Never mind,' said Saran. 'You're getting grey, Benny, but that's better than going bald like our Lewis. How is Annie and the children?'

'Fine; when are you coming up to see us in our new house?'

'Some day... who did you say was coming to the threeatre?'

'Louis Calvert.'

'Well, well, he must be an old man. He was a fine actor; when did you say he was coming?'

'The week after next.'

'Then I must try and go to see him. Where's he been all these years, I wonder?'

'I think he's been in America. Well, I must be off.'

'Yes, look after your work, my boy, for there's little enough of it about. I don't have to get up in the morning for anybody now.'

'Isn't Charlie working?'

'There's nobody working here – except Lewis, of course. He's got his bit of business.'

Benny grunted. There was little love lost between him and his brother Lewis, who had the trick of making his nose express his contempt for his eldest brother whenever they chanced to meet anywhere. Never spoke as they passed by, but Lewis' nose moved in a way that left but little room for doubt in the eldest brother's mind regarding his standing in the younger brother's estimation.

'Yes, I know he has,' Benny said as he pulled on his new driving gloves. 'I've seen him fairly often doing business, as you call it, on the street. It's a wonder to me the police haven't...'

'Mind your own business, Benny,' his mother told him.

'Oh, all right. All the same, I think it's a bit thick to drag a blind man into it.'

'What are you talking about?'

'You know what I'm talking about, mam. He's got Ossie hanging about the new urinal in Pontmorlais Square all day and every day taking slips for him.'

'That's where you're making a mistake, Benny. Ossie takes no slips from anybody, though if you want to know the truth – though Ossie gets well paid for it – all he does is to hang about there so as Lewis can unload money and papers that Ossie brings straight up here to me.'

'And risks imprisonment in doing so.'

'He risks nothing, nobody working for Lewis has to risk anything, for the police... never mind, off you go to your work, Benny. You look after your own boys, and I'll... how are they getting on at the college?'

'They're getting on all right.'

'I'm glad of that. Tell 'em to come up and see me when they're home next. Give my love to Annie.'

'You didn't mean that, Saran,' said Harry after Benny had gone.

'What didn't I mean?'

'That what you said about giving your love to Annie.'

'P'raps I didn't.'

'You know you didn't.'

'All right, then, I didn't. She's a bit too much of it.'

'In what way?'

'In every way – but don't let's bother about her.'

'You're wrong, Saran. Annie's all right, and you know it. You listen too much to Jane, who is far from being fair to Annie.'

'P'raps you're right again. And Louis Calvert coming to act in the threeatre after all these years.'

'Was that right what Benny said about Ossie being on the street for Lewis, Saran?'

'What if it is?'

'Well, it's not right, that's all.'

'Harry, please don't bother your head with matters of this sort. This is something between Ossie and Lewis, and my Lewis never in all his life done the dirty on anybody. Ossie's got a houseful of children, and his bit of pension and what he gets for making a few baskets isn't enough to keep that lot. So Lewis...'

'Ossie must trust...'

'Yes, I know he must; but when Lewis pays him well and looks after him, then I don't see much harm in him trusting a bit in Lewis as well...'

'But all this gambling, Saran.'

'Well, in the pitchers, Harry, you can see the best in the land doing it on racecourses and in Monte Carlo and all sorts of places...'

'Doing what?' cried Glyn as he came in after having been to the Labour Exchange.

'Gambling,' said Harry.

'Never gambled in my life,' said Glyn.

'You've done worse,' said Saran.

'If you mean the drop of drink, woman, then let me tell

you that these boys of yours can drink their share. True, I drank a drop of beer when I was their age, but I used to work twelve hours a day, which is more than they do.'

'Ay, you drank every night of the week because you had too much to do; and they drinks because they haven't got anything at all to do, because they're fed up.'

'Where they get the money to get it with is what puzzles me. I expect it's by gambling – and p'raps worse.'

'Now, Glyn, don't you try to say…'

'Well, they're out all hours of the night; a man can't lock his door and go to his bed tidy as he should do. So they're either whoring half the night…'

'They calls it Love in the pitchers, Glyn,' Saran informed him.

'All right, funny one. Then p'raps you can tell me what they call this in the pictures,' he said, throwing his now useless unemployment card and a form on to the table.

'What are these?'

'Well, you know everything…'

'I'm asking you what they are, Glyn?'

'It's my no-good dole card, and a form to fill in for my old-age.'

'I never dreamt you was as old as that. Are you as old as that?'

'The man told me that I should have been on the old-age pension months ago, and that I'd be lucky if I didn't have to pay back all the extra I've drawn since I was old enough for the old-age.'

'Then you can tell him that he'd be luckier to get it. Yes, I expect you are old enough. How old is our Benny?'

'I don't know. Somewhere between forty and fifty, I expect.'

'Don't be... and yet he must be. Half a minute now. Isn't Harry here as old as you?'

Glyn looked across at his heavily whiskered brother-in-law who was sitting in the best chair in the house – the most comfortable chair, anyway – and he was always in it. 'He's years older than me, I expect,' he sourly said.

'I know I'm not,' said Harry.

'Anyway, I expect you're old enough to draw the old-age if Glyn is,' said Saran. 'I must get Benny to look into this for me.'

'And what about yourself?' said Glyn.

'I'm not near as old as you are. But I must get Benny to see about the forms for you and Harry at once.'

'What about something to eat?' said Glyn.

She almost grieved herself until she was ill when she discovered that Harry could have been drawing old-age for about six months before he did. 'Never mind,' she said to Harry, 'you're all right now, now that you're drawing old-age. None of 'em here can say they're keeping you now – not that any of 'em have ever said it,' she hastened to inform him.

She went to the theatre to see the actor who had delighted her way back in the old days. 'He's an old man,' was all she said to Jane on the way home from the theatre after she had seen Louis Calvert in a play she didn't much care for. 'Yes, an old man,' she said again as they were all sitting down to a cup of tea in her house before separating for the night.

'Who's an old man?' said Lewis, who was nursing his pain on the stool near the fire.

'The man we've been to see in the threeatre tonight, Louis Calvert, a man I took most of you in the shawl to see act. I remember him in *Proof* – yes, that was easily his best part. Oh, he was lovely in that. Another cup of tea, Jane?'

'No more for me, thank you, mam.'

'I'll have half a cup,' said Sam's wife.

'They're going to run a liberal candidate,' cried Charlie as he rushed into the house. 'And he's one of our young liberal speakers. What do you think of that?'

'Think of what?' said Lewis.

' "Think of what?" ' repeated Charlie. 'Well, you're a bright lot, you are. Perhaps none of you know that there's going to be a general election?'

'When haven't there been elections?' said his mother. 'Nothing but elections since the war. Will you drink a cup of tea, Lewis?'

'No, thanks.'

'Well, I'm off,' said Jane as her father walked in full of excitement also.

'Your Ossie's just gone up the road – you'll catch him if you hurry,' he told Jane, then he went on to ask: 'What do you think?'

Lewis groaned, rose from where he was sitting and said: 'I'm off out.'

'At this time of night?' cried his father.

'Shut up – get me my light overcoat and soft hat from the wardrobe, mam.'

'Certainly, my boy.'

'Well, I'm damned, here's a time to go out, if you like,' said Glyn as he heard the door slam behind Lewis. 'Where's Harry?'

'In bed. What do you want him for?' asked Saran.

'I don't want him, but I'll have the armchair now that he's out of it.' He went and sat down in the armchair.

'Did you see Sam anywhere?' Sam's wife asked him.

'Sam, indeed. Yes, I've seen him; seen too much of him. Trying to dig up a communist candidate to fight our man, that's...'

'Who's your man?' Saran asked.

'She's trying to be funny again,' Glyn explained to the others. 'My man's Wallhead, and you know it. And here's Sam, my own son, working like hell to bring a communist out against him. And here's this feller,' he went on, pointing the finger of scorn at Charlie, 'helping Lloyd George...'

'Isn't he dead?' said Saran.

'Isn't who dead?'

'Lloyd George.'

'Well, of all the women... what makes you think the man is dead?'

'Well, I haven't heard much talk about him for a long time now.'

'Oh,' said Charlie, 'so if people stop talking about a man, he's dead, is he?'

'Well, as good as dead,' replied his mother. 'And specially when he's...'

'Don't bother with her, Charlie,' advised his father. 'But let me tell you, boy...'

'Did you say that Sam had gone home?' asked Sam's wife.

'I don't know where he is, neither do I care a damn. I've finished with Sam.'

'Well, I think I'll go,' said Sam's wife. 'Good night all.'

'Good night, my gel,' said Saran.

'And I've as good as finished with you, too, Charlie, after this,' Glyn said. 'To think that a boy of mine is going to support a man who is going to fight an election on money that he...'

'Do you two want any food before I go up to bed?' asked Saran.

'Yes, I want some food,' said Charlie.

'Then come and get it – and you, Glyn. Will you finish off that bit of belly-pork we had for dinner?' They said they would, so she put it before them and saw them started on their supper. 'And no shouting after I've gone up to bed, remember,' she warned them. 'Harry isn't sleeping any too well these nights.'

'Harry, Harry,' muttered Glyn as she went upstairs. 'And if it isn't Harry it's Lewis that can't sleep for the pain.... And I've had this pain in my side for years. A man won't be able to speak above a whisper in his own house before long. But listen, Charlie – and you mark my words, for I've known Lloyd George longer than you have – knew him before you were born. He used to be all right when...'

Saran evaded all the attempts of her menfolk to get her into the places where election meetings were held until eve-of-the-poll night, when her Charlie lured her into the Drill Hall, where the final rally of the liberal forces was being held, by telling her that she would hear Lloyd George himself speaking as plain as if she were in the same room as him. All that Charlie said about the Green Book and the Brown Book – and the far more wonder-working Yellow Book – went in through one ear and out through the other, but she was excited over the prospect of hearing Lloyd George speaking as plain as if she were in the same room as him. So she went, and so did Jane and Sam's wife, and who should they see on the platform with the candidate and other big liberals of the district but Benny and that stuck-up Annie. Yes, there they were as large as life on the platform.

'Humph, it's a wonder she haven't got them boys of hers with their plus fours on up there on the platform with her,' said Jane.

'Shut up,' Saran told her. 'Which is the candidate?' she asked a man who was showing people to their seats.

'The tall gentleman on the right of the chairman, madam,' he said.

'Looks a tidy man,' said Saran to Jane and Sam's wife. 'Well, I hope the one that gets in will get the pits opened up again. Your father says that his lot will do that quickest, and Charlie says that this lot with their Yellow Book will do it quickest. Then Sam...'

'Look, there's our Charlie carrying more chairs on to the platform,' said Jane.

'So it is,' said Saran. 'He've worked night and day for this lot. But there, he always did think the world of Lloyd George.... What's that thing they're fixing in front?'

'A loudspeaker, of course,' said Jane. 'Oh, look at him there on the platform talking to the candidate as large as life.'

'Who do you mean?' said Sam's wife.

'Why, that brother of Annie's, him that was a conchie when the war was on. Just like his damned cheek, I think, to go and stick himself up in front of a crowd like this now that...'

'Cheek? Nothing of the kind. Shut up,' said Saran to Jane.

'But he was a conchie, wasn't he?'

'And what if he was? Ain't we all conchies now?'

'I'm not, anyway.'

'Well, I am – and you should be with Ossie like he... shut up so as we can hear what that man's saying.'

'... where he is addressing an eve-of-the-poll rally in support of his son, Major Gwilym Lloyd George. (Applause)... his speech is being relayed from there to all the constituencies in Wales where a liberal candidate is fighting. In less than two minutes from now we shall have the pleasure of listening to thc voice of our Leader, the greatest Welshman...'

'Like hell he is,' from somewhere at the back.

'Order, order,' roars the crowd.

'Sir,' says the chairman patiently, 'we can agree to differ in terms more in keeping...'

He breaks off as a signal from a man standing on the left of the stage is followed by a sound similar to the sound of the tipping of coal from trams on to the screen which separates the large from the small.

'Now, silence, please,' cries the chairman, who sits down and turns a hopeful face in the direction of the loudspeaker from which the sounds are issuing. Every member of the huge audience also looks hopefully, many reverently, a few adoringly, and one – the interrupter at the back of the hall – cynically in the direction of the loudspeaker, which for a considerable time gave out what was taken by those prepared to give the apparatus the benefit of the doubt – as the applause of the enthusiastic thousands gathered to listen to the Leader in person at that very moment in faraway Pembrokeshire. Then those with the sharpest ears were able to pick up a word every now and then, words which came as the words of one who was being buried alive after having been half strangled. Again and again the sound accepted as applause crackled and crashed into the eardrums of the defenceless audience, as the chairman – like the good chairman he was – smiled encouragingly at the loudspeaker and nodded his head as though he could hear perfectly every word of a most interesting speech. But, as the liberals present had been told often enough by their socialist opponents, you can't fool all the people all the time; and though the chairman did his best to convey to the audience the impression that the speech was coming through OK – he even said 'Hear, hear' each time anything remotely resembling the sound of a voice emerged from the crash and crackle – the light-minded and least attentive section of the huge audience began laughing and jeering, gave the show the bird, as the saying is.

And after about ten more minutes of crackling and crashing the gallant chairman had to admit defeat. He stood up after he had had a word with one of the Marconi squad which had previously relayed the Leader without a hitch from ever so many places to ever so many more places, and he explained to the audience, did the chairman, that atmospheric disturbances along the Pembrokeshire coast and around Swansea Bay and points east had combined with other things to prevent that huge audience from hearing our Leader's speech. But he was pleased to say, there were several excellent speakers, including the candidate himself (loud applause), who would fire the last shots in what had been a wonderful campaign, a campaign from which Liberalism would, he felt certain, emerge victorious.

'What a bloody hope,' shouted the interrupter at the back, laughing cynically.

'Order, order. Turn him out. Did you ever hear such language? One of those old communists, I expect. And listen to him laughing.'

Stewards hurried to where the man was in the grip of uncontrollable laughter, and started hustling him towards the exit.

'All right, I'm going,' he told the stewards, brushing their hands away as he walked towards the exit steps, and everyone thought he was gone, and the chairman was on the point of calling upon one of the many excellent speakers on the platform, when the interrupter reappeared on top of the first short flight of exit steps and shouted over the heads of those in the audience at those on the platform: 'Homes for heroes, wasn't that it? Then where the hell's mine? That's what I want to know, where the hell's mine? Ask Dai Diddleum that. And ask him how he'd like to be unemployed since 1921 same as...'

By this time the policeman stationed at the entrance to our Drill Hall had rushed down the stone steps to help the stewards who had made a beeline for the interrupter from all parts of the hall; and this time, thank goodness, he had to go up them steps and out of the hall quicker than any man ever had to, and the policeman wanted to take his name and address, but the chief steward said: 'Never mind, now that he's gone.'

So the chairman was at last able to call on the first of the many excellent speakers he had there on the platform with him, and it was a lady speaker he called upon, a lady speaker who, after she had told the audience what a fine man their candidate was, went on to say that it was all very well for the socialists to talk about the boss class, but what about those members of the boss class that were standing as socialist candidates in different parts of the country? And how could they call themselves socialists when they were worth millions and wore diamonds at receptions, and had town and country houses such as those in which…

'Come on, let's go to the pitchers,' said Saran, rising.

'I'd like to hear the candidate,' said Sam's wife.

'Anyway, it's too late to get the full programme,' said Jane, who was a woman who believed in getting her money's worth.

'Who's paying?' Saran wanted to know. 'Come on, we'll be in time for the big pitcher and p'raps the comic as well.' And off they went to the pictures.

The theatre held out bravely until the pictures started talking, then it had to go over, and Saran was sorry, for she liked going to the theatre more than she liked going to the pictures.

'It's all pitchers now,' Saran said to Lewis when she got

home one night after seeing *The Singing Fool* in the place where she had for a generation sat and listened to flesh-and-blood performers. 'It was all right,' she went on, 'but it didn't seem right somehow in the threeatre, where... what's the matter, Lewis?'

'Nothing much.'

'I heard tonight that the Dowlais works is closing down.'

'What the hell odds if it does?'

'What odds? You'll soon find out what odds in your business, for you'll find it'll make a big difference to you.'

'Not it; the less they've got, the more they'll gamble in the hope of getting a bit.'

'P'raps you're right. Sit down and finish your supper.'

'I've had enough. How much money had I better take to this speal?' he asked nobody in particular as he rose and pulled a fat wad of one-pound notes out of the fob pocket of his trousers.

'Is it likely to be a big speal?' asked his mother in a way that would have surprised Uncle Harry had he been there to hear her, and would have surprised her fellow members of the Sisterhood even more had they been there to hear their most dominant Sister. For she spoke as one who was an authority on such matters.

'Yes, there'll be some dough there,' said Lewis, as he counted off some of the notes. 'Well, I think twenty nicker'll be enough. Here, put this lot away,' he said as he handed five times as many notes as he had decided to take to gamble with to his mother.

'You'd better take this lot with what's upstairs to the bank tomorrow,' she advised.

'I will if I'm up in time.'

'If you're not, then I'll go and pay it in; don't like having so much money about the house. Here, put this muffler on.'

'Thanks. If you happen to see that Ossie before I see him in the morning you'd better tell him to lay off the bev' until he finishes what he's well paid to do every day. If he can't, then I can get any God's amount as'll be glad to. That's the way it is,' he grumbled as he first buttoned up his well-cut light overcoat and then set his hat on his head at what he considered was the right angle, 'you give your relations a chance to earn some easy money, and before you know where you are they're taking liberties. Our Charlie...'

'Charlie was all right until you...'

'Until I caught him at the touch. Yes, and our Jim touched me for quite a bit before he went to join our Tom up Oxford way.'

'Every penny Jim took you had back from me, so...'

'Yes, but you're not Jim, are you?'

'Neither are you any better than him or Charlie because you've managed to get hold of a few pounds off the street where men are...'

Lewis laughed now that he had his mother going. 'Oh, so you've got your hair off, have you? Because *I've* got hold of a few pounds, you say. And what about you, partner? If Uncle Harry...'

'You'd better go before I...'

'I'm off, partner, for unless I'm mistaken I can hear the old man and his little Ossie singing their way up the long, long trail. Wish me luck, mam.'

'No, I'll wish you no luck after the way you've gone on

about Jim and Charlie, two boys that are every bit as good as you any day.'

'All right, they are. Now wish me luck.'

She smiled and wished him luck, then he hurried out so as to avoid meeting his father and his blind brother-in-law, both of whom were singing as they drew near to the house in which Saran was waiting to show Ossie the door, and to send him away home to Jane and his children. But he wouldn't be driven away that night, for he was the bearer of startling news, he thought, and he wouldn't go until he had unloaded it on Saran.

'What do you think?' he cried no sooner was he in through the door. 'We've got the tin hat put on us now with a vengeance. Haven't we, old man?'

'Ay, but not so much of the "old man",' growled Glyn.

'What's put the tin hat on you now again?' Saran asked. 'Here, don't trouble to make yourself comfortable,' she cried as Ossie beat his father-in-law to the armchair.

'Wait a minute till I tell you,' said Ossie. 'It isn't us two, but everybody's had the tin hat put on 'em this time. You know Meth Hughes, him as is boss of the rail-bank in Dowlais works?'

'I ought to,' said Saran.

'Well, we met him in Rose and Crown tonight, and the first thing he said was... what do you think?'

'He said that the Dowlais works was closing down.'

Glyn looked at her hard and said: 'But how the hell did you know?'

'It's stale news,' she told them.

'Not so stale,' said Ossie, 'for Meth – and he'd know as

soon as anybody – hadn't heard a word about closing down until today. And it's a clean sweep they're making, for all the bosses and the chaps in the offices are to have notices as well as the men. Finished for good and all, Meth thinks, and if that's the case, then it's domino on this district. The rates'll go up, and then our rents'll go up – yes, it's the tin hat right enough.'

'We'll live then,' said Saran. 'Do you want any supper, Glyn?'

'Of course I do, woman.'

'Then come and have it. And you get on home to yours, Ossie.'

'Leave the chap alone, woman.'

'Did you hear what I said, Ossie?'

'I'm going.... But isn't it a bugger, though?'

'What, now?'

'The Dowlais works closing down.'

'Oh...'

'For there'll be damn all left then, see – well, only them couple of pits down the bottom end of the district.'

'Ay, we'll have to eat bloody grass before the finish, Ossie,' sighed Glyn wetly.

'And drink water, and that'll be terrible for you two,' said Saran.

'You'd better push off, Ossie, for this woman is trying to be funny again.'

'I'm going. Did Lewis leave any instructions for the morning?' he asked Saran.

'No; he only said that if you haven't got sense enough to keep off the booze until after you've finished what he pays you to do, that he'll have to see about getting another man to do the job.'

'Oh, I know who that is. Don't I. Humph, it's that bloody little Phil Griffiths again. Carrying tales to Lewis about me in the hope that Lewis'll give me the peddler and take him on instead. And after I've been paying for beer for the little swine every day of the week. That's what you get…'

'Do you know what you'll get if you don't go home?'

'I'm going.' And go he did.

Glyn only had a shilling on him when he and Ossie turned into the Pelican shortly after five o'clock, so after they had had two half-pints apiece they were stumped, for Ossie seldom had any money, his Jane saw to that.

'Well,' said Glyn after he had looked into his empty half-pint for about a minute, 'we must try and strap a few pints here, for we've got no money left to raise the latch elsewhere. But I'd rather try Ned than the missus.'

'Then try him,' said Ossie.

'I would if he was behind the bar, but I haven't seen anything of him since we came in.'

'There isn't many here, is there?'

Glyn looked the length of the semicircular bar. 'There's only old Dick the grinder besides ourselves, and he's been nursing the same half-pint ever since we came in here. Seems like as if he's waiting same as us for Ned to show himself behind the bar.'

'I thought it was quiet here,' said Ossie. 'And this used to be such a good house, didn't it?'

'Well, here goes to try her for a couple of half-pints, anyway,' said Glyn as he rose and went up to the bar behind which was the landlord's wife. 'Could you fill us these couple of half-pints until...'

'Sorry, I can't,' sharply interrupted the woman. 'The last thing Ned told me was that I wasn't to pass another drop over the counter until the money for it was in sight.'

'If Ned was here he'd strap us a few drinks in a minute.'

'Then you'd better wait until he comes in to ask him.'

'Will he be long?'

The woman looked at the clock. 'No, I don't think so.'

'Where's he gone – funeral or something?'

'No; he's down at the court for non-payment of rates.'

'Don't say lies.'

'I wish I were saying lies.' She sighed. 'Yes, he's there right enough; so are about a score more of the publicans... Oh, here he is.'

'Hullo, Ned,' said Glyn.

'Hullo, Ned,' said old Dick the grinder as he moved forward to the bar with his empty half-pint measure in his hand.

'What do you want?' the landlord asked suspiciously.

'I was – we was just asking the missus if she'd fill us a couple of half-pints until – until Saturday,' said Glyn.

'I never goes anywhere else when I've got money, you know that, Ned,' said Dick the grinder. 'So if you'll let me...'

'The missus told you, didn't she?' growled the landlord.

'She – she said that you'd left orders not to serve anybody without the money,' admitted Glyn, 'but I didn't think that that applied to old customers like me and Ossie.'

'Or me, either,' said Dick the grinder. 'For you know, Ned...'

The landlord laughed loudly and sardonically. 'Old customers, ha, ha, ha. Money, ha, ha, ha. For the love of Mike! Do you know where I've come from?'

'The missus was saying something about you having to go to court about the rates, but we knew she was only joking,' said Glyn.

Again the landlord laughed offensively. 'Certainly she was only joking. I haven't been to court... it's only a bloody rumour. No more have another score or two of the licensed victuallers of this borough. No, it's only a rumour, chaps. We've got tons of dough, we have. And being as the rates are only twenty-seven and a tanner in the pound, we find no difficulty in... of course I've been to the bloody court...'

'All right, keep your hair on,' snapped Glyn, annoyed by the landlord's ironic barking. 'All I asked for was two lousy half-pints but you can keep 'em now. Come on, Ossie; we'll know where to take our money from now on.'

'Yes, and so will I,' said Dick the grinder.

And the three of them were on the point of leaving when the landlord shouted after them from behind the bar: 'Here, half a minute. Come on back here and sit down.' Then to his wife: 'Fill 'em a pint apiece.'

'You know what you said, Ned,' she reminded him.

'Yes, and I know also that I shall go bloody potty here if I have to stay and look at an empty bar much longer. So fill 'em a pint apiece, I tell you.'

'Fill 'em yourself; and if I'm not mistaken someone's filled you quite a few somewhere this day. You haven't been all day in the court, that's certain.'

'What if I haven't?' said the landlord as he took hold of

the handle and started filling a pint. 'Now, suppose you get into the kitchen and fry me a bit of something to eat. Go on.'

She went grumbling off to the kitchen.

'These bloody women... here you are, chaps,' said the landlord as he pushed the three pints of Harrap's fresh he had just filled across the counter to Glyn and Dick the grinder. After he had carried a pint to where Ossie sat alone in the corner, Glyn returned to lean against the bar, from behind which the landlord, having as good as bought an audience, had already begun telling his troubles to Dick the grinder. 'Rates twenty-seven and a tanner in the pound, and they expect me to pay 'em out of the lousy two barrels a week I'm getting rid of – well, three barrels a week at most. And nearly half of that on strap. Do you know what, I'm owed bloody pounds. Pounds – what am I talking about? I'm owed hundreds of bloody pounds, but what's been chalked behind that door won't pay rates at twenty-seven and a tanner in the pound. As I told 'em in court today; none of the other publicans had the guts to say a word. But I told 'em, I did – even though a fat swine of a policeman tried to shut me up. This borough, I told 'em, is made up as follows. Ten out of every hundred are ratepayers and ninety out of every hundred are rate-receivers. Do I get the bloody dole? I asked 'em. No fear I don't, I told 'em. Yes, and I told 'em a few more things. I proved to them that they've bled us publicans white, but they can't get blood out of a stone...'

'Give us a pipeful of 'bacco, Ned,' said Dick the grinder.

The landlord took a brass tobacco-box out of one of his pockets and handed it to Dick, who said: 'That's a fine tobacco-box, if you like. Look at it, Glyn. It isn't often you see such work on brass. Look at the scroll and...'

'It was my father-in-law's,' said the landlord. 'And what do you think he used to draw when he kept this house?'

They didn't know, neither would they venture a guess.

'Well, I'll tell you. Never less than twenty-two barrels a week.'

They registered astonishment.

'Yes, and when I took the place on after he died I was drawing as much as twenty barrels up to the time Dowlais works closed down. It was then I started to go bad, but even then I used to manage to make a go of it by making up for a rotten week on the Saturday when Merthyr Town was playing home, for there used to be a few thousand passing my door going to and coming away from the match, as you know, and as I told 'em in the court today. Then Merthyr Town went under and that was the last straw as far as this house is concerned...'

'But you've got the dogs going in the Park instead,' Glyn pointed out.

'Dogs, be damned. Don't talk to me about the dogs. The dogs are no damned good to us. They go up there, the unemployed in their thousands to the twopenny bank, and the few that's working – teachers and so on – to the shilling enclosure; and most of 'em comes away skint. Don't talk to me about the dogs. And what do you think? I seen a poster as I was on my way to the court this morning that was appealing to people to come to a meeting which is to start a campaign against the brewers and drink. Would you bloody well believe it?'

'Some of 'em wants prohibition,' said Dick the grinder.

'Well, they've practically got it in this borough, haven't they?'

'Will you...? You'll be paid before another day's over my head. A half-pint apiece'll do if you don't feel like letting us have another pint apiece,' said Glyn. 'Ossie's got a few shilling to draw, haven't you, Ossie?'

'I've got four an' six to draw in the morning,' said Ossie. 'If I see Lewis I'll get it tonight, I expect. I had a tanner on Bracket, copped at eight to one, it did...'

'So you'll have it tomorrow at the latest, see, Ned,' Glyn assured the landlord, who filled them another pint apiece, but Dick the grinder only managed to get a half-pint out of him before he continued his tale of misfortune.

'And they're threatening to sell us up. Well, let 'em; then I can draw the bloody dole, have a bit of my own back, become a rate-receiver for a change, and be able to sleep again when I goes to my bed at night. I haven't slept as I ought to for bloody years, indeed to my God I haven't.'

'Then what about me?' said Dick the grinder. 'I'm damned lucky if I get a couple of butcher's knives and a scissors to grind a day – about a bob all told. And out of that I've got to pay for my kip...'

'Your food's ready when you are,' said the landlord's wife sourly as she came back into the bar from the kitchen.

'Right, I'll be there now...'

'You couldn't...?'

'No, he couldn't,' snapped the landlord's wife.

'I wasn't talking to you,' Glyn told her.

'No, but I'm talking to you,' she told him.

'You may as well fill 'em another,' said the landlord as he went into the kitchen.

'There you are, you heard what Ned said,' said Glyn after he had gulped down what remained in his pint.

'Never mind what Ned said,' she told him as she snatched at the empty pint and rinsed it clean and wiped it and put it away with the other empties.

'Then we may as well push off, Ossie,' said Glyn.

'May as well,' said Ossie.

And off out they went, leaving Dick the grinder sitting with just a drop at the bottom of his half-pint, and the landlord's wife glaring at him from behind the bar.

CHAPTER 17

HOME, SWEET, SWEET HOME

'You'll have to eat dinner in your own homes this Christmas again,' Saran told Jane and Sam's wife as they were all three returning home loaded from a shopping and begging expedition about teatime Christmas Eve. Saran had not begged for herself, but as certain newspapers had collected funds to buy parcels for their deserving and distressed readers, she thought she might as well have one of the parcels as not. So she had told white lies to get out of the newspaper fund and from the Quakers' relief organisation what she afterwards shared between her Jane and her Sam's wife, and they both could do with all they could get, goodness only knows. But, thank God, Saran said to herself, they're both all right this Christmas again, for they've both had a bit of help from the Legion as well. Yes, they're all right, all mine are all right – thank God.

'I shall have my work cut out to do for them as is coming from away,' she went on to tell her Jane and Sam's wife. 'And so will you both.'

'You talk as though we had a dozen apiece coming home for Christmas from away,' said Jane. 'We've only one each coming home.'

'Well, it's good to have one coming home,' said Saran. 'Then all our Benny's boys'll be home, I expect.'

Jane sniffed. 'Will that one who got his BA, him with the Ronald Colman moustache that went teaching to London, be home, I wonder? I hate the sight of that boy.'

'You've no cause to,' said Saran, 'for the boy's a good boy; and so's the other boy Annie got in the college. He got his BA too, so Annie told me, but he's staying on in the college till he can win more honours to it, she said; for it's easier for him to get a job when he gets the honours put to the BA. And her other boy is going to college soon.'

'I wonder will she send that high and mighty girl of hers to college as well?' sneered Jane.

Saran changed the subject. 'Our Tom and his wife and our Jim are going to have a long and cold ride through the night to get here,' said Saran as some sleet began to fall and to be blown by the wind into their faces.

'And so will my boy, for he's coming by bus, too; and he's got farther than Tom and Jim to come,' said Sam's wife.

'My boy's coming by train,' said Jane, 'and I'm glad he is in this weather, for he's farther away from home than any of the family.'

'He's no farther away than my boy,' said Sam's wife, 'for my boy's right away the other side of London.'

'What odds where they are, as long as they get home safe and in time for Christmas?' said Saran.

'I shall want you all to come up and see me after dinner, remember,' said Saran. 'Benny and Annie are coming up for a bit, and I expect the boys will be with 'em…'

'Won't she be too busy entertaining her la-di-da friends up at number eleven The Walk to spare time to come and see you?' said Jane.

'She never has been too busy on a Christmas Day up to now to come and see me, anyway,' said Saran.

'And Mrs Owen's boys are coming home on the same bus as my boy,' said Sam's wife.

And they climbed slowly, with the wind blowing the sleet into their faces, up the hilly road to where they lived not far from each other in the district situated on an eminence above the town; and with what little breath they had to spare they talked of the families which, like themselves, were preparing for the reception of the exiles who had been forced to seek their living in places far away from their native home. And by the hundred they were being speeded home to spend Christmas with their own people in what they affectionately spoke of as 'good old Merthyr'. In chilly and smelly buses, in crowded trains, and a few unlucky – and yet lucky – ones having a lift in a lorry back to good old Merthyr.

'Your uncle Harry is worrying his guts out up there because the doctor won't give him leave to get out of bed and out of the house as far as the workhouse to be at the inmates' party,' Saran was saying as they arrived at the door of Jane's house, where they were met by five of Jane's seven children, who were anxious to know what their mother and granny had brought them from town. Having handed over to them that household's share of the load she had helped to carry up from the town, Saran wished her Jane good night and continued on her way with her Sam's wife as far as her door, at which she was relieved of all she was carrying by her Sam's children, and then she went on her way home alone and empty-handed, yet very thankful in the knowledge that two of her children and their children were provided for in a way that enabled them to look forward with pleasure and thanksgiving to the day on which their Saviour was born.

'Yes, God is good,' Saran murmured as she turned into her own house about the time that the bus which was bringing her sons back from exile was passing through Chepstow.

She had arranged the sleeping accommodation as on the previous Christmas. Tom and his wife were to have her room and her bed, and she didn't begrudge her feather bed to Tom's English wife, for if ever there was a decent woman, then it was she, Saran thought. And it would only be for a few nights, anyway. Then Jim could sleep with his father in one of the beds in the double-bedded room, and her two more homely sons, Lewis and Charlie, in the other bed. Then there was Uncle Harry in the little room, and she'd shift very well for a few nights on the old couch in the living room. Lewis went on something awful about her giving up her bed, but she soon shut him up. So she had put a new bedspread on her bed, and with Jane's help had made it look lovely for Tom and his wife. And now she was waiting for them, and for her Jim.

'Ain't they here yet?' said Glyn when he arrived home shortly after chucking-out time.

'No.' So after he had had a bit of supper he went to his bed.

'Haven't they come yet?' asked Uncle Harry when she took up his nightly hot milk well peppered.

'Not yet.' So he supped his hot milk up and was soon asleep.

'What, Tom and Jim not here yet?' cried young Charlie – though he wasn't so young, either, but being her youngest he was still being referred to as 'young Charlie' – when he rolled in about midnight with a couple of bottles in his overcoat pockets; and he'd already had far more than was good for him.

'Not yet,' said Saran. 'You'd better get to bed before they see you in that state. So if you want something to eat…'

'Why, I'm all right, mam. A few drinks, that's all. And I brought these couple of bottles so as Tom and Jim could have a belly-warmer after the ride…'

'You leave me to warm their bellies for 'em. Do you want anything to eat?'

'No, had some chips as I…'

'Then off to bed you go.'

'But I…'

'Shut up, and take those shoes off. Off with 'em. Now get upstairs quietly, for I expect your uncle Harry's sleeping.'

'All right; but don't forget to tell Tom and Jim when they come that I remembered to bring a drink home for 'em.'

It was half past one when Lewis came home in an unusually good humour from a party where he had won the best part of a tenner from three Jew-boys with whom he had played solo.

'Jim and Tom gone to bed?' he asked his mother.

'They're not here yet. Shall I put you something to eat?'

'No, thanks. I ate more than I should at the party. Oh, mam, you'd have laughed. I was playing solo – one, two, three shillings and a kitty – with Max Bernstein, Aby Freedman, and the Kosher butcher's red-headed son...'

'How is it you always play cards with Jews?'

'Because I like playing with 'em. Do you remember the Jew-boy that I used to play cards with when we were lying next bed to each other in hospital? Mam, couldn't he play crib! But tonight, single calls we were playing, and the kitty kept mounting up. The red-headed kid had to double it once when he got beat for solo, Max had to double it twice when caught on a misere and beat on a bundle, and Aby had to double it twice for shouting with nothing in his hand just to stop me lifting it with a couple of stone-wall solos. The three of 'em were determined that I, the Gentile, shouldn't lift the kitty; but I got it all the same. I was dealer this hand, mam – oh, and what a misere I had; we all had good hands. Aby, it was his first shout, called solo; then Max goes misere, and me with as fine a misere as ever you seen in your life – and then the red-headed kid calls a bundle. Now it was my last shout, so I shouts an open misere – and I got there. Ha, ha, ha, you should have seen their faces as I was picking up that kitty...'

'I hope nothing's happened to the old bus,' said Saran after another look at the clock.

'Oh, and the way they squealed when I said I was packing up with a tenner of theirs in my sky...'

'There they are,' cried Saran as she ran out into the passage to meet her two sons and her English daughter-in-law. All over them, she was, and talking good Welsh and so-so English alternately. 'You'll 'scuse me talking Welsh to the boys, my gel,' she said to her English daughter-in-law, 'for I can't help it – and I'm not saying anything wrong about you.'

'I know you're not, mother,' said her daughter-in-law from England.

'Ah, but you don't know,' she said jokingly.

'Let them take their things off and then come and have a warm,' shouted Lewis, who rather liked his English sister-in-law.

'Certainly,' said Saran. 'Come on, give me your things, and I'll put them in the front room out of the way. I thought you were never coming. How are the children, my gel?'

'Fine,' said her daughter-in-law from England. 'They're worrying mother this Christmas again.'

'You must bring 'em down to me next Christmas,' said Saran as she poured boiling water on the tea in the teapot.

'Well, they won't come by bus if they do come,' said Tom. 'Oh, mam, what a journey. The draught perished our feet, the smell of petrol and the stink from the lav...'

'Oh, never mind now that we're here,' said Jim. 'Where's dad? And how is he?'

'Oh, he's all right,' said his mother. 'Same old pain in his side, though. You know, the one he forgets all about as soon as I give him enough to raise the latch.'

They all laughed as they sat down to what Saran had prepared for them, and as they went on eating they asked their mother about this, that and the other person as though they were hungrier for news than for food. Jim and Tom talked to Lewis, whilst Saran conversed in her best English to her daughter-in-law from England until the clock struck four. Then she sent them all to bed.

The old house was like a football ground all day Christmas Day, from the time Jane's children and Sam's children and Benny's children ran up first thing in the morning to pay their respects, right up to the last thing at night. Talking and eating and drinking and smoking, for there was plenty of everything, thank God. Oh, and what a crowd was there during the hours between dinner and tea. They crowded the front room, the living room, the scullery, and Glyn and Ossie drank standing up in the passage what they had brought back with them from the Salutation, where they had spent the first of Christmas Day's two short drinking sessions.

Benny and his wife came in Benny's new car to pay their respects; their boys whom Lewis and Jane couldn't stand had paid their respects to granny with their cousins earlier in the day.

'I've no doubt that you had an exciting time up your way during the recent general election,' Benny's wife was saying to her English sister-in-law.

'No; it was quiet enough around our way.'

'Oh, we had a lot of fun here,' said Saran as she went on pouring 'just a cup of tea, that's all' for the tea-drinkers present, 'for we had a new lot standing here this time.'

'A New Party candidate,' explained Benny's wife.

'One of Mosley's lot,' explained Jane.

'He said parliament was no good,' said Sam's wife.

'Talking-shop, he said it was,' Saran said. 'Me, Jane and Kate went to hear the man. Looked a tidy man...'

'Here, that woman didn't come all the way from Oxford to talk blasted politics,' shouted Glyn on his way to where he thought Saran had hidden a flagon behind the earthenware bread-pan in the pantry.

'Where are you going, Lewis?' asked Saran as her son, with a bored expression on his face, rose from where he had been sitting and threaded his way through the crowd in the living room.

'I'm going up to sit with Uncle Harry for a while.'

'Ask him if he'd like a cup of tea.... Oh, lord, let's send some of these children off to the pitchers out of the way; then p'raps we'll be able to move about and hear ourselves talk.'

The children were glad of the chance to go.

'What about you coming with us to the pictures tonight, mam?' said Tom.

'Yes, what about it?' said Tom's English wife.

'I've never been to the pitchers on a Christmas Day yet, and I'm not going to start. But you go – I'm going to have a quiet evening with Harry up in his room.'

'Well, it won't do you any harm to have one night away from the pictures,' said Glyn as he returned to the living room after a fruitless search of the pantry and other hiding-places for the flagons he was sure Saran had hidden somewhere. 'You very near live in the pictures.'

'Yes, you're fond of the pictures, aren't you?' said Benny's wife.

'I like 'em well enough to go to 'em about three times every week,' said Saran.

'What do you think of that? – three times a week,' Glyn growled.

'Yes, my week's pitchers costs me tenpence all told; two pints in one night costs you a shilling,' Saran told him.

'There was a very fine picture in the Palace last week; were you there last week?' asked Benny's wife.

'I expect I was,' said Saran, 'for I mostly goes to 'em all.'

'Then you must have seen it; I'm referring to the picture Pauline Frederick was starred in.'

'I may have seen it,' said Saran. 'Another cup of tea, Annie?'

'No, thank you. It's about time...'

'What do you think of that for a woman?' Glyn asked them all. 'She "may have seen it". She goes to pictures, and she don't know for sure what she's seen after she's been there. If that isn't...'

'Well, Glyn, you're right for once. I goes to the pitchers, and if you asked me next day what was there I couldn't tell you. That's funny, when you come to think of it, though, isn't it?'

'No, not funny at all,' said Glyn, 'for you go until you don't know one picture from another.'

'I do go often, it's true, but no oftener than I used to go to the threeatre. Yet I'll remember some of the things I seen in the threeatre if I lived to be a hundred. I'll never forget – no, not if I live to be as old as Methuselah – that Vezin I seen acting in the Temperance Hall when I was a gel. No more can I forget Louis Calvert, Leonard Boyne, Mrs Bandman-Palmer – nor that man that played *The Grip of Iron*.'

Benny's wife laughed before saying: 'What a thing to remember.'

'P'raps it is a funny thing to remember, a man strangling 'em two at a time till the froth fell from their mouths down on to the stage. But there it is; I remember him and many more that I seen acting in the threeatre, though I can't remember the pitcher I seen last week. The people in the threeatre seemed to leave something with me that the pitchers don't.'

'Well, shall we go, Benny?' said his wife. Before receiving an answer she said to Tom's English wife: 'So I can expect you to tea with us one day before you go back. Come on, Benny. So glad to have seen you all again. Thank you,' she said as Benny helped her on with her heavy winter coat with collar and cuffs of fur. Sam's wife watched her being helped into her coat with wide-open eyes, and Jane sniffed loudly, and said as soon as the woman's back was turned: 'Thank God *she's* gone. We'll be able to breathe now.'

'What about a song, Ossie?' said Glyn. 'I expect you're pretty dry, like myself, but sing something to keep us alive.'

'Ay, give us a song, Ossie,' said young Charlie.

'Don't make a fool of yourself, Ossie,' said his Jane.

But he sang for them, all the same. A comic song he sang.

'What do you think I heard today, mam?' cried Jane as she

ran into her mother's house the morning of the very day the unemployed were first allowed into the Penydarren Park for twopence to see the greyhounds run.

'I'm sure I don't know.'

'Try and guess,' said Jane, sitting down to get her breath, for she was very fat, and she had run all the way up to tell her mother the news. 'But there, you wouldn't guess in a hundred years. Who do you think is married and the father of a baby?'

'If you tell me I'll know.'

'Our Hugh's boy down at Senghenydd.'

'Never.'

'He is, I tell you.'

'Who told you?'

'A chap from down there who brings his dogs up to run in the Park told Ossie in the Owen Glyndwr.'

'Ah, but did that chap know for sure it was our Hugh's boy?'

'Of course he did; told Ossie that he used to know Hugh well.'

'Well, well, Hugh's boy married. I must be getting on, then.'

'Yes, bound to be getting on when you're a great-grandmother.'

'It's years since I heard anything from down that way...'

'Oh, and Ossie told me something else, told me that our Lewis is mad about our Charlie going to stand up on the twopenny bank up at the dogs to bet. Reckons that somebody's behind Charlie, and talks about getting all the bookies in the shilling enclosure to go on strike to make them as owns the track stop the small-money bookies from working the twopenny bank.'

'Yes, I know all about it, for I've had them at it hammer and tongs here this morning up to about five minutes before you came in. Lewis thinks he's everybody up the dogs; but if the unemployed on the twopenny bank wants to have a few coppers on a race, and they can't pay a shilling to get where Lewis and the big bookies are, then they're as much entitled... hush, here's Lewis coming in again.'

'Here, where's that Ossie of yours?' he shouted angrily at Jane.

'Gone down to his pitch, I think,' she replied.

'He'd better be unless he wants to find himself back basket-making again. Yesterday, when I was looking for him to unload what I had on me, he was bevvying with the old man in the Owen Glyndwr. If that happens again it'll be just too bad for him. Always the same when a man gives his blasted relations a break, they...'

'Now, simmer down, Lewis, my boy,' Saran told him, 'for I've had quite enough of your grousing this morning. To hear you talk is enough to make anybody think that you're keeping us all.'

'Humph, if I didn't do more towards the keeping of you than that little Charlie of yours does it would be God help the lot of you. And now he cuts in with them as are trying to rob me of my living.'

'Nothing of the sort. If he didn't stand up to bet on the twopenny bank, you know damned well that plenty of others would. So why not let him work for you, taking in the copper bets from the unemployed whilst you carry on in the enclosure taking the big money.'

'Because I won't on principle. If people want to bet, then let 'em pay to come and do it with the right people in the enclosure.'

'How can the unemployed pay a shilling every night of the week to come there? And, remember, them as is unemployed likes to see the dogs running as well as them as is working and got money to pay their way into the enclosure.'

'Dogs running, be damned,' shouted Lewis. 'Nobody wants to see the damned dogs run; people comes to bet, and that's all. For all they'd care you could run the dogs through little tunnels out of sight...'

'All right, stop shouting. I don't want your uncle Harry to hear all this kind of talk in the state he is up there. And I won't have you shouting at Charlie, either, because he tries to make a few shillings up on the twopenny bank...'

'If I thought that he was standing up for you I'd...'

'Yes, you'd do a lot, wouldn't you? Now, go on about your business before Sherman's runners will have picked up all there is to pick up down town. It'll be Ossie that'll have to wait for you, I'm thinking.'

'Sherman's runners won't get my clients' money...'

'Jane,' said Saran as she turned away from Lewis, 'we'll do the upstairs today instead of tomorrow, but not your uncle Harry's room. I'll do that myself...'

'I'm going,' said Lewis.

'Yes, go. And after we've cleaned upstairs, Jane...'

'I said I'm going,' shouted Lewis.

'Time you did,' said his mother without looking at him. 'We'll rub a few towels through, Jane, then there'll be less for... What do you want?' she asked as Lewis brushed his fat sister aside and planted himself in front of his mother.

'You know what,' he said childishly.

'No, I don't.'

'Don't you?' he said, looking at her appealingly.

'All right, good luck,' she said.

'Yes, but I'm not having it flung at me like that. Say it tidy.'

She smiled indulgently on the middle-aged bald-headed man who stood looking down at her with the eyes of the baby she had let draw milk from her for long after he had learnt to walk. Same Lewis, she now thought. 'Good luck, Lewis bach.'

'Now I'm OK,' he said. 'Here, Jane, here's a tosharoon to buy yourself into the pictures with for a week or two,' he cried as he tossed half a crown on to his fat sister's lap.

'And have it flung in my face after that I've had it,' said Jane, but not before she had grasped the half-crown.

'See that you keep that Ossie of yours up to scratch,' was what he said as he was going out.

'Here, what about mam?' Jane called after him. 'You haven't given her anything.'

Lewis stopped at the front door to laugh and say: 'She's got more dough than ever I'm likely to have.'

'I'd like to know where it is, then,' said Saran. 'Go about your business, boy. The first race'll be over before you get halfway around your... once he's had his shout out, he's as soft as the rest of you,' said Saran to Jane as

Lewis started hurrying down into town as fast as his perforated belly and other physical souvenirs of the war would allow. 'Now, let's get on with the upstairs before any of the others get back to hinder us. And not so much row, remember, Jane, for your uncle Harry's none too well today again. My, but you was lucky to drop in to get that half-crown. You'll have to fork out for yourself to the pitchers tonight. As good as gold, Lewis is.... No, not that bucket, it leaks. You'll find a new one in the scullery. Yes, as good as gold he is. Your father gets his shilling out of him as reg'lar as clockwork every day; and Sam... where is Sam keeping himself these days, Jane? I haven't seen him since Sunday.'

'He's up the outcrops after coal most days...'

'Oh, is that where he's been? Then I can expect him here to sell me a couple of bags. We'll take Kate with us to the pitchers tonight; you can pay for her out of that half-crown.'

'Indeed I'm not paying for her. Her husband isn't blind and helpless like... Sam can go and get coal and sell it...'

'Yes, and Ossie gets more out of Lewis than Sam gets by selling coal. But come on, gel, or we'll never finish the upstairs.'

Harry was as good as finished, any day, anybody could see that. He was stuck in bed all the time now, and Saran had to look after him as she would a baby. And she liked looking after him and mothering him, though he was a funny baby to look at with those matted whiskers of his.

'Uncle Harry gets to look more like Karl Marx every day,' laughed Sam one day as he came down into the living room after having been up to pay his respects to the old wreck upstairs.

'Who is Karl Marx?' Saran asked her Sam. 'One of your communionist lot?'

'He was,' Sam said. 'He wrote that Communist Manifesto that I lent to dad, and which he lost for me.'

'I tell you I gave you the damned thing back that night I met you in the Black Lion after we'd been to hear Tom Mann speak in the Miners' Hall,' said Glyn. 'And if you don't believe me, you can ask Ossie...'

'I don't want to ask Ossie or anybody,' said Sam, 'for you never gave it me back, dad.'

'Well, of all the...'

'What kind of thing was it?' asked Saran.

'What?' said Sam.

'The thing you say your father lost.'

'Thing. He's talking about a book, woman.'

'Oh, an old book. I thought you'd gone and lost something of value b'longing to him. How much was it, Sam?'

'I had it for threepence off one of the comrades.'

'Then tell the comrade to get you another,' she said as she handed him a sixpence as his wife dropped in, looking awful bad, Saran thought.

'Jane told me to ask you if you was going to the Palace tonight,' she said. 'Greta Garbo is there this week.'

'Which of 'em is that?' said Saran.

'Why, Greta Garbo, of course. Her that was in...'

'Never mind who she is, for I'm not going, anyway.'

'But you haven't been more'n a couple of times all this summer.'

'I know I haven't; neither am I going to go until your uncle Harry gets better than he is now.'

And though Kate coaxed and coaxed, and though both she and Jane on their way to the Palace to see Greta Garbo that evening turned in to try and persuade Saran to accompany them, she refused to leave the house. 'I'm going to sit with your uncle Harry,' she told them. 'So off you go.' And off they went without her.

What she could see in sitting up in the bedroom night after night with Uncle Harry was more than Jane or Kate could see, for there was Uncle Harry propped up in bed so as he could look out of the window, and Saran sitting in the chair re-footing socks and stockings and doing most of the talking. Harry kept on sighing as his eyes encountered what he saw to make him sigh through the window, and as he thought of all the things he had done during his life which he ought not to have done. Saran, who had never had much time to do any thinking about what she had done which she ought not to have done, kept on talking as Harry went on sighing. He sighed most heavily on towards the evenings when he could see through the window the score or so of ill-dressed youths who spent most of their time playing faro for coppers on the piece of waste ground about fifty yards distant from the house, and when he looked beyond them to where the crowd of unemployed roared at the dogs from the twopenny bank of the Penydarren Park.

'They're still at it,' he would sigh as his eye fell on the youths gambling.

'Oh, those boys. Why bother your head about them? Do you know who I seen down town today?'

'Yes, but the sin – and the waste. Awful it is, Saran.'

'Awful, no, though p'raps it's not right for 'em to be always playing cards out by there, but there isn't a handful of copper among 'em all. So why worry? Yes, when I was down town today...'

'There are the others now,' sighed Harry as the crowd roared its encouragement to the dogs just slipped down in Penydarren Park.

Saran lowered her knitting into her lap and said sharply: 'Are you going to worry yourself into your grave over these things? Haven't I told you until I'm sick of telling you that these things don't matter much. If them poor boys down there – or them over in the Park – had anything better to do, they wouldn't be doing what they're doing, and what seems to worry you all the time. Everybody can't be like – well, like you, Harry. Having no work to go to, they drink what little they can get, play cards like those boys there, and go to the dogs like that lot shouting down there. And twice as many again as is there goes on Saturday nights to where they can stand to watch the boxing for sempence; for they feel they've got to have something to make 'em forget how useless they are to themselves and everybody else. Now, here's these old boys of mine... but don't you worry about 'em, Harry bach. You get better, that's enough for you to do. And you are getting better, that's easy to see. And when you're better you'll be able to go and see them as are dying to see you once more up in the workhouse. I sent the 'bacco and snuff like you said and I sent the Spanish black rock for old Charlie Rowlands. And that's what I was going to tell you. I seen old Jerry Sullivan pulling the workhouse firewood trolley through the town today, and he told me that old Charlie Rowlands... do you feel like going to sleep?'

'I do feel a bit sleepy, Saran.'

'Then have your hot milk first, then I won't have to wake you.'

She made his hot milk and gave it to him out of the tablespoon, and after he'd drunk it all – every drop – he went to sleep like a baby, he did; and she tiptoed down the stairs to her other work.

CHAPTER 18
Carrying On

Saran was telling her Jim about it when he was having a bit to eat soon after he had arrived home from where he was working up around Oxford to spend the August Bank Holiday with her; her Tom and his English wife and their children having decided to spend the August Bank Holiday with the English wife's people somewhere in England that Saran knew nothing about. Still, she was thankful to have one of her exiled sons home with her, and as Sam's boy and Jane's two boys – for the Labour Exchange had sent another of Jane's boys into training which had resulted in his getting a job in the place where the Murphy sets are made – were home as well, it wasn't going to be such a bad holiday after all. And she was telling her Jim about it.

'Yes, we've had another 'lection here since you was home Christmas. And four different lots trying for the seat that came to be empty because of that poor man Wallhead dying. Oh, Jim bach, you never seen such times. Meetings everywhere from morning to night. There was our Sam's lot, the communionist…'

'Oh, hell, *communists,* woman,' cried Glyn. 'I'm sick and tired…'

'Well, our Sam's lot, whatever you like to call 'em, had a man out this time. And so did your father's lot…'

'Ay, and we got him in,' crowed Glyn, 'though Sam and his lot…'

'Then Benny's lot had a man out, and Benny's wife…'

'Ay, she's a nice bitch if you like,' said Glyn. 'Says she's a national liberal, and yet she goes and supports a Lloyd George lib…'

'Can't the woman support who she likes?' said Saran. 'But never mind her for the time. How many lots is that I've said was standing?'

'Three,' said Jim, lighting a fag.

'But there was four. Let's see, now… oh, Jim, is it true that you're thinking about getting married to a gel up there where you're working?'

'He's got his own mind to please, haven't he?' said Glyn.

'Who told you about it?' Jim wanted to know.

'Tom's wife said in the letter to Jane…'

'Oh, it's her, is it?'

'Then it's true?' said Saran.

'What if it is, woman?' growled Glyn.

'Nothing – as long as I know, that's all. I was telling you about the 'lection, Jim…'

'He don't want to hear about the election,' growled Glyn,

who was waiting to take Jim to where there was a better drop of beer to be had than could be had around Oxford – or anywhere in England.

'Yes, I do want to hear about it,' said Jim.

'But it was all in the *Merthyr Express* that we sends you every week,' Glyn reminded him.

'Yes, but reading about it is not the same as...'

'Your father's in a hurry to take you out to spend your money on drink for him and that Ossie.'

'You're a bloody liar, woman.'

'Then shut up until I've told the boy. What was that other lot that had a man out at the 'lection?'

'Well, being as you seem to know all about it...'

'I'm asking you what was the other lot with your lot, and Sam's lot, and our Benny's lot.'

'The ILP, if you want to know.'

'Ay, that's the other lot, Jim. The ILP – good speakers they had. There was one man with long hair – but he wasn't the candidate, Champion Stephen was the candidate...'

'Champion Stephen be damned. Campbell Stephen, woman.'

'I knew it was something like that. Then there was S. O. Davies, your father's man; and Wal Hannington, he was our Sam's man. A man from London he was. Then there was our Benny's man.... What was his name, Glyn?'

'John Victor Evans. I'm off out for a walk.'

'Sit down, and I'll take a stroll with you after I've had a bit of a spell here with mam,' said Jim.

'You should have met him as he stepped off the bus, Glyn, and then you could have taken him straight to the pub.'

'Look here, woman...'

'You and your "*woman*"! Can't you say anything else but...?'

'Go on telling me about the election,' suggested Jim.

'There's not much to tell. I went with Jane and Sam's wife to some of the meetings, for there was women speaking at most of 'em, but it was our Sam's lot had the one that capped the lot. An old woman... what was her name again, Glyn?'

'Mrs Despard, do you mean?'

'Ay, that's the one; nearly a hundred years old, our Sam says she is. They was holding her up by the arms, like the Bible says Moses was held, when she was speaking from the top of a chair in the open air down by the public buildings. And didn't she go for your father's lot. Then there was that other woman that spoke for your lot, Glyn, the one wearing a cloak like some of the women that used to come to the threeatre.'

'Mrs Bruce Glasier.'

'That's her. And there were young women, too. That Jenny Lee, and ever so many more.'

'And who did you vote for, mam?' Jim asked.

'None of 'em, my boy.'

'Now, what do you think of that, Jim?' asked Glyn, expressing his utter lack of comprehension of a woman who, when given the chance to, failed to exercise a hard-won right. 'Here's a woman who hasn't got sense enough to use her vote, yet to hear her talk you'd think she knew everything.'

'I know enough to suit me,' said Saran. 'Anyway, who

was I to vote for? I heard the four of 'em, and each one warned me that if I voted for either of the other three, that it would be all up on me. So it was three to one against me whichever way I voted.'

'More bookies' talk,' growled Glyn. 'Come on, Jim, let's go.'

'Sit down, Jim,' said Saran. 'Your father thinks I'm nothing more than a damned fool when it comes to voting, but I've seen a lot of voting in my time. I remember Pritchard Morgan and D. A. Thomas when they was in their prime, and I heard talk of the things they was going to do then. Ay, and I heard talk of the things Keir Hardie was going to do for us when he came down here from Scotland. He was a nice man; and so was the man Wallhead who came after him. And now Wallhead is gone again; all them men are gone. I've seen 'em come and go, same as I've seen people that used to go to the British Schools here made into lords and ladies, and they're gone, too. I've heard your father and you boys talk about this miners' leader and that, and what they had done and were going to do; but all the same I had to beg my way through the '98 strike, and I'd be on my backside now like most other people around here if I hadn't had sense enough to look after the bit that came my way during the war. I've come a long way – in my old backhanded way – to where we are today. I've lived under the old Queen and a couple of kings since her time, and under God only knows how many governments of all sorts. And here we are. Your father with his "woman" this and "woman" that tries to make me out a damned fool – but I've learnt something. And if I couldn't do better than some of the… hullo, Jane… oh, here's Ossie, your father's boozing-pal, come to fetch you, Jim…'

'Never mind about boozing-pal,' cried Ossie. 'I've got a bet with your Sam, and you're the one to settle it. He reckons that your Benny is gone fifty, and I…'

'Benny's not fifty until next birthday,' said Saran.

'Then I've won,' said Ossie.

'Half a minute,' said Glyn, 'I'm not so sure. Benny was born on the twenty-fourth of November, eighteen…'

'I know when he was born,' said Saran, 'and I know that he's not fifty until next birthday.'

'Then it's time you had your golden wedding, isn't it?' said Jim.

'What's a golden wedding?' said Saran.

'What people gets when they've been married fifty years, of course,' said Jane. 'You ought to know that, our mam,' she added.

'Well, I didn't.'

'Humph, golden wedding,' grunted Glyn. 'I'm lucky to get the price of a half-pint…'

'Jim, take your father out of my sight before he breaks my heart with his grousing,' said Saran as the house began to fill with callers. Sam and his wife and their boy from away, and Jane's two boys from away, and their other children; then Lewis and Charlie ran in for a bite before going off to bet at the dogs, so between everything Saran was pleased when Jim and his father and Ossie and Sam went out to have a few drinks. None of Benny's people called that day, and Uncle Harry, of course, was upstairs out of the way.

'If there was another war broke out tomorrow, I'd go to it like a bloody shot,' Sam surprised all the members of the family by saying towards the end of the little party Saran gave at her house on the evening of her Benny's fiftieth birthday. Benny was the guest of honour, of course, and it was his son, the one with the honours to his BA, that started Sam off by referring to some resolution never to take part in any war that had been passed at his college. 'Yes, like a bloody shot I'd go,' Sam repeated.

'Well, there's no need for swearing,' said Benny's wife.

'Nor for shouting,' said Saran, 'for your uncle Harry is pretty bad up there tonight.'

Sam lowered his voice to say: 'You can pass as many resolutions as you like, but if things keep on as they are there'll be half a million ex-servicemen like myself ready to change into uniform whenever we're wanted.'

'More fool them,' said Saran.

'How's that?' said Sam. 'Isn't it better to chance being blown up or bayoneted...?'

'This is a nice birthday party,' said Lewis, who hated to hear talk of bayonets.

'Sorry,' muttered Ossie as he knocked over the glass of beer he was feeling for.

'It's all right,' said Saran. 'Fill him another, Glyn.'

'Certainly,' said Glyn, who filled another for himself as well.

'But things will improve now that we've had the commissioners' report on South Wales,' said Benny.

'What is he going to do for South Wales?' asked Saran.

'It's the Government that'll have to do it, but what the commissioner recommends is the transference of all surplus labour of men and boys under forty-five years old to more prosperous districts, and also to...'

'Where are the districts that wants our men?' asked Saran.

'Well, there's...'

'Yes, Benny, there's blasted fools as don't know what they're talking about. Send the men away, indeed.'

'Woman, you're too handy calling people fools.'

'What else are they when they say every man under forty-five should be sent away to take a chance 'mongst strangers who've got plenty to do to look after their own. Our men and boys'll go themselves, without being sent, to wherever there's a dog's chance of earning enough to live on. Haven't Tom and Jim, and Jane's two boys, and Sam's boy, and thousands more like 'em gone from this district? Of course they have. Let the Government do something for the place as'll make it possible for those as are left to make a living here. That's what they want to do and that's what they'd have to do if everybody was like me; for I'd hang on here until – well, until I had to eat grass – before I'd let them ship me away to where it's little, if any, better. Transference, did you say he wanted? Well, I've transferred all I'm going to transfer. Two in the Senghenydd explosion, two to the war, as good as three when you take into account Benny's arm and...'

'Never mind the rest, mam,' said Lewis.

'And Tom and Jim gone up England to work. Now I'm going to keep the couple I've got left...'

‘Too true you are,’ said Charlie, who had been taking glass for glass with his father and Ossie.

‘Yes, too true I am – that’s if you’ve got sense enough to hang on...’

‘If you can find a better hole...’

‘Shut up, Charlie,’ Saran told him. ‘I’m talking serious. We’ll never go short, for I’ve got enough to see us through, that’s if we die tomorrow,’ she hastened to add jokingly as she noted the way her children and her in-laws looked in her direction.

‘Is there any more beer?’ said Glyn.

‘I think we’d better be off now, for it’s getting on, and Doris and her young man are coming to supper,’ said Benny’s wife, fearing that the party to celebrate her husband’s half-century was on the way to becoming a drunken do, though as a matter of fact it was far from developing into anything of the kind. But she collected Benny and her sons, thanked Saran for having so honoured her husband and off she went.

‘Well, now that they’re gone, what about some more beer, and a song from Ossie?’ said Glyn.

‘No beer and certainly no songs here,’ Saran told him. ‘Harry is not going to be disturbed by any of your row. Here’s a shilling, go and make beasts of yourselves down at the Anchor whilst me and Jane and Kate clear up here.’

‘But woman, there’s three of us, and a shilling...’

‘What three of you?’

‘Well, here’s Sam...’

‘Here you are, here’s a tosh,’ said Lewis, handing his father a half-crown as he passed on his way to his room to dress to go out for the night and part of next morning.

‘Ah, that’s something like, that is,’ said his father as he looked at the shining half-crown. ‘Now we shall be able to have something like a drink. Come on, Ossie boy. Fall in, Sam.’

‘Don’t be late, Sam,’ said Sam’s wife. Sam said ‘right-o’ as he followed his dad out of the house, with Ossie’s hand on his right shoulder.

Harry was worse, and Saran hardly ever left him now, and when she had to, to attend to her household duties or to get a little sleep, she was relieved by Lewis, who was a most dependable and efficient male nurse, she was surprised to find. It was obvious to all that the end was near, and the family without a single exception rallied around Saran. Benny’s wife was the only one who brought flowers every morning for Harry’s little room, all the others came love-laden. Harry was not conscious of anyone’s presence for about a week before he died, but at the last hour he did open his eyes and say: ‘Saran.’

‘Yes, here I am, Harry,’ she said in the Welsh tongue.

His hand tremblingly moved across the top quilt of his bed until hers met it halfway and held it. And they held hands for a long time before he at last said: ‘You do – believe, Saran bach – don’t you?’

‘Certainly I do,’ she assured him. ‘I always have. God is good, that’s what I’ve always said.’

His grip on her hand tightened and he sighed contentedly. ‘Yes – God is – good,’ he murmured. He began to breathe in faint gasps, as a blown puppy does, and the only word she caught before he breathed his last was the word ‘Mam’. He had gone. She sat for long with the body that had housed his turbulent spirit before she rose and put the hand she had been holding back under the quilt. Then she went down and into the living room, where Lewis was sitting alone. His familiar and hellish pain was giving him gyp, yet he forgot it as soon as he saw his mother's face, on which he saw for the first time the expression of utter helplessness.

'Mam,' he cried, springing to her side and helping her across to the armchair.

'He's – he's gone, Lewis,' she murmured.

Lewis smoothed her hair.

Benny saw to everything, though it was Lewis that paid for the taxis and the motor-hearse in which his uncle Harry's remains were conveyed to the cemetery, where they were buried in the same grave as his mother's. 'Gentlemen only', and only the gentlemen of the family at that, were at the funeral. Saran didn't let Benny write to tell the boys working up Oxford way for fear they would go to the expense of journeying down to the funeral. 'Write to tell 'em afterwards,' she said.

As the funeral was about to start off from before the house Saran was standing looking out of the front window with Benny's wife and Jane and Sam's wife and some of the children standing respectfully behind her. Saran was smiling sadly as the motor-hearse and the cars filled with her men following slowly started off.

'S'long, Harry bach,' she murmured as she stood and watched the funeral out of sight around the corner. Then she swallowed hard and led the way back into the living room.

Foreword by Mario Basini

Born in Merthyr Tydfil and educated at Aberystwyth University, Mario Basini worked as reporter, feature writer and columnist for the *Western Mail*. He is a former Welsh Feature Writer of the Year and a Honorary Fellow of Aberystwyth University. He broadcasts frequently on BBC Wales and is the author of *Real Merthyr*.

Cover image by Archie Rees Griffiths

Archie Rees Griffiths (1902–1971) was born in Aberdare but brought up in Gorseinon on the outskirts of Swansea. He worked in the Mountain Colliery and the tinplate works at Gorseinon before attending Swansea School of Art (1919–1924) and the Royal College of Art (1924–1927). His paintings are a record of industrial life in Wales during the first half of the twentieth century, foreshadowing the literary reaction to the period, and formed part of a group that included Evan Walters and Vincent Evans who made a committed attempt to portray Welsh rural and industrial life in realist terms. Griffiths was a Marxist and a Christian, themes that are often reflected in his work and choice of subject matter. He continued to work throughout his life but received very little public recognition after the 1930s and found it increasingly difficult to make a living from his art. He died in London in 1971.

LIBRARY OF WALES

The Library of Wales is a Welsh Assembly Government project designed to ensure that all of the rich and extensive literature of Wales which has been written in English will now be made available to readers in and beyond Wales. Sustaining this wider literary heritage is understood by the Welsh Assembly Government to be a key component in creating and disseminating an ongoing sense of modern Welsh culture and history for the future Wales which is now emerging from contemporary society. Through these texts, until now unavailable, out-of-print or merely forgotten, the Library of Wales brings back into play the voices and actions of the human experience that has made us, in all our complexity, a Welsh people.

The Library of Wales includes prose as well as poetry, essays as well as fiction, anthologies as well as memoirs, drama as well as journalism. It complements the names and texts that are already in the public domain and seeks to include the best of Welsh writing in English, as well as to showcase what has been unjustly neglected. No boundaries will limit the ambition of the Library of Wales to open up the borders that have denied some of our best writers a presence in a future Wales. The Library of Wales has been created with that Wales in mind: a young country not afraid to remember what it might yet become.

Dai Smith
Raymond Williams Chair in the Cultural History of Wales
Swansea University

LIBRARY OF WALES

FUNDED BY

CYNGOR LLYFRAU CYMRU
WELSH BOOKS COUNCIL

SERIES EDITOR: DAI SMITH

1	Ron Berry	*So Long, Hector Bebb*
2	Raymond Williams	*Border Country*
3	Gwyn Thomas	*The Dark Philosophers*
4	Lewis Jones	*Cwmardy & We Live*
5	Margiad Evans	*Country Dance*
6	Emyr Humphreys	*A Man's Estate*
7	Alun Richards	*Home to an Empty House*
8	Alun Lewis	*In the Green Tree*
9	Dannie Abse	*Ash on a Young Man's Sleeve*
10	Ed. Meic Stephens	*Poetry 1900-2000*
11	Ed. Gareth Williams	*Sport: an anthology*
12	Rhys Davies	*The Withered Root*
13	Dorothy Edwards	*Rhapsody*
14	Jeremy Brooks	*Jampot Smith*
15	George Ewart Evans	*The Voices of the Children*
16	Bernice Rubens	*I Sent a Letter to My Love*
17	Howell Davies	*Congratulate the Devil*
18	Geraint Goodwin	*The Heyday in the Blood*
19	Gwyn Thomas	*The Alone to the Alone*
20	Stuart Evans	*The Caves of Alienation*
21	Brenda Chamberlain	*A Rope of Vines*
22	Jack Jones	*Black Parade*
23	Alun Richards	*Dai Country*
24	Glyn Jones	*The Valley, the City, the Village*

'This landmark series is testimony to the resurgence of the English-language literature of Wales. After years of neglect, the future for Welsh writing in English – both classics and new writing – looks very promising indeed.'

M. Wynn Thomas

WWW.LIBRARYOFWALES.ORG

LIBRARY OF WALES
titles are available to buy online at:

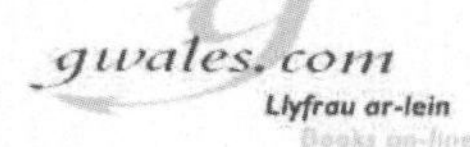